SANTA

D0607253

Rules of Engagement

"I'll go upstairs and change into dry clothing."

"You'll stay here and put on my robe."

"I must consider my reputation."

"Lady, if you don't get those clothes off, I promise to leave your reputation in shreds."

It was obvious by his lowered head and rapid-fire response he had lost all patience, and this time she opted for wisdom. "You kissed me before." She held out her hands, palm up. "You must promise that if I do this, you won't try and kiss me again."

"Miss Lockhart, the only thing I promise you is that I will get the truth from you one way or another." He pointed. "Now get back there and strip off."

Other Books by
Christina Dodd

CANDLE IN THE WINDOW
CASTLES IN THE AIR
THE GREATEST LOVER IN ALL ENGLAND
A KNIGHT TO REMEMBER
MOVE HEAVEN AND EARTH
ONCE A KNIGHT
OUTRAGEOUS
PRICELESS
RULES OF SURRENDER
THE RUNAWAY PRINCESS
THAT SCANDALOUS EVENING
SOMEDAY MY PRINCE
TREASURE IN THE SUN
A WELL FAVORED GENTLEMAN
A WELL PLEASURED LADY

CHRISTINA DODD

Rules of Engagement

Book Two of the Governess Brides Series

AVON BOOKS
An Imprint of HarperCollins*Publishers*

This is a work of fiction. Names, characters, places, and incidents are products of the author's imagination or are used fictitiously and are not to be construed as real. Any resemblance to actual events, locales, organizations, or persons, living or dead, is entirely coincidental.

AVON BOOKS
An Imprint of HarperCollins*Publishers*
10 East 53rd Street
New York, New York 10022-5299

ISBN: 0-7394-1138-1

Printed in the U.S.A.

With thanks to George Burns, Bob Hope,
and especially Jack Benny,
who taught generations of Americans how to laugh.
Humor never dies, it just gets recycled.

Miss Pamela Lockhart and Miss Hannah Setterington,
Proud proprietors of

The Distinguished Academy of Governesses

~~Are desperately attempting to make their endeavor a success and~~
Offer the finest in governesses, companions and instructors to fill any need
~~Without being too fussy about the details of the position~~
~~Although they certainly won't do anything immoral or illegal~~
Serving fashionable society on this day
July 1, 1840

This was the best day of the month, payday.

Miss Pamela Lockhart gave a light-hearted skip as she made her way toward home. The residential London street might be prematurely dark from the rain, she might be chilled and wretched, and once again she'd had to try to teach tone-deaf little Lorraine Dagworth how to play "Twinkle, Twinkle Little Star" on the pianoforte, but she had easily collected the month's fee from Lorraine's mother. She had also, after a bit of struggle, collected from the aristocratic Lady Phillips. And finally she had given Lord Haggerty's son his dancing lesson and—while fending off both the younger man's groping and the older man's offer of an ignominious affair—secured the month's reimbursement without offending either of the loathsome gentlemen.

Yes, a governess's work proved difficult and occasionally abhorrent, but payday, glorious payday, made it all worthwhile, and as Pamela cut through the filthy, garbage-filled alley, she tipped up her head to the raindrops and laughed aloud—and stumbled to a halt.

Something snagged her skirt. A protruding board, perhaps, or . . .

A sharp point jabbed at her back and a rough voice snarled, "Give me that purse ye've got hidden in yer bosom, miss, an' I might spare yer life."

Pamela froze, heart pounding. That object . . . a knife! A thief held a knife to her back. He might stab her. She might die.

He wanted to steal her money.

The knife prodded her, and the man snarled right in her ear, sending the stench of gin and tobacco on the puff of foul breath. "I said, give me that purse. No denyin' ye've got it, miss. I saw ye at th' greengrocers payin' fer them pretty strawberries."

She clutched the bag with her purchase. Rain sluiced endlessly down. No one remained in sight; everyone with any sense had hurried home to sit before his fire and toast his toes. Only she remained, bait for this footpad who planned to steal her beautiful, hard-earned, just-collected cash.

The blade jabbed again, and the thieving fiend grabbed her arm hard enough to bruise it. "Are ye a half-wit? I said give me yer money or I'll kill ye."

Frustration roiled within her. Frustration, anger and despair.

The knife jabbed deeper. She felt the pop of threads as it cut through her gown and corset cover.

She snapped, "Let me think about it."

Miss Hannah Setterington smiled at the nervous eighteen-year-old girl seated before her desk in the study. "I can find you a position," Hannah said. "That is what we do here at the Distinguished Academy of Governesses. But because we supply only the finest governesses to the *ton*, and you have no experience as yet, you must work through our rigorous month of training. This teaches you to deal with the situations that arise with children and with your employers."

Still damp from the rain, the girl shivered a little and glanced longingly at the flames that leaped in the hearth. "Thank you, Miss Setterington, but . . . I've just arrived from the country. I have nowhere to live and . . . I can't pay . . . for any schooling . . ."

Her choked dismay almost brought a tear to Hannah's eye. She'd been young like this once, unsure, desperate . . . running away. She was older now, wiser, in control of her life, but she could never completely leave behind the memories. Rising, she said, "Let's talk over here. It's cozier." She led the way to the grouping of chairs beside the fire and indicated a seat, then waited while young Miss Murray composed herself. "You do not pay for our training, and you will remain here, under our roof, while you participate in it."

Miss Murray frowned in suspicion. "Why would you be so kind without reimbursement? I'm from the country, but I'm not stupid. I'm a good girl."

"I'm glad to hear that," Hannah said steadily. "But we do expect reimbursement. In return for your bed, board and instruction, we will place you in a position and collect the fee which your employer will pay us for the guarantee of a learned and accomplished governess."

"Oh." Settling back into the chair, Miss Murray said, "I . . . I suppose that's reasonable."

"Quite. The first week of your training is a time for us to get to know you, to decide if you are the high caliber of governess we want to represent and for you to decide if this is the career you wish to follow."

Miss Murray snuffled into her handkerchief. "I have no choice."

"One always has a choice." Hannah was not one to countenance self-pity. "We represent females in every capacity. Sometimes one teaches young children better than older children, sometimes one proceeds better as a finishing governess, sometimes one is superior as a companion to the elderly."

Miss Murray brightened. "I hadn't considered that. I used to care for my grandmother, and I liked that very much."

Hannah nodded. "You see. We have already discovered a direction for you. We do provide companions, and also daily and weekly teachers of pianoforte, needlework and dancing. We here at the Distinguished Academy of Governesses pride ourselves on finding an instructor for every need."

She heard a knock on the front door—a still infrequent occurrence and one that brought her to her feet. The butler would of course open the door, but he had instructions to bring any customer to her immediately.

Hannah said, "Our housekeeper waits for you at the head of the stairs. Mrs. Knatchbull will show you to your bedchamber, where you may unpack, and tomorrow you will join our other two students in learning to be the type of governess our school is proud to call our own."

Miss Murray recognized a dismissal when she heard one. She bobbed a curtsy, gathered her bag and went to the door. The girl was well bred and courteous, if unsure, and with training she would prove an asset to the school.

Smiling timidly, Miss Murray stood aside to let the butler Cusheon by. Then she stopped. Her mouth dropped open. And she gawked at the gentleman who trod on his heels.

Indeed, Hannah judged it a lucky circumstance Miss Murray had reacted as she had, or Hannah herself would have been the one dumbfounded. The gentleman, dressed in the height of fashion, was marvelously, languidly, seductively handsome. Tall and long-legged, he wore a dark blue suit that amply displayed his breadth of shoulder. He carried a gold-headed cane and wore gloves of leather dyed to match his suit. His black hair, trimmed close against his collar, hung in loosely curled and rumpled splendor over one side of his forehead. His aristocratically proud nose had been broken at one time—probably from a fall off his pony, Hannah decided uncharitably. His eyes were so soft and brown a woman could lose herself in them, yet a sharp intelligence operated beneath their fathomless depths, for he summed up Miss Murray and dismissed her in a single glance. Then his focus sharpened on Hannah. He didn't wait for Cusheon to introduce her, but bowed curtly. "Miss Setterington, I presume?"

Hannah took an instant dislike to the man. Rude, abrupt creature. "Yes, and you are . . . ?"

"Devon Mathewes, the earl of Kerrich," Cusheon proclaimed, and only one who knew the old butler well could tell that the earl's presumption exasperated him.

The earl disdained to notice Cusheon's displeasure, nor did he remain to observe Hannah's curtsy. Instead, he strode forward into the study and trusted she would follow.

Of course she did follow, and Cusheon took up his guard at the door.

"How may I help you, my lord?" She made her way to her chair behind the desk.

Sinking into a chair in front of the desk, Lord Kerrich proclaimed, "I need a governess."

The front door of the townhouse again opened and quietly shut. Hannah hoped it was Pamela, for it was raining and almost dark. She worried about her friend and fellow owner of the Distinguished Academy of Governesses, out on the London streets day after day pursuing the jobs that kept the academy alive during its first crucial months.

But Hannah dared not take her attention off her client—a

widower with children, she presumed. "You wish to hire a governess, and you have come to the right place. We supply only the finest governesses. How many children do you have?"

He reared back as if offended. "Good God, I don't have a child!"

Hannah paused in the act of sitting. "My lord?"

"Don't you understand, woman? I need a child, too."

CHAPTER 2

At the sight of Hannah's confusion, Lord Kerrich raked his fingers through his hair, mussing it completely and making himself, for some obscure reason, even more attractive. "A child. I need a child. I have a great wish to be seen as re-spect-able." He carefully sounded out *respectable*, as if women who taught children couldn't easily assimilate big words.

If his explanation was supposed to make Hannah comprehend, it did not, but it occurred to her he didn't care whether she understood his dilemma, only that she understood what he wanted. Which she still didn't.

"If you could elucidate a little more, my lord?" she prompted.

His teeth snapped together—white teeth, evenly spaced, Hannah saw—and he glared as if she could somehow be blamed for his predicament. His voice stung with mockery as he explained, "There are those in our country who see me as . . . improper. A rake. A philanderer. In other words, unsuitable to associate with . . . decent people."

Through the doorway, Hannah saw a woman's silhouette. Pamela *was* back, and hovering just out of eyesight.

"To be seen as respectable matters to you?" Hannah could scarcely believe that. He didn't seem the type of man to whom public opinion mattered.

"A man who is ruled by the beliefs of the ignorant is a shadow of a man. In fact, one might call such a man a woman." He chuckled as if he had amused himself.

Hannah did not chuckle.

He didn't require even that imitation of politeness. "But I am a banker. My grandfather founded Mathewes Bank. He would be most disappointed if my reputation proved to be of detriment to that institution for which he labored for so long and assiduously." Cupping his cravat in his hand, he said, "Indeed, I will not allow *anyone* to tarnish the family name of Mathewes."

His sentiments sounded almost admirable, almost a vow, although Hannah cynically wondered if he truly worried about the bank, his grandfather and his family name, or if his personal income was his primary concern.

"It is a sad day in England when a man who keeps a mistress is seen as more respectable than a man who embraces a wider range of females." He chewed his fine lip.

"An obvious injustice."

He disregarded her sarcasm. "Indeed. So I want an orphan. I'll take him into my home, make it look as if I have been overcome with the milk of human kindness. I'll keep the foundling long enough to secure Her Majesty's favor once more, and in the meantime you can't expect me to care for him on my own!"

Hannah understood his plan now, and caught her breath at the callousness of his intent. "You wish to hire a governess to go to an orphanage and get you a temporary child to befool society and the queen? My lord, I wouldn't be able to sleep an eye-wink if I—"

Pamela stepped into the doorway, into the light. She

looked like a drowned rat, with hair scraggling into her face and her eyes glaring like a demon's. Glaring at Hannah. Nodding vigorously, she pointed at the seated Lord Kerrich, then at herself.

Hannah shook her head *no*.

Lord Kerrich thought she was shaking her head at him, and he lounged back in his chair and smiled, exposing those perfect white teeth. "Come, Miss Setterington. Scruples? You can't afford them. You started this academy a mere two months ago, and to the best of my knowledge you've placed only one governess full-time. She is marrying Viscount Ruskin this Wednesday, if I read the invitation correctly, and as his wife she is unlikely to bring you further income. You and your other governesses are working piecemeal as dance instructors or some such."

He knew far too much, and Hannah was torn between staring at him and observing Pamela as she continued her little pantomime.

"I listen to gossip, Miss Setterington. There is a great deal of gossip about your school, little of it kind. You need me. You need my money." He pulled his wallet from his pocket and placed a check upon the desk.

She didn't want to look at the neatly scripted handwriting, but she couldn't help it. Even upside down she could read it. One hundred pounds.

She was glad she was sitting down.

She and Pamela didn't have to have the money. With what Pamela had collected today, they could survive for another month. But . . . they had three female young mouths to feed, three young minds to shape. Only then could Hannah and Pamela find them employment in respectable households and collect a placement fee. Cusheon and Cook and Mrs. Knatchbull depended on Hannah and Pamela, also. Even Hannah had developed the habit of eating on a daily basis. As long as nothing untoward happened in the next month, they could place the new girls, and the future of the Distinguished Academy of Governesses was secure.

As long as nothing untoward happened . . .

"That is how you work, isn't it? You charge a placement fee and guarantee satisfaction in the governess one hires? Well, I will give you an additional fifty pounds right now for the suitable governess, and fifty pounds for procuring a suitable orphan. In addition, I'll pay all expenses the governess incurs in finding the child. I don't know what the going rate to buy an orphan is these days, but I can afford it. Twenty-five pounds a month for the governess while she works for me, and at the end, when I succeed in convincing Queen Victoria and her wretchedly formal consort that I am the man to"—he caught himself on the verge of an indiscretion—"well, when I am once again in Her Majesty's good graces, I will pay a final compensation of two hundred pounds."

Hannah barely restrained her gasp. Pamela did not, and Lord Kerrich heard it, Hannah was sure. He didn't turn, only smiled. "You see? Even our clandestine listener believes it a great amount and worth the effort."

He was correct. Pamela danced with impatience, silently demanding that Hannah accept for her. But Hannah had to object. "My lord, you mentioned the queen. I cannot in conscience take part in deceiving our sovereign!"

He glared. "I'm not going to harm her, I'm going to help our monarch—as I have done all these years. It's for her own good."

Somehow, Hannah believed that. This man, with his cold eyes and proud face, had an honor of his own. It wasn't an easy honor, or a humane honor, but he carried it as part of the fabric of his being. In a lower voice, she said, "But your plan is so heartless."

He reared back in his chair, his dark, perfectly formed eyebrows raised in astonishment. "Heartless? Why heartless?"

"Unless you plan on adopting the child."

"That's going a little far."

"So you're going to lie and tell him he's to be adopted, then renege?"

"I see no choice. A child can't be trusted with the details of my plan." Placing his cane firmly on the floor, he placed both his hands atop the ivory knob that formed the handle. "Miss Setterington, he'll have every advantage while he lives with me, and he'll be out of the orphanage for a time, at least. You cannot say this is a bad thing."

Hannah agreed. She had been a lady's companion not so long ago, and the lady had been a compassionate woman. Hannah had had occasion to visit a few orphanages to deliver clothing and food, and they were uniformly dreadful places. "But afterward, to be forced to go back . . ."

Waving a long, gloved hand, Lord Kerrich agreed. "You do have a point, and a good one. I'm a compassionate man."

Obviously, he was not, and just as obviously he was oblivious to the fact.

He continued, "I concede you are correct. I'll help the youngster learn a trade and find a place for him in my household. It will be the least I can do." He leveled a stern glance at Hannah. "But first he must help me win the queen's favor. Now—as to my requirements."

"For the orphan?"

"No. One orphan's much the same as another, I suspect. My requirements for the governess."

He might be the handsomest man Hannah had ever met, but he made her head whirl with his assumptions, his requisites and his loathsome ruthlessness. To deal with him was to deal with the devil, yet he bore an air of implacability that convinced her that open defiance would have unpleasant repercussions. Yes, she was familiar with lords who imagined themselves so superior they could do as they wished regardless of the unhappiness they caused, and yes, she knew well that unless she employed tact, she and the Distinguished Academy of Governesses would be much the worse for it.

"Do you wish to interview our selection of governesses?" she asked.

"I will tell you what I need and you will get it for me."

She was relieved, for their current selection included only her and Pamela. "What do you need?"

"A plain woman, one not given to fantasizing, one with her feet firmly planted on the ground. An older woman." His full mouth compressed into a thin line. "An older woman who has left all hope of marriage, or even romance, behind."

I don't know of a governess like that. Hannah wanted to cut him down to size so badly! But Pamela now waved her hands emphatically, demanding the job as if she weren't the feminine counterpart of the handsome Lord Kerrich. Had she gone mad?

When Hannah hesitated, his teeth clamped together. "Come, Miss Setterington, you know the reason. I am sick of being the object of lovelorn sighs. I have to put up with it in my own household—one needs scullery maids, the housekeeper assures me. But if I must spend time with a governess, and I will have to, then I want to be assured she will not be making cow eyes at me or, God forbid, sneaking into my bedchamber and peeling down to nothing. Which just happened with the senior upstairs maid who one would think knew better."

"One *would* think so." Hannah might have been tempted

to laugh, but he was so sincere—and so conceited.

Actually, if not for his demand that the governess be plain, Pamela was the perfect candidate. She had little use for men. In fact, she could have wed many a time, but always she had refused, and haughtily, too.

But she liked children, and they liked her. Why she was willing to be part of a scheme that must end in a child's heartache, Hannah didn't understand. Rising, she cut the interview short. "I will see if I can find a governess to fill your needs, my lord, but I make no promises."

He rose also, and smiled at her with such charm she almost staggered under the influence. And she didn't even like him!

"Try," he suggested. "I'm not in the position to help you gain respectability—quite the opposite, I'm afraid. But the money will help buy you time until you have established credibility on your own. Which"—he cocked his head and examined her from head to toe—"you will do. You have the air of someone who succeeds at whatever she sets her hand at."

"Thank you, my lord." Would that that had always been true. "I will inform you of my progress soon."

"By next Tuesday," he said. That gave her a week. "I'll expect a governess to present herself on my doorstep."

She nodded. He strode out the door. Pamela had faded into the shadows of the entry to avoid meeting him, and as he left he looked neither left nor right.

Hannah stood behind the desk, and Pamela stood behind the stairway until Cusheon had closed the front door on Lord Kerrich.

Then they paced forward, meeting in the entry like armed adversaries.

"What do you mean by telling him you made no promises?" Pamela asked. "I'll do it!"

"Your love of money will get you in trouble yet, Pam! You can't mean to go through with his scheme. Lord Kerrich proposes a despicable plot to convince Her Majesty of his decency when he obviously has none."

"In my youth . . . I had occasion to make Her Majesty's acquaintance."

Hannah gaped. Hannah knew Pamela's parents had been wealthy and well connected, but never, never had Pamela revealed how far she had fallen when the tragedy had overtaken her.

Pamela continued softly, "Her Majesty was then and I'm sure is now a person of much good judgment—obviously, if she is threatening Lord Kerrich in some manner. And she is surrounded by every wise adviser—Lord Melbourne and now Prince Albert. I think we can trust she will be protected from his machinations."

Hannah couldn't believe Pamela had kept so much of her background hidden, or that she clearly meant to stop now, after revealing such a tantalizing hint of former glory. "Do you know Lord Kerrich, then?"

Pamela had a gray cast to her skin that dulled her normally bright blue eyes, and her brief laugh contained a tinge of hysteria. "Long ago we met briefly. He won't remember."

"But—"

"He is far too important to recognize me." Pamela lowered her head as if the weight of her memories were too much to carry. "I had a different name then."

Pamela chose to go by her mother's family name, rather than her father's. Hannah didn't blame her, but she was expecting too much if she thought Hannah wouldn't be curious. "Please, tell me—"

"Don't press me."

Hannah heard the note of finality, and subdued the innumerable questions that clamored to be asked. "As you wish. But even if you are safe from identification, surely you also must think of the child. He will be hurt, no matter what Lord I'm-so-handsome says."

"I'll protect the child."

"You love children!"

Pamela turned on her in a fury. "I said, I'll protect the child!"

Hannah stepped back in astonishment.

Pamela's fury faded quickly, leaving her shivering in great convulsions. "We need the money."

"Come to the fire, dear." But Pamela didn't move, and Hannah insisted, "We are not so desperate as that!"

"Yes, we are," Pamela said in gritty perturbation.

Taking her shoulders, Hannah asked, "What's wrong?"

Pamela jerked herself free and trudged into the study, discarding her drooping bonnet onto the floor.

Hannah followed, picking up the hat, shocked that her normally tidy friend could be so careless. "Pamela?"

Pamela ran her hands through her hair, pulling off the white net and quite a few pins in the process.

Hannah winced. That must have hurt, but Pamela didn't seem to notice. She just stood before the fire and held her hands to it even though she still wore her soaked kid gloves. Something had happened. Something hideous. But Pamela seldom told her troubles.

Asking would get Hannah nowhere, so she tried guile. "How can you pass as a plain older woman?"

Pamela raised her gaze from her now-steaming gloves. "When Lady Temperly expired and willed you this house, she left her clothing, did she not? I will wear it."

"Lady Temperly was tall! She topped you by two inches, and she had a pronounced dowager's hump."

"Yes. That will do." Pamela stripped off the gloves and

tossed them on the settle. "I'll wear some pale powder and glaring rouge, just as the older women do. I'll pass. I have to."

"And what about those families who have previously employed you? What will they say when they see you so disguised?"

"I'm a governess, not a social butterfly. As always, I'll remain in the background, and in any case, I've always worked outside of London. The chance of seeing someone who will recognize me is slim."

"Pamela, what's *wrong*?"

Pamela rubbed the place between her eyes as if in pain. "Do you remember when Charlotte, you and I were all desperate for employment, and we decided to try and make a go of the Distinguished Academy of Governesses? How we hoped we could help others find appropriate places of employment and make our fortune at the same time?"

"Yes, of course I do." Desperation had led Hannah to propose the plan. Desperation and ambition, for if the three friends didn't discover some way to make a living not dependent on the whims of the *ton*, they would never have control over their fates.

Pamela, even more than the other two, wanted the Distinguished Academy of Governesses to be a success, and she had worked like a madwoman to obtain temporary positions so Hannah could find suitable candidates and begin the teaching process.

"This school is my only chance to end my life in some kind of prosperity," Pamela said. "I won't give up on my dream now. Our dream."

Hannah realized what the problem *must* be. "It's been too much for you, hasn't it? You've been working too hard, going from house to house teaching those dreadful children.

You'll take anything to avoid doing it any longer, but I told you, Pamela, I would be glad to—"

"No!" Pamela took a deep breath, then grasped Hannah's hand. Taking her fingers, Pamela carried them to a place on the left side of her back. "Here."

Hannah found a tear in the soggy woolen gown. A tear that went deep, past Pamela's corset. "What . . . ?" Pulling her fingers away, she stared at the spot of crimson that stained one finger. "Pamela?"

"It happened on the way home."

"Cusheon!" Hannah shouted, then took Pamela's arm. "You must sit down. You're hurt."

"I'm not, really. It's just a pinprick." But Pamela allowed Hannah to lead her to the chair. "I gave in as soon as the point touched my flesh."

Cusheon arrived at a run. "Madams?" Seeing Pamela's pale face, he shouted for the housekeeper.

Mrs. Knatchbull bustled in with the two older trainees in her wake.

"We need bandages," Cusheon commanded. "And hot water. At once."

"I was robbed. I lost all the money for the last month." Pamela's firm chin quavered. "Unless I take this position, we are ruined."

His butler announced her with an air of gravity befitting a woman of her age and situation. "Lord Kerrich, Miss Pamela Lockhart from the Distinguished Academy of Governesses is here."

Kerrich looked up from the accounts spread before him to stare critically at the lady making her way into his large, book-lined study. A fire burned in the grate, candles flickered in candelabras placed throughout the room, the heavy velvet curtains were open over the tall windows to let in whatever light there was, but the gray and cloudy day made it difficult to observe all the particulars of her appearance. Yet the scent of lavender preceded her as she walked briskly toward him. Then the candlelit circle of light around his heavily carved mahogany desk embraced her, and for the first time in a fortnight his heart lifted. There was no mistaking it—Miss Setterington had indeed produced a governess who fit his needs. Dour, unattractive, yet not so old she would scare the child.

And Miss Setterington had produced this miracle one day earlier than his deadline. He never doubted the power of money.

Rising, he bowed. "Miss Lockhart."

She curtsied, then examined him quite as if he were a recalcitrant pupil and she his instructor.

Lifting his monocle, he returned the favor. She bore a worn, hideous, flowered carpetbag of mammoth proportions, large enough that the handle dangled off her wrist and the bottom bumped at her knee. She carried a black umbrella with a primitively carved wooden handle. Her ill-fitting purple dowager gown hung about her shoulders and showed damp spots from the monotonous rain, yet she sported a generous bosom and neat waist.

Ah, but he was well acquainted with the corset tricks women used to conceal figure defects and enhance deficiencies. Undoubtedly, Miss Lockhart was acquainted with them, too.

She wore tinted spectacles, he noted, a sign of weak eyes and excessive learning. Her complexion was bloodless and her lips pale. Her brown hair was pulled back so tightly from her face that any sagging around the chin and neck had been reduced—another feminine trick, and one that would scarcely fool a connoisseur such as himself. A tangled, spidery thin net of gray lace covered her hair, and she sported an absurd decoration that looked like nothing so much as two knitting needles stuck in right angles through the knot at the base of her neck.

He dropped his monocle and seated himself. "Perhaps you'll do," he said.

She nodded and without waiting for an invitation, seated herself in the old-fashioned Hepplewhite chair before his desk. The style fit her. "I was going to say the same for you."

He scarcely refrained from laughing out loud. She reminded him of his grandfather, a gentleman who had been unwilling, by God, to take insolence from one so undeserving as a mere thirty-year-old grandson.

His amusement evaporated. Because of his grandfather he was doing this. Because of his grandfather and the bank and the family name, which must not suffer for his cousin's weakness and . . . and which did not deserve to be made a laughingstock. His fists clenched at the thought of that laughter. "You have brought references."

"Of course." Plunging her hand into the capacious carpetbag, she brought forth three closely written sheets and handed them across the organized piles of paper on his desktop. "I have nine years' experience with children, and as you see, I've worked for quite exemplary families in various counties around London. Lady Byers, especially, was pleased with the results of my instruction. Her daughter was quite wild when I came into the household, and when I left she was desolated."

He looked the letters over cursorily. They were from good, solid country families, mostly in the southern counties. All claimed that Miss Lockhart taught children with extraordinary skill. He didn't care. He only cared that she fulfilled his requirements. "I assume Miss Setterington has conveyed my needs."

"Yes." Miss Lockhart placed the carpetbag at her feet. "I am to buy you an orphan and train it as your companion."

Hm. Put like that, it didn't sound so dreadful.

"So you may win some"—she looked around his lavishly appointed library—"wager, or some such, which will bring you yet more lucre."

That sounded dreadful. Fiercely resentful of the implied rebuke, he rose to his feet.

But she held up her hand. "Save your facile indignation, my lord. Unlike other women of my acquaintance, I understand that handsome young aristocrats, as well as hoary old merchants, can develop a taste for the acquisition of possessions. Indeed, I would call such an attribute part of the honored English way of life." She smiled in a kind of pale imitation of humor. "Even ladies desire their share of the fortunes. For that same reason, indeed, am I here."

Still he stood and stared at this annoying woman. That damned Miss Setterington had managed, in her disapproval, to make his mission sound more palpable than this old maid in her approbation.

"I can assure you, I will shield the child from any hurt," Miss Lockhart said.

"The child?" Why was she babbling about the child?

"Yes. I assumed your momentary hesitation had to do with worry for the orphan. In fact, you look rather dyspeptic over the fate of the little dear." Miss Lockhart blinked at him from behind her tinted glasses.

Blinked at him, or winked at him?

Her actions recalled him to his purpose. Lifting the candelabra from his desk, he strolled around the desk and shed its light full in her face.

She looked down, her thin nostrils pinched in disdain—or perhaps in dismay. For Miss Lockhart was not as old as he'd first assumed—not that he could depend on age to protect him from unwelcome advances. His initial impression of Miss Lockhart's governess-sternness faded, leaving him to think her merely an unattractive female, firmly on the shelf and, perhaps, desperate to jump off and into any available masculine arms.

More specifically, into his arms.

A simple test would prove him wrong . . . or reluctantly right. Coldly he moved to secure his own peace of mind. Looming over her, he displayed the kind of virile confidence women seemed to find utterly appealing, and waited for her to look up.

At last she did, but if she was impressed, she gave no outward indication. "Could I prevail upon you to put the candelabra down, my lord? It is very bright and I fear you will drip wax on my second-best gown."

"Your second-best gown? It is so attractive," he lied glibly, "I thought it your best gown."

She viewed him as if he were a candidate for Bedlam and moved her skirt from beneath the flickering candles. "I wear my best gown on Sundays, my lord. When I, like all Christian woman, go to *church*."

A reprimand, one aimed at his dissipated conduct. "Then it is simply the lady wearing it who creates the illusion of unparalleled beauty."

Ignoring his graceful figure, she reached into the carpet-bag at her feet and brought forth a ball of yarn and the start of a black woolen knitted . . . thing. "How excessively likely."

Hm. She didn't sound particularly sarcastic, nor did she seem struck by his charms. Was she pretending disinterest, or was she truly the dried-up old prune he required? Placing the candelabra off to the side, he perched one hip on the desk and leaned toward her. "As I expressed to Miss Setterington, I feel the child will be better off serving me than being left in a home for foundlings. It was the thought of my deceit which caused a twinge of conscience."

Her cheeks sucked in as she pursed her mouth. "I see."

He smiled with winsome, if feigned, interest. "Yet I find myself wondering how conscience-ridden you are, Miss Lockhart. An attractive woman, in the prime of life, must not always wish to care for the children of others. Surely you must wish for your own."

She snapped at him. There was no other word for her unrestrained impatience. "What I wish for is no concern of yours, my lord. Your only interest should be in my character and my efficiency. Now." Reaching behind her head, she plucked the long sticks from within her coiffure, threaded them through the knitted thing and proceeded, before his astonished eyes, to knit. "Miss Setterington told me of your generous offer of salary. Yet you'll excuse me if I not only confirm the amount, but discuss my living arrangements."

Words failed him for a few precious moments. Miss Lockhart was an eccentric, then, the kind of absurd spinster that England produced in abundance.

The needles clicked without pause. "Bed and board, of course, Lord Kerrich, and in a decent room, well ventilated." She looked around, appraising his study. "*This* is a pleasant room, with many beautiful decorations and, more important, I can't feel a draft. This chamber is larger than it needs to be, but I imagine, like me, you detest a close room. A close room promotes ill health, and a woman on her own cannot be too careful of her health. Also, I'll have a fireplace that doesn't smoke. I'll have a half-day off every fortnight, no exceptions. I expect to be allowed to go to worship every Sunday, and to take the child, too. I believe a righteous heart is necessary for a successful upbringing, and—"

He interrupted out of sheer necessity and to complete his test. "My dear Miss Lockhart. Dear, dear Miss Lockhart." He laid his hand over one of hers, stilling her incessant knitting. "You must know you needn't worry about the placement of your bedchamber. I will . . . personally . . . approve your room not far from my own."

She looked at his hand in cool disfavor, then up at him. Behind the tinted lenses, her heavily lashed eyes narrowed. "I beg your pardon?"

"These details are of no consequence. You shall have whatever you wish, and I look forward to working . . . closely . . . with you on the teaching of the orphan." He blinked his own not-inconsiderable lashes at her.

With deadly accuracy, she used the knitting needle to rap his hand hard enough for him to snatch it back and rub the bruise. She then raised the needle and skewered the knot at the base of her neck. Thrusting the unfinished knitting back into her bag, she said with awful severity, "Young man, although I cannot believe my ears, I do understand you. It is the curse of my pulchritude to be besieged by male attentions, but I refuse to unquestioningly accept my fate. Much as I would enjoy your generous salary, I must decline your attentions and the position."

My God, she was perfect. Impervious to his charm, so sure of herself, her morals and, amazingly enough, her allure, she could not be swayed from her righteous path. "No! Please, Miss Lockhart, you have made your principles quite clear to me. Rest assured that our association will be that of employer and employee, no more." With Miss Lockhart, he knew the orphan would be molded and cared for and he would be safe alone in his bed.

She viewed him suspiciously. "And my requirements for this position?"

"All will be met."

"You will be able to restrain your animal tendencies?"

With excessive gravity, he agreed, "As difficult as that will be, yes."

"I wish to state my opinion, my lord, although I've never met a man who was reasonable enough to listen to reason."

Oh, this should be prime. "Go ahead."

"It would be better if you married."

"You women all think alike. That is just what Her Majesty told me."

"Marital union, I am told, provides a man an outlet for those inconvenient passions that afflict them. But I suppose you have only a short amount of time before the queen's demands must be met?"

"She has given me three months."

"Three months in which to become respectable?" She looked at him and laughed, a bitter croak of disdain. "Even I believe that is unfair. Yes, you have no recourse except to bring a child into your home, for no woman in her right mind would marry a man like you without extensive courting and vows of fidelity, written and signed in blood."

He straightened from his lounging position. "No woman would refuse me."

"You jest, my lord."

"There isn't a woman alive who can't be seduced by a handsome face, a title or a fortune, and without conceit I can say I possess all three. Really, Miss Lockhart. You have proved resistant to seduction, but what if I offered marriage?"

"That is a stupid supposition. If I were the most beautiful woman in the world, you would still not offer me marriage. Every man claims his passion leads him, but if that were true, they would marry as they wished and not where they must."

"But if my passion led me to you, you would have me for my face and form."

"Men do not love from the fullness of their hearts, and handsome men are worse, for they are spoiled."

"Then you would have me for my title."

"I come from noble stock. I know that title does not confer honor or constancy or integrity."

Deliberately, he played the snake in the garden, and offered the irresistible apple. "Then you would have me for my fortune."

She faltered.

As he knew she would. "Ha!" Tucking his knee into his cupped hands, he leaned back and surveyed her with satisfaction. "I was right."

She looked at him and saw something in his face—and what could it be, damn it!—that stiffened her resolve. "You are wrong. I have managed to refrain from running away with any of the men who make me offers, and I would not trade my dreams for a life with you."

"Your dreams must be grand."

"Not grand, but they are mine." Standing, she hefted the bag on her arm. "And I am done with this fruitless discussion."

"Yes." He couldn't believe he had allowed himself to be lured into such banter, and with such an ugly, disagreeable creature. "You understand what you should do?"

"I will find your orphan and bring the child here. Since I suspect you wish the child to have some fraction of deportment, I will train it—"

He slid off the desk and away from her. "Quickly."

"Yes. Quickly. Then . . . we shall proceed as you wish."

"You'll acquire the child by the end of the day."

"It is after the noon, my lord. I will settle into my chamber and look over the arrangements of your schoolroom today. Tomorrow I shall find us a child."

Taking Miss Lockhart by the arm, Kerrich briskly escorted her toward the door. "Then everything is settled."

"The major details, at least. I dislike taking your time."

"Good." He needed to go back to the figures on the sheet, which were good, damn it. Better than good, and Queen Victoria was a fool for ever doubting him. "Tell the housekeeper to put you in the bedchamber adjoining the schoolroom. If you find that unsatisfactory, make improvements as you wish. I'll tell the woman your wishes supersede all else."

The governess stopped just short of the door. "The . . . woman?"

"The housekeeper." He scrambled to remember her name. "Bertha or Betty or some such."

The governess didn't move. "Is she new to your household, then?"

"Relatively. Seven years. Ten. I don't know." What did the blasted governess want? Why didn't she leave?

She readied to speak, and already Kerrich recognized the spark in her eyes. He had somehow displeased her. She would render a tongue-lashing. He would bestow a set-down. And the woman would know her place.

But a tap at the door saved her the much-needed reprimand.

"Enter," he called impatiently.

Moulton—the butler who was so much more than a butler—stepped through and announced, "My lord, Mr. Lewis Athersmith."

His cousin had answered Kerrich's summons at last.

Kerrich and Moulton exchanged satisfied glances; now their plan could proceed.

"I'll be out of your way," Miss Lockhart said with schoolmistresslike briskness.

"Yes." The sight of the whey-faced, pinch-mouthed, purple-clad governess only reminded him of the staggering run of misfortune he had experienced. He didn't understand how any of it had come to be. A mere month ago, everything had been as it should. He had his title, his fortune, his income, his good looks, his health, an upstanding family, a mistress in his bed, debutantes to flirt with, the respect and good will of everyone in the *ton*, the fear of his enemies . . . all was right with the world.

Then his favorite horse had come up lame, the senior upstairs maid had appeared in his bedchamber stark naked, his mistress had taken umbrage and left in a snit, he'd suffered the catastrophic interview with Queen Victoria, he'd fled to Norfolk imagining that there in the peace and beauty of his country estate he would be able to conceive of a way to appease the queen and her pompous consort.

Only to seek shelter during a rainstorm, and find that infernal contraption in an abandoned hut.

He hadn't even known what it was at first. And him, a banker! Then he had realized, and at the same time he realized his danger. My God, if the villains caught him! He had run from that hut, given instructions that everyone on the estate stay away from the area, and ridden to the train station at top speed. In London, he had gone at once to the correct officials to report the crime and demand they take action—only to discover it was not so easy.

And that was Lewis's fault.

He and Miss Lockhart met his cousin in the entry.

"A new butler, Kerrich?" Lewis watched as Moulton walked away. "I thought you'd never retire old McCutcheon."

"He's off visiting his daughter for the moment," Kerrich lied.

Catching sight of Miss Lockhart, Lewis bowed, his blond hair flopping over his furrowed brow. "I'm sorry, ma'am, I didn't see you."

Miss Lockhart curtsied, and Kerrich reflected bitterly that she probably approved of Lewis. Kerrich and Lewis were of an age, but while Kerrich knew without conceit that he had been blessed with most of the good looks, no one who looked at Lewis would think him anything but good. A cleric, perhaps, or a professor. In the Mathewes family, Lewis had received all the sincerity, resolution and intensity.

Who would have thought those very attributes would lead to his downfall?

"My lord, who is this lovely young man?" Miss Lockhart asked, approval in her ringing tone.

"My cousin, Mr. Lewis Athersmith. Lewis, this is . . . the governess."

"The governess?" Lewis appeared stunned.

"The governess." Let Lewis make of that what he wished.

But the woman pointed her umbrella at Kerrich like a tutor taking a pupil to task. "Lord Kerrich, what is my name?"

"What? What?" He looked hard at her. The light and shadow of the entry sliced at her face. She looked almost menacing and, to his astonishment, her features revealed a trace of beauty. He looked harder. Faded beauty. "You are Miss Lockhart. Why?"

Enunciating clearly, she commanded, "Do not forget my name again."

In astonishment, he stared at her as she curtsied again to Lewis.

Lewis smiled as he returned the obeisance one more time with a little too much enthusiasm. "I look forward to meeting again soon, Miss Lockhart. Any woman who dares take my cousin to task must be a formidable woman."

Miss Lockhart preened. There was no other word for it, and if Kerrich's life hadn't become such a tangle, he would have discharged the female before the farce was truly begun. But he knew full well finding another governess of the proper age and disposition would be well-nigh impossible, and so he ground his teeth as Miss Lockhart approved of Lewis. Approved of him just as everyone in Kerrich's family had always approved; even Kerrich's beloved grandfather had held up Lewis as a shining example for Kerrich to follow.

"I am now in residence here, Mr. Athersmith, and it will

be a pleasure to further our acquaintance." She turned to the butler. "Mr. Moulton, I wish to see the housekeeper. At once." And she marched away on the butler's heels.

"She's an odd thing." Lewis turned his attention on his cousin. "But no odder than you. A governess, cousin?"

Kerrich practiced the tale he had made up to cover his sudden and suspicious philanthropy. "I'm adopting a foundling, a lad I met on the street."

Lewis stared at him as if not quite sure of his hearing.

"The boy's courage and manliness captivated me."

"Courage and manliness." Now Lewis looked down with a deprecating smile. "Of course."

Kerrich could see he had put his foot wrong already. As far back as their childhood, he had been the daring one, the charming one, the one who would inherit the money, the estates and the title. Lewis had been the studious one, the one who had graduated from Oxford with honors, the one for whom everyone predicted a shining future.

Yet what the hell kind of behavior was he indulging in? And why? Not that it mattered; as head of the family, Kerrich could not allow their name and honorable reputation to be dragged through the mud. But still he determined to know why.

So with an affection utterly at odds with what he truly felt for his mutton-headed relative, he led the way to the comfortable grouping of chairs around the fireplace. "Sit down, Lewis."

Lewis slowly sank into the chair, his blue eyes cautious.

And *guilty*. Damn it! Why hadn't Kerrich noticed that before?

He answered his own question. Because he hadn't seen Lewis for months. Heaven knows, he hadn't missed him, and it hadn't occurred to him he ought to be scrutinizing Lewis's activities. Lewis was the son of a vicar, for Lord's sake! Lewis was supposed to be honorably employed by Lord Swearn preparing his heir for Oxford, not engaging in criminal activities!

When Kerrich thought about it, he just wanted to shake Lewis until he saw sense, then send him back to the family estate in Norfolk where Grandpapa would shake Lewis until this madness had passed. But somebody had to find out the details of Lewis's offenses, learn the names of his accomplices, and more important, of the master criminal, and handle the matter. That somebody was Kerrich. So he sank into an armchair opposite his cousin and with a serious mien said, "I have a proposition to offer you."

If anything, Lewis became more cautious. "You, cousin?"

"There's trouble at the bank." Kerrich weighed his words with care, choosing them for the optimum effect. "I can't go to anyone but a family member. I need you to come and live with me. Work for me." Lewis began to speak, but Kerrich held up his hand. "Please, hear me out. I know you already have a position"—Lewis had been terminated, but Kerrich pretended not to know that—"and it will not reflect honorably on you to depart at such a time, but I find myself in a dreadful situation, one with dire consequences."

"You, cousin?" A faint smile played around Lewis's mouth.

"I know I can't in good faith ask that you abandon your post for me, but I do depend on your affection for Grandpapa."

Lewis's smirk disappeared. "Why would any problem of yours affect Lord Reynard?"

"Because it is my grandfather's bank. He started it, he worked there even after entrusting the running of it to my father, he trained me after my father's death. I know you hate the figures and the finance, and I know you swore you would never labor therein, but I pray that your affection for Grandpapa will overcome your distaste."

There it was again. Guilt, writ for Kerrich to see. Hadn't Lewis thought how his crime would strike at Lord Reynard's heart? Or was he so lost to all scruples he didn't care?

When Lewis didn't at once respond, Kerrich continued, "I know. You will say Grandpapa isn't your grandfather, but a great-uncle. Yet I think you feel affection for him, and while he would never mention it, you also owe him your education."

Under the weight of the guilt Kerrich piled on, Lewis's resistance caved in. "Yes," he said. "I owe your grandfather everything. If I judge your problem at the bank to be as grievous as you claim, then of course I will help you."

"It could not be any more grievous," Kerrich answered. "As you know, we print our own banknotes for distribution in Norfolk."

Lewis nodded. Probably he didn't dare open his mouth for fear confession would come flying out.

So Kerrich told Lewis what he already knew. "Someone is counterfeiting our banknotes."

CHAPTER 4

Boys were such obnoxious creatures. Pamela pondered that truth as she searched the eager crowd of orphans gathered around her in the refectory. Each was showing off, each trying to get her to choose him to be taken away from the sterile environs of the orphanage, and the little boys' antics reminded her of the big boy's antics she'd recently observed.

The big boy being Lord Kerrich, and his antics yesterday being the silliest bit of posturing she'd ever seen in an adult man. Yes, he was handsome, wealthy, and titled. Yes, his smile could charm the birds out of the trees. No, she didn't care.

No more than she cared about the whistles and tricks the lads used to assault her ears and call attention to themselves. Kerrich's charms were as obvious and wearisome as his cousin's were refined and studious. Kerrich could learn a lot from Mr. Athersmith.

He would not, of course. Pamela remembered observing Kerrich at Kensington Palace and diagnosing him as a vainglorious young man with a high opinion of himself. He hadn't changed. He thought himself above the common run of gentlefolk. She could only hope that someday someone—some woman—would put him in his place. And that she was around to see it.

One of the eight-year-old boys began to sing in a high, sweet voice. He was gifted, and with training could become a great vocalist, but although Kerrich disclaimed interest in his orphan, Pamela suspected she knew what he wanted: a manly boy, one he could slap on the shoulder.

A responsible and well-paid governess should try to give Kerrich what he wanted, so she steadfastly ignored the talented boy, and also girls who sat on the stairway with their faces pressed between the banisters. Too bad, for Pamela had a weakness for the unloved, the outcast, the leftover children. She understood them so well.

"Hey!" One of the larger boys shoved the younger ones aside. "I'm Chilton. I be a good 'un. See?" He rolled up his sleeve and flexed his muscle. "I could carry yer coal and black yer stove better than any o' these other fellows."

"Cannot." Brave and furious, one of the younger boys shoved back. "Ye're bigger, but ye're lazy."

Chilton doubled his fist. "Am not."

Another boy shoved him from the back, and the toughest boys tumbled to the floor in roiling turmoil.

"A feisty bunch, aren't they?" Mrs. Fallowfield, the orphanage director, tried to put a good front on the brawl.

Without a reply, Pamela stepped back to avoid the fracas.

Seeing her disapproval, Mrs. Fallowfield clapped her hands and ineffectually shouted for order. The blowsy woman had no control over the children, but only the desperate or corrupt took a position such as this, and Pamela judged this woman to be both. Certainly she had been more than willing to sell Pamela one of the boys without ever asking what his fate would be. She had only demanded her price.

Pamela's gaze wandered to the outskirts of the crowd. One boy of perhaps ten stayed back from the rest, watching the fracas with hazel eyes too wide for his thin, smudged face. His dirt-brown hair hung just to his shoulders, he wore a smock of some kind and held a broom, and while the fighting knot of boys hid his lower body, Pamela thought him pathetically thin.

Raising her voice above the cacophony, Pamela asked Mrs. Fallowfield, "What about that youth?"

The director looked surprised. "That's not—"

But Chilton had heard, and he staggered erect, wiping his bloody nose on his sleeve. "Youth?" Collapsing back onto the floor, he brayed with laughter. His merriment was apparently contagious, for the other boys started sniggering, the girls hooted and stomped their feet, and even Mrs. Fallowfield had trouble controlling her amusement.

The lad looked as if he'd been slapped, and not for the first time.

Apparently Pamela had inadvertently made him a laughingstock. She gestured him over, and as he made his way toward her, she understood.

The lad was a lass. What looked like a smock was actually a rag of a well-worn dress. Her skinny wrists stuck out from the sleeves and the hem had been let down until there was nothing left, and still her stocking-clad ankles were revealed. Why her hair was short, Pamela didn't know, but the cut obviously had brought other misunderstandings, other mockery. The poor girl was near tears, and fighting not to let the others know they had hurt her.

Pamela understood. Well did she remember her early, ugly duckling years when everyone mocked her for her gangly legs and incredible clumsiness. She herself had been the butt of many a joke, as well as the celestial joke of all time—she had grown into a beautiful swan.

She wanted to assure the girl that only too soon the boys would give anything for one smile from her lips, but she couldn't promise beauty or confidence or strength of character. Not growing up in such a loveless, toilsome environment. So Pamela tucked her hands behind her and asked, "What's your name, dear?"

"Elizabeth, ma'am." The girl bobbed a curtsy. "Elizabeth Hunter."

"How old are you, Elizabeth?"

"I have eight years."

Eight? She was eight? For all her pathetic thinness, the girl was tall and promised to get taller. No wonder she slumped her shoulders. Pamela ached to comfort her, and her fingers writhed as she clasped them together to restrain the impulse. "How long have you been at the orphanage, Elizabeth?"

The room was silent now as everyone listened to the exchange.

While Elizabeth was obviously nervous, still she met Pamela's gaze without flinching. "Over a year, ma'am, since my parents died of the fever."

"Ah." Unlike the other children Pamela had met here, this child spoke with a crisp, educated accent, and now she knew why. "Were you sick, too?"

"Yes, ma'am."

That explained the haircut, for everyone knew long hair sapped the strength, and cutting it was a common therapy to cure a fever. Pamela gave a comforting smile. "Well, Elizabeth Hunter, I apologize for thinking you a boy."

Rising from the tangle of boyish arms and legs, Chilton staggered up, running into Pamela on the way, and sneered right into the girl's face. "Yeah, Beth, you're such a milksop you could never be a boy."

"Really?" Quick as a striking snake, Beth grabbed his

ear and twisted, bringing the big boy to his knees. "At least I'm not a thief. Give it back."

Pamela watched in bewilderment.

"Ow ow ow." He clawed at Beth's hand.

Beth ignored the pain. "Give it!"

He struck out at her.

She extended her arm all the way, stood out of his reach, and gave his ear another twist.

At last Chilton delved into his pants and brought out Pamela's silver watch.

Rage roared through Pamela. When he had bumped her, he had lifted her watch—the one thing she still owned that had been her father's—from the small pocket sewn into her skirt. The restraining ribbon had been cut, the whole operation done so skillfully she hadn't even noticed.

Beth let Chilton go, but something of Pamela's inarticulate fury must have shown in her expression, for he dropped the watch and scampered backward.

Beth caught the timepiece before it hit the floor, and wiped it on her apron. "If you've got a handkerchief, ma'am, you can place it within the folds until you can properly clean it after being in *his* pants."

Mrs. Fallowfield aimed a blow at Chilton's head as he sidled past. "Ye little reprobate, now Miss Lockhart will think I'm raising ye to be a pickpocket!"

Was Pamela such a buffoon, then? Robbed of a month's wages by a vile footpad, then of her watch by an orphan boy?

"Ma'am?" Beth held the watch extended.

Deliberately, Pamela used her handkerchief to reach out for the watch.

Beth flinched as if expecting a slap.

Pamela stopped and looked around at the silent crowd. They hated Beth. In her speech and her appearance she was different, and now by her actions she'd made them all look like thieves. Would Beth be punished for her good deed? Flicking a glance at the fuming Mrs. Fallowfield, Pamela knew the woman would blame Beth for revealing the crime, not the boy for committing it.

Taking the watch, she slipped it and the handkerchief into her reticule, then stripped off her right glove. With her tongue, she wet her thumb and rubbed the smudge off Beth's chin. Mind made up, she said, "I'll take this one."

Beth's eyes grew round and lustrous.

A flurry of whispers broke out from the orphans.

"That one?" Mrs. Fallowfield couldn't restrain her scorn. "Ye came fer a lad!"

Beth lost that brief luminosity, and she glanced from Mrs. Fallowfield to Pamela.

"I've changed my mind."

Like a thwarted shop assistant, Mrs. Fallowfield didn't give up. "Beth's no good fer ye. She's insolent an' . . . an' proud. Thinks she's better than anyone else."

"Yes. I can see that," Pamela said brusquely as she opened her pocketbook. "I believe you said three pounds sterling for an orphan under ten years of age."

"Fer a lad!"

Pamela should have known the woman wouldn't easily yield. Spearing her with a glance, she said, "Girls are worth less. So two pounds."

Beth clasped her hands together at her chest, as if hope was taking roost in her affection-starved heart.

Mrs. Fallowfield's mouth flopped open. "Naw," she squawked. "Five pounds. Five fer that little hussy."

Pamela pressed three pounds into Mrs. Fallowfield's hand, and for all the woman's denials her fingers closed eagerly over the coins. "Three pounds, as we agreed." Taking Beth's hand, she led her toward the door.

Mrs. Fallowfield hurried after them. "Ye'll be sorry. Ye'll bring her back in a day complainin' about her."

Beth flung open the outer door as if sweet freedom itself waited in the misty morning air.

As Pamela stepped onto the narrow steps, she smiled her chilliest smile at Mrs. Fallowfield. "Then you would have the undoubted pleasure of telling me 'I told you so.' "

My God, what have I done?

The footman held the umbrella as Pamela urged Beth up the steps into Lord Kerrich's carriage. She followed Beth and seated herself on the forward-facing seat, where her doubts assaulted her full force. How could she have so impulsively taken a girl from the orphanage, when she knew quite well Kerrich desired a boy? Her reckless act of defiance might result in her dismissal—a dismissal she and the Distinguished Academy of Governesses could ill afford.

In silence, she stared at the dirty, badly groomed and gawky child before her.

But the silence lasted only as long as it took for the coachman to set the horses in motion and Beth to fall to her knees in the cramped space. Snatching Pamela's gloved hand in hers, she kissed it, and in a timid, earnest voice she said, "Thank you, miss. Thank you for your kindness in taking me away from that place. I never thought I could hope again, and now I can and I swear, miss, swear on the graves of my mother and father that I will do everything you want. I'll be good. I won't cause you any trouble. You won't even know I'm there, I'll be so good."

"Oh, please get up!" Appalled by the child's lavish gratitude, Pamela tugged her fingers away. Once again, Beth had reminded Pamela of herself as a child, endeavoring to be whatever her father wanted, to do whatever her father wanted. Not even the constant lessons he taught—that nothing she did could please him for long—had ever stopped her from trying. For her mother's sake, she strove desperately to make him happy, and for her own sake, too. She had lived in the hopes of hearing his praise and desiring his smile.

She wouldn't subjugate this child to that kind of torment.

"If you knew what I've got you into, you might not be so grateful."

Awkwardly, Beth sidled onto the seat opposite. Her hazel eyes were big and fearful. "I know. The master wants a lad."

"That, too." *The master doesn't really intend to adopt you.* The confession hovered on the tip of Pamela's tongue, brought forth by the guilt her deception caused her. Guilt she hadn't experienced until she'd put a face to the girl. The hopeful eyes. The pale lashes. The broad forehead and sweet chin. The teeth, new and too large for the childish face. The cheeks, meant to be round and full, but thinned with omnipresent hunger.

But what was the use of telling Beth of the consequences that might be visited on her so far in the future? They'd be lucky to make it through this day without Kerrich demanding Pamela fetch him a different child. "Actually," Pamela said bracingly, "he never told *me* he wanted a boy. That was an assumption on my part. Your qualifications make you a much better candidate for His Lordship's purposes than any of the other children."

"Qualifications, Miss Lockhart?"

Pamela smiled at the child rocking with the motion of

the carriage as it traveled the rainy London streets. "Yes, indeed. You are polite and well spoken. Lord Kerrich will be able to display you to his friends without fear you will embarrass him."

Beth's grubby fingers twisted in her lap. "He's going to want to display me to his friends?"

"Lord Kerrich will be proud of you," Pamela explained. "He'll want to introduce you."

"Oh." Beth bit her lip, then confessed, "I'm rather shy. The other children make fun of me because of it."

The wretched colored glasses were sliding down Pamela's nose, and as she pushed them back up, she remembered—she wasn't young Pamela, the governess thieves and employers took advantage of. She was stern, no-nonsense Miss Lockhart, so unattractive Kerrich had been openly relieved when she hadn't responded to his flirtatious advances. The character she played had enough stiffness in her spine to give courage to an entire orphanage of bashful children, and that character wouldn't allow Beth to succumb to nerves now. Not when the child had just escaped the foundling home and still faced the gauntlet of Kerrich's examination. Drawing herself sternly erect, Pamela said, "Nonsense. You are not shy. Look at how you calmly introduced yourself to me after I had mistakenly assumed you were a boy. And view your bravery in recovering my watch! No, young lady, you are not shy. You are a lion in the face of adversity."

Beth drew back from Pamela's bracing manner. "I am?"

"Certainly." The carriage swung onto Hyde Park Gardens and stopped before Kerrich's townhouse.

"Maybe I'm only brave when bad things are happening," Beth said cautiously.

Pamela nodded with all the firmness of a seasoned mentor. "A clear indicator of courage." Young Timothy, the footman, opened the door. He held the umbrella in one hand and offered his other hand. Taking it, she stepped out and turned in time to see Beth tumble out on her heels. "Ah. A chance for our first lesson. One always allows the footman to lend a hand when descending a carriage."

Beth looked up at the impassive, liveried servant. "I can get out without his help." Then, perhaps thinking she had hurt his feelings, she said to him, "But thank you anyway, mister."

The footman's mouth twitched with suppressed laughter.

Yet he liked the child's courtesy, Pamela could see that by the stiff little bow he gave.

Kerrich *had* to keep her. Pamela fell further into the role of masterly Miss Lockhart. "Very good. One should always thank the servants, by name if possible. He is Timothy."

"Timothy," Beth repeated.

"Now stand up straight, shoulders back."

Beth straightened.

"Come with me, and remember—you are a lion."

"Yes, Miss Lockhart." Beth answered bravely enough.

But her little hand crept into Pamela's, and Pamela looked down at her and smiled with encouragement. "That's the spirit!" she said, although Beth had paled so much the smudges of dirt stood out on her cheeks.

The footman with his umbrella sheltered them as they started up the stairs toward the massive double door that was the entrance to Kerrich's townhouse.

Beth's steps dragged. "Miss Lockhart? Is this a boardinghouse or a hotel or . . . what is this place?"

Pamela stopped, brought face to face with the massive task she'd set herself—to prepare a foundling for a masquerade to fool society. To fool the queen who, from Kerrich's throwaway comments, knew him and his mechanisms only too well. Pamela, used to entering the homes of the wealthy, counted Kerrich's home and its trappings as among the greatest she'd ever viewed. Beth, raised by middle-class parents, living in a squalid orphanage, was ill prepared to deal with this kind of affluence.

But Beth was a child. Children adapted easily to change—or so Pamela told herself. With a gesture that encompassed the broad stairway, the Roman arches above each window, the brooding stone eagle carvings set in the brick façade, she said, "This is Lord Kerrich's home."

Beth lifted her chin and looked up, up, to the roof four stories above the street. "Does he have a large family? Children?" She pleaded for information as if she suddenly realized how little she knew of the man who held her fate in his hands.

"Never fear, he has only a cousin, whom I met and who seems a good gentleman. I understand from Mrs. Godwin, the housekeeper, that he is staying for a time with Lord Kerrich. I don't know about any other relations." She didn't, she realized. She hadn't cared about Kerrich's family, only about herself and how he and his money could serve her.

And that was fair, she told herself sturdily. She cared about him as much as he cared about her. Although it did seem Beth had a good plan to acquaint herself with her patron before being introduced to him.

"Is Lord Kerrich nice?" Beth asked.

That Pamela could answer without qualm. "Very nice indeed, when he decides to be." She rapped on the door, and nodded at Moulton when he opened it.

"Is this the child?" Moulton asked as Pamela led Beth into the foyer.

"Is this the master?" Beth asked in a voice of awe.

Moulton, stuffy and pretentious, unbent enough to whisper, "No, miss. I am the new butler."

"You're the butler?" Beth examined his austere features and magnificent suit, and she made her admiration known with one reverent word. "Never."

Pamela smiled as she unpinned her hat and handed it to the footman. Beth had charmed Moulton, for if he had been a grouse he would have ruffled his breast.

Instead he examined Beth's shabby appearance with undisguised horror and advised, "Lord Kerrich is in the study. Miss Lockhart, I would strongly suggest you wash the child before presenting her to the master."

So he, and undoubtedly all the servants, knew why their elegant domain had been invaded by a child.

"Yes, she needs a bath."

"Not likely," Beth muttered.

Pamela paid her no heed. With every intention of whisking her upstairs, she guided the child into the foyer.

But Beth skittered to a stop as the interior of the house opened up to her view. The large and towering entrance gleamed with polished wood floors and massive hand-tied Oriental rugs in deep colors of rose and royal blue. Two footmen flanked the outer door, each so still in his blue and gold livery he might have been part of the furniture. Gilt-framed mirrors decorated the white-painted walls, reflecting the light from the crystal chandelier and the diamond-shaped windowpanes. Fresh-cut flowers blossomed everywhere. A stairway rose up the middle and split at the top to become a gallery where one could scrutinize the comings and goings of the household.

A series of chambers led off the foyer. As Beth crept forward, she peered into the morning room, the breakfast room, the library, and her gasps sang in the silence. Pamela followed, observing the child's wonder with a fascination of her own. It was like watching the girl open her first present on Christmas morning, and Beth's wide eyes and trembling awe only reinforced Pamela's determination to keep the orphan.

Then Beth peeked into the open door of Kerrich's study, and she scurried to hide behind Pamela.

Pamela glared at the gentleman who stalked toward them, a broad-shouldered silhouette against the fading light behind him.

"Miss Lockhart, is that the child?"

Beth clutched at Pamela's skirt.

Without effort, Pamela found herself transformed into the strict Miss Lockhart, acting—and reacting—to his egotistical lordship. "My lord, this is indeed your child."

"Bring it in." With the confidence of a man who was never refused, Kerrich turned his back and returned to his refuge.

Pamela marched forward, towing Beth behind her. Stepping into the doorway, she said, "The child would be better served if allowed to bathe and change before meeting you."

"No."

Kerrich's flat refusal put Pamela on her mettle. "Very well." Clasping Beth's hand, she drew her gently into the study, then urged her forward with a hand in her back.

Kerrich had taken up position with his hip on his desktop, long-limbed, graceful, and as unintentionally attractive as he had been yesterday on purpose. His gaze considered first Pamela, then slowly moved to rest on Beth. His eyes sharpened, and he straightened from his fashionable slouch. In a furious, betrayed tone, he said, "Miss Lockhart, *that* is a girl."

"Very astute of you, my lord," Pamela approved. Heavens, how good she was at this pretense of pedantry and restraint! "Amazingly enough, the only other choice in gender the orphanage contained was that of a boy."

"Why *didn't* you get a boy?"

"None was suitable."

"What do you mean, none was suitable?"

"Beth is the only child in the foundling home with the necessary qualifications."

"The necessary qualifications?" He commanded attention by his arrogant pose and imperious tone. "Woman, what the devil are you talking about?"

"My lord, your rough speech is unacceptable in the presence of two ladies. Unlike Beth's, whose speech is unmarked by street cant." Pamela paused and let that sink in.

From the foyer came the sound of a knock on the outer door.

Kerrich examined Beth again. "Surely there was some lad there who—"

"No." Pamela's gaze clashed with his. "Also, Beth's manners are impeccable. And she is honest. I will make no comment on the state of *your* honesty."

Beth whimpered, a pitiful whisper that halted the two combatants.

Moulton tapped at the open door. "My lord?"

Kerrich paid his butler no heed, but he did take note of the child's unease, for he tempered his tone. "What am I to do with a girl?" he asked.

"Just what you would do with a boy, I fancy," Pamela answered. "Show her off. Become a character of kindness and respectability."

"That's stupid!"

Pamela truly enjoyed retorting, "I have thought so all along."

Kerrich narrowed his eyes at her. "Miss Lockhart, you overstep your bounds!"

Voices came from the foyer, and the drift of fresh air told Pamela the outer door was open. "Forgive me, my lord.

I thought most men enjoyed having a woman agree with their pronouncements."

Beth tugged at her sleeve, and Pamela leaned down so she could whisper loudly. "Please, ma'am. We're supposed to be convincing him I'm the tyke for him."

Pamela slid her gaze toward him. He'd heard, of course, and of course he felt no compunction about grinning his delight at Pamela's discomfiture. "A boy," he announced, "would go to the horse races with me. And to the fights. And to the club."

In deference to Beth, Pamela tempered her impatience. "You have a reputation as a rake. Take Beth where you would take your own daughter. To the park. To a Shakespearean play. To the fireworks."

Moulton took a hesitant step into the chamber. "My lord?"

"In a minute, Moulton!" Kerrich said irascibly. "Miss Lockhart, such an itinerary would bloody bore me to death!"

Her patience, always thin with foolish gentlemen, snapped again. "Think, my lord! You mourn the chance to entertain yourself by teaching a young man the dissipations you revel in? The queen does not attend the horse races or the fights."

"What do you know of Her Majesty's habits?"

"As much as you, if you would only—" Pamela brought herself under control before she could betray herself and her past to the overly arrogant gentleman. "I know she is recently wed, and I know her consort is quite somber. And it doesn't take a great deal of thought to realize that the queen, like any right-thinking woman, would not be impressed by your philanthropy when it involves teaching young men to wager!"

Moulton stepped into the foyer and stared, then stepped back in and fidgeted.

Kerrich didn't appreciate her frank, and without a doubt correct, evaluation of his plan, and he did what all men do when their fallacies are pointed out to them. He sulked. "This child is useless to me."

Evidently, Beth decided she had to take a hand in her own fate, for she spoke directly to him. "Excuse me, sir. I'm not useless. I know how to do lots of things, and if you let me stay, I'll learn how to be the brat you're looking for." Her voice was shaking, yet she stared Kerrich right in the eye. "But you have to let me stay first. I promise to do whatever it is you want me to do, if you'll just give me a chance."

Kerrich glanced at Beth.

Please. Pamela wanted to plead with him. *Look at her. See past the dirt and shyness to the courage and spirit.*

But his eyes narrowed, and his color built. "Miss Lockhart, you must imagine that I am a soft-hearted imbecile to try and foist such a ruse on me. Is she your sister, perhaps, or a cousin you dabbed with dirt and hoped would wring my heartstrings? I am not so gullible!"

Beth jerked her hand out of Pamela's and put her fists on her hips. "Are you calling her a liar? She's a nice lady, and she rescued me!"

For one horrible moment, Pamela thought Beth would try to box his ears. Catching her shoulders, she held her close and said, "Truly, my lord. I met Beth today for the first time. I do not seek to deceive you in any way." But her voice faltered on that assurance, since her very appearance was a deception.

Kerrich noticed, of course, and stood up as if he would throw them both out personally.

But from the doorway of his study came an old man's hearty voice. "Hey, lad, do you have a hug for your old grandpapa?"

CHAPTER 6

"Gardner Mathewes, the marquess of Reynard, has arrived," Moulton intoned, as if any idiot couldn't see Kerrich's beloved grandfather standing in the doorway.

"Grandpapa!" Kerrich stood, totally flummoxed by the unexpected appearance. "Why didn't you warn me you were coming?"

"Warn you?" Lord Reynard chortled. "You sound like a lad caught out in a prank. Why should I warn you, young Devon?" He peered up at his grandson through the same brown color of eyes Kerrich saw in the shaving mirror every morning. "Have I come at an inconvenient time?"

"Not at all." *The worst.* Nevertheless, a flood of affection engulfed Kerrich at the sight of the old man. Regaining his wits, he strode forward and embraced his grandfather, and felt the poke of old bones where muscle used to be. He looked down at his grandfather—the grandfather who used to be his height—and said, "You know I always welcome you."

"Bloody right." Lord Reynard embraced him back, and he must have been peering over Kerrich's shoulder because he said, "Pardon me. I didn't see these lovely young ladies."

"What lovely young ladies?" Kerrich turned to see Miss Lockhart standing with that ridiculous girl-child she wanted him to take in.

"Well, lad, don't dither. Who are these lovely young ladies?" Lord Reynard asked, and he couldn't have sounded more delighted to see the shy little foundling and her sour-puss governess.

Because of Kerrich's obligations this . . . onerous female . . . had come into his life. He glared at Pamela, fully aware he had approved of her only the day before. What had been in his mind?

Duty. Family honor. Queen Victoria saying, *Lord Kerrich, if you don't cease your frivolous pursuit of women and show yourself to be a serious, responsible gentleman, I can no longer allow you to retain those parts of my personal fortune in your bank. You should marry, as I have done, produce children, and become respectable—or else.*

And he, being a stupid fool, had sneered and asked, "Or else what? What worse could you do then to take your fortune away from my safekeeping?"

Well, she'd told him. The queen's *or else* had haunted his nightmares for years, and to discover someone knew his secret! And to have it be Victoria herself!

Taking matters into her own hands, Miss Lockhart introduced herself. "I am Miss Pamela Lockhart." She bent her head low as she curtsied to Lord Reynard, making a point of displaying a great deal more respect to the elderly nobleman than she had to Kerrich. "Lord Reynaud, it is an honor."

"Miss Lockhart." Lord Reynard rubbed his chin thoughtfully. "Have we met?"

"Perhaps, my lord, but a good many years ago and very briefly."

Lord Reynard stared at her as if dredging up memories

long disused. "I used to know the Lockharts from Somerset. Are you related to them?"

Startled, Kerrich looked at Miss Lockhart. She was one of the Somerset Lockharts?

But Miss Lockhart didn't meet his gaze, or his grandfather's, either. Instead she looked down at the carved Chinese carpet and without emotion, said, "Yes, my lord. Alice Lockhart Ripley was my mother."

"Ah." Lord Reynard stiffened, then bowed slightly. "Hadn't heard about your father's death until recently. Let me extend my condolences."

"Thank you, my lord."

Kerrich was shocked. Miss Lockhart, as unnatural a female as he had ever met, reacted not with grief but with what looked like resentment, even embarrassment. His father had died when Kerrich was ten, and Kerrich well remembered the choking grief of loss. How could Miss Lockhart be so cold? And why was his grandfather looking so dismayed?

Injecting a falsely hearty note into his voice, Lord Reynard asked, "What are you doing here with my grandson? He's a rascal, you know. You'll have to watch yourself."

Kerrich barely refrained from snorting, then scrambled to fulfill his diplomatic duties. "This is the governess."

"The governess." Lord Reynard's wrinkled lips puckered.

If anything, Miss Lockhart grew more pallid and peevish. "Yes, my lord. I make my way in the world by teaching children."

"Good. Good," Lord Reynard said obscurely. Placing one hand on his cane and one hand on Kerrich's arm, he said, "I've been rattling around in that demmed coach for hours, and I'd like to take a turn about the room."

"As you wish, sir," Kerrich said.

With a short, dignified bow, Lord Reynard said, "Ladies, excuse us a moment. Don't leave."

They made a circuit of the room, passing Kerrich's desk, the grouping of armchairs before the fire. As always, Kerrich was shocked at the disintegration of the tall, proud mentor of his youth. The stoop of Lord Reynard's shoulders had grown so pronounced he had to lift his head to look Kerrich right in the face. In the past three years he had stopped carrying the decorative cane hooked over his arm and begun using it to support his every step. His rheumatism had grown worse with each winter, and a rainy day like today made him hobble and grunt.

At the farthest end of the room, out of Miss Lockhart's earshot and in the alcove with the bookshelves and the tall, curtained window, Lord Reynard paused and leaned one hand against the ledge as if exhausted.

"Are you well, sir?" Kerrich asked, putting his arm around him.

"Fine as can be expected. Most men of eighty-four are drooling in their silver cups, not chasing their female caretakers around their beds." He tapped his forehead. "And I'm still sharp as an icepick up here."

"For which I am very thankful." Usually. In his present circumstances, his grandfather's acumen could be the cause of great discomfort.

"Just brought you here to warn you . . . Burgess Ripley was charming, handsome, witty, and he abandoned his daughter and wife. Blackguard left them destitute."

"Good God." Kerrich looked at Miss Lockhart. She was kneeling before Beth, straightening the child's clothing and speaking quietly. The child was smiling at her as if she were a vision of beauty, and not some acerbic middle-aged spinster, and Kerrich couldn't even find it in his heart to insinuate that Burgess Ripley had fled to avoid his daughter's acrimony. With the child and with Lord Reynard she seemed almost . . . sweet. "Why did he leave them?"

"Always had a wandering eye. Went to live with some doxy on the continent. The mother died, leaving poor Miss Ripley—or as she calls herself now, Miss *Lockhart*—alone, and I believe the girl wasn't yet sixteen."

"That must have been twenty-five years ago. She should be over it by now."

"Not *that* long."

Not that long in his grandfather's timeframe, Kerrich supposed, but the injury done to Miss Lockhart by her father had obviously soured her on the whole male gender. "Then I will not inquire more about her family background."

"The Ripleys used to be much in society. I'm surprised you don't remember the family."

"I think that was probably before I attended parties." But was it? Something nudged at his memory . . . something about that night at Kensington Palace . . . swiftly, he turned his mind away. He made it a habit never to contemplate that night at Kensington Palace.

"For a bright young man, you're occasionally quite obtuse," Lord Reynard observed.

"I?" Kerrich prided himself on his intelligence. "No other man at the bank can judge the market as I can and invest so profitably. No man comprehends the vagaries of trade, and I'm damned good at predicting the ebb and flow of currency. You know. You taught me."

"I taught you the importance of recognizing faces and remembering names, too, my lad, but you've never thought that a significant skill, and for that you're a fool."

Stung, Kerrich said, "I remember people of consequence."

Lord Reynard stopped again and faced Kerrich. "People

of consequence change every day. I started with nothing, lad, just the title you now bear and a strong determination to conquer whatever horizon I crossed. I started at that bank at thirteen and owned it before I was thirty, but I remember every slight I received from the people of consequence of my day. And where are they now?"

"Dead?"

"Cheeky." Lord Reynard grinned. "Yes, most of them, but they fawned on me before they died. I made a point to forget their names, and favors were not given to those who slighted me in my youth. Somewhere in your organization there is a youth working for you who looks up to you and is stung by your inattention. Your failings are going to catch up with you, and soon, I predict."

"I'll put my mind to remembering names, Grandpapa." They started toward Miss Lockhart and the child again. "Just as soon as my life returns to normal."

Lord Reynard dismissed his promise with a flip of the hand. "Oh, that'll never happen now."

They returned to the spot where Miss Lockhart and Beth stood waiting. Lord Reynard stared at them searchingly, then asked the question Kerrich had been waiting for. "What do you need a governess for, lad?"

"I'm adopting a foundling." Kerrich braced himself for questions.

"*This* foundling?" Lord Reynard cocked his head and examined the girl.

That wasn't the question that Kerrich expected. He thought that Lord Reynard would demand to know why.

Instead he again asked, "This foundling?"

His grandfather's tolerance knocked him off-balance, and Kerrich glanced at Miss Lockhart. She watched him with bright, interested eyes, as if she couldn't wait to hear his decision whether to take Beth or demand another, and all the while knowing he was trapped. Trapped by his grandfather's fortuitous arrival and by the sour knowledge he'd been losing the earlier fight anyway.

He capitulated with little grace. "Yes, this foundling. This is—" Damn, what was the brat's name?

Lord Reynard stared significantly at Kerrich.

Kerrich wished he remembered this one name at least.

"I need a seat, lad."

Kerrich hurriedly brought him a chair from before the desk.

Lord Reynard sank down on it. Then in as kind a tone as Kerrich had ever heard him use, Lord Reynard asked, "Child, what are you called?"

"I'm Elizabeth Hunter. Beth." She curtsied without being told, but trembled at the attention focused on her.

"So, Beth, what do you think of my grandson? Are you like all women, and think he's a young charmer?"

Beth's eyes widened as if the question astonished her. "Oh, no, my lord. I don't think he's young at all."

Miss Lockhart whipped her handkerchief out of her sleeve and hid her lips behind its ample folds. As if that could disguise her amusement at Kerrich's expense!

Kerrich glowered directly at her, forcing her to meet his gaze, and when she did he experienced a shock. For he might consider this female a termagant, but when merriment shone from her eyes he found himself seeing the humor in the situation. Only the most celebrated of sirens could make a man laugh at himself, yet he found himself almost smiling back. Almost. By God, in the far distant past had Miss Lockhart been a femme fatale?

Lord Reynard paid heed to neither his grandson nor Miss Lockhart. "And my grandson's certainly not a charmer, heh?"

"Well, I don't know." Beth scraped the carpet with her

toe and looked bashful, making Kerrich wonder if he'd imagined her earlier fury on Miss Lockhart's behalf. "He seems kinda—"

Miss Lockhart earned her pay for that day, at least, when she interrupted Beth's disclosure. "Beth is yet so new to the household, she has scarcely had the pleasure of being showered by Lord Kerrich's charms as the rest of us have."

Kerrich barely refrained from wiping his brow. He could imagine how his grandfather would react if he knew Kerrich had accused a lady whose family had been among his acquaintances of dishonesty and deceit.

"However, Beth will get to know His Lordship, for Lord Kerrich will be spending part of each day in the nursery with Beth and me."

Kerrich's pleased regard faded. "What?"

Miss Lockhart pulled Beth close to her side and smiled down at her. "I don't know if Lord Kerrich has told you the tale of this child, my lord, but her quick wit saved a very precious pocket watch from a nefarious pickpocket."

Beth tried to protest. "But not—"

Gently Miss Lockhart laid her hand over Beth's mouth. "I know, dear, you don't like the praise, but you deserve it." She beamed at Kerrich. "Just as Lord Kerrich deserves praise for so honorably bringing Beth into his home."

Lord Reynard slapped Kerrich on the shoulder. "Quite right, lad. Admirable thing to do."

The old man knew very well this was overly generous; why didn't he point out that a simple reward or a job in the kitchen would do as well? His admiration boded ill. It boded very ill indeed.

"So, Beth, you deserve the chance to get to know Lord Kerrich. He is, after all, in your debt." Miss Lockhart eased her hand away from Beth's mouth, and when Beth remained mute, Miss Lockhart said to Lord Reynard, "Lord

Kerrich has been most insistent that he show his appreciation for his little heroine by getting to know her and taking her to all the wondrous entertainments London has to offer."

Kerrich smiled, but with tightly clenched teeth. "But I had also expressed my concern that, as a businessman, I cannot spend my whole day in the nursery."

"My lord, you want to exhibit an open, easy relationship with this child."

He glared at her, a muscle twitching in his cheek. "That is certainly what I want to do."

"For that, you will have to spend time getting to know her. I will expect to see you up in the nursery every day." Miss Lockhart looked him straight in the eyes and spoke fiercely. *"Every day."*

He knew he was trapped, but he also knew how to negotiate. Focusing on the female to the exclusion of everyone and everything in the chamber, he demanded, "How much time?"

"Two hours a day."

"Any *particular* time?"

"As you have rightly pointed out, my lord, you are a busy man." No mean negotiator herself, Miss Lockhart stared right into his eyes. "When it's convenient for you, I beg you would inform me."

His blood coursed warmly through his veins. "I'll let you know my schedule."

"And I will arrange ours accordingly."

Satisfied with the compromise, he stepped back to find that Lord Reynard watched them through bright eyes, and Beth had sidled toward the door as if she expected them both to explode.

"Aren't you afraid someone will think the girl is your love child?" Lord Reynard asked.

Kerrich swung on his grandfather in horror. "A love child? Impossible! Everyone knows that I am damned vigilant when it comes to—" He stopped, aware that, under Lord Reynard's prodding, he had ventured into forbidden conversational territory.

But obviously it was not a worry; Miss Lockhart looked confused. Poor old maid. She probably thought rhythm was something performed by an orchestra and a French sheath was a fashionable pocketbook.

Clearing his throat, he said, "Surely no one would think I'm taking my own illegitimate child into my home."

His grandfather chuckled purposefully.

Kerrich rubbed his forehead. "Yes, of course they will. Can't a man perform one philanthropic gesture without becoming the object of gossip?"

"Not when that man is a handsome rake of marriageable age," Lord Reynard answered.

Righteously indignant, Kerrich said, "Over the years, I have contributed to many charities."

"Drafting a check in the sterile environs of your office, son, is quite different from taking on the pain and joy of raising a child." Lord Reynard bowed to Beth. "Although I'm sure with this admirable young lady, the joy will far outweigh the pain."

Beth dipped into a little curtsy.

Bloody damned right the joy will outweigh the pain, Kerrich wanted to say. *Especially since, when this farce is over, she's going to be trained for some useful employment and I'll have nothing more to do with her.*

But he couldn't afford to be that honest. "I will deny the rumors straight out."

Lord Reynard laughed aloud.

"No, you're right," Kerrich answered the unspoken derision. "That will add fuel to the rumors."

Again Miss Lockhart showed herself capable of earning her considerable salary and bonus. "*I* will keep the rumors at bay."

In surprise, the two men considered her.

"I will be with you always. Wherever you go with Beth, I'll go, too. Not only as a chaperone, but also as a source of gossip." Smiling coldly, she folded her hands at her waist. "Let us not deny the rumors, my lords, let us start them. Direct them. I drop a hint here, confess a tidbit there, and soon it will be all over London that Lord Kerrich is adopting the orphaned daughter of . . ." She hesitated.

"Of one of his staff who was killed performing some good deed for him."

Kerrich could scarcely believe the words had come from Beth. Lifting his monocle, he stared at her. She didn't look any different. Still grimy, still shy, and if anything a little surprised at her temerity.

"Won't that work?" Her voice squeaked a little higher than normal.

"It will work very well." Miss Lockhart smiled with admiration.

"Realistic." Lord Reynard approved. "Makes it sound like Devon is doing this out of guilt rather than out of goodness. You're a clever gel."

Beth smiled. Two dimples appeared in her thin cheeks and her eyes came alive with pleasure.

"Two very clever females." Kerrich was not amused, and he let his cold gaze linger on Miss Lockhart as he considered the ramifications. "Very clever indeed."

CHAPTER 7

With schoolmistresslike briskness, Miss Lockhart said, "If that is all, my lords, we'll be out of your way. Our little foundling needs a bath."

"Do not," Beth muttered as she was herded out the door.

The silence left behind lingered while Kerrich and Lord Reynard stared after them.

Then Lord Reynard rapped his cane on the floor. "Excellent character in a woman. Good-looking, too."

"Yes." Kerrich hadn't realized his grandfather's vision had failed so badly.

From the entry, Lewis spoke, and he sounded disgustingly cheerful. "Salutations, Miss Lockhart. Who might this young lady be?"

"This is Beth. Beth, this is Lord Kerrich's cousin, Mr. Athersmith."

Kerrich heard the whisper of Beth's greeting.

A lass. He could imagine what Lewis was thinking after hearing Kerrich's story of the tough street boy he admired.

Kerrich strode to the door and as the governess and the child climbed the stairs, he glared at Lewis. "I thought she was a boy." His tone dared Lewis to challenge him.

And Lewis, good-lad Lewis, pretended it was totally customary for Kerrich to make such a mistake. "Yes, I can see how that might happen." He wore a greatcoat, a pair of rugged boots, and a broad-brimmed hat pulled down over his eyes.

Looking him over, Kerrich asked, "Going somewhere, cousin?"

Lewis explained himself without any obvious resentment. "I have some errands and it's raining again."

"Take the carriage."

"I would not presume—"

"No presumption at all," Kerrich said, all the while thinking that Lewis would not presume because Lewis didn't want his activities traced. "I wouldn't have you suffer any tribulations. I realize you are working for me as a favor."

Lord Reynard's voice echoed from the library. "Who's working for you, boy?"

Lewis blanched. "Your grandfather is here?"

"Please," Kerrich mouthed. "Tell him nothing."

In a jerky motion, Lewis nodded, then as Kerrich stepped back, he strode forward and into the library. Kerrich looked out into the entry and saw Moulton silently acknowledge that someone would be following Lewis. Satisfied, Kerrich turned back to his library, to his cousin and his grandfather, and to the desk where the book of dummy accounts rested.

Holding his hat, Lewis stood before Lord Reynard. "Sir, how good to see you! I didn't realize you were coming."

"No one did." Lord Reynard reached out his hand. "At my age, surprising my relatives is perchance the only thrill I can handle."

Lewis took the proffered fingers and squeezed them, but to Kerrich's critical gaze he did so awkwardly and as if he suffered acute discomfort. "A pleasant and unexpected gain for both Kerrich and me, then."

Kerrich unlocked the desk, and with carefully simulated slyness, he slid the book of accounts into a drawer. He locked it within, making sure the metal rattled against the lock, then he pocketed the key.

Lewis observed every move.

"So you're working for Devon now," Lord Reynard said. "I thought you were working as a tutor for . . . who was it you were working for?"

Lewis answered with a little too much brevity. "Lord Swearn."

"I thought him a good man." Lord Reynard fixed his gaze on Lewis. "But obviously you don't agree."

Lewis had the grace to look uncomfortable. "No! Sir! Lord Swearn was perfectly equitable."

"I always say the only two ways to know a person is to work for them or marry them. Didn't the family treat you well?"

Lord Reynard had Lewis scrambling now. "Sir, they were quite generous. Always kind."

"You were preparing the eldest boy for Oxford, I believe."

"Yes, sir."

"Then the youth you taught was a dunce or a wastrel and blamed you for his lack of progress."

"No, sir, young Mr. Fotherby was quite responsible."

Lord Reynard thumped his cane on the floor in small, rhythmic motions. "I don't understand, then. Why did you leave?"

Lewis stiffened further with each pointed question. "I simply . . . thought it time I served my time in the family business."

"You left in the middle of preparing that lad for Oxford to work in the family business?" Lord Reynard turned to

Kerrich, who had been observing with fascination. "Boy, don't we still own a bank?"

"We do," Kerrich said.

He turned back to Lewis. "You hate numbers. You always swore you wouldn't work in the company business."

"I have matured."

"Hm." Lord Reynard gave him a long look, then smiled widely. "Good for you, son. Glad to see you've joined us."

Lewis staggered slightly as he relaxed.

Yes, Kerrich thought. *You hated that interrogation, didn't you?*

"Thank you, sir," Lewis said. "How long will we have the pleasure of your company?"

"I've decided to take Devon up on his invitation to spend time with him in London. Thought I'd go to the United Service Club, see if any of my old friends are around, talk about the world of finance and how it's all gone to hell since we got too ancient to run it." Lord Reynard grinned.

Kerrich wavered between elation and dismay. While it was God's own truth Kerrich always loved to see his grandfather, he found the timing of this visit suspicious. Lord Reynard so seldom ventured out these days. Why had he come? Had he heard a rumor? Or, God forbid, did he know the truth?

And if Kerrich was bedeviled, he could imagine the disquiet Lewis experienced as he faced the man who had put him through Oxford, knowing he was doing his best to bring the bank to ruination and the family to disgrace.

Or perhaps he had gone so far down the road to damnation he no longer cared.

"Sir," Lewis said, "I'm sure your friends will be glad to see you and catch you up on the gossip. I look forward to seeing you often, sir."

"Aye." Lord Reynard withdrew his hand and waved

Lewis away. "I recognize a plea for dismissal, and I know you have more important things to do other than to greet an old man. Go on, we'll talk later."

"I look forward to that, sir." Lewis bowed. "Since you have just come, you'll be wanting to visit with your grandson now, anyway." He bowed to Kerrich, too, and exited quickly—too quickly in Kerrich's critical opinion.

"He never calls me 'uncle' anymore." Lord Reynard's shrewd old eyes watched the place where Lewis had disappeared. "He calls me 'sir,' and when he's speaking to you about me, he calls me 'your grandfather.' "

"He seems quite conscious of being the grandson of your sister, sir. We might have treated him like a beloved relative, but to everyone else he was barely a part of the family."

"There's nothing more dangerous than a man who allows others' perceptions to form his character. Something's not right. Not right at all."

Kerrich wished Lord Reynard had made the observation years earlier, when Kerrich could have somehow stopped this debacle that threatened so much of their lives. "I'm sure it's nothing to worry about."

Lord Reynard whipped his head around and glared. "Don't patronize me, boy. I'm old, not stupid."

So much for easing his grandfather's mind. "No, sir. I apologize."

"You'd best watch him."

Of course Kerrich agreed, yet he could scarcely confess why.

Lord Reynard stroked his rough, wrinkled chin. "But perhaps that's why you have employed him, heh?"

"You are very astute, sir." Kerrich set a crystal paperweight on some of his less-interesting correspondence, then looked up at a wail from above stairs.

"What was that?" Lord Reynard asked. "It sounded like a banshee."

Mystified, Kerrich shook his head. "Perhaps the child?"

"Only if they were killing her."

The noise did not repeat, so Kerrich suggested, "Let's go sit by the fire."

Willingly Lord Reynard heaved himself out of the hard-backed chair for the promise of a cushioned one. "She's a spirited filly, that one."

"Who . . . oh." Did every conversation have to center around *them*? "Which, the child or the governess?"

"This young lady you're courting." Lord Reynard leaned one hand on Kerrich's arm and one on his cane, and started toward the fire.

Kerrich's head whirled. "What young lady?"

"Your pretty governess!"

"Now, wait, Grandpapa—"

"What other reason would you have for adopting a child? You're a rake, but you certainly wouldn't take a lady of good background as your mistress. So you obviously want that governess in your home so you can plead your suit at your leisure."

"You mean—Miss Lockhart? To wed?" Lord Reynard's speculation rendered Kerrich incoherent.

So that was the reason Lord Reynard had not interrogated him about his sudden turn of philanthropy. He thought Kerrich wanted to take Miss Lockhart to wife! And Kerrich could deny it, but what other reason could he give his grandfather for taking Beth into his home? For foisting her on society and lying about her origins?

"A woman like that wouldn't have a man like you without persuasion." Lord Reynard waggled his finger. "You'll have to work to win her."

Kerrich tried to see the best way out of this morass, but

could come up with nothing better than "I don't want her!"

Lord Reynard backed up to the fire and rubbed his rear. "Then what the hell is a girl of respectable family doing living in your house?"

"I'm . . . looking her over." *As good a tale as any.* "I know I'll have to wed soon, and I have a list of what I want in a wife."

"Do you?" Lord Reynard coughed—or did he chortle? "Tell me about this list."

"I'll show you." Striding to his desk, Kerrich sorted through his files until he found it. "Basic requirements, really. She should be of good family. That goes without saying."

"Without saying," Lord Reynard repeated.

"She should have a strong sense of what is proper, be instructed on the duties of a hostess, be intelligent and, of course, be pliant and live to please me."

Lord Reynard stared at him, and by his expression Kerrich suspected he would not be praised for a list that he thought to be quite forward thinking.

Finally Lord Reynard asked, "Why don't you just buy a collie?"

"Because I can't get an heir on a collie," Kerrich snapped. "Did I mention my bride should be fecund?"

"Now there's something that's difficult to discover without prematurely tasting the delights." Lord Reynard closed one eye and tilted his head. "You didn't mention beauty, so I must assume you are too clever to make your decision based on mere pulchritude."

Without volition, the picture of Kerrich's perfect woman rose in his mind. "She should have long brown hair, wavy when released from its braid, beautiful skin with a faint golden tint to it, curves that would crash a phaeton, and eyes of the most angelic blue . . ."

Lord Reynard's question broke the spell. "What about love?"

Kerrich dismissed that with a wave of his hand. "Oh, I can make her fall in love with me."

"You could make any woman fall in love with you, heh?"

Kerrich shrugged. "Every man has to be an expert at something, Grandpapa."

"Even Miss Lockhart? Do you fancy you're up to the challenge of making her fall in love with you?"

"If I wish—although I'd rather you didn't tip her off as to my intentions."

"Of course not! I mounted a few fillies in my time. Surprise is of the essence." Looking at the Oriental carpet beneath his feet, Lord Reynard seemed lost in thought. At last, he raised his head and asked, "Are you still mouthing that dull-witted resolve not to love?"

Kerrich wanted to groan. When, at the age of eleven, he had first sworn not to love, Lord Reynaud had been philosophical, even indulgent. But as the years had gone on and Kerrich had stuck to his resolution, Lord Reynaud had tried more and more to dissuade him. Kerrich understood Lord Reynard's reasons. He wanted to see Kerrich happy, and he wanted great-grandchildren. "I've never met a woman who made me want to abandon my resolution."

"If you did, you'd run as fast as you could in the opposite direction, like the coward you are." Lord Reynard groaned as he sank back into the comfort of his armchair. "These old bones can't bear the jolting of a coach like they used to. Bring the whisky when you come back, my lad."

"The doctor says you shouldn't be drinking spirits." But Kerrich fetched the bottle and two glasses as he spoke.

"Damned old fool," Lord Reynard condemned the doctor in one pithy, often-repeated phrase. "I've been drinking whisky all my life. That's why I'm still here, hale and hearty and eighty-nine years old."

"You're bragging again," Kerrich answered mildly as he placed the glasses on the table between the two armchairs. "You're only eighty-four."

"And a better man than you'll ever be." Lord Reynard watched as Kerrich poured. "I didn't have to adopt a child to get one. I made my own."

"You just got caught with your pants down, that's all." Kerrich handed over a glass. "And not until you were thirty-four, either, so I've four more years."

"Yes, your grandmother never admitted it, but I think she arranged to have her father catch us. I'd scarcely stormed the portal when he—"

Kerrich flinched away. "Please, Grandpapa! I don't want to know."

Lord Reynard grinned at Kerrich's squeamishness. "How do you think your father got here, lad? He was not angel-borne, or found under a cabbage leaf."

"If I choose to believe so, I think you should let me have my illusions." Kerrich slumped in his chair.

Taking the glass, Lord Reynard lifted it high. "To your grandmama, the smartest woman ever born and the woman I loved."

"To Grandmama." Kerrich joined in the toast to the woman he remembered as stern and disciplined, although his grandfather seemed to have completely different recollections, none of which Kerrich wanted to acknowledge.

After Lord Reynard had drained the glass, he held it out to be refilled.

Kerrich complied, knowing full well the old man would sip this one through the afternoon and into the evening.

"A man of years has to survive on memories." Lord Reynard sounded sentimental.

Lord Reynard's sentimentality was always suspect and usually at Kerrich's expense, so he retorted, "As old as you are, you should have memories to last you a good long time."

"Ah, lad, you shouldn't grudge me my reminiscences, especially when you're the only one I can reminisce with. All my friends and my enemies are dead, my only child is dead, your mother's off somewhere with that gigolo of hers—"

"Italy, last I heard, and that gigolo is making her very happy."

"At your expense."

"Worth every penny." Kerrich lifted his glass to the dowager countess of Kerrich. She was his mother and he loved her, but resentfully. Every time he saw her, he remembered his father. His father was the wisest, kindest, best man he'd ever met, and his mother hadn't even waited a year after his death before she'd found herself another man. She said she suffered a broken heart. Kerrich thought she had chosen an odd way of healing it. No, Mother was the kind of complex, intelligent woman Kerrich had made a career of steering clear of. Give him the burbling, empty-headed ones who played for pleasure without a thought to the consequences; Kerrich's life was easier with his mother in Italy.

The glow of firelight danced on Lord Reynard's bald head and cast a golden gleam on the fringe of white hairs around his ears. "Speaking of old memories and getting caught with my pants down, do you recall that famous incident at the duchess of Kent's dinner party in Kensington Palace—"

"No!"

Lord Reynard's teeth gleamed in a grin. "You always were sulky that you were actually at the palace that evening and still missed out that fabulous display. Where was it you were? With the other lads skulking about in the gardens?"

Kerrich didn't want to talk about it, but better than anyone he knew how impossible it was to change the course of conversation once his grandfather had begun to reminisce, and especially about this. Over the years, his grandfather had recalled this incident repeatedly and enjoyed it every time. "Yes," Kerrich said. "We were in the garden, plotting to scare the girls."

"Ah, yes." Lord Reynard nodded wisely. "Every young man's desire, to scare the girls."

"At seventeen, anyway."

Another shriek traveled through the air and trailed off in a high, suffering note. Kerrich and his grandfather exchanged glances.

Raising his voice, Kerrich called, "Moulton, what *was* that?"

Moulton appeared at the doorway. "My lords, it would seem Miss Beth objects to the act of bathing."

"Is she fighting?" Kerrich asked.

"I understand from the upstairs maids that Miss Lockhart is drenched as well."

"Poor Miss Lockhart." Kerrich didn't bother to subdue his grin.

"Poor Beth," Lord Reynard said. "She's going to keep you hopping."

"Nonsense, a little water will do them both good."

While he spoke, Moulton made a gesture to Kerrich that indicated success. Then he bowed and retreated.

So the butler had sent someone to follow Lewis. Kerrich had done what he could to protect his cousin from arrest, but all the culprits needed to be found, and soon, for while the Mathewes Bank could temporarily bear the loss of revenue, the Bank of England took it ill that English pound notes had also been counterfeited, and more ill that it had been done on their special watermarked paper with their special, difficult-to-make ink. That meant someone had gone right into the bank and stolen the supplies. If the matter wasn't resolved soon, the business would be reported to the prime minister, Queen Victoria would undoubtedly find out, her money would be withdrawn and Kerrich still would have no guarantee Her Majesty wouldn't open him to ridicule before the whole of society.

"What a night that was," Lord Reynard said.

Recalled to the moment and confused, Kerrich asked, "What night?"

Then Lord Reynard chortled like an evil fairy.

"Oh. That night."

"Old King William was there, under protest, of course, since he detested Her Grace of Kent."

"Who doesn't?" Kerrich took a swallow of liquor. "Even Queen Victoria has little use for her mother these days."

"Yes, indeed. Quite a scandal, that. Yet one can't blame our young sovereign. Her Grace was—is, I would wager—bitter, and with little real care for her daughter except as princess royal."

"Mark my words, Prince Albert will bring about a reconciliation. Queen Victoria's consort is a very proper sort who expects certain behaviors from those about the royal family, and from Victoria herself." Kerrich tasted bitterness himself, and not just from the drink he sipped.

"Albert's right. Days are long past when a monarch can do what he likes. For a girl to be so estranged from her mother looks bad. And let's be frank. Victoria's gender works against her. Women are always subject to megrims and fits." Lord Reynard set down his glass and folded his hands over his belly. "You can't depend on a woman. I wish Victoria a long reign, but I scarcely depend on it."

Kerrich was more than willing to discuss Queen Victoria,

her political situation, and any number of other fascinating topics, but not surprisingly Lord Reynard could not be distracted.

"Yet who would have believed, on that night twelve years ago, that she would be queen, married and with child so soon?" Lord Reynard threw his head back and closed his eyes as if he could see the scene even now. "Do you remember? King William at one end of that long table, the duchess of Kent at the other, and all the rest of us between them trying to keep them from coming to blows."

"I wasn't allowed to dine with the adults yet, Grandpapa." But Kerrich did remember, for he, as well as the rest of Victoria's youthful visitors, had been allowed to mingle in the second floor drawing room. When their parents went in to dine, these progeny of the noble guests had peeked at the table set with fine plate and sparkling dinnerware. Then they'd been sent away to a separate room to eat and entertain one another.

Kerrich had been seventeen, the oldest of the three adolescent boys and, in his own opinion, quite superior to the girls for all that one of those girls was the acknowledged heir to the English throne. Another of the girls had been fifteen, a beauty with bright blue eyes and a long swirl of hair the color of caramel. He had tried to be pleasant to her—hell, he had tried to charm her—but she acted as if he were a beast of which to be wary and retreated to another room. In disgust, he had rounded up the two other boys and taken them into the garden.

Where in a fit of pique, he paced and thought and, finally, conspired to be as contemptible as that girl seemed to believe. He plotted to give her a scare.

"Her Grace had arranged for fireworks, so the servants left open the drapes." Lord Reynard smiled fondly. "Thank God, or we might never have seen that magnificent sight."

"Thank God," Kerrich echoed insincerely.

Leaning across to him, Lord Reynard slapped him on the knee. "You're jealous that you didn't see it. And you were in the garden, too. You should have looked up, lad!"

"I got sick, took one of the horses and went home." Kerrich stuck by the tale he'd been telling for twelve years.

"No matter. The fog might have obstructed your view. It kept swirling past the windows like will-o'-the-wisps, catching the candlelight and then dancing away when it heard the king and the duchess quarreling."

"The dampness covered everything," Kerrich acknowledged. The trellis. The roof. And the windowsill looking into the chamber where one girl, the handsome girl and apparently a house guest, undressed for bed . . .

"That young man provided the kind of entertainment one can't pay for." Lord Reynard cackled in that reminiscent sort of way that made Kerrich want to writhe. "Hanging there from a broken trellis, in front of the dining chamber windows, upside down, his pants ripped off except where they were caught on that one boot . . ." Lord Reynard interrupted his speech to laugh.

Laugh long enough that Kerrich hoped he was done.

But no. "His arms hanging over his head. His free leg kicking. And in the light of the candles, that white arse shining like a full moon." More laughter.

Kerrich smiled with so much simulated mirth that it hurt.

"And when he twirled in a circle, we saw all the constellations, too." Lord Reynard slapped his thigh and roared at his own wit.

"How droll," Kerrich said.

"Yes. I tell you, boy, that comet had a long tail."

Kerrich wanted to cover his face.

Still chuckling, Lord Reynard shook his head. "The old boot of a duchess screamed in shock, but I noted, as did everyone, that she kept quiet until we'd seen the full exhibition. And the king quipped . . . the king quipped . . . ' 'Tis the first time I've ever seen a full moon on a foggy night.' "

"King William always did have a way with words," Kerrich said.

"Not really. He wasn't much of a king or a quipster, but the gazettes used that phrase and drew so many versions of that lad hanging upside down." Lord Reynard pointed his bent, arthritic finger at Kerrich. "Do you know I collected all those lampoons and kept them?"

Kerrich took a good, long swallow of whisky. "No, I didn't know that."

"We never did find out who that young man was."

Kerrich sat up a little straighter. "I thought you said it was obviously some lowborn prankster."

Lord Reynard put his finger beside his nose and nodded. "Her Grace said so, and the others took up the cry, but I tell you, lad, that beneath the shirt tails that hung over his face and made him impossible to identify—"

Kerrich felt ill.

"I caught a glimpse of jacket. More than that, before he fell I looked hard. That jacket was well made by a good tailor." Lord Reynard looked right into Kerrich's eyes. "If you hadn't already taken the horse and gone home, I would have thought it was you."

CHAPTER 8

Kerrich arranged the pillow behind him on his bed, leaned against the headboard and with half a mind reviewed the real account book for the bank. Yes, he could see where the counterfeiting had caused a slow but steady drain in the bank's finances. He wanted to shake Lewis for this. But he couldn't. Couldn't, because Mr. Veare said he could not.

Closing his eyes, Kerrich leaned back and thought about the grim-faced gentlemen in the small office of the Bank of England. Kerrich had gone in to demand that someone find and arrest the villains counterfeiting and distributing his banknotes, and in turn the gentlemen—who had been called in from the government—threatened to arrest Kerrich for allowing counterfeiting of Bank of England currency on Kerrich's estate.

The gentlemen didn't care that Kerrich declared his innocence; they simply watched with hard eyes and told him he should be more mindful of what went on on his lands. They informed Kerrich that Lewis was part of the counterfeiting ring, and when Kerrich had not believed it, they brought forth the evidence in the form of Lewis's signatures on the purchases of ink and paper—the forgeries of Kerrich's banknotes had apparently been practice, and done with easily traced supplies—and most convincingly, on a printing press.

Kerrich couldn't understand; still didn't understand what had made his virtuous, dutiful cousin turn to crime. Lewis had been a brilliant scholar, finishing a degree in divinity.

Kerrich ground his teeth. Divinity, for God's sake. There was irony.

On graduation, Lewis had been offered several positions—as a clergyman, as a professor's assistant. He might soon have been offered a chair of his own, but he had chosen instead to prepare young noblemen to enter Oxford. Seeking his true vocation, Lord Reynard called it. Laying waste to his chances, Kerrich more rightly named it. But it didn't really matter. Lord Reynard had granted Lewis a yearly stipend so that his beloved sister's grandson would never be in need.

So what had Lewis done to need so much money? Had he been gambling? Was he keeping a lightskirt on the side? Was someone blackmailing him?

And what difference did it make? For counterfeiting, Lewis could dance at the end of a hangman's rope, and the gentlemen from the government had made it abundantly clear that unless Kerrich uncovered the entire counterfeiting ring, and that apparently included at least five men and their leader, Kerrich could dance with him. The Mathewes family could be wiped out because of Lewis's stupidity.

So, acting on those gentlemen's instructions, Kerrich had hired Lewis, given him information, given him access to a dummy account book for the bank, asked his advice—and watched him. The government had planted men in Kerrich's household, and Moulton was their leader. He didn't work for the government, but had his own sleuthing firm. He not only directed all operations, but made quite a passable butler. Under Moulton's direction, one of his men or one of the government men followed Lewis everywhere. To the theater. To the business district. To the docks.

It had all been for naught. Lewis had lost them every time.

Kerrich slid lower in his bed, a broad, massive affair with a mattress long enough that he could stretch out his legs all the way and wide enough that he could upholster it with three women, although he hadn't done that since his youth. His bedchamber shimmered with color, the rich blue-purple of iris, accents of scarlet, glints of gold. The fire was burning merrily in the grate, although it was a warm night. Now flames shot out, curling fantastically in puffs of orange dragon fire.

I've fallen asleep. I'm dreaming, he realized, pleased with the acuity of his deduction.

A good dream, he recognized a moment later. A very good dream.

A woman stood before the hearth, her back to him, her hand resting on a chair. She was silhouetted against the flames and she was, of course, what made it a good dream, for she was stark naked.

But unlike all the other naked ladies who had lately invaded his bedchamber, this one was perfection.

This wasn't the senior upstairs maid. This was youth and a maiden's innocence and beauty incarnate. Her caramel-colored hair was piled atop her head in a swirl that defied gravity, and glinted with sparks of amber and chestnut. For a woman, her shoulders were broad, yet soft and golden, and the long indent of her spine led his gaze inevitably to the cleft of her bottom.

What a bottom it was. The globes were full, yet tight and high, the kind he would hold in his hands as this woman straddled him and rode him for hours, for days. She wouldn't tire, not this woman of abundant charms. Nor would he, for his erection throbbed as it had when he was a half-grown lad getting an eyeful of one girl's forbidden graces.

As always in a dream, he couldn't move, so he forced himself to call out, "Come on, then. Give me what you've always promised."

And she turned, providing a glimpse of full breasts, the indent of navel in the smooth flesh of her belly, the triangle of hair that hid the petals of nature's sweetest rose.

Just as in real life, he stared at her body until his eyes ached and it occurred to him that she wouldn't walk toward him or kiss his lips or place her naked form against his until he looked at her face. Women, even dream women, were funny that way.

So with painful effort he lifted his gaze from the smooth, rose-colored nipples to her face—and screamed.

That man was sure staring at Miss Lockhart funny.

Lord Kerrich hadn't stared at her like that yesterday, and Beth didn't understand why he would be all big-eyed and suspicious today. It wasn't as if Miss Lockhart had mucked up her looks or anything. She wore a gown that bunched around her shoulders, a brown one today. Her tinted spectacles slid down her nose, and when Lord Kerrich strolled into the classroom carrying his cane, wearing a monocle, and dressed as dapper as bedamned, she still got that sour expression like he gave her a bellyache.

"My lord." Miss Lockhart stopped smack in the middle of the spelling lesson and curtsied. "We didn't expect you so early. It's not yet gone eleven."

"Couldn't sleep," Lord Kerrich said, as grumpy as you please.

Beth had stood when he came into the room, and when

he stopped before her, she curtsied, feeling almost jaunty in the pink dimity gown, which was only a little faded and was actually ironed, and the white pinafore with the ruffles on the shoulders.

He just looked her over and pronounced, "You're clean. Stay that way."

"Yes, my lord." An idea occurred to her, and she was so taken with it she dared say, "If I stay clean, I don't have to have any more baths, do I?"

"Oh, no." He shook his head. "You're not involving me in that battle. Miss Lockhart, teach something. I have things to think about." Marching to the rear of the classroom, he paced back and forth, and every time Beth glanced his way he was looking at Miss Lockhart like she scared him.

Beth fidgeted in her desk. She already knew all this corn about reading and writing, but Miss Lockhart called this a review, so Beth was free to examine Miss Lockhart and figure out why Lord Kerrich was gawking so.

Of a surety, this morning with the sun shining through the big windows, her face looked eerie, too pale with pink color on her cheeks, but all in all she had the demeanor of a lady, the lady who had taken Beth from the orphanage and given her a chance at a new life.

Beth knew how to be grateful. She would do anything for Miss Lockhart. She'd learn all that stuff Miss Lockhart said she needed like Latin and pianoforte and history and literature and sketching. She'd dress in these fine new clothes that one of the maids had found for her. And somehow, she wouldn't be ascared anymore. After all, Miss Lockhart had called her a lion. So Beth would be the foundling Lord Kerrich wanted. Tough. Brave. Better than a boy.

Luckily, being better than a boy wasn't difficult.

"So." Lord Kerrich came and stood over Beth's desk, and interrupted Miss Lockhart right in the middle of

T-H-R-O-W and T-H-R-O-U-G-H. "You don't like to take baths."

The pen felt awkward in Beth's hand, so she put it in the stand and looked up, way up, to Lord Kerrich's face. "My mum used to make me take baths. She about scrubbed my skin off, and so did Miss Lockhart." She tried to look as disgruntled as any lad, which wasn't hard because she really didn't like washing. "Why do wenches like water so much?"

"We *ladies"*—Miss Lockhart emphasized the word so much Beth got the impression she didn't like to be called a wench—"like to see clean children."

"The sight must be better than the feel," Beth retorted.

Miss Lockhart rapped on the desk with her pointer. "Don't be saucy."

"No, ma'am." Beth arranged the folds of her skirt.

But Lord Kerrich stared down at Beth, then up at Miss Lockhart, then back at Beth. In a conspiratorial tone, he said, "Ladies do make a fuss about a little dirt, don't they?"

Beth wanted to leap to her feet and shout her jubilation. She'd said a boy thing and he'd agreed with her!

Grabbing one of the big chairs, he turned it backward and straddled it. Leaning his chin on the back, he asked, "What else makes you want to yell?"

He made her nervous, looking at her so hard, but over his shoulder Miss Lockhart was nodding encouragingly, so Beth gathered her courage and tried to think. *What made her yell?* "When Mrs. Fallowfield put me in the closet, I yelled and kicked the door."

Miss Lockhart began to clean the chalk off the slate-board.

"Who's Mrs. Fallowfield?" Lord Kerrich asked.

"The old bitch what directs the orphanage."

"Beth!" Miss Lockhart drew herself sternly erect. "Such expressions must never cross a lady's lips."

"That's right, Beth." Lord Kerrich looked like he was going to explode, his face twinkly with laughter. "The correct phrase is, 'The old bitch *who* directs the orphanage.' "

Miss Lockhart's eyes flashed so bright Beth could see the wrath right through the tinted lenses. "You know very well what expression, Beth."

Beth didn't dare play the dunce, and she nodded and whispered, "Yes, Miss Lockhart."

Miss Lockhart answered his earlier question. "Mrs. Fallowfield is the director of the orphanage, my lord."

"She sounds like a dreadful old . . . wench," Lord Kerrich observed. "Why did she lock you in a closet?"

"Because I cried at night and woke the others." Beth didn't want to talk about that, so she hastily added, "I yelled when I set my apron on fire."

"You set your apron on fire." Lord Kerrich repeated what she said as if he couldn't quite comprehend her.

"You know. An apron, like this one." She held up the white cotton pinafore. "I didn't do it on purpose. I was just little. Mum was cleaning the grate, and I thought the coals look pretty, so I scooped one up with the shovel and put it in my pocket."

"Good gracious." Miss Lockhart put her hand over her mouth.

"This can't be true," Lord Kerrich said.

"It is, too." Beth glared in indignation. "When the flames started busting out, my mum grabbed me and rolled me on the floor and pounded me with a rug. And look!" She rolled up her sleeve and held out her arm where a ripple of purple marred the skin. "I got burned."

Standing, Lord Kerrich kicked his chair away. "Miss Lockhart, I can't do this!"

Miss Lockhart lifted her dark brows. "My lord?"

"This is too hard. What if I get fond of that child and she sticks another coal in her pocket? What will happen to *me* then?"

Miss Lockhart looked like her belly was aching again, and she kept opening her mouth, then closing it, as if she didn't know what to say.

Beth knew what to say. "I was little when I did that. I don't play with fire anymore."

"You can't fool me," Lord Kerrich said with chilly precision. "Children get hurt all the time."

Miss Lockhart must have gotten her words back, because when she started talking it was a tirade to amaze. "You're right, my lord. She could get hurt. Somehow. She could need care. And should you, in your munificence, become attached to her, you might get hurt by her suffering. So I'll just go and tell Lord Reynard that you have no intention of following through on your commitment. Shall I?"

Lord Kerrich pointed his finger at Miss Lockhart. "You dare!"

Miss Lockhart sniffed. "And I believe there's some matter to be taken care of with Her Majesty, too."

"Miss Lockhart, you take too much upon yourself."

"I am just trying to remind you what you have at stake here."

"I know what I have at stake here."

"Then keep the course, my lord, and you will succeed. Waver now, and you are a craven."

"No one calls me a craven."

"Perhaps someone should call you illogical for thinking a boy orphan would be less likely to hurt himself and thus you."

They were acting like two of the lads at the orphanage, and just like at the orphanage Beth scrambled to distract them. Grasping the hem of Lord Kerrich's fine black coat, she tugged at it. "I yelled at the horse races when my papa took me."

Lord Kerrich stopped shouting and shaking his finger. He looked down at Beth with something like amazement. "Your father took you to the horse races?"

She nodded.

Miss Lockhart said, "Oh, no."

Lord Kerrich ignored her, coming to kneel at Beth's side. In a pleasant, coaxing voice, he asked, "Did you like the horse races?"

"I loved them." Beth didn't have to pretend. Her enthusiasm swept her along. "The smell of the dirt and the straw and the way people jumped up and down and all the shouting and sometimes if I asked nice the owner would let me pet the horse—"

"You cannot take that child to a horse race," Miss Lockhart said.

Leaning back on his heels, he cupped his chin and examined Beth—but not unkindly. As if he was interested. Then he sighed. "No. I suppose not."

"But—" Beth said.

"No." Miss Lockhart stood firm.

Beth slumped in her seat. It wasn't fair. Papa had taken her. Why couldn't she go now? With Lord Kerrich? It would make him like her, and so she would tell Miss Lockhart later.

"Where did you go to the horse races?" Lord Kerrich asked.

"The Hippodrome."

"It's not a good track," he said. "The clay is so heavy the best jockeys refuse to ride on it."

She kicked the leg of the desk.

"And it's on the outskirts of a slum. Surely you saw the

pickpockets and thieves that frequent the place."

"Yes." She shot him a scornful glance. "But Papa and I couldn't go to Ascot, could we?"

"I suppose not."

A thought came to her, and she sat straight up. "Do you own a horse, my lord?"

Lord Kerrich shook his head. "No. No racehorses."

Miss Lockhart pushed her glasses up on her nose. "Praise be for that."

"But you own a horse? A real horse? Is it tall?" Beth squirmed with glee. "Is it chestnut? I think they're the prettiest, but Papa liked the dappled grays."

"I have a chestnut." Looking more like a fairy godfather every moment, Lord Kerrich grinned at Beth. "*And* a dappled gray. In fact, I own a team of both."

In her rush of joy, Beth forgot she wanted to please Miss Lockhart and build a kinship with Lord Kerrich so he would keep her. She thought only of the horses, the beautiful horses. But it was almost too good to be true, and she couldn't help asking suspiciously, "You wouldn't be fibbing to me, would you?"

Throwing back his head, he laughed out loud, a great, ringing laugh that made Beth want to laugh along.

But not Miss Lockhart. She came and stood over the top of them, and glared down her nose at him as he knelt at her feet. "My lord, this is not what I intended."

"What did you intend, Miss Lockhart?" He drawled so slowly he sounded like Chilton when he was being a wiseacre. "That I should take needlework lessons with Beth?"

"There are men who would be much improved by the lessons of patience and gentility learned along with needlework."

"*I* am not one of them." Slowly, he rose, stretching himself upward until Miss Lockhart's nose reached just about to his collarbone, and he looked down toward her.

They both wore such insufferably superior expressions that Beth was hard-pressed not to giggle.

"I'm taking the child for a ride in the park." He held out his hand to Beth, and she took it without hesitation. "If you plan to go along, Miss Lockhart, you'd best change into suitable riding gear."

CHAPTER 9

A groom led Beth's mare on leading reins, Lord Kerrich followed on a chestnut gelding, calling out encouragement and comments, and Pamela brought up the rear—figuratively as well as literally, in her opinion. She knew she ought to be glad that Beth and Kerrich had found something in common, something about which they were mutually enthused. But an hour in the stables being introduced to every horse was not what she had had planned for the first day of Beth's lessons. And riding through the park on this old nag who could scarcely plod along! Somehow it didn't seem equitable.

In all fairness, Pamela had to admit part of her dissatisfaction came from the variety of aches she had acquired last night during the bathing battle with Beth. Right now, as her mare followed along the path radiant with tawny blossoms and miniature pinks, she felt every bruise clear to the bone.

As Kerrich moved up to ride beside Beth, Pamela watched him suspiciously. Just as she suspected, he allowed the stableboy to hand Beth the reins.

"No," Pamela called. "This is her first ride!"

But they pretended she was too far back for them to hear her, and when she kicked at the nag's sides and tried to get it to trot, she encountered nothing but a snort of exasperation from the horse. She, Pamela Lockhart Ripley, was left behind because of an old nag.

As if she *were* an old nag.

Slumping back into the saddle, Pamela resolved to speak to Kerrich as soon as they returned to his home about his abominable disregard for Beth's safety. That was if the child didn't fall off, although Kerrich kept her to a walk, kept close to her side, and kept the stableboy along her other side. Then they disappeared around a bend.

Part of Pamela's fretfulness was pure exhaustion. She hadn't slept well the previous night, although, just as Lord Kerrich had promised, her bed was comfortable, her sleeping chamber well-ventilated and next to Beth's, and she had been awarded every privilege. Much as she hated to admit it, Hannah was right. Pamela felt guilty. Guilty and desperately afraid someone would see through her disguise. It wasn't that it bothered her to make a fool of Kerrich. No, the cocky boy had clearly grown into an overbearing man. But Lord Reynard was another tale.

Tightening the bow under her chin, she hoped that the riding hat Moulton had scraped up for her shaded her face enough to hide the lines where her pale powder and red rouge met the true colors of her skin. When she'd applied her disguise this morning, she hadn't planned on riding in the sunshine . . . and because of her secret guilt, she could scarcely bear to look at herself in the mirror.

Yes, Lord Reynard made her feel guilty. He had peered at her with interest, and she could have sworn he was on the point of remembering her. Remembering her as being young and pretty, not the middle-aged spinster his grandson so disdained. But he hadn't, and every time she thought about it, she almost fainted in relief that he hadn't recognized her, and felt guilty—there was that word again!—that she should be tricking a man of his years. Then she worried that he had recognized her, and for some nefarious reason of his own kept his mouth shut. Yet what nefarious reason would such an old man have for abetting her in her disguise?

The answer was—he had no reason. That she even worried about it proved Kerrich had influenced her so that she spied conspiracies everywhere. Kerrich was a menace to sense and honor.

And safety. Pamela rode around the bend and looked ahead on the path. Cats and mittens, that was Beth stretched out there in Kerrich's arms!

She experienced an unwelcome jolt of fear. What if the poor child was hurt? Then Kerrich would truly wish to send her back, and demand a new child, a tougher one this time.

This time she didn't abide any headstrong disobedience from the horse, but kicked it into a trot until she could get to the child—and the man. "What happened?" she asked in a ringing tone.

"We didn't stand you up fast enough to avoid her censure," Kerrich told Beth. His top hat rested on the grass beside him, and the bush behind him framed him in green and dappled him with sunshine. With Beth in his arms grinning at him, he looked like the subject of a Watteau painting instead of the careless rake Pamela knew him to be.

Beth rubbed her head. "I'm fine, Miss Lockhart."

The stableboy rushed to help Pamela dismount, but she swung out of the saddle before he could reach her. "You bumped your head."

"That's not what hurts the worst, but you'll yell at me if I rub that." With Kerrich's arm under her elbow, Beth rose, and tottered momentarily.

Pamela rushed forward, anxious as a mother, but Kerrich turned his shoulder and blocked her.

"Anything broken?" Kerrich led Beth a few steps along the side of the path. "Anything sprained?"

"No. I can ride more!"

Pamela swallowed a surprise upswelling of tears. Surely it was nothing more than the fear of her plan going astray with Beth's injury. It couldn't be that she already felt a surfeit of affection for Beth. And certainly not hurt that Kerrich had rudely turned her aside. In that decisive tone that came so easily, she said, "That's enough riding for this afternoon."

Beth whined, "Ah, Miss Lockhart . . ."

"Walk a little farther. Work out the bruises." Kerrich let go of Beth and with his hands on his hips and his head turned as he observed the child's progress, he said, "So, Miss Lockhart, you don't ascribe to the theory that she should get right back up on the horse?"

And for no reason, Pamela found herself struck mute by his magnificence.

He stood there, displaying his profile. Each bone in his face thrust at the tanned skin, speaking boldly of his noble heritage. His chin was stubborn, his nose jutted forth, his forehead was high. His lips . . . ah, his lips were soft and full, sensual and inviting. His fine black woolen riding suit fit him beautifully, sketching the width of his shoulders, the breadth of his chest, his narrow waist and his disconcertingly long legs. He was the most handsome man she'd ever met—and she noticed it! She, who despised men on principle and handsome rakes in particular, suddenly observed this man's physical charms in the same way any adulterer leers at a pretty girl.

She scarcely knew how to respond, only that she should hide her thoughts under a façade of words. "Knowing how to ride will do her little good should you decide to dismiss her, my lord."

Why now? Why him? Perhaps it was because, when he wasn't looking at her, she no longer felt the pressure of being the older, genderless Miss Lockhart. But she must remember that Kerrich was a libertine. A liar. A manipulator.

This morning she had been so busy despising him and wanting to please him at the same time, she hadn't reacted to his sheer, absolute glamour. Now she saw it, saw him, and in a total twist on her usual emotions, she was embarrassed to have him see the riding raiment she had thrown together. One of Lady Temperly's black woolen mourning gowns. An old-fashioned olive-green jacket. And a riding hat forgotten by one of Kerrich's ladies and never retrieved. As if it mattered what Pamela wore!

In an impatient movement, he slapped his riding crop along his boot. "As you justly pointed out this morning, my grandfather's involvement leaves me no choice except to keep the child."

Her unanticipated interest in Kerrich's appearance horrified her. What was worse, her interest would horrify *him.* He would be afraid she would appear nightly in his bedchamber *sans* clothing. And she dared not declare she would not, for just an hour ago she would have sworn no man's charms could move her. Her moral fiber was under assault; she must battle the onset of shallow longings!

Kerrich glanced toward her, and in a sudden shift his voice oozed honey and persuasion. "The child's got a good seat, surely you could see that, and who didn't have a tumble or two when they were learning to ride? She'll learn all kinds of proper lessons from you, Miss Lockhart, of that I have no doubt, but let me teach her to enjoy herself. I think there's been little enough pleasure in her short life."

"Yes." She was still in a daze, fumbling for her former rationality and worrying that he was showing not just a fleeting interest in Beth, but genuine sensitivity. "That's true, but—"

"Good, then we're agreed." His regard focused beyond her. "Look, there's Lady Smithwick and two of her daughters riding toward us. Let us introduce Beth to them."

His proposal snapped some sense back into Pamela. "We can't do that, it's too soon!"

He didn't take his gaze away from the three ladies riding with their groom, and his smile widened as they got closer, but his voice snapped with authority. "Miss Lockhart, while I know you consider me a fribble, what I am doing is important to both me and my family. I am fighting a battle against time and Beth's spill has the makings of a gratifying accident."

Pamela did consider him a fribble, she did believe he was fighting a battle against time and Beth's spill did have the makings of a gratifying accident, for they could use it to spread the word about the child. Nevertheless, she felt she had to voice a protest. "But, my lord, those are Fairchilds."

"Yes, blatherskites, and that's the best thing that can be said about them." He glanced at her. "Miss Lockhart, we have no way of getting out of meeting these ladies, and I recognize the hand of fate when I see it. Kindly bring Beth to me so she may be introduced, and let them carry the rumor of my philanthropy back to society!"

"Yes, sir." As she walked toward the place where Beth stood watching, Pamela knew Kerrich was right on all counts. No dreadful damage could come of this encounter. It was only her pride that desired a perfectly behaved child and her compassion that perceived Beth's incipient anxiety.

"Ho, there." Kerrich bowed as the ladies rode closer. "A lucky appointment, indeed!"

Stepping between them and Beth, Pamela quickly finger-combed Beth's shoulder-length hair and wished the child wore something besides a serving maid's cast-off clothing. Yet to Beth, she projected complete confidence. "Lord Kerrich wishes that you meet Lady Smithwick, Miss Fairchild, and her sister. Let us quickly make you tidy and take you to meet the kind women."

Beth's eyes darted from side to side. "I don't want to."

"Nonsense," Pamela said in a bracing tone. "You will charm them, and Lord Kerrich is there to help you. Besides"—she turned, put her hand on Beth's shoulder and shepherded her slowly forward—"it's good practice for you, and later when we return to our schoolroom, you may ask me any questions you have about the experience."

Beth's voice sank to a whisper. "What if I do something wrong?"

"We are in the park. No one expects more than just courtesy, which you have in abundance."

Kerrich obviously had set the scene, for as they approached, the beautiful young ladies and the plump older one were smiling at the child with the vivacity of confirmed gossips who realize the greatest tidbit of the entire year may just have fallen into their laps. Pamela dropped back as they reached Kerrich's side, and watched as Beth curtsied and smiled timidly and responded to their questions in a demure voice.

"She's a pleasant little thing," Lady Smithwick said in an approving tone. "It's so good of you, Lord Kerrich, and so indicative of your good nature and high moral fiber—"

Pamela was proud that she refrained from snorting.

"—to take her into your home when you don't even know if she is descended from bad stock."

Kerrich wrapped his arm around Beth before she could step forward. A good thing, Pamela thought, since her small, skinny fists were clenched. Projecting her voice with the calm authority of the Miss Lockhart she had become, Pamela said, "But Lord Kerrich does know the child's background. She is the daughter of an ancient but poverty-stricken family in the North. Her father was a trusted assistant, killed while performing a heroic deed in Lord Kerrich's service."

The ladies looked crestfallen.

In an overly loud whisper to her sister, the younger Miss Fairchild said, "So she's not his bastard?"

Lady Smithwick snapped at the girl, "Certainly not! I never thought such a thing." Which was an obvious lie. Turning back to the party on the ground, she trilled, "Lord Kerrich, God will undoubtedly bless you for your kindness."

"Yes, but you'd better not bring her out again until the seamstress has finished her new garments." The elder daughter covered her mouth as she giggled. "She is dressed like a serving maid!"

Kerrich still held Beth, although now he appeared to be hugging her rather than restraining her. "You are ever wise, Miss Fairchild. Of course, I take your advice."

As they rode away, Kerrich smiled and bowed, Beth and Pamela curtsied.

For a long moment, Kerrich looked down at Beth, then angrily turned on Pamela. "Miss Lockhart, this is your fault. Why did you not tell me Beth needed clothing?"

CHAPTER 10

"I cannot believe you allowed me to take that child to the park in those clothes." Feeling decidedly peeved, Kerrich sat in the delicate chair in the elegant, mirrored surroundings of Madame Beauchard's fashion salon, waiting for Beth to come out in the latest gown of Madame's choosing. "Why didn't you tell me she was in rags?"

"You exaggerate, my lord. Those garments were provided by a young maid from your very household who had outgrown them."

Her extravagant patience grated away at his normally dispassionate disposition. "A maid's clothing? I took her into public wearing a maid's clothing? Miss Lockhart, this is a disgrace I will long remember."

With a snap that few dared to practice on him, Miss Lockhart said, "You have eyes to see, my lord. If Beth's clothing displeased you, you had only to speak."

That woman.

Some people said dreams had meaning. He didn't believe it, of course. Dreams were nonsense, sometimes pleasant, sometimes horrifying, but never anything more than the meandering of an idle mind. But last night's dream! Those fleshy tints. Those high breasts. Those shapely legs.

That face. Miss Lockhart's face!

Out of the corner of his eyes he could see her. She sat beside him, only her knitting needles in motion. However, she radiated her own irritation, although how she dared he did not understand. "As if I would bother to notice the child's garments," he retorted. "That is what the governess does!"

Miss Lockhart gave a shrewish huff. "What a governess does, my lord, is guide a child through the intricacies of learning and conduct, not ride a miserable old nag on an ill-advised expedition!"

"Miserable old nag?" he repeated. Interesting that she saved her greatest scorn for her steed. Did Miss Lockhart fancy herself a rider? "You sound as if you would wish to be mounted on a finer horse."

The knitting needles clicked faster. "That is not the point. The point is that I had not yet considered Beth's wardrobe for I did not yet know where you would keep her or in what capacity." When he would have spoken, she overrode him with a strong, "*Also*, it never occurred to me you would wish to purchase an extensive wardrobe for a child you plan to discard when she had succeeded in getting you what you want."

Shocked, he asked, "Do you think me a catchpenny, then? This is as if you were saying I wouldn't purchase a uniform for a footman I hire only for a party."

The knitting needles faltered. "A . . . footman."

"Or some such." Perhaps comparing a foundling to a footman seemed a bit cavalier to Miss Lockhart, but her doubts in his beneficence wore thin. "I assure you I am famous for the fairness and honor with which I treat my staff. Have you had anything to complain about?"

"No, my lord."

"Your rooms are as you requested? Your half-days off are scheduled as promised? You have a nursery maid assigned to you to perform the inconsequential tasks of child care?"

"Yes, my lord. Thank you, my lord."

"Well, then." Satisfied he had made his point, he adjusted his cane across his lap, crossed his ankle over his knee, and allowed his monocle to dangle from his fingers. "I promised the foundling would be given training in some trade, and so she shall be."

"No one could expect more of you."

Was she mocking him?

He should look at her to see, but all day long, by dint of staring toward her or over her shoulder, Kerrich had avoided looking directly at Miss Lockhart. Which was foolish, and could not continue, but he had to admit to a certain cowardice.

This was his grandfather's fault, of course. Grandpapa had congratulated Kerrich on his wisdom in courting Miss Lockhart. Grandpapa had implied Miss Lockhart was an attractive woman. And now, because of a silly dream caused by his grandfather's suggestions, Kerrich squirmed in the presence of Miss Lockhart. He had lusted after this crone who was not only unattractive, but older.

Unfortunately, or perhaps fortunately, the full-length gilt-framed mirrors hung every few feet along the wall, reflecting their seated images at him from every direction. So he risked a glance at those hands, busily engaged in knitting.

He hadn't seen them without gloves before, and he noted how smooth they were, unmarked by spots, with skin so transparent he could observe the blue tracery of veins and so delicate it moved like fine, pale silk.

How very odd. In his observations, he had noted the first place age showed was in a woman's hands.

Madame Beauchard recalled him from his contemplations. "My lord, here is our little miss." She ushered Beth out of the dressing area in the newest selection, a simple yellow morning gown.

Leaning forward, he examined the child's apparel with the same intense interest he showed when selecting his own garments. "The style, yes. It is appropriate for lessons." With his fingertip, he touched Miss Lockhart's upper arm and noted a firmness of flesh he had not expected. "Don't you agree?"

"Most appropriate, my lord." Miss Lockhart inched away from him.

"But the color!" he continued. "Madame Beauchard, what were you thinking?"

"As always, my lord, you are right," said the modiste in her fake French accent. "Yellow is not the young lady's color." Then, slyly, she added, "Just as it is not yours, my lord."

Lifting his monocle, he fitted it to his eye and stared at Madame Beauchard. Did she dare to insinuate . . . ?

With the ease of a consummate liar, Miss Lockhart once again told her tale. "That is correct, Madame Beauchard. Beth looks like her father, an assistant at Lord Kerrich's bank who died while performing a heroic deed in Lord Kerrich's service."

"Her father?" Madame Beauchard looked at Beth, and Kerrich could see her reluctantly discarding her more fascinating speculation.

"Yes," Beth said. "Papa died saving Lord Kerrich's life."

"Beth!" Miss Lockhart failed to hide her amazement when she heard this new addition to the yarn.

"Didn't he?" Beth squeaked.

Kerrich rescued the child, and his character. "I am eternally grateful to your father."

Miss Lockhart recovered from her surprise and answered with composure, "Yes, Beth, but you sounded as if you were bragging, and I'm sure it was more than Madame desired to know."

"Never fear, my lord," Madame Beauchard said. "Everyone would tell you I am the most discreet of the fashionable couturiers."

Kerrich's incredulity overwhelmed him. "You?"

Madame Beauchard contrived to look hurt.

"Madame, I would take it badly if you were to question the child." He looked meaningfully at Beth. "She gets upset when reminded of the circumstances of her father's death."

Beth took the hint, and sniffed and knuckled her eyes.

Looking alarmed, Madame snatched her hand off Beth's shoulder. "Of course not, my lord. I have no wish to make the *petite fille* cry." Gingerly, she patted Beth. "Come along, *cherie*, let us dress you again for Lord Kerrich's inspection."

They disappeared behind the curtains.

Miss Lockhart put her hideous knitting into her bag and thrust her knitting needles back into the knot at the base of her head. "I should go back there."

"No."

"But, my lord, if Madame Beauchard does question Beth . . ."

"She won't. She hates children except when they bring her income and she knows if Beth becomes agitated our session will be cut short. I predict Beth is even now being stuffed with sweets and praised for her beauty." And besides, while many were the occasions he had sat here waiting for Madame to bring forth his mistress and her clothing for his approval, he had never found such a delicious way to pass the time before. If not for that damned dream, tormenting Miss Lockhart would be quite the finest diversion he'd ever discovered.

Miss Lockhart relaxed back into her chair, but those hands, those soft, pale, slender hands, plucked at her atrocious black woolen skirt as if they could not be still.

Funny, that. She had given him the impression of imperturbable composure and strict control. What had she to be nervous about?

Perhaps he made her uncomfortable, although he wondered why. Perhaps he should prod her further, and *discover* why. "The tale of Beth's father gets more improbable with every telling. It should have been thoroughly thrashed out before we stepped foot out of the house. You should have thought of that."

Her hands stopped their wanderings across her skirt, grabbed a fistful of material, and squeezed. "My lord, I did advise against taking Beth out today."

"But you also advised we get to know each other and develop a rapport. I believe we have accomplished that. Wouldn't you say, Miss Lockhart?"

Her knuckles stood out white on her hands. "Yes, my lord."

"So I was right in suggesting that we ride. Good." Idly, he swung his monocle from its silver chain and contemplated how best to discomfit her. "Do you ride well, Miss Lockhart? Or is that private information which should not be shared with a dissolute gentleman such as myself?"

"I have not said I consider you dissolute."

"You have not told me whether you can ride, either." As the moment of silence stretched out, he amused himself by wagering whether she wished more to ride a fine steed or to put him in his place.

Finally Miss Lockhart admitted, "I can ride."

"Then I will mount you appropriately." Realizing what

he had said, he wavered between laughter and horror.

She stiffened, and in the most stifling of tones said, "You are the epitome of graciousness, my lord."

Laughter won. A soft chuckle which lent him the fortitude he needed to look at her.

That face. In his dream, it had been grotesque, painted, cruel. Today it just looked . . . unnatural. In this feminine environment with its clear light, its gilt mirrors, its crystal chandeliers, Miss Lockhart appeared gawky and rumpled, badly fitted in an old-fashioned jacket and dress.

"I will buy you a gown." The words were out of his mouth before he realized what he had said, but at once he understood what was driving him. This female didn't understand the role of woman in civilization. Ladies were supposed to be soft and beguiling. They were supposed to talk a man around, flirt and tease, win their way with wiles. Maybe, if he could just get her out of those purple and brown and black monstrosities that she wore and into some agreeable color, she would no longer assault him with words—or, at least, he wouldn't mind so much when she did.

But of course Miss Lockhart didn't react like a normal lady, with flutterings and gratitude. No, she looked like a Gorgon, one of those Greek females with snakes for hair, who had just viewed herself in the mirror and turned to stone. He was surprised she could even move her lips to refuse him. "Lord Kerrich, such a suggestion is unacceptable."

He didn't know what made him do it. Maybe just pure incorrigibility. Probably it was that frigid expression of abhorrence that curled her lips. Certainly he was exorcising that abomination of the dream. But he leaned back in his chair and looked her over carefully. "A plainer style, just as I suggested for Beth, would lessen the impact of your impressive torso." Actually, under closer scrutiny, the shape of her body beneath the ill-fitting gown appeared to be genuine, not the result of corset trickery, and almost Gothic in its arches and buttresses.

"Perhaps you didn't hear me, my lord. It would not be appropriate for me to accept a gown from you."

"A nice pale blue, I think, would be less contrast to your extraordinarily pale skin." Good God, that looked like a trace of rice powder in the crease of her neck. She wasn't actually putting on powder to make herself paler!

Beth caroled from the door, "Look. Look what I have to wear!"

Before he turned to view the child, he stared carefully at Miss Lockhart. It was true. She did wear rice powder, and red rouge unless he missed his guess—and he never missed. Good God, he'd seen many a woman who powdered and painted to ill effect, but never had he seen a woman so obliterated beneath the laminate of cosmetics.

"Lord Kerrich, Beth and Madame Beauchard wish you to decide on this newest selection." Miss Lockhart sounded calm under his scrutiny, but again her nervous hands betrayed her agitation, and she withdrew a man's silver watch on a chain from her jacket pocket and opened it as if her schedule had been quite demolished. Probably it had, and probably she blamed him.

Beth wore the same pale blue he envisioned for Miss Lockhart, in batiste, with full skirts, long sleeves and white lace at the collar and cuffs. Her eyes were shining, and she touched the skirt with reverent fingers. "I haven't worn an ironed dress since my mother died, and today *all* the dresses have been ironed."

Miss Lockhart tucked her watch away and cleared her throat as if to clear away a lump of emotion. "From now on, we'll make sure all your gowns are ironed."

"Yes. Oh, please." Beth twirled on her toes again. "At Lord Kerrich's, even the scullery maids wear ironed aprons!"

"Even the scullery maids take baths once a week."

Miss Lockhart's excursion into sentimentality hadn't lasted long, Kerrich noted.

Beth grimaced, then shrugged. "Oh, as you say. As long as I can wear these fine togs."

The child knew how to strike a deal. Kerrich admired that.

"Not togs," Miss Lockhart said. "Call them clothes, or garments, or apparel."

The woman knew how to pick her battles. He admired that, too.

He also knew how to pick his battles, and battling with Miss Lockhart over whether she would accept a gown was futile. For the moment, he would capitulate—and if Miss Lockhart understood him at all, she would recognize the danger in his yielding.

Fortunately, Miss Lockhart understood him not at all.

They sat in silence while Beth changed again. Once more, Miss Lockhart brought forth her knitting, and this time he wondered if she worked not from the rigid belief that idleness bred corruption, but to hide her impetuosity.

"What are you making, Miss Lockhart?"

"A wrap, Lord Kerrich."

Flat. Easy. Interesting . . . Knitting was the work of peasants, and he would wager Miss Lockhart had little experience with it. "How long have you been knitting, Miss Lockhart?"

Her hesitation betrayed her. "Years."

"You must have many pieces of work to display."

"No, my lord."

Ha! He had her. "Why not, Miss Lockhart?"

"I give them to charity."

She sounded like the same old censorious Miss Lockhart, but as he watched her fingers moved awkwardly, the needles fought each other, and she tangled the black yarn into a knot.

He smiled. How pleasant to know he had the ability to hamper the composure of so formidable a woman.

Then Beth came dancing out in a white, ruffled gown with a blue velvet sash.

Twirling his finger, he indicated the child should turn, and when she had, he said, "Yes, I suppose she must have something like this for afternoon parties, but let's keep it to one, shall we? At her age, the furbelows are too much and detract from her handsome face. Simplicity is the key."

"*Oui*, my lord." Madame Beauchard smiled with ever-great and greedy delight. "You are correct as always. From now on, we will eschew the ruffles."

"But I get to keep this one?" Beth stood on the toes of one foot, then on the toes of another, like a ballerina impatient to dance.

"Yes, that one," Kerrich said.

Beth curtsied and grinned, went to the mirror and pirouetted, then reentered the dressing area.

"Damn, now I suppose I will have to take her to the ballet." Kerrich sighed heavily. "I detest the ballet. All those girls dancing around on their toes. As Grandpapa says, if they wanted taller girls, why didn't they hire taller girls?"

Miss Lockhart asked, "Is that supposed to be a jest, my lord?"

"My grandfather thinks so."

"Then I will laugh when he tells me."

Why did she treat him as she did? With everyone else, she seemed an amiable woman. Indeed, in the brief time she'd been in the stables, she'd charmed the stableboys. But she didn't like him, and he was such a genial man. Kind. Thoughtful.

He caught a glimpse of himself in the mirror. Handsome. Dashing. She couldn't hold that against him, could she? She couldn't assume on such a thin basis that he was cut from the same mold as her father?

He resolved to ask, but when he turned to look earnestly into her eyes he met only his own reflection on the tint of her glasses. He wanted to take them away from her, and in irritation he said, "I find it difficult to talk to those spectacles."

"Talk to me, then, if you must."

Her knitting had smoothed out; apparently sniping at him soothed her.

"Why do you wear them?"

"I must," she answered.

"You can't see without them, then." He reached for the metal frames. "How bad is your vision?"

She flinched backward and warded off his hand with her arm. "I can see. But the light hurts my eyes."

"Surely sunlight, only."

"All light."

Behind the tinted glasses, he saw her eyes guiltily shift to the side. The jade was lying to him! He couldn't imagine why, and he didn't need this kind of nuisance. A child, a governess, a counterfeiting ring, the queen with her ugly threats . . .

He was trying to accomplish something here. Miss Lockhart didn't appreciate it. So . . .

"That last dress the child wore was handsome."

"Very handsome."

"So she shall wear it when we shall give a party to introduce Beth to the other children."

"That is an excellent idea, my lord." Miss Lockhart beamed as she approved of him—momentarily. "In about a month—"

"A week."

"I can't prepare her in a week!"

"And I don't have a month."

"My lord, this is not a game."

"I begin to suspect you are the one unaware of that fact, Miss Lockhart. One week, or you and she are of no use to me, and you both shall be out on the street!"

CHAPTER 11

Pamela woke and sat up with a sense of panic. Someone was frightened. Suffering from a nightmare. Screaming. Beth.

Pamela blinked in the dim light of the night candle flickering in the sconce on the wall.

The nursery. Kerrich's house. Beth.

Swiftly she rose, wrapped her robe around her, took the candle and hurried into the bedchamber beside hers. There she found the child. Beth was awake now, sitting straight up, hands clasping the blankets up to her chin. She stared forward, fighting the night phantoms with a trembling discipline that told of a frequent need for such strength.

"Beth." Sticking the candle on the holder, Pamela seated herself on the mattress beside the girl, moving slowly so as not to startle her. "It's Miss Lockhart."

Beth's gaze moved toward her, eyes open so wide the whites showed around each iris. She nodded, a jerky motion, to indicate she recognized her governess, but her teeth were clenched. She couldn't speak.

With a tender touch, Pamela smoothed the child's hair off her forehead. "You're awake now. Whatever you dreamed about is gone."

Beth fought for words, squeaking fearfully until she managed to say, "I know. I dreamed about my mother."

She wasn't the kind of child to cast herself on Pamela's bosom and howl, but a lone tear trickled from the corner of her eye and down her cheek. Pamela wiped it away, her heart squeezing with sympathy pains.

"I miss her so much." Beth curled her knees toward her chest.

"She was your mother. Of course you miss her."

"It's been a year." She held the blankets in bunches close to her mouth. "I should be over it by now."

Such a thought could have never come from the child. That was some adult speaking. "Who told you that?" Pamela asked.

Beth swallowed. "Mrs. Fallowfield. She hated it when one of us started crying because . . . then we all did."

Pamela didn't know what made her admit it. Perhaps she felt an adult responsibility to comfort the child. More likely it was hearing her own tale told by one who cried out her pain rather than holding it within. Or perhaps it was Lord Kerrich's threat echoing in her mind, and the knowledge that if the party tomorrow was a failure, she and Beth would be alone together, and out on the street. But no matter why, Pamela said, "Many years ago, my mother died. Sometimes I still dream."

Beth stared at her. "Do you cry?"

"Always. She was very ill before she died and I . . . I tried to help her get better." Pamela swallowed over the familiar lump in her throat. "I couldn't."

"Oh, me too!" Beth dropped the blankets and scrambled out of her cocoon. "I mean, nothing I did helped. And Papa. He was sick, too. He used to take me places while Ma cooked, and he taught me about the horses. I miss him so much. And Ma . . . she was always there, she hugged me and made me feel better, and now when I dream about her she's always sick, and *I* have to hold *her*, only she doesn't feel better. She dies."

"That's the worst part," Pamela whispered. "All my good memories are overshadowed by the great anger and the crushing sadness."

"If I could just dream about her hugging me, just once . . ."

Pamela couldn't resist that appeal, and she gathered Beth to her and rocked her.

Pamela loved children. Incorrigible or sweet, boisterous or shy, she always found a way to wrap them around her little finger, and that way was love. She talked to them, listened to them, teased them, played with them, taught them, and they responded, returning her love twelve-fold. Yet as a governess, she had always been careful to protect her heart, never forgetting that the children she taught were not her own, for always she would have to leave them.

Yet with Beth Pamela found a common ground.

Beth snuggled closer, no longer crying but giving and sharing now.

In the twelve years since Pamela's father had deserted her and her mother, she had never told anyone about her nightmares. Nobody else would have understood. Beth did.

Beth needed love. Beth needed a place. Beth needed everything that Pamela had had in her youth and that had been torn from her by her father's abandonment. Kerrich could give her that. Pamela couldn't. Pamela couldn't even stay with Beth because of this wretched disguise she'd donned, but she could do one thing.

She would finagle and encourage and coax Kerrich into keeping Beth as his own. And if that didn't work—she'd blackmail him.

Beth's sleepy little voice broke into Pamela's musings.

"Miss Lockhart, you look so different at night."

Pamela caught back a gasp. In her own robe without the wretchedly tight hairstyle and the dreadful powder, she would look different. She glanced down at Beth's upturned face. The girl was staring at her as if enchanted, and Pamela slid her fingers over Beth's lids to shut them. "Your eyes are tired."

"No, they're not." Beth sighed and snuggled closer. "I like you, Miss Lockhart. No matter what, promise me we're going to be together."

Pamela caught her breath.

"Promise . . ." And Beth slid into sleep.

Beth really, really wanted to smack little Billy, Lord Chiswick, right under his fat chin as he grabbed the last piece of cake off the gaily decorated sideboard and stuffed it in his mouth. She longed to watch the blue sugar frosting go up his nose and hear the other children jeer at the stinky, squabby, ten-year-old viscount. But she knew Miss Lockhart would disapprove. *No, dear,* she would say, *it doesn't matter that he called you an insolent beggar who doesn't know her place. You still can't put your knee in his chest and force-feed him mushrooms until he turns into a bloated toad.* And even more than Beth wished to teach Bully-Boy a lesson, she wished to make Miss Lockhart happy.

Beth stopped glaring at Bully-Boy and glanced through the columnar portals into the large, beautifully furnished sitting chamber. There the adults sat on shiny, polished chairs and brocade-upholstered sofas to listen as Miss Fotherby accompanied herself on the harp and sang. There Miss Lockhart sat in the back row, looking very ugly and very strict, and frequently observing the children's activities in the antechamber. And there, behind and to the side, stood

Lord Kerrich leaning against the wall, staring at Miss Lockhart's profile.

During the week of frenetic preparation just past, he'd been staring at her a lot. Sometimes he looked annoyed, sometimes he looked puzzled, but he always *looked,* and that gave Beth hope. Because Beth had seen through Miss Lockhart's disguise. Beth didn't know why Miss Lockhart wore all that stuff on her face or dressed with such daft dowdiness, but Beth had made her plans. Lord Kerrich was rich. Miss Lockhart was poor. Lord Kerrich was selfish. Miss Lockhart told him so. Lord Kerrich was handsome . . . and so was Miss Lockhart. So all Beth had to do was get them together, talking and fighting, and show Lord Kerrich Miss Lockhart's real appearance. They'd get sweet on each other for sure.

"Hey." Bully-Boy pinched her arm. "I want more cake."

Beth ignored him. In the orphanage, she'd had a lot of experience ignoring knuckle-draggers—and some experience fighting them. What interested her now was how Lord Reynard watched his grandson and Miss Lockhart, just like Beth was. The old man was a shark, no doubt about it.

Mr. Athersmith was there, and he only watched Miss Fotherby with a long expression and this earnest, cow-faced devotion. He lived here and worked every day with Lord Kerrich, which should have made him important, but he wasn't. He was nothing more than a hoddy-noddy, the kind of man who slipped around and acted modest and humble when he really thought he was better than everyone else.

Lord Kerrich's family party was a success. The sun was shining, a breeze had whisked away the coal dust in the air, the windows were open, and everyone was happy today.

Bully-Boy pinched her again, hard. "I want cake. Go get it."

Everyone was happy except this brat, and nothing could make him happy.

But Beth would try one last time. Miss Lockhart would have approved of Beth's manners when she said, "I'm so sorry. We're out of cake. Perhaps you'd prefer a pastry or an ice."

"No." He thrust his round, ugly face right into hers. "I want cake."

Two of the visiting governesses leaned against the entrance to the corridor and gossiped. Beth's other guests, about a dozen children ranging in age from six to nine, sat lined up against the wall, plates balanced on their knees, forks suspended in the air, watching Beth with hopeful expressions.

"I said"—Bully-Boy gave her a push—"I want more cake. My mother says you're just a servant, anyway. So go to the kitchen, servant, and get me more cake."

She glanced toward the adults again, sitting sideways to her and intent on the singing.

Quick as a wink, she hooked her foot behind Bully-Boy's knee and pulled his leg out from under him, then in one swift, continuous motion she stepped toward the wall and found a seat.

Bully-Boy staggered sideways into the sideboard decorated with silver, lace and marzipan. With a clatter that stopped the music, he grabbed the tablecloth and brought the food and dishes down on himself. Breaking the shocked silence, he gave a screech so high only dogs could hear it.

His mother rushed in immediately, thus proving she was a dog.

Miss Lockhart was right on her heels, and nursery maids and governesses arrived from all over the house.

Pink ices, yellow lemonade and brown macaroons formed a colorful paste all over Bully-Boy's black wheyface suit with its short jacket and sissy breeches, and his mouth was a round, bawling ring in the circle of his pallid face. Beth wanted to laugh. Instead she managed an expression of horror and amazement that closely matched the ones worn by the adults. At least she hoped it did. She hoped she didn't look like the other children. Those dunces clapped their hands over their mouths or giggled as Bully-Boy kicked and squealed like the piggy he was.

His mother was on her knees beside him, the nursery maids were wiping at him and he was screaming, "She did it. She pushed me!"

His mother looked right at Beth. "I knew it." Her voice carried over the tumult. "That child is a vulgarian, a commoner, and not fit to associate with the finer people."

In an innocent little voice, Beth said, "But I didn't push him." She elbowed the girl next to her, a smart-looking tyke for all she wore more ruffles than a bedcurtain. "Did you see me push him?"

The girl didn't even stop to consider. "She was sitting here with me." Then, ducking her head, she whispered, "Billy's a plague and you showed him."

Luckily, no one heard her and Beth maintained her guise of wide-eyed innocence.

A guise that Miss Lockhart saw through with one long look. But Miss Lockhart wouldn't betray her. Beth knew that, just as she knew Miss Lockhart and Lord Kerrich would get married and adopt Beth, and make beautiful babies, and they'd all be a real family.

Kerrich joined the crowd to watch the fracas with admiration and amusement. This wasn't the kind of party he usually gave, or even usually attended. In fact, he made it a point to avoid any party attended by children, especially these afternoon ladies' parties where young people were given the chance to mingle with others of their age while their mothers exchanged gossip and the few men who attended listened to an obligatory piano—or in this case, harp—recital, then fled to the game room and smoked to clear the perfume from their lungs.

They were headed that way now—Lord Swearn and Lord Colbrook, Mr. Tomlin and Lord Albon, Grandpapa and Lewis, and Chiswick's father, Lord Pitchford, all of them sneaking out like the desperately bored knaves they were.

Kerrich longed to join them, but this was his party, his idea. He glanced at the mess in the children's chamber. He had to stay, at least this bit of a fracas livened it up.

Chiswick's mother turned on him. "It is the fault of your misguided charity that we have been forced to clasp this asp to our bosom."

Kerrich bowed. "What asp is that, my lady?"

"That . . . thing." Lady Pitchford pointed her trembling finger at Beth.

Beth, who looked as pristine as a china-faced doll, and who Kerrich had seen blot out Chiswick with one smooth motion. "Did any of you see Beth hurt little Chiswick?"

The children and the governesses shook their heads, the governesses because they hadn't been watching and the children because they hated Chiswick. Either reason seemed good enough for Kerrich. "There you have it, my lady," he said. "Young Chiswick slipped."

"That's not what *Billy* says!" said the lady who once had been a candidate on his list of suitable wives.

"Ah." Kerrich raised his monocle and looked disdainfully at Lady Pitchford. "But Beth is two years younger, two stones lighter and female. Are you saying my girl beat up your son?"

"She had the advantage," Lady Pitchford said. "She's a gutter brat!"

Annoyance swept away Kerrich's façade of good humor. No one was going to pick on *his* damned foundling. "A gutter brat is what she is not. She is the child of a respectable family. Her father saved my life, and it is not charity that brought my dearest Beth into my home, but gratitude for the valiant spirit which lives in her." He challenged the assemblage with his gaze. "I would take it ill should anyone else descend so low as to abuse the dear lass."

No one from the crowd in the sitting room accepted the challenge. They murmured noncommittally and broke off into little groups, chatting about the weather and the newest fashions. The governesses went to their charges and began making little fusses about them to cover their previous neglect. And Miss Lockhart helped Chiswick to his feet and finished wiping him down.

"He's not hurt," Kerrich heard Miss Lockhart telling Lady Pitchford. "Although it would be best to get him home so the laundry maid could clean his costume."

"They're his favorite garments!" Lady Pitchford's voice trembled.

Kerrich felt no pity for the woman or her son. Letting his monocle dangle from its silver chain, he said, "As clumsy as he is, he must change thrice a day. You'd best limit his sweets, my lady, or it'll be a sore-backed horse that carries him."

Miss Lockhart pulled him aside and like the vengeful flame scorched him with her quietly spoken words. "My lord, let us have no more of that. The lad is not deaf, and such ill-mannered comments must surely smite an already paltry spirit."

"But he hurt Beth."

"I know. But a child who is raised with cruelty learns only cruelty, and one can only imagine what life has created such a wretch."

"You are very compassionate, but I believe it is groundless. The child is just spoiled!"

"Perhaps." She leaned closer. "But I saw Beth's activities as clearly as you, so please extend your courtesy to Lady Pitchford and Lord Chiswick as they leave."

Being justly reprimanded brought him no more pleasure than being unjustly denounced, Kerrich found. In fact, it was worse, for it meant he was wrong—and that was a position in which he seldom found himself.

Miss Lockhart left him standing there as she went to Beth. "Come, dear," he heard her say. "We should bid farewell to your guest and extend the hope that any future visit will proceed more peacefully."

To Kerrich's surprise, the good-byes went smoothly under Miss Lockhart's iron rule, with Beth easily performing her hostessing duties and Chiswick giving no more than a whimper as he backed away from her handshake.

And although Kerrich hated to give the appearance of obeying Miss Lockhart, he found himself following Lady Pitchford and her son into the foyer, offering up his apologies for the ill-fated scene and extending his insincere hope that they would visit again one day.

The very worst came when the door shut behind them and Miss Lockhart said approvingly, "Well done, my lord! That was exceptionally generous and well mannered of you."

He lifted his monocle, glared down at her and with withering sarcasm said, "Miss Lockhart, I do not know what I did before you came."

"Nor I, my lord." Lifting her skirts, she followed Beth up the stairs to the children's play chamber. "You may thank me for my guidance later."

That woman. Annoyance ate at Kerrich. Miss Lockhart was either returning his sarcasm with interest or, what was worse, thought him honestly indebted for her tutelage. He stalked through the sitting room, smiling with false affability at his guests and scarcely noticing that they cowered when he spoke to them. He didn't need anyone to teach him his manners. Miss Lockhart had been hired so the foundling he was using in his scheme would cause him no trouble, and she had best remember that.

So he would go where the men had gone to drink and play cards. The game room. Standing in the doorway, he stared at the gentlemen who had so gladly abandoned him to the scene with Lady Pitchford. Grandpapa held court in a wide cushioned chair. Lewis diffidently stood off to the side, not playing cards, not conversing, the odd man out as always, although Kerrich thought that his own doing rather than any snobbery on the part of his visitors. And the others, his guests, his compatriots, his friends . . . he glared. There had been a time, and that time only a month ago, when he had laughed at these men. He'd listened to their complaints for years, and he'd called them henpecked. In thrall to their wives.

If Kerrich thought about it, he might begin to see similarity between these men and himself, especially with Miss Lockhart's voice still ringing in his ears. It was not to be borne.

"Kerrich, come in!" Lord Reynard called out. "These gentlemen were just asking me about your sudden philanthropic bent."

"Actually, I believe my exact words were, 'What in the hell is Kerrich doing taking on a child and a governess?' " Lord Swearn sat at the card table waiting for his next hand. The man was fifty, with hair growing out of his ears and none on his head. One might assume a man of his age would know better, yet he and Lady Swearn had produced a child just last year. He couldn't even claim an old man's foolish indulgence for his young wife, for they'd been married twenty-five years and the baby was the youngest of seven.

"Yes, man. You've been an inspiration to me. No wife, no children—a peaceful life." Lord Pitchford grinned as if he were kidding, but no one thought he was joking. After all, his wife and child were gone and he still lingered, leaning against the sidetable, puffing on a cigar and looking large and self-satisfied. But Lady Pitchford knew how to cut him down to size. When she started talking, he shriveled and moped like a chastised lad.

"I told 'em why you took little Beth, but they just squawked like the bunch of peahens they are." Lord Reynard good-naturedly insulted the men he'd known since they'd been—as he often called them—snot-nosed brats.

"That's all very well for you to say, sir," Lord Colbrook said. "You haven't got a wife."

"Aye. And I miss her."

Colbrook flushed at Lord Reynard's crisp tone. "Sorry," he muttered. "Didn't think."

"You haven't the equipment to think." Kerrich tapped his forehead.

Colbrook nodded morosely and dealt the cards. He happily did as his wife told him, for even he acknowledged her wit and brilliance outpaced his own.

"The point is, Kerrich, you could have given the child a good life without taking her into your own home. And that witch of a governess!" Mr. Tomlin swallowed his whisky as if the mere memory of Miss Lockhart caused him pain.

Before his marriage, Mr. Tomlin had been only the wild, moneyed son of a half-noble merchant. Well did Kerrich remember the times they'd had on the town. They had drunk, they had wenched, they had fought, although Tomlin had been a miserable fighter with a tendency to get in the way at just the wrong moment.

And now? Bah, he spent the evenings at home with his pretty young wife, or chained to her side through all the proper entertainments as they sought to cement their place in society for the sake of their children.

And Lord Albon, silent and plucking the cards off the table with the concentration of a dedicated gambler, was the same as all the rest. Strong and resolute in his life outside the home, yet there within its walls, he bent to his wife's wishes when any real man knew he had to keep a firm hand on the reins.

Fools, all of them. "So, Tomlin," Kerrich asked, "aren't you the man who called himself ecstatically happy in his marriage? Who told me I ought to find myself a wife? Have children? Are you now saying it's not as wonderful as you would have had me believe?"

"It's just as wonderful as I told you." Tomlin picked up his hand of cards. "But there's one thing that makes it that way, and you're not getting *that*."

"A little frigging makes it all worthwhile, does it?" Kerrich accepted a brandy from the footman, and watched as Lewis poured himself another one and filled it to the top. Lewis wasn't a heavy drinker. Did the presence of Swearn, his former employer, make him uncomfortable?

"More than a little, if you're lucky," Pitchford said.

The married men all laughed as if they knew something Kerrich didn't.

But Kerrich could shut them up. "How often are you lucky, Pitchford?"

Pitchford's fatuous grin faded.

"Besides," Kerrich said, "when I've an itch I can buy a woman to scratch it."

"Not with that little lass in the house, you can't." Lord Reynard had strict notions of a gentleman's proper behavior, and he never hesitated to air them.

"I'll go out for it, sir," Kerrich assured him.

"What's wrong with the governess?" Lord Reynard asked. "If a man's got eyes to see, she's a demmed fine figure of a woman."

A few discreet coughs and curled lips followed his statement.

Lord Colbrook had arrived late enough to miss Miss Fotherby's harp recital—deliberately, no doubt—and he asked, "What *is* wrong with the governess?"

"Nothing, if you like that corpselike complexion." Then Tomlin realized he'd maligned Lord Reynard's opinion of her, and glanced at him in alarm.

"Miss Lockhart has her moments." Lord Reynard spent most of his days at the United Service Club, talking business with his old friends, but Kerrich had several times caught him chatting with Miss Lockhart.

"I'd say she's *had* her moments," Albon said. "Now are we going to play cards, or talk?"

"Lockhart." In one of his annoying mannerisms, Colbrook flipped his cards back and forth, back and forth. "Lockhart, Lockhart. I know that name. Wait a minute—is she that Ripley daughter? Can't remember her first name, but the family was from Somerset."

"Pamela Lockhart Ripley," Lord Reynard said. "Yes, that's her."

Colbrook gave a crow of laughter. "Then you're all jesting me. You buffoons!" He smacked Albon on the arm with his fist. "The incomparable Pamela is here, in this very house? Kerrich, you dog, no wonder you adopted the orphan. Tell me, have you stormed the citadel yet? I understand it's well-fortified and never been breached, but if anyone can do it, you can!"

Everyone stared at Colbrook. Everyone except Lord Reynard, who with an enigmatic smile gazed into his drink.

"Colbrook, what are you babbling about?" Tomlin asked.

"She's famous. Beautiful woman. Untouchable." Colbrook wiggled his eyebrows. "Or has been until now, eh, Kerrich?"

Kerrich sipped the brandy and ignored the niggle of discomfort. "Actually, she's quite plain."

"That's polite," Swearn observed.

"No." Colbrook didn't believe it. "You nodcocks are jesting with me."

"Fetch Miss Lockhart for us," Kerrich commanded the footman.

With a bow, the footman left.

Kerrich leaned against the wall where he had a good view of the chamber's inhabitants. Those at the card table played their game, the slap of the cards the only sound in the room, but the ones who had met Miss Lockhart grinned at the thought of the coming entertainment. Lewis poured another drink for himself, and Kerrich could cheerfully predict he would have an aching head in the morning.

With a groan, Pitchford sank into a chair beside Lord Reynard, muttering, "Gotta rest before I go home."

Kerrich knew he should be anticipating Colbrook's surprise, too, but he didn't like this . . . this case of mistaken identity. Colbrook's error only reminded him of his impression in Madame Beauchard's fashion salon—that Miss Lockhart was more than she seemed. But how could she be? She had been hired through Miss Setterington. He'd viewed her references. What could the woman be hiding?

She appeared in the doorway, a female of medium height and undefined age. A female Lord Reynard thought handsome and fitting to be Kerrich's bride. The men stopped their game, dividing their attention between her and Colbrook, and if anything her visage grew more severe. Advancing on Kerrich, she curtsied. "You sent for me, my lord?"

"Yes, I did." He scanned her countenance, composed, cold, yet tinged with wariness. Not unnatural, he told himself. Most women were chary when bearding a group of men in their den. Over her shoulder, he saw Colbrook sitting pop-eyed while the others did a poor job of smothering their merriment. What had seemed a simple idea when he'd called for her now seemed cruel and contemptuous. With no explanation, he said, "You may go now."

Confused, she hesitated.

"Now," he repeated.

With a curtsy, she glided from the room at the same dignified rate with which she had entered it.

If Kerrich could have, he would have spared her the laughter that broke out as soon as she crossed the threshold.

"Now that we've got that cleared up, can we play cards?" Albon demanded.

"You see, Colbrook, what a beauty she is?" Tomlin teased.

"There must be some mistake," Colbrook said. "There must be two Miss Lockharts."

The others hooted.

"Well, there must!"

"I hope there's not two of *her*," Swearn said.

"She's ugly." Tomlin squinted as if the sight of her had hurt his eyes. "Kerrich, how can you bear to have her about?"

Incredibly, Kerrich found himself saying, "She's not so bad."

"Not so bad, eh?" Lord Reynard sounded intrigued.

"Not to look at, of course. Although she's not hideous." All eyes were on Kerrich, and he wisely refrained from mentioning that on her, at least, spectacles were handsome. "I like to talk to her."

In unison, at least three of the men exclaimed, "You like to *talk* to her?"

"When did you become a choir?" Kerrich gibed.

"What's the matter?" Swearn asked. "You haven't ever met a woman you like to talk to?"

"No."

"Come to think of it," Pitchford said reflectively, "neither have I."

"That's because you have no conversation," Kerrich roundly condemned Pitchford. "I do like to talk to her. Miss Lockhart doesn't care about my looks or my money, she tells me the truth in all things."

Tomlin leaned back in his chair. "So she *is* like a wife."

Albon threw down his cards in disgust. "I give up. You lot will never play, and this is a good hand, too."

All the other players threw their hands on the table.

"You know what she said today?" Kerrich was starting to enjoy himself. "She chided me for being rude."

"You're damned rude all the time," Swearn said.

"Never had a woman say so before," Kerrich rejoined. "I like having a woman converse without being coy and flirtatious." He realized he meant it. "When she first met me, I looked her over and said, 'You'll do,' and she said, 'I was thinking the same about you.' "

The men guffawed.

"She dared?" Colbrook's eyes were wide and awed.

"She's dared more than that over the last few days. Haven't been slapped down so rudely since I wore knee breeches."

"I like her already," Tomlin said.

"You would." Kerrich exchanged a grin with him. Tomlin was, after all, still Kerrich's best friend.

"You're infatuated," Swearn said.

"Don't be ridiculous. She's not my type. I go for handsome, sleek, silly women, not overly pale, sharp-tongued termagants."

Lord Reynard cackled. "You're in love at last."

Kerrich swung around on a surge of anger.

But this was his grandfather. Although Lord Reynard had the right, he seldom took the advantage and made comments about Kerrich's emotions. When he did, Kerrich always laughed them off. Why was Kerrich furious now? "With all due respect, sir, I don't love any woman. Although I suppose if Miss Lockhart were here she would tell me I have a duty as host to circulate among the more feminine of my guests."

"Better do what she says, man, or she'll thrash your little arse," Pitchford mocked.

"I intend to." Placing his drink on the table, Kerrich bowed to the company, then said, "You, Pitchford, had better to go home to your wife, or she'll have the servants bar you from your home."

Pitchford slithered deeper into the chair, and with a smile

Kerrich went in search of the ladies. They were, after all, more important to his plans than ever the men could be.

In the drawing room, the servants offered refreshments to any guest with a thirst or appetite, and there he found the ladies, whispering with their heads together. At the sight of him, they hastily separated.

As clearly as if she were speaking in his ear, he heard Miss Lockhart's voice saying, *We cannot force the* ton *to embrace Beth, so we must show our ease with the situation and hope their acceptance follows. Remember your goal—Her Majesty must have a good report of you.*

Miss Lockhart. She haunted him.

Summoning his charm, he wandered in and bowed to each of the ladies, who watched him with expressions that varied from wariness to disapproval. "Lady Albon. Lady Colbrook. Lady Swearn. Mrs. Tomlin. And Miss Fotherby." He greeted Lady Swearn's daughter, a fresh-faced maiden destined to be one of the diamonds of the next season following her presentation at court. "Let me take the chance to thank each of you mothers for bringing your children to meet Beth. I'm aware that the only reason you came was because of the faith you put in my judgment."

"How so, Lord Kerrich?" Lady Swearn's reputation for bluntness was justified.

"That I would have a good reason for bringing a child into my home." He gave a self-deprecating laugh. "Of course, you know me well enough to realize that a confirmed bachelor like myself would only bring the child into my home if she be of acceptable parentage and especially if she be well-behaved."

Lady Swearn drew herself up. "That scene just passed—"

"I apologize, but I understand little Chiswick did something similar last year . . . I don't remember the details, in the past I paid so little attention to the children . . ." Kerrich frowned and acted puzzled. "Perhaps you can remind me?"

Three of the four faces before him lit up. Lady Swearn fixed him with a gimlet eye, and he knew she had the strong suspicion he was speculating.

With much success, it appeared.

Lady Colbrook and Lady Swearn were of an age, but where Lady Swearn was the consummate mother, involved in every facet of her children's lives, Lady Colbrook had already guided her two children into successful marriages. Thin, beautiful, coolly intelligent, Lady Colbrook loved to gossip, relished the humor in most situations, and dressed in the height of fashion, but her distaste for cruelty was evident when she burst out, "Are you talking about that scene where he pushed Althea Sledmore's daughter off the veranda? Althea will no longer allow any of her children to attend a function to which he is invited."

"Probably Lord Kerrich heard about the time we caught the little fiend licking all the cakes at *my* Michaelmas celebration," Mrs. Tomlin said.

Mrs. Tomlin was young, yearning to fit into the society in which she found herself, and so aggrieved by Bully-Boy's prank Kerrich swallowed his laughter. "No, I definitely would have remembered that."

"Then it was the time he chased all the girls into a corner, turned his back and pulled down his breeches to show them . . . to show them . . . his nakedness!" Lady Albon said.

Kerrich's mirth hardened into aversion. "Why did he do that?"

Lady Swearn's impressive bosom heaved with indignation. "Because he's a nasty lad and if his father wasn't wealthy he would be an outcast."

"You are too hard on him, Mother," Miss Fotherby said

in a soft voice, and her china-blue eyes were wide and guileless. "He's just a little lad."

From the doorway came Lewis's voice. "Perhaps the boy had heard the old tale of the young man dangling outside Kensington Palace *sans* his unmentionables."

Miss Fotherby gasped, and Lady Swearn harrumphed, but the other ladies received Lewis's risqué, laughing reminder with obvious amusement, and they parted to let him into their midst.

Kerrich allowed the footman to pour him some of the ghastly pink punch.

"Mr. Athersmith! That is such an old story, and you are naughty to recall it," Lady Colbrook trilled.

"But I do recall it." Lewis bowed, the artistically arranged hank of his blond hair overhanging his forehead, his cheeks flushed ruddy with drink. "Everyone likes to reminisce about it—especially my dear great-uncle, Lord Reynard. He was there that evening, you know."

"No, was he?" Mrs. Tomlin moved closer. "I always thought it was just a fable."

"You are too young to remember when it happened, my dear, but that was the season I was presented and there was talk of nothing else. The satirists had a grand time with the whole incident, drawing cartoons that showed the duchess and her humiliation and the king and his guffaws." Lady Albon lifted her fan and whispered behind it. "There was even speculation that the king had arranged for the viewing as a gesture of his resentment of the duchess."

"A full moon on a foggy night." Lady Colbrook touched her aristocratic nose with her lace handkerchief and a whiff of exotic perfume wafted Kerrich's way. "It was quite the talk of the city for months."

"I believe my cousin was there, too."

Lewis claimed the relationship with such emphasis, Kerrich couldn't help but wonder why. Why, when he had previously done all he could to distance himself from Kerrich and his grandfather, was he now parading his noble antecedents with such ostentation?

Or did he suspect the truth?

"Isn't that right, cousin?" Lewis prodded him.

Kerrich had much experience in deflecting such queries. "I was there, but I'm sorry to say I can't add to the tale, since only the royal party observed the actual . . . incident."

The ladies tittered.

Kerrich bowed, noting that Lady Swearn had captured her daughter's arm and had moved a little apart from the group. Of course. Lord and Lady Swearn had removed Lewis from his position as tutor to young Fotherby, probably because Lewis had been distracted by his descent into crime. Probably Lady Swearn was uncomfortable with the contact. On the other hand, Lewis seemed intent on impressing everyone with his wit and connections.

"Did they ever discover who . . . er . . . dangled there?" Mrs. Tomlin asked.

"No, and please remember my child's age and innocence," Lady Swearn admonished.

"I didn't mean . . . I didn't mean . . ." Mrs. Tomlin blushed deeply.

"No, of course you didn't." Lady Swearn scowled. "I blame Mr. Athersmith for bringing up the subject in front of a young girl."

The pointed reprimand startled Kerrich, and a glance at his cousin showed Lewis was flushed with mortification. So it was as Kerrich had surmised; Lewis's expulsion had not been congenial.

"Forgive me. Excuse me." Lewis bowed himself out the door.

The ladies exchanged knowing glances.

"Oh, Mother." Miss Fotherby rung her hands. "He only meant to entertain us."

Lady Swearn still held her daughter's arm as if the girl might escape. "No matter. It's time we collect the other children. Your father wants us to journey to our estate in Suffolk tomorrow, and he'll join us when he can. The company in London is thin."

"Well, thank you!" Lady Albon, a countess and the highest-ranking female there, feigned offense.

"You know what I mean. Those of us who are here in the summer are either leaving soon or just arrived, and while we're here we pine to be in the country on our estates where it's not so dreadfully hot." Lady Swearn flipped out her fan and vigorously fanned herself.

Kerrich did not point out that the beads of perspiration on her forehead were probably an indicator of her age rather than the temperature. Instead, he tried to defuse the situation by agreeing, "Yes, I've finished my business in London"—that business being the so far futile observation of Lewis and his acquaintances—"and I do believe I will pack up the household and Grandpapa and return to Norfolk tomorrow week"—in the hopes Lewis would meet with his criminal friends on the estate. "Perhaps our paths will cross."

At that civil remark, Lady Swearn looked more dismayed. "Yes. Perhaps."

Taken aback by her scant courtesy, Kerrich could only stare.

Lady Colbrook seemed oblivious. "Lilly, I'm so glad you're going to the country. I have so longed to visit you there."

"Of course." Lady Swearn blinked. "You're welcome anytime, although I wish I understood your sudden affection for the countryside."

"No, an older woman." Moulton lowered his voice. "A lady of consequence, one of your guests. It would seem that rather than pursue his criminal activities, Mr. Athersmith has been pursuing an affair."

"But . . . what about Miss Fotherby?"

"I don't know, sir."

Of course he didn't, and just because Lewis had been thwarted in love didn't mean the noddy-pate wasn't tracking a little wild tail. "We have had a man following Lewis to illicit assignations?"

"Indeed, and I believe that's the reason why we've had no luck discovering his contact. We pay no attention to the arrival and departure of women."

One of his guests. Kerrich's lips curled in disdain. Just like his mother. Proof there were no ladies in society who remained true to their marriage. "Who?" he demanded.

"My man didn't know, sir. Handsome, he said, and considerably older than Mr. Athersmith, but her hair was covered and . . . well, really, sir. In our business, the fairer sex is of no consequence."

The night candle was lit, the nursemaid now slept at the other side of the bedchamber and, satisfied that everything was as it should be, Pamela smoothed the covers over the peaceful child. "Sleep well, little one," she whispered.

"Is she asleep?" a voice asked behind her.

With a gasp, she spun around, her hand to her heart.

Kerrich stood behind her, hands on hips, looking down at Beth. "My lord, what are you doing here?" she whispered.

"I thought I would check on the child." His coat and waistcoat and collar were gone, leaving his shirt open at the neck, and his expression of piratical satisfaction was

"I enjoy your company," Lady Colbrook said warmly.

"Don't feel sorry for me because I'm lonely," Lady Swearn answered. "I have plenty of company with the children. Now come, Penelope."

Miss Fotherby dragged behind her mother, a mortified beauty.

Lady Swearn halted in the doorway. "By the way, Lord Kerrich—your foundling is charming."

Their departure left a little silence behind.

Then Lady Colbrook broke it with a brisk "You can't blame Lady Swearn. Penelope is her oldest daughter, and they have such hopes for her."

"Yes, she's a beauty," Mrs. Tomlin agreed.

"With her background and fortune, she could easily snag a marquess." Lady Albon cast a meaningful glance at Kerrich.

In his time, Kerrich had had his share of meaningful glances as related to young ladies, but this one seemed different. Deciding to fling himself on their collective mercies, he said, "I confess, there was much about that scene I didn't understand."

The silence came back, stronger and more uncomfortable, as the ladies exchanged glances.

Then, by some mysterious manner, they elected Lady Colbrook as their spokesman—as they always did, for the lady's strength of will made her a natural leader. "Didn't you know? Mr. Athersmith lost his position with the Swearns because he fell madly and unsuitably in love with Miss Fotherby."

CHAPTER 13

"What a mess." Kerrich looked around the foyer.

Beside him, Grandpapa leaned on his cane. "Not too bad, considering what a good time the children had."

Kerrich thought his grandfather must be seeing a different house than he was. A few of the children hadn't the breeding or the supervision to keep to their designated areas, and toward the end they had ranged through the house like a swarm of locusts, dropping food, losing hats and handkerchiefs, breaking vases. The library was the only chamber left untouched by the festivities, and that because of a sturdy lock. With any luck, this was the last party Kerrich would have to give for children.

"I'll tell you, Grandpapa, when I have children they're going to mind their manners."

Grandpapa cackled. "I said the same thing about your father, and your father said the same thing about you, and look at how that turned out."

Swiftly indignant, Kerrich said, "I would say I am quite well behaved."

"Now."

Kerrich wanted to sputter indignantly, but he knew better. He had been a hellion.

"I'm not used to all this excitement. I'm going to see my bedchamber." Grandpapa started toward the stairs. "When I'm gone, Moulton can stop skulking in the shadows and come to speak to you."

Surprised, Kerrich looked around.

"Good evening, my lords." Moulton stepped out from the corridor that led to the kitchens.

"You have a talent for skulking," Grandpapa said. "You ought to start a firm for sleuths. I think you'd do very well at it."

Kerrich and Moulton exchanged alarmed glances, for of course that was exactly what Moulton had done years ago, and so successfully the government contracted with him when they needed someone to pose as butler in a noble household. As he was doing now.

His hand on the banister, Grandpapa turned and said, "Don't look so alarmed, gentlemen. I'm old, but I'm not given to blathering. Your secret is safe with me." Then he made his slow way up the stairs.

Kerrich briefly put his hand to his head, then he led the way into the library.

"He's a sly one." Moulton's voice rang with admiration.

"Easy for you to say. He's not your grandfather." But Kerrich couldn't deny his pride. Trust Grandpapa to see the truth of the situation. "Moulton, where is my cousin?"

Moulton straightened. "That would be what I came to discuss with you, sir. He left in the middle of the party. My man followed, of course, and perhaps an hour ago they saw him meet with someone."

Kerrich leaned forward eagerly. "So we're getting somewhere."

"No, my lord. He met with a woman."

"A woman?" Kerrich's mind leaped to Miss Fotherby. "A very young woman?"

vaguely disturbing. "It was an exciting day for her. Will she sleep undisturbed?"

"If she doesn't, I sleep in the next room."

He glanced toward the door. "If she wakes tonight, the nursemaid will be here for her. Today's party went well. Tonight we'll compare our experiences." Placing his hand on her shoulder, he turned her toward the door. "We must plan our future strategy."

So although she was tired and wanted nothing more than to cast off Lady Temperly's second-best black party silk, she went with him down the shadowy hall, down the stairs, and into his library. He was right, they did need to talk.

Surprisingly, she looked forward to it. She didn't know why, except that with him, she could say whatever she wanted. With him, she was a middle-aged, unattractive woman who, when she spoke her mind, was nothing more than irritating and capricious. She experienced a wonderful kind of freedom in talking with Kerrich, and when this position was finished, she would miss that.

Standing in the middle of the library, she looked around. "This is your favorite chamber."

He glanced around as if startled. "Yes, I suppose. It's comfortable."

It was more than comfortable. It exuded that homey, lived-in, cherished atmosphere a room gathers after years of care and affection. One should have been able to shout down its length and get an echo back, but alcoves and window seats broke up the span. The bookshelves contained fine ceramics and fanciful blown glass and old-fashioned marble busts, but mostly they sported rows and rows of leather-bound books that invited the reader to plumb their depths. Two fireplaces shed their warmth and illumination. The furniture was sturdy, of cherry wood and dark mahogany, made for a man's comfort with deep upholstery of forest green and russet. Kerrich's desk dominated the chamber with its massive breadth and heavy lines. He spent both his work time and his free time here, and much like a wary mouse, Pamela felt dubiously honored to be invited into the lord's lair.

"Have a seat," he invited. "May I pour you a sherry?"

She hated sherry. She always had, but ladies drank sherry and she was a maiden who tried to avoid calling attention to herself.

Not now. Between her disguise and Kerrich's forbearance, she was freed of such unnatural restraints. Sinking into a well-padded and brocade-upholstered chair close to the open window, she inquired, "What are you having, my lord?"

"Ale sounds good."

"Ale it is."

He looked startled, but it was an indication of how thoroughly she had fallen into the role of eccentric that he went to the door and called, "A pitcher of ale and two mugs." Coming to the window, he sank into a chair opposite hers. "So you like ale, do you?"

"I don't know, I've never had it."

He smiled, a blossom of amusement that opened his countenance. Pamela would have sworn this was not his usual, calculated-to-enchant smile, but genuine and pleasant, although she hated to use either word in conjunction with Kerrich.

"My grandfather says one should always try something new occasionally," he said. "It keeps the mind sharp. Although I would say yours is sharp enough."

Stupid to be flattered by his praise; the man sowed charm like a farmer sowed seed—liberally and in the hope some would grow into a likely crop. But somehow his smile convinced her he thought her special. Frightening to think she was as susceptible as any other woman.

Timothy carried in a silver salver, placed it on the table between them, and asked, "Shall I pour, my lord?"

Still watching Pamela, Kerrich waved a hand, the young footman poured and bowed, then delivered the beverages and bowed again.

Pamela cradled the mug, a ceramic monstrosity of dubious Chinese origin. "Thank you, Timothy."

"What?" Kerrich craned around as the footman paced from the chamber. "Timothy, is it? Yes, thank you, Timothy."

When he was gone, she asked, "How long has he worked for you?"

"All his life, I would think." Kerrich sighed dolefully, understanding her drift by her tone. "Which is worse, that I didn't know his name or that I didn't thank him?"

"I tell Beth that courtesy should be automatic."

"Humph." Lifting his mug, he swallowed half in one gulp.

When he wiped his mouth on his sleeve, she smiled; it was so very manlike and almost endearing in its instinct.

He saw the smile and perhaps didn't care for it, but he said only, "What do you think of the ale?"

She sniffed the brew, then took a cautious sip. "It's very . . . rich." It coated her tongue with a taste of something bitter that had been roasted—and made her grimace.

He laughed at her expression. "There's nothing more English than ale. How come you've never had it before?"

"I lived quite a sheltered life as a girl."

"And since."

That's right. He thought her an older woman. "Yes, and since. How is it that you do drink ale?"

"For all that my grandfather comes from noble stock, he

was a poor lad and that's all his family had." Lifting the mug, Kerrich said, "Drink up. The next cup will taste better."

One of the signs of Kerrich's great wealth was the plethora of candles throughout the house, and here, tonight, it was no different. But they faced the window, the candles flickered behind them and this alcove was shadowy and almost intimate.

She took a gulp of ale. If only she had brought her knitting. The handwork placed a barrier between them, although why she thought she needed it, she couldn't conceive. One unaffected smile, no matter how delightful, was not cause for alarm. "So, my lord. What did you wish to discuss?"

This next smile was not nearly so appealing, although she couldn't put her finger on the difference. "I thought today was a rousing success," he said.

"So it was."

"What?" He cupped his ear.

A little louder, she reiterated, "I thought today was a success."

"I didn't quite hear you. Could you repeat that?"

At last she comprehended his odious scheme. She didn't need her knitting to place a barrier between them. Not as long as he insisted on hearing *I told you so*. With all the dignity of her station, she said, "My lord, I admit your stratagem to find acceptance for Beth was efficacious—"

"Effi . . . what?" he teased.

She ignored him. "But at the same time daring—and foolhardy. If Beth had done something unacceptable—"

He hooted. "If? That stunt she pulled on young Chiswick was not what I understand to be socially acceptable. But damn, it was funny."

"My lord, your profanity is unnecessary!"

"You are correct. Forgive me." But he was still grinning as he took the pitcher and poured both mugs full again. His shoulders rippled beneath the fine white lawn, his thighs strained against the cloth of his black trousers, and his perpetual cynicism seemed softened by the candlelight.

Apparently, she admired his form even when he was laughing at her. Distressing, and so common. Again she had been tested and again she had found herself so like those weak-willed women who fell before temptation that she scarcely knew where to look. Out the window seemed the safest, and she fixed her gaze on the street where the gas lamps flickered and carriages occasionally drove by, their wheels clangorous on the stones.

Reseating himself, he said, "So we are agreed that I was right to insist on a party and you were wrong."

That jerked her attention right back to him. Hotly, she denied, "I was not wrong, I was—"

"Wrong. The opposite of right is wrong. So you were wrong." He smiled at her, an absolutely smug grin that made her itch to scratch his eyes out, then before she could argue he said, "I have to return to Norfolk next week."

As a distraction it worked well. "You're returning to the country?" She took a drink to moisten her suddenly dry mouth. "You're abandoning your plan?"

"Abandoning . . . no, of course not! Perhaps I would be better to state that the household is returning to Norfolk next week. You and the child will go with me to Brookford House."

"Really?" Her mouth curved with pleasure. "I don't believe Beth has ever been to the country. I look forward to introducing her to its pleasures."

"Yes, I have several suitable mounts there, and the hostler is an excellent riding teacher. In fact, he taught me to ride."

She smiled politely. It wasn't the riding that excited her; it was the chance to show Beth off in the more informal atmosphere of the countryside. "This will work very well with your plan, my lord."

"I don't know about that. Beth would be exposed to more society in London, but I must spend time at my bank. I have asked Grandpapa, who assures me he will accompany us, and, of course, Lewis will go also." On repeating his cousin's name, Kerrich's voice developed a note of disdain.

A note she did not care for. "Your cousin is a respectable man."

"You are wrong again," he said.

Stung by his derision, she asked "Why? Because he is quiet and shy, and not given to chicanery or debauchery?"

"Unlike me, you mean?" Placing the mug on the table, he leaned his hands on his knees and glared. "Miss Lockhart, you are a simpleton."

"You hired me." She lifted her hand when he would have retorted. "A slanging match will avail us nothing, my lord. We must agree to disagree about your cousin, my intelligence and a whole host of other matters."

"You're a governess. You do not recognize a mature man."

"Lord Kerrich, I *am* a governess. I recognize that most males do not mature, they simply grow taller." Unwise, of course, to retort so wittily, and she waited, interested to see if he would behave like a typical roué and pout or threaten.

He surprised her; he nodded soberly. "Yes. When you look at what some women marry, you realize how much they must hate to work for their living. However, when it comes to my cousin, try not to put too much stock in your own infallibility. You don't like listening to 'I told you so.' "

A sincere Kerrich was even more dangerous than a

charming Kerrich, and she changed her mug from hand to hand and surreptitiously wiped her damp palms on her skirt. "I'll try to remember that."

"My concern tonight is how our move to the country will influence our plans to complete my apparent reformation. While we're at Brookford, we'll have parties, host hunts, whatever it takes to keep Beth and me in the center of attention."

"I'll do everything in my power to make a success of this, my lord." She made her vow solemnly, in homage to their current accord.

"Of course you will. You're getting paid for it."

CHAPTER 14

Kerrich saw her flinch and at once realized his mistake. "Forgive me, Miss Lockhart. I forget, sometimes, that not all women are like my mother."

She had again raised her cup, and now she stared at him over the rim. "Your mother?"

Damn! He shouldn't have mentioned his mother, but Moulton's tale of Lewis and his liaison had inevitably brought her to mind.

Was it possible Miss Lockhart hadn't heard? The story was common knowledge. Only *he* never spoke of it, for to do so might betray how vulnerable he had been when he was little. Crying to see his youthful ideals destroyed. Crushed by a betrayal he had never imagined.

Now he was older. He knew how to protect himself, and anyway, this woman wasn't like all the others. She could keep a confidence. Weighing his words, Kerrich explained, "My parents married at their parents' behest. My mother was the daughter of the bank's former president, an incompetent man. My father was the son of the man whose abilities had taken it from him."

"That is Lord Reynard?"

"Yes, my grandfather." Again he poured his cup full and took a drink. "My parents were wed in the hopes that their union would cement the association and that they might find love together."

"And did they?"

"Yes. My father loved my mother and my mother loved herself."

"Oh." Miss Lockhart pleated her skirt. "How unpleasant for you."

"Nonsense. Until he died when I was ten, we seemed a happy family." He couldn't believe he was confessing so much, and eloquently, too. Surely he had never even thought this before. "After his death, she couldn't wait to throw off her mourning."

"I'm sorry." She really seemed to be. Her eyes were sad, her chin tilted down.

He hastened to reassure her. "Don't be. I'm glad it happened. It opened my eyes, prepared me for a life without illusions. No one takes advantage of me."

She nodded. "Yes. I understand that it is advantageous to be inured to hurt, but the process is painful and regardless of what you say, I am sorry for the boy you were." She began again to speak, but stirred as if her thoughts made her sore and raw. "Your mother. Is she—"

"In Italy with her current lover." It seemed important that he assure Miss Lockhart of his insensitivity. "And that, my dear, is where I am happy to have her."

"You hate her."

"Of course not!" He ran his finger around the rim of his mug. "She isn't worth my hatred."

"I don't know if that makes you a better person than me, or not."

She spoke so quietly he barely heard her, and abruptly

he remembered the tale Grandpapa had told of her situation. "Your father left."

"You've . . . you've heard the gossip?" Her voice squeaked at the end. "*All* the gossip?"

Obviously, he had made her uneasy with the mere mention, although he would have thought the passage of time would have eased her distress. Although it hadn't eased his. Ah, he understood Miss Lockhart better than he wished.

Taking care to appear interested, but aloof, he said, "My grandfather told me the tale. A difficult and unhappy development for you, especially in your youth."

"For me?" She glanced at him, glanced again, and the clenched fists in her lap relaxed. "Yes, for me, but"—she looked at him once more as if to reassure herself—"it was my mother who truly suffered." Reaching into the pocket of her skirt, she drew forth the silver watch he'd observed before. "This is my father's, the only thing I have left of him."

"You keep it to remember him by?" he guessed.

Flipping open the ornately designed cover, she looked at the face as if she could see her father's features within. "No. I keep it so I will remember the pain a superficial, unfaithful man can cause. My mother loved my father very much. She died of loving him—and missing him." She smiled without humor. "I imagine you approve of that kind of devotion. Most men do."

"I see it as further proof that love is an ambush. It lures you in with a pretty decoy and catches you like a trap catches a poacher, and you're stuck there until you bleed to death." He looked down at the brew, wondering how such a little bit of ale could have loosened his tongue so thoroughly.

She blinked, and he realized why she looked different this evening. This was the first time he'd seen her without her tinted spectacles. Her bare face was softened without the metal and glass cage that protected her eyes. And her eyes were large, blue, and in this light, the skin around them was surprisingly unlined. She must have been a pretty women in her youth, and her youth was definitely not as long ago as he had thought. In fact, she could be his age. He was on the verge of asking her, which proved how far gone he was with drink, for no woman would answer that question truthfully.

But she saved him the trouble and her the lie by saying, "So, to avoid marriage, you took in a foundling. The question is, why would the queen think *you* would be better off married?"

"You don't understand Victoria—that is, Queen Victoria. She likes me."

"But . . . why?"

"Why does she like me?" He was amused. "Because I always treated her well."

Miss Lockhart raised her eyebrows.

"Normally. I treated her normally." He took a drink of ale, savoring the keen flavor. "When we were young."

"What is normally?"

"I didn't fawn over her because she was going to be the queen, I treated her as if she were just a girl."

"A girl you liked?"

"Just an annoying girl. A tagalong girl. She is nine years younger than I am. A silly girl. Nothing more." He remembered the child Victoria had been, and remembered, too, his heedless affection. "She was lonely. Her mother kept her apart, guarded her every moment, so when I teased her, she liked me."

"I still don't understand why she wants you married."

"She's young, but she's royal. She believes her way is best." He saw when Miss Lockhart comprehended his meaning. "She married, she's ecstatic, she's settled down, and her way is the only way. She's going to save me from myself."

"I suppose someone needs to. Forgive me, my lord, but I confess to an unquenchable curiosity. How is Her Majesty blackmailing you?"

If you only knew. But no. He'd kept his secret for too many years. This easy conversation with a thoughtful woman would not bring forth that confession. Yet he felt no qualms in telling her part of the reason. "Many years ago, my grandfather convinced King William to put an amount aside for the crown princess Victoria in Grandpapa's bank. The original sum provided a solid base for the bank, and my grandfather invested it wisely. I have continued the tradition, and the resultant sum is considerable. A boon for Victoria, and a boon for us."

"So she has threatened to remove the principal and the bank will fail."

Offended, he snapped, "Of course not. I am a good manager. The bank is on solid financial ground. But you have to see that I object to being threatened because of my reputation. The queen demands I find respectability, and she defines respectability as a wife and the prospect of family. I think I can convince her respectability is responsibility."

"You consider marriage the sure route to misery."

"Not really." He stroked his chin, a gesture he had adopted from his grandfather. "The trick to marriage is not letting expectations get in the way. A man needs to understand why women get married, that's all."

Her mouth drew down in typical Miss Lockhart censure. "Why, pray tell, do women get married?"

"For money, usually." He could tell she was offended again, but with Miss Lockhart, he didn't have to worry overly much about offense. After all, she didn't. Besides, he thought his assessment quite fair. "I don't blame them. The world is not fair to a spinster. She has no recourse but to work or starve. So if she's asked, she marries."

Obviously, Miss Lockhart did not consider his assessment fair. She slapped her mug on the table so hard the crockery rattled. "Do you have any idea how insulting you are? To think a woman is single because she has never been asked, or if she is married, she has done so for monetary security?"

He found himself entertained and very, very interested. "Ah, I've touched a nerve. Are you telling me there is a man alive who dared to propose to you?"

"I am not telling you anything." But swept along by her passion, she did. "A man can convey financial security, but whither thou goest, I shall go, and all that rot. A woman has to live where her husband wishes, let him waste her money, watch as he humiliates her with other women, and never say a word."

"Men are not the only ones who break their vows."

"So fidelity is a vow *you* intend to keep?"

Of course he had no intention of keeping that vow, when he was forced to make it, and falling into that trap which had so neatly snared his father. "I've supported more women than Madame Beauchard's best corset-maker. If I let marriage stop me, think of the poor actresses who would be without a patron."

She wasn't amused. "So nothing about your wife would be sacrosanct, not even her body. Your wife will cherish dreams that you never know about, and even if you did they would be less than a puff of wind to you."

Women had dreams? About *what*? A new pair of shoes? Seeing a rival fail? Dancing with a foreign prince? But Miss Lockhart wasn't speaking of the trivial, and he found himself asking, "What are your dreams?"

"You don't care. Until I spoke, it never occurred to you that a woman could have her dreams."

"That's true, but you are a teacher, and already you have taught me otherwise." Leaning back in his chair, he gazed at her and with absolute sincerity said the most powerful words in the universe. "Tell me what you want. I want to know about you."

She had no defense to withstand him. She leaned back, too, and closed her eyes as if she could see her fantasy before her. "I want a house in the country. Just a cottage, with a fence and cat to sit in my lap and a dog to sleep at my feet. A spot of earth for a garden with flowers as well as vegetables, food on the table, and a little leisure time in which to read the books I've not had time to read or just sit . . . in the sunshine."

The candles softened the stark contrast between her white complexion and that hideous rouge. Light and shadow delineated her pale lips, showing them in their fullness. Her thick lashes formed a ruffled half-circle on her skin. When she was talking like this, imagining her perfect life, she looked almost . . . pretty. "That's all?"

"Oh, yes."

"That's simple enough."

"Yes, very simple. And mine."

Careful not to break into her reverie, he quietly placed his mug next to hers. "Why do you want that?"

"That's what I had before—"

She stopped speaking so suddenly he knew what she had been about to say. Moving to the side of her chair, he knelt on the carpet. "Before your father left?"

At the sound of his voice, her eyes flew open and she stared at him in dismay. She *had* been dreaming, he realized, seeing that cottage, those pets, that garden, and imagining a time when she could sit in the sunshine. Her countenance was open and vulnerable, and his instincts were strong. As gently as a whisper, he placed his fingertips on her cheek. "There's one dream you didn't mention, and I can make it come true." Slowly, giving her time to turn if she wished, he leaned forward . . . and kissed her.

And he would have sworn that, at the last moment, she tilted her head to receive him.

Certainly she closed her eyes. He closed his, too, savoring her lips, soft and full, warm and giving, separating for him with such sweet ease he experienced a surge of tenderness. Her breath matched his in rhythm and flavor. He could almost taste her . . . and then he did taste her. He half-expected Miss Lockhart to withdraw at the first touch of his tongue, but whatever ice he had thought encased her melted. Gradually he increased the pressure, further opening her lips. He moved his fingertips into her hair, cupping her head, rubbing her in the slow, sensual movement pretty women liked.

Miss Lockhart liked it, too. She leaned into his hand, a slow shift that indicated gratification and begged for more. Her hands had been resting in her lap; now they fluttered up and around like bewildered birds unsure where to perch. Capturing them, he moved them up and placed one on each shoulder. Each fluttered again, then settled warily.

At first her hands were only a spot of warmth along his muscles. Then, as if shyness gave way to curiosity, they crept down to the joint of his arm, and there they smoothed the cloth across his skin. Her fingers sought out his bones, exploring the thrust of them with little, circular movements.

She pleasured him so well with her timid, unsure movements that the compulsion seized him to pleasure her yet more. Rising from his crouched position on the floor, he put one knee on the seat beside her skirt and lifted himself above her, tilting her head upward, baring her neck . . .

dominating her. He slid his mouth away from hers, along her jaw and to the place behind her ear. The taste and scent of her face powder filled his head as he kissed her there, and heard her inhale and felt her fingers clench.

Now her hands crept back up, massaging and probing, making him want to purr like a giant cat in thrall with its mate.

Taking her earlobe in his mouth, he bit gently, and when she cried out in surprise, he licked it as if in apology.

Her body knew the truth. That was no apology, it was provocation. She moved in the chair, a ripple from top to bottom, an inducement of its own.

And he, rake and roué, never resisted temptation. Still he held her head as he outlined the shell of her ear with his tongue and probed it and blew a light draft of air, but his other hand slid down to her bosom. In his mind he cursed the silk and ruffles that stood between him and his goal, but he pressed firmly and found a breast that pressed firmly back.

My God, she was perfect. Generously blessed, rounded, solid. The weight in his hand made him want to see and to taste, and the resulting tumult drove him from a gentle seduction toward a greater, more pressing desire. He needed to take this woman. Not just kiss her ear and caress her breast, but thrust himself inside and satisfy himself in her arching body.

Her hands slid toward his neck, and he stopped on an inhalation, waiting, waiting . . .

And she appeased him. She delved under the edge of his shirt and touched—oh, God—his bare skin. Then she stopped.

Why? Did she surmise how very much he had wished to put her hands elsewhere? On a place lower and of more interest to him?

Or was she shocked by her own temerity?

He wanted to direct her, to tell her to continue, but he wanted to kiss her more. He sought her lips and found them, opened them and discovered it was as if he'd never kissed her. He had appeased no appetite, conquered no desire. She tasted as new and delightful as she had before, and she kissed back with a charming spectacle of reserve and eagerness.

Curiosity drove him. He released her breast and explored lower, to her waist, bound by a corset yet agreeably small, and down further, to draw her hips to him . . . but damn, she wore petticoats and they got in the way.

He released her mouth. "Miss Lockhart." Vaguely he was aware that it was silly to call her that. "Pamela. Take off these clothes and let me—"

They opened their eyes at the same time.

They both jumped, and she gave a shriek.

She was ugly. What had he been thinking? She was ugly. Yes, he liked to talk to her. Yes, that overly pale complexion and those dark glasses had grown on him. Yes, she sported a grand body. Yes, the candlelight had softened her appalling coloring, but . . . she was ugly.

And from her expression, she thought no better of him.

"Miss Lockhart, I didn't mean—"

She placed her hands on his chest and pushed. "Get off."

But for some damned reason, he didn't want to. His knee crushed her skirt, his hand held her head, he prevailed over her physically if not mentally, and he liked it. This woman needed to be managed and commanded, made to do what was right for her, for now, and not live in some faraway dream that might never come.

Then he gained control of himself. When a man assumed authority over a woman, he was trapped forever, and the next thing along was love, and he would not love. Again he scrutinized Miss Lockhart.

In fact, she was the cure for love.

He stood up and stepped away, then for some damned reason bowed as if he could stick formality in front of him like a shield.

She stood, too, but painfully, like a woman who had been led to desire and abandoned.

No. He would not feel guilty.

She drew herself up in the stern motion he'd come to recognize as uniquely Miss Lockhart. But this time he saw pride enough to carry her through the door—but no farther. "I don't know why you did that, Lord Kerrich, but I think that to mock me with kisses is a cruelty I ill deserve."

"I didn't kiss you to be cruel. I did it because . . ." He scrambled for a reason that would save them both face. "Because I wanted to make sure you hadn't succumbed to my handsome face and elegant figure." Strutting toward the door, he did a fine imitation of a popinjay. "I feared you might be planning a visit to my bedchamber—"

"To your bedchamber? What have I done to make you think that?"

"Nothing. But you've been here over a week, and I find that is the length of time it takes most women to fall in love with me."

"In love with you!" Her raised voice and dubious tone were an affront. "You, sir, are a coxcomb."

"I only tell the truth." Not all the truth, but some of it. "I wanted to discourage your intentions."

Her eyes narrowed. "By kissing me?"

"I can tell a great deal by a kiss"—for instance, that you have never been well-kissed before—"and I now know that you, Miss Lockhart, might be tempted by the flesh but have a stalwart nature and will resist. You cannot be had by seduction."

"Certainly not!"

They stared at each other, and he chafed. There were lies in kisses, and greater lies in words, but they had told each other too much. They understood each other too well. None of this should have happened—and he was the instigator of it all. What *had* he been thinking? And why, even when he was looking at her, seeing all her faults, was he still plagued with curiosity about this frumpy, homely, outspoken female?

She broke eye contact. "If your experiment is over, then I will go to bed. *Alone.*"

"Yes. Excellent. Sleep well." He was talking to her back, and when she had cleared the threshold he hurried to the pitcher and poured his mug full. He drank it in one long draft, then poured the last of the pitcher in his cup. It was only half-full, and feeling foolish, he emptied the half glass she'd left into his cup, too. He wanted it all. After what just passed, he needed it all, and he had no desire to look at Moulton or that footman what's-his-name or anyone else who would answer his call. They might see on his countenance his confusion, and he couldn't bear that.

Seating himself, he slouched in his chair and stared out into the street. All he could see was Miss Lockhart's upright, curvaceous body walking out the door, and remember how she had felt beneath his hands. And wonder . . . and wonder . . .

Beneath those frumpy clothes, she was hiding a magnificent body.

He sat straight up. She was hiding . . . her figure. She was hiding her age.

He had looked into her eyes. Tumultuous eyes, the color

of the sky when hatching an autumn storm. Frightened eyes. Angry. Evasive.

She was hiding . . . what else was she hiding? Tomorrow, he would find out.

CHAPTER 15

But tomorrow was Pamela's half-day off, and she could scarcely wait to leave Kerrich's townhouse and hasten to Hannah.

She meant to tell her friend everything; her pleasure in the conversations with Kerrich, her confession of her dreams, Kerrich's odd behavior—that kissing!—and her own feeble acquiescence.

How, when she'd opened her eyes and seen his face, so handsome, so odiously confident, it was as if she viewed her worst nightmare brought to life. She, Pamela Lockhart, had been kissing Lord Kerrich, a man whose sexual exploits no doubt put her father's to shame!

Oh, yes, she needed to confess to someone and have someone explain her own behavior.

But when she arrived at the Distinguished Academy of Governesses and Hannah greeted her with glad cries, Pamela found herself mute. Hannah's affection, her kind brown eyes, her keen wit and enduring friendship made her the perfect friend, and how did one tell a friend that one had run mad?

She used the servants as an excuse to gather her thoughts,

greeting them and expressing her gratitude at their care of Hannah. She found herself carried along to the study and seated in the most comfortable chair right before the fire. Hannah presented a letter from Charlotte, and she read it with the sincere hope that Charlotte's new husband would somehow gain the wisdom to love her as she deserved. She found herself reluctant to put it down, and reread parts of it, but at last she could delay no longer. She looked up at Hannah with a smile.

"Take off that ridiculous powder and that abominable rouge." Hannah handed her a handkerchief. "I can't look at you that way."

Pamela laughed and went to the mirror, and with a basin of water provided by Cusheon, she cleaned her face until the Pamela she knew so well had emerged.

But she had changed. There was an anxiety about the eyes, a hopeful smile tugging at the mouth, and Pamela knew she had only to turn and say, *Lord Kerrich kissed me.* Instead she returned to her seat and said, "That feels wonderful."

"You are so beautiful, and to think you have been forced by that man's unreasonable demands to hide your beauty . . ." Hannah shook her head.

"Actually, it's quite enjoyable in an odd way. No one ever notices me." *Except Lord Kerrich, who kissed me.*

Hannah leaned forward in her chair and demanded, "Tell me everything."

Lord Kerrich kissed me. "My post is going well. Beth is a dear, not timid, and always willing to do anything we require of her just for the chance to remain in Kerrich's home." Cusheon brought the tea tray, and Pamela thanked him.

As Hannah poured, she frowned worriedly. "Will she be crushed if Lord I'm-so-conceited doesn't keep her?"

Lord I'm-so-conceited kissed me. "I'm doing everything I can to teach her skills and at the same time encouraging him to spend time with her." Pamela laughed, and she flattered herself it sounded normal. "Believe it or not, they have much in common. They both adore horses." Accepting a plate, Pamela exclaimed, "Cusheon! My favorite teacakes. Thank you!"

"Pleased to have you back, miss." Cusheon bowed and began his slow retreat to the foyer.

Hannah leaned back and cocked her head as she teased, "Is he still heedless enough to believe you are an older, unattractive spinster?"

Yes, but he kissed me anyway. "He's a man! Men see what's on the surface and no more."

Cusheon had gone only so far as the entrance, and he harrumphed.

"Except you, Cusheon." Pamela smiled at him. "All the wisdom of the male gender resides in you."

He bowed again and went back to stand guard by the doorway.

"Is he cruel to you?" Hannah asked in an undertone.

"Kerrich? No, not at all. He's really not as awful as we first feared." *Not even when he kissed me. He did it well.* "He explained all the circumstances for this deception he is practicing."

Hannah was always curious. "What circumstances?"

"You know I can't tell you that. You'll just have to trust me. He has his reasons." *Why was she defending a man who had kissed her? And then told her he had done it as a test?* Looking around the slightly shabby study, Pamela deliberately relaxed. This was her home. She was speaking to one of her best friends. She *could* confess her actions here, and she would.

Instead she found herself saying, "Nevertheless, I'm so glad to be here where I can be myself."

"Pamela, I know you. You're not looking me in the eye. You're nervous and jittery." Hannah shook her finger at her. "You're not telling me something."

He kissed me. "I'm not?" Her voice squeaked.

"You don't want to say it because to do so would force you to admit you were wrong." Hannah donned the stern expression of a governess. "You lack confidence that he will do right by the child when the deception is done."

"No! I know he'll do something for her. He's not a liar, he's just . . . unwilling to love. Possibly, or rather probably, he won't keep her as his own, but there was never much chance of that, was there?" And Pamela's heart ached for Beth. "But he seems to be fond of her, or as fond as that man can be of any female." *Except that he likes to kiss them, and he has recognized I'm a female. And I want to confess all—but I don't. I'm frightened by him and appalled at myself. Am I really as weak as my mother?*

The thought horrified her. She had loved her mother. Her father had irrevocably wronged her mother. But her mother shouldn't have died for love. She should have lived for her daughter's sake and for life's sake.

"I suppose that dealing with such a man is enough reason for you to be consumed and weary." Hannah patted her hand. "You're doing the best you can in difficult circumstances."

"As to that, I am. I threw together a party in a week, and although Kerrich's servants are well trained, the burden of organization was on me. Naturally," Pamela said with complete immodesty, "the affair was a smashing success, and I wouldn't be surprised but the queen has already heard word of Kerrich's beneficence. We might have that final payment sooner than we anticipated." She rubbed her hands together in mock greed. Then she craftily brought up the subject dearest to Hannah's heart. "But I didn't come here to talk about me. You must tell me how the Governess School is progressing." *For it seems I can't tell you that Lord Kerrich kissed me.*

Hannah's eyes glowed, and she launched into an exuberant detail of hiring out a trainee at a profitable rate.

It was the knowledge of the school's budding success that comforted Pamela as, two hours later, she pulled her plain woolen shawl around her shoulders and hurried back to her assignment. Hurried and suffered a vague anxiety—and a nebulous delight.

The anxiety she could explain. Although it was just past noon, the high overcast clouds allowed a watery summer light, and since that vile thief had robbed her she hadn't walked the London streets alone. Well . . . except that very morning when she had walked the same distance to the Governess School.

But to be so delighted to spy Hyde Park Gardens! To feel her heart jump when the tall, wide edifice of Kerrich's townhouse came into her sights. To feel comfort within the confines of her reapplied disguise. Ah, that was an anticipation that sincerely dismayed her. Kerrich was like her father. He was! And she feared she reacted to the dissolution and the charm as she had reacted to similar traits in her father; despising him for the dissolution, and trying to please for a glimpse of the charm. Had she changed not at all from that young, adolescent girl who had gone to meet the princess at Kensington Palace and stay there with her for a night?

She had tried so hard to make the princess like her, and the princess's mother, too. Not because they mattered to her. Oh, no. Because her father had told her to charm them. Because her father had decided that if his daughter could please them enough, they would wish to have her for a companion for the princess, and he would have influence on an important and a susceptibly female household.

She had failed, of course. The Duchess of Kent had allowed no one to influence her daughter except herself. Pamela's mission had been doomed from the start. Her father's displeasure had been a foregone conclusion. But she had tried anyway, tried so hard she had scarcely noticed the handsome, flirtatious young Kerrich.

Well, she noticed him now.

Oh, of course Kerrich wasn't totally like her father. He had no mistress as far as she could tell, and he seemed dedicated to his bank rather than the pursuit of loose women. Was it those feeble virtues that had won her around so thoroughly that she had kissed him?

As she approached the townhouse, she straightened her shoulders. The edgy guise of Pamela had to be discarded. Each step up to the grand double doors brought her closer to Kerrich, to Beth and to the challenge they faced. She couldn't allow Kerrich to distract her with his need to conquer any woman he saw—and that could be the only reason for his inexplicable behavior—so she reminded herself it was up to her to support the Governess School until the time when it could totally support itself. Strengthening her resolve, she again became Miss Lockhart, governess of iron. For Beth, she had to be brave. To Lord Kerrich, she had to be unassailable. She would never again let him kiss her to satisfy his curiosity.

Grasping the grand brass knocker formed in the shape of an eagle claw, she pounded firmly.

Timothy answered the door and in tones of surprise—one might even call it horror—exclaimed, "Miss Lockhart!"

"What?" She swept inside the grand foyer and reached up to unpin her hat.

He stared at her, wide-eyed and uneasy.

She couldn't imagine what about her had created such dismay. She glanced in the mirror and started, then realized the pale, red-cheeked creature there was indeed *she*, and the *she* Timothy was used to seeing. "Am I late?" she asked.

"No!" He squirmed. "No, in fact, we had hoped that you would be . . ."

She lifted her eyebrows to him. "Be?"

"That will do, Timothy." Moulton walked into the foyer in his peculiarly smooth gait. "I will assist Miss Lockhart now."

"Y-yes," Timothy stammered. "Thank you, Mr. Moulton."

Pamela handed her hat to Moulton and waited for him to acquaint her with the progress of Beth's activities. She had left a full list of things Beth should do with the nursery maid, Corliss, although she expected they would have completed only a part. After all, there was no substitute for the discipline of a real governess.

However, Moulton inquired, "How was your half-day, Miss Lockhart?"

"Quite enjoyable." Indeed, she admitted she had greatly enjoyed the chance to sit with Hannah and for a few brief hours, be herself. Yet she couldn't lie to herself. All the time she was with Hannah, the thought of Lord Kerrich and kisses lingered in her mind. Perhaps he had kissed her because he felt sorry for her, or because he had to conquer every woman in his sphere, or out of curiosity—but she *would* stop thinking about it!

And she would take care to stay out of his grasp.

So she was glad to be back. "Did Beth give Corliss any trouble?"

"Not at all. Corliss is quite capable." He took Pamela's shawl as she slipped it off. "What did you do on your half-day?"

"I visited my friend and comrade at the Distinguished Academy of Governesses, Miss Hannah Setterington." She put her hand on the banister. "And now, I'll—"

He interrupted. "Is all going well with your venture there?"

Moulton was usually so proper and distant, a man who showed his competence in every way, and even as she answered she wondered at him. "Very well. Miss Setterington placed one of the governesses we have trained in quite a comfortable home."

"Jolly good. That must make you happy."

She wasn't imagining it. He *was* acting oddly. Trying to ease away, she took the first step up the stairs. "But it's time to go back and work with Beth. We have much to do before we can accept an invitation."

Snatching up the silver salver that sat in the foyer, he showed her a complement of sealed, formal sheets. "These came this afternoon. That must give you a sense of accomplishment."

"Yes, and they prove Lord Kerrich was right in demanding we give the party." A fact he had not hesitated to point out—not long before he kissed her.

But the next time they spoke, and Pamela did not at all worry about seeing him after those kisses, she would not hesitate to point out Beth was the kind of foundling the *ton* could embrace—polite, sunny, grateful and obedient. Only Pamela understood the pressure those expectations brought to bear, for she felt them, too. During their next outing, Beth dared not put a foot wrong, and that especially included knocking down little boys, regardless of the provocation. Oh, there was so much to teach the child, and so little time!

Again she took a step, and Moulton asked, "Which invitations are you going to accept?"

It was on the tip of her tongue to remind him that he worked for Kerrich, as did she, and Kerrich would decide which invitations they would accept. But again she wondered at his chattiness, and again she remembered Timothy's dismay, and suddenly a great light shone in her mind. Shooting the question at him with all the lethal intent of a gunman, she asked, "Did Lord Kerrich take Beth for a ride this morning?"

Moulton scooted backward.

She took the step back down, and repeated, "Moulton, did Lord Kerrich take Beth for a ride this morning?"

Moulton's gaze fell away. "Yes, Miss Lockhart."

"Is she hurt?" she asked harshly. Kerrich had been a marvelous riding teacher for Beth, and while on horseback Kerrich and Beth thought as one. They talked about gait and size, breed and color, and Beth even argued with Kerrich, spiritedly quoting her papa. But both he and Beth had chafed at the sensible restrictions Pamela's presence had placed on them. She could only imagine what risks they had taken today.

"No!" Moulton took a difficult breath. "Miss Beth was hale and healthy last time I saw her."

From the doorway of Kerrich's study came Mr. Athersmith's voice. "Are you afraid of a woman, Moulton?"

When she had time to think on it, Pamela knew she would be startled by the look of venom Moulton shot toward Mr. Athersmith. "No, sir."

"But you're stalling." Mr. Athersmith drawled so slowly

and so obnoxiously he must have imagined himself to be a patrician. "Go ahead and tell her."

She understood Moulton didn't want to be the bearer of bad news. She was a servant, too; she knew how frequently the messenger was crippled. So she said, "Mr. Athersmith, *you* will tell me where Lord Kerrich has taken my charge."

By his complacent smile, it was easy to see that was just what Mr. Athersmith wanted. "He took her to one of the most improper places a man can take a girl-child." His blond hair fell over his forehead in a well-trained, captivating curl. "He took her to the horse races."

CHAPTER 16

Pamela stood on the step outside the coach and surveyed the area around the racetrack with disdain. A hillock rose on the plain, and from the cheering coming from the other side, she would guess the racetrack could be viewed from there. Here, carriages were parked in rows along the flat. Coachmen and footmen stood guard around them, for residents of the nearby London slums slinked back and forth, waiting for a chance to strip off a wheel or take any belongings within. Horses ridden from the city were walked by their grooms, and she noted two horses in particular. She had followed them throughout Hyde Park. No mistake—Kerrich and Beth were here, the Hippodrome was indeed the eyesore she heard it called, and although she didn't know where to start looking for her charge and the despicable man who had brought her hence, she would not let ignorance stand in her way. And when she found them . . .

"Excuse me, miss." A hunched and miserable Timothy had been sent to protect her from the more unsavory elements in the crowd. "It looks like rain. I don't know my way around the area, but if you permit me, I will take the umbrella and go look for his lordship and Miss Beth and—"

"And what?" Her eyes snapped with annoyance. "You will give His Lordship the upbraiding he deserves?"

"N-no, Miss Lockhart, but—"

"*I'll* find them and bring them back." She marched off toward the sound of cheering coming from the tall mound, threading her way through the maze of carriages.

Timothy caught up with her, clutching his black footman's umbrella.

She was not afraid of Lord Kerrich. Last night, it was true, Lord Kerrich had kissed her. But that did not make her a stooge, or subjugate her good sense to any prank Kerrich chose to pull. He claimed he kissed her to test her moral fiber. Today he would face the very same, upright, ethical Miss Lockhart who had first marched into his study, and he would find himself at a loss.

At the gate a knowledgeable-looking blackguard clad in a top hat, a dirty gold waistcoat and the occasional tooth lingered outside, and she thought he might help her—for a price. In her sternest tone, she said, "Excuse me, sir. Where will I find the horse races?"

Her sternest tone failed to impress this individual. He looked her over from top to bottom, leered moistly and wiped the spittle off his chin with the back of his hand. "Th' 'orses are right over that 'ill, an' a pretty lady like yerself will be wantin' a toff-gennaman like me t' keep 'er company whilst she bets on th' fillies."

Timothy stepped up to her side, his fists balled.

"No," she declared, "I most definitely do not."

Timothy stepped back.

She took a breath and almost smothered from the stranger's rank odor of gin, tobacco and unwashed clothing.

"Unless you know your way around the track and know where the gentlemen gather."

The sharpie tucked his thumbs in the top of his trousers. " 'Deed I do."

"Miss Lockhart!" Timothy said.

She paid him and his shocked outcry no heed. From the look of the gathering clouds, a storm was rolling across the countryside, and she wanted this task done quickly, so she told Sharpie, "I want you to find Lord Kerrich."

"Lord Kerrich, is it? What's 'e got that I 'aven't, I'd like t' know?"

Sweeping him with a cool gaze, she said, "Cleanliness, for one thing. Can you find him or not?"

Sharpie's gaze shifted toward her reticule. "Can ye pay me or not?"

"When you find him."

"Two quid. 'Alf now, 'alf then."

"One quid, half now, half later."

He stuck out his hand, clad in black woolen gloves with the fingers worn out, and she carefully counted out her own coins. "Timothy," she said. "Make sure this gentleman doesn't run off with my money."

Timothy was a nice boy, but *he* earned less than a pound a week. Clapping his hand on Sharpie's shoulder, he said, "I'd take it badly if you ran."

"Won't be doin' that." Sharpie showed his meager mouthful of teeth. "Want me other coins, I do." He set off toward the entrance gate.

He leaned into the booth and chatted up the girl taking the money, then beckoned Pamela over. "As a favor fer me, Mary 'ere is goin' t' let ye in fer only one quid. Each."

Pamela turned to Timothy. "What is the standard admission to a horsetrack?"

"Ten shillings." He glared at Mary, who in turn glared at the sharpie.

Who clutched the cloth over his chest and said mournfully, "Can't trust nobody these days. Ye've broken me 'eart, Mary, dear, tryin' t' swindle me an' this fine lady. Now let us in fer free an' we'll not report ye t' th' authorities."

Men, Pamela thought morosely as she followed him through the gate. *It mattered not what station in life they occupied. They all saw a woman as a pigeon to be plucked and then*—she sneered at the back of Sharpie's filthy neck—*to be kissed. Then they thought you wouldn't notice when they spoiled all your hard work by taking an innocent little girl to the racetrack.* Well, if that had been Lord Kerrich's plan all along, he was in for a rude awakening today.

Pamela and her two escorts climbed to the top of the hill. A gust of wind greeted them, and the scent of the storm off the Channel, but below them they found the racetrack, and the people—lots of people, all staring breathlessly at the oval cut in the grass at the foot. Horses pounded past on the track, rounded the curve, came toward them, then rounded the other curve—and it was over.

Her mouth pursed as if she were indeed the redoubtable Miss Lockhart, Pamela observed, "A very brief pleasure."

"But a pleasure indeedy," Sharpie assured her.

All around them, spectators cheered or wailed, depending on the outcome of their wagers. Stakeholders moved from group to group, collecting money and distributing it, and pocketing a little. Well-dressed gentlemen mingled with men like Sharpie, and Pamela could not see a lady anywhere. Except for . . . well, those were not ladies.

Sharpie stood craning his neck like a fledgling looking for its dinner. "Yer Lord Kerrich is likely t' be standin' wi' a crew o' noblemen just like 'im. Convenient. Makes it easy fer th' pickpockets t' find 'em, ye see."

Timothy grabbed his jacket just above the waist.

Sharpie glanced at him. "Aye. That'll 'elp 'em t' find yer stash, too." With a leap, he started down the hill.

Pamela wrapped her shawl more tightly around her to protect against the wind gusts and followed him into the crowd. Timothy panted at her heels.

"Come on, come on," Sharpie called. Then as suddenly as he started, he stopped.

Pamela looked around, expecting to see Lord Kerrich and Beth somewhere close. But surrounding her were men staring forward, straining to see . . . the scents of crushed grass and coming rain, of excitement and despair, rose in waves. In the deepening silence, she heard the pounding of hooves as another cluster of horses raced before them. Then it was over, the cheering and wailing began again, and as if she had caused the lapse in their search, Sharpie said, "Come *on*."

The farther they descended, the more they moved among well-dressed gentlemen. Pamela's presence garnered several sharp looks, but she paid no heed. At last near the foot of the hill, they reached a wooden barrier, chest height, where gentlemen leaned to watch the races. That is where they saw Kerrich and Beth.

Sharpie waved a grandiose arm. "There ye are, miss. Lord Kerrich an' 'is little girl an' those gennamen . . ." He squinted.

Beth stood on a wooden box by the rail, flanked by the stableboy. Kerrich was off to the side, monocle in place, talking to three men in black suits with gray beaver hats. These gentlemen, even to Pamela's inexpert perception, seemed out of place in the raucous crowd.

As Sharpie's gaze rested on them, his black-toothed smile faded. He took a step back.

"Wait for your fee," Pamela commanded.

Instead, Sharpie started backing up more and more quickly. At last he turned tail and ran, occasionally glancing back as if the devil were on his heels.

Stunned, she watched him go, not knowing what he saw but recognizing his very real fright. She looked toward Kerrich and his friends again, and her ire rose. Kerrich paid Beth not a bit of attention, leaving her on her own except for the stableboy, who was no more than sixteen. And with a storm coming, too!

She started toward the culprits. "Lord Kerrich!" She injected her sternest tone into her voice.

Kerrich saw her bearing down on them, tipped his hat to the strange gentlemen, tucked his monocle in his pocket, and came toward her without a sign of guilt or dismay. Without a sign of affection. Certainly not as if he was the man who had kissed her after she had confessed her dreams, and implanted another, wilder fantasy in her mind.

That was fine with her. She didn't like him anyway.

"How could you?" She marched toward him until they were face to face. "How dare you?"

"I dare a lot of things. However, I'm fear I am unclear on what you're huffing about now." His upper-class accent positively crackled with consonants, and he viewed her with pointed disdain.

"You bring that baby here"—she pointed at Beth, who smiled and waved—"and abandon her so you can speak to some ne'er-do-well gamblers"—she gestured toward the black-frocked gentlemen—"and when I catch you you show not even a smidgen of shame."

"Bosh! That baby knows more about this horsetrack than I do, I was never more than ten feet away from her and those gentlemen are not ne'er-do-wells."

"That is why they have scurried off like the cockroaches they are?"

Kerrich glanced at the place where they had stood. They had disappeared into the crowd, although their path was obvious. The men through whom they passed leaped aside like sailors avoiding scurvy. "They had business elsewhere."

"Buffoon business."

He bared his teeth in a grin. "Watch yourself, woman. You may have kissed me, but that does not give you the right to be insolent."

She caught her breath. He could have slapped her and she wouldn't have been so shocked. "Lower your voice," she commanded, and in a furious whisper said, "Kiss *you.* I did not kiss you. You kissed me, and an awkward experience it was."

"Ultimately."

Good. He agreed with her. She was glad. She didn't want him to recall those kisses fondly.

"Nevertheless," he said, "I am your employer, an aristocrat and a man, and for all three of those reasons I deserve your respect."

She turned toward Beth, who had leaned her elbow on the railing and now viewed them as if they were street players performing for pennies. A few others in the crowd observed the scene unfolding before them, too, but most were looking toward the darkening sky.

Thanks be. She couldn't bear to provide a spectacle for these gamesters. Lowering her voice, she said, "For *those* reasons, you have it."

Into the sudden hush of a race, his voice was loud. "Miss Lockhart, the reason I'm here at the racetrack today is to speak to those gentlemen who, like me, are involved in banking and monetary pursuits. We had important business.

I could scarcely dismiss them because I had a child with me."

The race ended, the gamblers began their clamorous pleasure and melancholic dramatics, so she enunciated clearly. "Then you shouldn't have brought the child."

With his hands on his hips and his feet apart, he glared down at Pamela. "I had to."

Contemptible man. "Don't try and make me feel guilty for being derelict in my duties. Beth had her nursemaid to care for her, and I arranged with Moulton to have an alternate should something happen to Corliss."

"You misunderstand. You are welcome to your half-day off, and Corliss was on her post when last I saw her."

"Was Corliss weeping?"

"Corliss? Weeping?" He reared back as if offended by the very thought. "I don't know. Why would I notice *that*?"

His complete indifference fired her resentment. "When I saw her, she was crying because she knew I would be angry with her."

"With her? Why would you be angry at her? When I decided to take Beth, she couldn't have stopped me."

"So I told her." Pamela heard another pounding of hooves and, surprised another race could occur so quickly, she glanced down toward the track. No horses rounded the oval. Then she realized—what she'd heard was the grumble of thunder. "But a simple nursemaid comprehends what you obviously do not."

"Miss Lockhart, this may come as a complete surprise to you, but I am a rake. A rogue. An extremely sought-after man, and I am tired of being treated like a child in need of discipline." He actually had the audacity to tap the bodice above her chest. "I know what is right. I know what is proper. I do not need you—or a nursemaid—to tell me."

"What you have done to Beth's reputation is what any

thoughtless rake does to a single female's reputation—you have tarnished it by taking her to an inappropriate activity." Pamela gestured toward Beth, and found her standing right between them. "Now no one else will ever want to adopt her."

"It's not a poser, Miss Lockhart," Beth said soothingly. "Lord Kerrich's going to adopt me."

The two combatants paused and stared at the girl.

Kerrich's jaw dropped. Then he turned on Pamela and glared.

With the combination of his irascibility and her dubiety, Pamela didn't know what truths might have been revealed then, but the threatening summer storm finally made its appearance with a flash and a fury. Driven by the wind, the rain smashed into them, plastering Pamela's gown against her, obscuring her spectacles, making her catch her breath at the instantaneous chill. Even the most hardened of gamblers scattered, clutching their top hats and running toward their carriages.

Pamela pulled the spectacles off. "We should go," she shouted, and a gust of wind blew the storm into her face.

"Yes, let's take this fight to more comfortable circumstances." Kerrich smiled at Pamela unkindly. "My library."

She scowled at him. Did he *mean* to invoke the memory of those disquieting kisses? Surely not. He had called them awkward.

Coming to stand behind them, Timothy blocked the wind as best he could and raised his umbrella. The gale immediately turned it inside out and sent him stumbling.

Beth yelled, "Lord Kerrich, tell Miss Lockhart why you brought me to the racetrack."

He glared down at the child through the deluge. "Because you asked."

"But you wouldn't take me at first." She bent her head against the driving rain.

Taking off her shawl, Pamela wrapped it around Beth's head and arms. "We can talk about this later."

For some reason, Beth was obstinate. "Tell her, Lord Kerrich."

"Not now!" Kerrich put his hand in the middle of her back and drove her toward the top of the hill and the eventual calm inside the carriage. "Anyway, Miss Lockhart does the proper no matter what. She isn't going to like me better for crumpling to your blackmail. Footman, take the child to the carriage!"

Snatching up a loudly protesting Beth, Timothy carried her off toward the carriages.

That left Kerrich and Pamela alone. Taking her arm, he propelled her forward. Her eyes stung and she wiped at them. As they topped the hill, the wind and the rain struck them straight on. Far ahead, Timothy was running with Beth toward the rapidy emptying posting area, and the coachman was securing the horses Beth and Kerrich had ridden to the back of the carriage.

"What a bloody damned mess," Kerrich said.

"Your fault," Pamela mumbled, although she knew she should not continue to provoke him. Then, as if in retribution, the gale slipped under the curved wing of her hat. Flipping off her head, it dangled down her back, held only by the ribbon under her chin. Pamela tried to return it to its place on her head.

"Take it off." Kerrich spoke close to her ear, sounding even more aggrieved than before.

She shouted. She had to, he couldn't have heard her above the storm's roar if she did not. "A lady is never seen in public without—"

"Oh, for God's sake!" Stopping, he turned her toward him, untied the sodden ribbons, removed her bonnet, and yelled, "Now is not the time to worry about the propriety of wearing that ugly hat."

The rain sluiced down right on her bare head. Snatching her hat out of his hand, she snapped, "It's not ugly."

"You're right." He brushed the water off of her cheek, then stared at his fingers. "It's hideous!"

"It's perfect for a dried-up old spinster like me." She nodded her head at him in final reproof, noting how oddly he gazed at her, then turned and forged on. Her hair straggled down and she shoved it back.

It took her a moment to realize he hadn't rejoined her. For some obscure reason, he remained in the same spot, standing in the mud and the wind and the rain.

Just when she thought the day couldn't get any worse, he was going to prove stubborn. She started back for him, and at the same time he started for her. She came to a halt; he strode forward with such purpose she thought he would walk right over the top of her. She tried to evade him, but he grasped her arms in his fists and held her against him, body to body. She looked up at him. He gave a curse, the kind of curse she had heard in the stables when they'd had a horse trample them.

"My lord," she exclaimed, uncomfortable with the closeness, confused by his fury. "I beg that you remember to whom you are speaking!"

"To whom *am* I speaking?" he demanded.

She didn't understand him. "Wh-what?"

"Miss Lockhart." He shook her, but he kept her so close against him that the punishment was nothing more than discomfort. "Miss Liar!"

Her stomach twisted.

He slid one arm around her waist, then with his other hand he wiped at her cheek and showed her his fingers. "Look at that, Miss Lockhart. Your disguise is all washed away."

CHAPTER 17

As the carriage pulled to stop before his townhouse and Timothy jumped down from the back and ran toward the building, Kerrich flung wide the door and shouted, "Don't bother getting us another umbrella. I've seen it all now."

"My lord?" Drenched, confused, distressed, Timothy stopped before the open front door and gaped.

Leaping right into a puddle, Kerrich placed the step himself, reached inside, grabbed Pamela's wrist and dragged her out into the gusting rain. The drops splashed against her face, and she wanted to hug herself against the cold, but he hauled her along as if he were a stevedore and she some kind of cargo.

Such handling did not endear him to her. Fiercely, she tugged backward. "What about Beth?"

Beth's voice chimed, "I'm here."

"She's right behind us." Kerrich whipped his head around and glared at Pamela. "*She* can have the umbrella. It's not as if *she* did anything wrong."

Snatching an umbrella from inside, Timothy hurried to lift the cover over Beth as she climbed the stairs.

Kerrich kept his hand around Pamela's wrist as he

pushed inside without ceremony. "I suppose you knew about this, too, Moulton."

"My lord? Knew about . . ." Moulton caught a glimpse of Pamela and his chin dropped. The most articulate sound he seemed capable of was a long, exhaled, "Ohh."

Candles flickered everywhere in the foyer: tall tapers, fat columns, all wax and all burning brightly, and when Kerrich looked back at Pamela he stopped short. She barely avoided sliding into him, and as incensed as he was, she suspected that kind of contact might be hazardous. She thought that if he had to wrap his arm around her to steady her, he might hold her too tight and all the precarious hostility between them would shatter into . . . well, she didn't know what it would shatter into, but something quite unpleasant. Like his kisses.

He stared at her, examining her bare face. "You can look like this . . ." His voice trailed off as if fury had made him incoherent.

"I doubt, my lord, that I sport any beauty now."

He loomed over her, a dark, scowling presence. "Compared to what you were before . . ."

She should have been worried. Instead she was antagonistic. Without hesitation, she told him so. "This whole affair is your fault, not mine."

Moulton's breath hissed between his teeth.

Kerrich did not stir. "You dare."

She drew herself up and gave him her severest Miss Lockhart scowl—only to find it no longer worked.

Impervious, he commanded, "Beth, go upstairs and find your nursemaid, what's-her-name."

"Corliss," Pamela said.

"Yes, sir." Beth curtsied.

Pamela glanced back in time to see the child skipping up the stairs, apparently not a bit perturbed at having her governess hauled off by a hostile lord. "Change out of your wet clothing at once or you will catch pneumonia," she called.

Beth waved and smiled.

Pamela was starting to find Beth's invincible good cheer suspect.

Kerrich towed Pamela toward his study, and she doubted any force in nature could have stopped him.

His grandfather stopped him.

Lord Reynard came out of the study, leaning on his cane, and in one glance took in the situation. "My, my, aren't we looking well, children." Holding out his arms to Pamela, he said, "You are as charming as I remember."

"Thank you," she said faintly. *How long had Lord Reynard known?*

Kerrich's head snapped around. "Where did you meet?"

"At one of my visits to Kensington Palace, son."

"Really?" Kerrich stared at her as if trying to place her.

No, please don't remember that.

Lord Reynard patted her back. "Go on in there and let my grandson yell at you. Don't put up with too much from him, now."

Spying an escape, she said, "I should go and change first."

Kerrich snatched at her and although she backed up, he caught her by the wrist again. "No," he said.

Lord Reynard smiled fondly. "That's right, boy. Hang on to her." And he hobbled off.

Kerrich shoved her over the study's threshold and snapped, "Get out."

For one marvelous moment, Pamela thought he spoke to her. Then she heard the squeak of a chair and saw Lewis, pen poised over the papers spread out on Kerrich's desk, gaze shocked and disbelieving. "Devon," he asked, "who is this lady?"

"Who do you think she is?" Kerrich demanded.

"She looks like . . . she appears to be . . ."

"For God's sake, man, just say it. It's Miss Lockhart!"

"Oh, my." Lewis rose, shoving the chair back so hard it struck the wall. "Oh, my."

"Yes, my boy orphan is a girl and my ugly old lady governess is a young belle. It seems everyone is a perjurer." Kerrich gestured widely toward Lewis. "Do *you* have a secret you would like to confess? I'm in the mood to be lenient with you. Miss Lockhart is the one who will feel my wrath."

Gathering his papers, Lewis stacked them and mumbled, "I'm leaving. I'll work elsewhere." He sidled around the desk. "I'll . . . um . . ." He gazed at Pamela as if he pitied her. "Best of luck, Miss Lockhart."

As he scurried out the door, Kerrich muttered, "Damned fool." Then he kicked the door shut.

Tugging on her captured wrist, she whirled to face him. "We are not circus performers, my lord. We are rational human beings and there is no reason to make a scene such as you have just made."

"No reason?" With his hands on both her shoulders, he propelled her forward to view herself in one of the wall mirrors. Seizing a candelabra from the table placed before her, he held the half-dozen flickering candles so close to her face, each hollow and ridge was revealed. "Look at yourself and risk telling me there is no reason."

Although some of the rouge remained in rosy spots on her cheekbones, most of the powder had washed away. Half of her hair hung loose and dangled onto her sodden shoulder. Her appearance was one of a young woman in distress—but it was that of a *young* woman.

He stared with renewed consternation, his brown eyes radiant with rage, his eyebrows a slashing statement of displeasure, his hair so wet and black it glistened with an almost purple sheen. "This is unbelievable," he said. Then, in a shout, "Moulton!" He headed toward the portal. "Moulton!"

The door opened almost in his face. "Sir?" Moulton still sounded confounded—and gleeful.

"Get me a basin with warm water. Soap. A cloth. A towel."

Moulton bowed. "At once, my lord."

"I have never seen him move so quickly." Pamela leaned against the table before her and examined her face.

"I doubt he's ever been as curious." Kerrich stared out into the foyer as if the answers were written there. "What maggot got into your brain to embark on such a ploy?"

"It's your fault," she repeated. "Do you think I would have done this if you hadn't demanded it?"

With scrupulous forbearance, he faced her. "I demanded it? *I* demanded you wear clothes like . . . that? *I* demanded you put knitting needles in your hair? *I* demanded you paint yourself white and red like some Oriental bowl?" His lips curled as he gestured toward her. "Do you even knit?"

Clutching the edge of the table, she met his gaze in the mirror and mocked his deep, clipped voice. "Oh, Miss Setterington, I want an *older* woman, an *ugly* woman, one who has given up *all* hope of a match. Miss Setterington, I'll give you *so much* money if you can just get me a woman who is indifferent to my *spectacular* beauty. I'm so *tired* of women *fawning* on me." She sneered right back at him. "And yes, I knit!"

"Virago!"

Moulton appeared in the doorway in time to hear Kerrich's insult and was arrested, foot in the air.

Kerrich took the basin and clothes. "Good. Now get me some blankets and a dressing robe. Two dressing robes."

"My lord?" Moulton's eyes bulged.

"Robes. Get them." Kerrich stepped back and slammed the door with his foot.

Pamela watched him stalk toward her. She was already too familiar with that long stride, that smooth pursuit of information, evidence . . . confession. He would never admit he was at fault. More than that, he would never even think he could *be* at fault. A resourceful woman would try to appease him.

She said, "I have done nothing more than be what you demanded. I can't help it if you're a conceited rogue."

Placing the basin on the table, he wet the cloth and wrung it out. For the first time, she realized what he intended. She tried to take the wet cloth from him, but he brushed her hands aside and moved so close to her, the table pressed against her thighs behind and he pressed against her thighs before. The wet gown and petticoats were not enough to shield her from his proximity, and she tried to evade him. But he got a grip on her chin and wiped at her face as if she were one of her own charges. Her forehead, her cheeks, her nose, her mouth—she could have struggled, but she suspected he would subdue her by any means necessary. That he would enjoy subduing her.

He unpinned her collar and tossed it aside, then washed her neck. Her skin tingled, although whether from chagrin or the scrubbing she'd received, she could not tell. Gripping his wrists, she said, "This is unnecessary."

Stepping back, he looked at her. "I would say it was most necessary." His voice slid down an octave. "Well, look at you."

He was looking at her, and she recognized his expression. She'd seen it in other men; she'd seen it in him. Gaze caressing, nostrils flared, lower lip thrust out as if contemplating a kiss.

"I am wet and I am muddy," she snapped. "My feet ache with cold and my hair is dripping. I am not the kind of woman to attract a connoisseur such as yourself."

He leaned forward and down so his face was just in front of hers and his breath brushed her skin. "It is good, Miss Lockhart, that you occasionally remind me of your teaching background."

She leaned as far back as she could. "What do you mean?"

"You have just informed me of my feelings." His eyelids drooped; he watched her lips. "Thank God, otherwise I might have mistaken this sensation for desire."

"No." Alarmed, she slid sideways and away. "No, it's not."

He didn't chase her, as she half-expected. But then, she was in his richly appointed library in his well-guarded house. He didn't *have* to chase her.

They stood in silence, staring at each other. Him, because he seemed to glean gratification from looking at her. Her, because she dared not take her gaze off him.

When someone rapped on the door, she jumped and gasped.

"It's Moulton," Kerrich said carelessly. He walked toward the door, not coming close to her.

She moved back anyway.

"He's brought the blankets and robes." This time he opened the door only a crack, not allowing Moulton even a glimpse of her, gathered the armload of wool and velvet, and again slammed the door with his foot.

Robes. Two dressing robes. She'd heard him demand them, but the injustice of this ill-timed discovery so overwhelmed her she hadn't realized why he wanted them. She still didn't understand why he wanted them. And she wouldn't do what he wanted, anyway.

"Here." He threw her a blanket and a rich dark green robe. "Go behind that screen. Strip down and dry yourself."

"I will not."

"You will or you'll catch pneumonia." He grinned at her as if he had the gall to be enjoying himself. "That's what you told Beth."

Then the grin disappeared and she realized he might be enjoying himself, but a tempest raged beneath the surface.

"Do as you're told or I'll do it for you."

This was worse than she realized. It *was* his house. She could scream till her throat was raw and no one would come to her rescue. And maybe she was being dramatic, but . . . there wasn't a male servant in this house who would blame him if he strangled her, much less stripped her naked. Men stuck together. She'd had proof enough of that in her life. "I won't be alone with you with nothing on but a robe."

He reached out for the bundle of cloth in her arms. "Then I'll keep the robe."

She had the good sense to step away. "You are behaving like a swine."

"I am behaving like a man who's been made a fool of." He gestured toward the door. "The servants are in the kitchen chortling right now. Lewis must be hugging himself to see me so humiliated. And my grandfather knew, didn't he?"

"No!"

"Yes! He's been making discreet hints about your age and beauty ever since he arrived."

"If that's true, it's not because of anything I said."

"It's because he knew. He recalled you. Who else recalls you?"

"Not you, obviously."

He sprang to attention. "We've met?"

She cursed her impetuous tongue. Recalling that occasion would be, at this moment, the height of folly. "If we have, it meant as little to me as it did to you. Besides, you don't care what anyone thinks. Remember?" Again she lowered her voice. " 'A man who is ruled by the beliefs of the ignorant is a shadow of a man. In fact, one might call such a man a woman.' " She chuckled in odious imitation of an odious man.

"You will stop quoting me."

Now she chuckled in real mirth. For the first time today, she had scored her point. "I'll go upstairs and change into dry clothing."

"You'll stay here and put on my robe."

"I must consider my reputation."

"Lady, if you don't get those clothes off, I promise to leave your reputation in shreds."

It was obvious by his lowered head and rapid-fire response he had lost all patience, and this time she opted for wisdom. "You kissed me before." She held out her hands, palm up. "You must promise that if I do this, you won't try and kiss me again."

"Miss Lockhart, the only thing I promise you is that I will get the truth from you one way or another." He pointed. "Now get back there and strip off."

She hadn't won anything. But he was on the verge of taking matters into his own hands, so she scurried behind the screen. Kerrich was right, the blackguard, she did want to be rid of her sopping clothes and most especially of her sodden leather shoes. And if she was going to obey his orders and her own wishes, she would have to be as quick as possible. She did not care to have him join her.

Twisting and squirming in the small recess behind the

screen, she unfastened the buttons on the back of her gown. With a quick glance to make sure she was unobserved, she pulled it off over her head.

"You must have known you would be caught," he called.

"Why?" She judged his voice to be over by the fire, and relaxed her vigilance a little. Untying her petticoats, she let them drop and stepped out of them. "Once you had ascertained I was the proper female for the job, you never looked at me."

"I . . . did . . . too."

She paid him and his indignation no heed. There was no chair so, sitting on the floor, she slowly and painfully worked the buttons out of the leather of her shoes. "You wanted the job finished as quickly as possible, so I knew I wouldn't have to pretend for long."

"I saw you. I knew there was something about you." He paused, then with absolute relish said, "I kissed you."

"I needed the money."

"From kissing?" He sounded like he was laughing.

"No, my jesting lord. From the success of your plan." Reaching under her pantalettes, she untied her garters and peeled off her stockings. A shiver shook her as the air flowed over her moist skin, and she wrapped the blanket around her. "As you have so kindly pointed out, my lord, women will do anything for money."

He drew breath, then exhaled in slow, long consideration. "Except you." The rapid-fire fury of his speech had become lazy contemplation. "*You* will not marry for money."

She had not slowed. She had not gained reason. She was still as furious as she had been at the racetrack, and she yelled, "I will not marry at all." Then she heard herself. Shouting, like some chippy of her father's. Looking down at her trembling hands, she gained control of her voice and said softly, "But there's no question of that, is there?"

"Oh, I don't know. That might be the answer to my problems. You're clever, you're from a good family, and if you're as lovely as Colbrook claims, I would have myself a wife of whom even Queen Victoria would approve."

CHAPTER 18

Pamela came barreling around the edge of the screen, ready to put Kerrich straight in his thinking.

But he stood before the fire, absolutely nude.

Nude. Presenting her his profile. His arms upraised, the muscles bulging in his upper arms. A towel over his head as he dried his hair. A whisk of black hair lightly covered his clean, glowing skin, especially from his chest to his groin. Especially around the protrusion which . . .

She closed her eyes, then without her volition found them open again.

His legs. His legs arched with muscle, too, healthy and long, and all over, the fire's golden glow lovingly licked his flesh.

She shouldn't look. She should go back behind the screen. Why had she even come out here?

He must have found her silence suspect, for he whipped the towel off his head and faced her.

She would have thought curiosity, vulgar curiosity, would lead her to look again at his body, or that mortification would make her scamper away. But his force of will compelled her to look at his countenance. At his slow, crooked smile, the way his drying hair stood in spikes around his face, the hawklike nose and the faint shadow of a beard across his chin. And his eyes . . . brown was too pedestrian a word, but they were brown. Dark brown. Yet tawny threads wove compelling accents, and his dark lashes emphasized the authority of that admirable, persuasive gaze. If a color could be labeled *sin*, his eyes were that color.

"Miss Lockhart." He spread his arms wide. "Do you like what you see?"

"Lord Kerrich, you have no shame." She used her most implacable tone, but she clutched the blanket more tightly about her and her gaze slipped downward. She had seen the occasional naked boy. She was, after all, a governess. But this was so completely different. Kerrich's shoulders were broad, his hips narrow, his proportions perfect for wearing clothes—or not. His fit figure, she surmised, was the result of much exercise on horseback and in the prize-fighter's salon. But what exercise had he performed to bring himself to such . . . virile dimensions? Most men did not appear to have an excess in their trousers.

For that matter, he hadn't appeared to have such an excess in his trousers. Was that stirring of his manly parts the signal that she should run away, regardless of her dishabille?

"No, I have no shame," he said. "I have no reason to, and as your future husband—"

Now she remembered. *That's* why she had come around the screen in a furor, and at his prompting her wrath rose again. "Marriage is not a humorous matter."

"I'll say."

"Nor a frivolous matter, to be decided by the shape of a woman's eyes."

From across the room, he flirted with her. A faint smile,

a slow blink, a slumberous look. "I wasn't thinking of the shape of your *eyes*."

Exasperating! "You know full well I would never wed a man such as you."

He tossed his towel aside and paced toward her. He was so . . . big. Dark. *Big*. She debated whether it would be better to hit him with her fists or retain possession of the blanket. Then he went past her, behind the screen, and came out with one of her dry towels.

With no idea of his intent, she failed to take evasive action. The towel covered her head before she could step away, and his hands followed, rubbing ruthlessly at her hair.

"What's wrong with a man like me?"

He stood behind her, far too close for comfort, so close she could smell the fresh, rain-wash scent of his body and catch occasional hints of enveloping warmth. Using one hand to try to fend him off, she said, "You're a rake. You're proud of it."

"Better hang on to that blanket or it'll fall," he advised. "Yes, I like women."

"Too many women." She decided this scouring of her scalp couldn't in any way be called a seduction, and took his advice. She held the blanket.

"How many is too many?"

"More than one." Daringly, she said what she'd always thought. "If a man was meant to have more than one lover, he would have more than one organ."

He burst into laughter, a wholehearted, generous laughter that made her feel witty and sparkling at the same time. But his next words stole her gratification from her.

"*At a time*," he said. "One woman *at a time*."

"So if you ever wed—"

"You."

Why did he keep bringing that up? To plague her, she supposed, for making his foolishness obvious to everyone who knew their situation. But the thought of marriage to anyone frightened her, and the thought of marriage to him made her fingers clench and her chest tighten. A handsome rake, gifted in seduction and having no respect for fidelity? Kerrich was her worst nightmare.

Doggedly, she continued, "If you ever wed anyone, then following the philosophy you have just espoused, you will have to reserve your consummations for your wife. Which you've already told me you do not intend to do."

The towel slipped off her face as he used it to rub the long strands of her hair between his palms. "No. A woman given that kind of fidelity will squander the gift in benighted ignorance of its value."

"That value being more than the fidelity a woman gives her husband?"

"A man is more able to appreciate the rareness of the boon."

"You talk circles around the truth." She stared deep into the chamber, seeing only the shadows and not the light. "You are just like my father."

"Now there's a rare insult." But he didn't deny it. "I have to wed you. I can't have you around the house if I do not, and I hate to see you lose the money which you so covet."

"If I wed you, I wouldn't receive a salary at all—although that doesn't seem fair, either," she said reflectively. "I would deserve some sort of compensation for my suffering."

The towel dropped to her feet and his hands slid to her shoulders. "You wouldn't suffer except perhaps the first time, and I flatter myself that I could bring you pleasure even then."

She whirled around, breaking his grip and facing him.

She'd come to appreciate the man she thought him to be, she realized, for she noted the loss of respect. "So you will make me pay for the privilege of working for you by forcing me into your bed?"

He viewed her thoughtfully, then walked around her as if she were an obstacle in his path. "That seems an extreme way of phrasing it."

"But I've heard it so many times before." She followed him. "Do you know what it's like to have to watch your every word, to keep your eyes downcast, to be as plain as you can be and still be grabbed at and touched and kissed?"

Just in front of the fire he leaned down, right in front of her, his spine stretching, his backside tightening, as he picked up his robe. "I can honestly say I've never been in that position." He walked toward his desk, pulling the robe over his shoulders.

Leaving her standing, staring at the spot where she had seen—not glimpsed, but *seen*—his slim, taut buttocks.

"Miss Lockhart?"

Dazed, she glanced up and watched him do as he had done on that fateful day when she'd come for an interview.

Facing her, he slid onto the desk. A few loose papers were scattered on its surface. A few fat folders were stacked neatly before the chair. He sat on one edge, his bare feet dangling, his robe wrapped loosely around him, his gaze intent. "You were saying that men give you trouble?"

"Oh. Yes." A bare body part was nothing. Her resentment was immense. She followed him, stood right before him, confronted him. "Men. They grab and touch and then, when you object, you're told you're a flirt. You enticed them." With slow emphasis, she said, "It wasn't their fault."

He almost touched her chin. Almost, but she jerked her head back.

He nodded as if he comprehended her fierceness. "That's

the worst of it. The noddy-pates always blame you."

"When I wouldn't have one of them." She drew herself up to her full height, grasping for dignity in a plaid woolen blanket.

"I can't claim to utterly understand. No one ever grabs at me."

She did. She didn't know where she got the brass, but she grasped his lapel and jerked it back so roughly her thumbnail scraped his skin.

Grabbing her hand, he said, "Ow."

"You're supposed to like it. Anything they do, you're supposed to like, because you're poor, young and worst of all, pretty."

"I am pretty, aren't I?" He rubbed her knuckles.

She didn't want his comfort. Wrestling her hand free, she thrust her head close to his and glared into his eyes. "They'll want to slobber on you."

"I don't slobber when I kiss."

"I know." Enfolding his head in her fingers, she pressed her mouth on his. The blanket fell to the floor, but it didn't matter because . . . because she was teaching him a lesson. Explaining her life through demonstration. She still wore her corset, her chemise and her pantalettes. It wasn't as if they hadn't kissed before.

Moreover, she knew what he was doing, the louse. He was letting her kiss him, urging her to take pleasure in the closeness between them and the softness of his lips in the hopes he could lure her into his bed.

Wrapping his fingers around her wrists, he held them while he pulled away. "You must stop."

Restraint? Good sense? She stared at him, into those brown and golden eyes, and found these new traits of his not in the least admirable.

Struggling, she freed her hands. "That's right. Protest."

Still he insisted on being wise. "You will be sorry if you don't stop."

This was about retribution, about revenge on all those other men who had tried to take advantage of their position to seduce her. Her anger at him, at the others, at this stupid masquerade and its ghastly unveiling still churned beneath the surface, but a judicious application of lust, she found, transformed that anger into pure, turbulent, dominating passion.

"You can't tell me what I feel," she said.

"I'm giving you a chance."

"Don't you see?" She brushed her palm along the muscles and sinews of his shoulder. "I'm showing you what it's like to be used like a woman."

"I'm a man." His voice had deepened.

"Yes." She opened the other side of his robe. "I saw."

She heard his intake of breath, a gasp of excitation as she looked at him, and she gasped herself. Things had changed. His body had changed.

In a strained voice, he said, "Men dream of a woman who will use them in just this manner."

Girls gossiped about men and the body part that could change size, but she'd never imagined the tales were true. Nor had she imagined, except in her worse nightmares, she would ever have the occasion to see the proof. But this was very curious, very gratifying . . . very naughty. His protrusion had lengthened, risen, grown in every way, thrusting forth from the nest of black, curling hair at his groin.

She stared. He wanted her. All the evidence was there, from the expanding dimensions to the drop of thick liquid that eased from the rosy end. If she wanted, she could make him suffer. Or she could use this rake, this man with the gift of seduction, to satisfy the old, nagging curiosity from her girlhood. She had never been tempted, but Kerrich tempted her, and when she contemplated him, he was perfect. He was guaranteed to bring her pleasure and then, like all rakes, he would be done with her. Kerrich wouldn't talk about forever. Not seriously. Not even his suggestion of marriage was serious.

Yet she could get a child.

Yet she would never have another, such exquisite opportunity.

What a choice.

"You're fulfilling my dreams," Kerrich warned her.

A choice that had to be made at once, with no time for wisdom or forethought.

Perhaps it was better this way. Because, with time and cool thought, temptation would be vanquished. There was no chance of that now.

With the tip of one finger she touched the drop of fluid at the end of his protrusion, dabbling in it, smoothing it over the satiny skin.

"Every dream I ever had." But his voice was almost inaudible. And, "All right, then. I did try."

Another drop seeped up. She slid her palm lightly over the head, gliding along on the liquid, exploring the groove, the cap, the ridges.

"Usually," he said hoarsely, "a woman touches a man in a less incendiary limb first."

She thought herself curious, but when she spoke, her voice sounded taunting. "Is that a rule?"

"Not if you don't want it to be." He'd dropped his robe off his shoulders.

"I've just never seen anything like this," she said.

He groaned.

She hadn't hurt him; she knew she hadn't, but she didn't understand what had caused such a sound of misery. "Lord Kerrich?"

"Just . . . keep touching me."

Ah . . . now she understood. She was tormenting him.

What satisfaction. Tentatively, she rested her palm on his hair-covered thigh, and when his muscles clenched she rubbed up and down. She closed her hand on his protrusion, holding it firmly, marveling at the skin so soft none of hers compared. "What do you call this?"

"Right now—I call it *master.*"

She chuckled.

He did not.

She caressed him with both hands, one on each limb. How peculiar, to have two such different textures so close on a single body!

His hands flexed on the smooth surface of the desk, then in a lightning-swift move, he reached for her waist. Shocked, she grabbed for his shoulders as he picked her up and dragged her up with him. Her knees landed on either side of his hips, on the folds of his robe. She sprawled atop him in an untidy heap. His private parts imprinted themselves on her belly. "Lord Kerrich, this is not—"

Enfolding her head in his hands, he pressed a kiss on her. Not like her kiss, or like his kisses of the previous night, but a kiss that possessed and overwhelmed. He thrust his tongue in her mouth, tasted her like a starving man, made her whimper and catch fire. How could he do that with his lips, his hands? How could he make her crowd against him, trying to get closer than the inside of his heart? She kissed him back, entangling her tongue, her breath, her passions with his.

Taking his mouth away, he said, "Let me." And tugged at her corset strings.

She had no faith that any man could do more than make a snarl of those strings, but Kerrich untied and unlaced at a speed any lady's maid would have envied. Of course.

Pamela hadn't accounted for his extensive experience.

So she bit his neck.

He jumped and muttered, "Savage."

She kissed the place to make it better.

He removed her corset completely and dropped it off the edge of the desk, leaving her clad in only her thin, cotton chemise.

She ducked her head and kissed his chest.

He lifted her breasts in the cups of his hands . . .

And she breathed in pure ecstasy. Sitting up, she tilted her head back and closed her eyes.

"I knew . . ." he whispered. "Sensitive all over." He rubbed his thumbs languidly along the delicate skin beneath, then skimmed up and over her nipples.

The pleasure made her clench her legs around him, rock to ease her excitement, and deep inside her womb tensed, waiting for something. For him.

How could she know so much? What feral instinct had her in its grip?

When he put his lips on her breasts, she whimpered. He sucked the cloth into his mouth, then smoothed it across her nipple and looked. "So pretty," he said. Then he wet the cloth again and suckled.

What she had felt before was nothing to this. This was sublime, a divine experience, pure happiness distilled into this man and his touch. She held him to her, raked her nails though his hair. He blew on the damp cloth and her nipples rose, tight and thrusting, pointing at him and demanding.

He yielded. He untied the ribbon at the full neck of her chemise and slid it off her shoulder. He brought her breast out into the open and stared at it, and she saw worship in his gaze. Tilting his head, he began to kiss the smooth skin beside her arm—and she pushed him away. "Let me show you what I want you to do."

In a disconcerted tone, he repeated, "What you want me to do?"

"Yes." Opening her hand over his collarbone, she pushed him down flat on the desk.

His robe was beneath his bottom, the hard wood beneath his back, and he gave a hiss as his heated flesh made contact with the cool surface. "I'm not going to let you tease me," he said.

"Yes, you are. You're going to let me take my revenge on you, and on every other shallow male who worships at the altar of beauty and ignores—"

He adjusted his hips beneath her, and for a moment she lost track of what she was saying.

At his mocking smile, she remembered. "Every shallow male who cares only for comeliness and nothing for the woman."

"But I can guide you until you're lost in pleasure."

She didn't want to be guided. She wanted to command. So with a half-fathomed idea that he would respond and submit, she untangled her arms and slowly worked the chemise off over her head. As soon as it had cleared her eyes, she saw him. The concentrated gaze he had bestowed on one breast doubled in intensity. His lips were slightly open, yet he breathed with difficulty. He was a man in thrall, and between her legs his protrusion stirred.

It couldn't get bigger . . . could it? Thank heavens she still wore her pantalettes. Her plain, clean, white pantalettes, symbol of purity, worn to hide her limbs from licentious rogues such as him.

Foresight and caution rose to plague her. Where was this going? When the anger had been exorcised and the passion spent, would she be the pitiable creature she feared?

"Miss Lockhart." Recovering from his daze, he rose to lean on his elbows.

That brought her back to this time and this place. She didn't want him to take charge. She didn't want to think sensibly. She just wanted to drive Kerrich insane. So, crossing her arms, she cupped each of her breasts in her palm and lifted them.

His elbow slipped and he toppled back.

With the deceitfully affable smile she had inherited from some distant, seductive female ancestor, she leaned toward him, bringing herself to his mouth. "Taste me," she whispered.

His resistance collapsed. Because what she wanted was what he wanted, too, of course. Because he couldn't believe his luck or her gullibility, of course. But of course, she didn't care. He did as he was told, and when he suckled on one nipple and caressed the other, she was in an agony of delight. She undulated her hips, finding the motion against him to be a voluptuous debauchery. She was no longer aware of being in the library, in the chamber she so enjoyed. Her surroundings had narrowed to a single area, the long, wide surface of the desk. She was aware of Kerrich, naked and illicitly handsome, of his mouth, seeking other places that would bring her joy, of his hand, ranging over her as if the touch of her gave him pleasure. From the throb in her loins, she knew that he gave pleasure.

She pressed the flat of her hands on his chest, feeling the coarse hair, the tensile muscles, the pulse of his heart. He was alive, and he made her come alive—with laughter, with fury, with rancor, with exasperation. With him, she felt all she hadn't let herself feel for years, and now she wanted him. Even if he hurt her. Even if it weren't proper. Even if she were being as stupid as every other infatuated lady.

Tonight would be for her.

When she untied the waist of her pantalettes, Pamela wasn't as efficient as Kerrich would have been. For all her bravery, her fingers were trembling.

So Kerrich helped her. When she regained sanity, she would be piqued that he handled female undergarments so adroitly, but right now she didn't care. He eased off her pantalettes, and she never suffered a moment of embarrassment.

Until she had to place herself on him again. Her bare thighs touched his bare hips and if she settled her weight, they would be almost . . .

"Why are you staring at nothing and moving your lips?" he asked.

She looked down at him, at that elegant countenance and the long, broad, bare body that served as her saddle. "I'm thinking."

His hand drifted up toward her chest, and as lightly as the first leaf-fall of autumn, drifted down her chest and onto her belly. "I wish you wouldn't."

"If I take this to its natural conclusion, what would that be?"

Now his lips moved, and nothing came out.

"I mean," she said, "what would happen afterward? Between you and me?"

"Whatever you want," he answered promptly. Too promptly.

He was lying, but she was appeased because he'd said what she wanted to hear.

"All right." Leaning over, she sank onto him. His chest against hers, their bellies touching, his rambunctious erection nestled against her . . . her skin ached with the gladness of touching him, and she settled deeper, relaxing, touching all of him with all of her and wishing she could touch more. "All right," she repeated, her lips so close to his her breath brushed his face. Then she kissed him as he had kissed her: demanding, coercing, leading him where she wished to go. She loved this. She wanted this. "Kerrich, please," she whispered.

What he saw in her face seemed to give him immense satisfaction, for he grinned, briefly and savagely.

Then he scooted beneath her as if trying to escape.

"No!" Instantly enraged, she sat up and dug her nails into his chest. "You can't leave me."

"I won't." He chuckled briefly, unevenly. "I can't." Taking a breath, he said, "Over here. Scoot over here."

Not understanding, she went with him as, helped by the robe beneath him, he slid across the desk. A few papers shuffled to the floor as he moved far enough to get into one of the drawers. The slide of wood against wood sounded loud in the quiet room, and the phial clattered as he drew it out.

Staring at the crimson bottle with its delicate cuts and lacy filigrees, she asked, "What is it?"

"Lean back." He grabbed one of the paper-filled folders

and stuck it under his head as a pillow, then uncorked the phial.

She wavered. She wanted this, yes, but she hadn't thought it out. How could she? She didn't know all the details. But to take the chance that he could look and see . . . there . . .

"It's oil." He poured a thin stream of platinum liquid into his cupped palm and waved it toward her. "Attar of rose. Can you smell it?"

She could, and the scent was rich and sensuous, redolent of flowers and opulence.

Corking the bottle, he shoved it aside without ever taking his attention off her. "When you lean back, I'll rub it on you. I'll do your belly first . . . have I told you how beautiful your belly is? Taut and the color of cream, with the indentation of your navel placed where the thumb of God pressed inward."

"You . . . you didn't see my belly."

He smiled again, blast him, that slow, knowing, erotic smile she had been admiring for . . . for too long.

"There is nothing about you I haven't noticed." He poured half the oil onto his other hand and rubbed his palms together. They glistened with temptation. "You are beautiful, and I want to touch your belly and your thighs."

With the oil, he meant. Such explicit intimacy shocked her, and at the same time moisture eased from inside her. Just like him, she realized. She must be eager, for she responded just like him.

Still the training of a chaste lifetime could not be subdued, and she said, "I thought this wouldn't take very long."

He laughed out loud. "Am I demolishing your schedule, teacher?"

"Yes." He was demolishing everything—and she would

worry about it *tomorrow*. No consequences. Not tonight. "Where else are you going to touch me?"

"Just where you think I will touch you." His sin-colored eyes glowed with promise. "Lean back."

Slowly, she leaned enough to arch her back.

"More. Put your hands behind you on the desk."

She stretched back, back until she looked up at the ceiling and all of her was bared to his gaze. That he was looking, she had no doubt. The man was incorrigible, and very, very good at what he did.

The first tender touch slid up her hipbone, then across to her navel, where it swirled and delved. Then his other hand, it had to be his other hand, touched her inner thigh and moved with infinite indolence up toward . . . "Sh . . ." he whispered. "Don't move. Close your eyes. Let me . . ."

His touch tousled the triangle of hair, ruffling every nerve. When he opened her, the air puffed against her. *Now. Now he'll pierce me with his finger.* Determinedly she shut her eyes. She could take it. She might suffer embarrassment. She surely would undergo discomfort. But at least she'd know if his performance lived up to his reputation.

Instead, he anointed her inner, delicate, bare skin with oil. It felt . . . good. More than good.

"What are you doing?" she whispered.

He didn't answer.

Her hesitation became anticipation as his hand progressed with ever narrowing circles toward her own tiny protrusion at the front. She knew how sensitive that was, yet he didn't quite touch it. Not yet. Not yet.

She found herself quivering, trying to entice him with tiny rhythmic movements of her hips, trying to get him to caress her there.

He didn't, drat him.

He continued that disturbing dance of skin against skin,

and all her predisposed notions drifted away. "Please." Colors shifted and glowed behind her closed lids. "Please, Lord Kerrich."

"Devon," he said.

She hesitated. Coupling was one thing, a breakdown of the social distance between them something else. She knew herself to be a lady of English society, stifled by too many rules, but . . .

Deliberately, he removed his touch. "Devon," he repeated.

She surrendered at once. "Devon. Please, Devon."

His fingers skimmed the places he had skimmed before, then with exquisite care, he plucked at the protrusion that was causing her such craving, and he both eased the craving and made her want more. Her hands searched behind, found his thighs, gripped them and rubbed them. "Kerrich . . . Devon . . . don't. Please. You're making me . . ." *Feel too much.* This wasn't the way it was supposed to be, was it? This irresistible, clawing desire, made more poignant by its startling newness.

If this was lust, why had she eschewed it all her life?

Blind with passion, she swayed, her whole body caught up in the bliss of having *him*, Kerrich—Devon—beneath her, titillating her with the clever hands of a connoisseur. Each muscle in her body trembled in anticipation, each touch jolting her and each touch making her want more. She wanted to beg him to do . . . do . . . whatever it was that came next. She couldn't articulate words anymore, yet she concentrated so hard on her yearning he must have overheard her, for his fingers glided farther back—and inside.

She arched up, avid, frantic, desperate. His finger slipped in and out, his palm rubbed against her, and she was ready. So ready. If he didn't stop, she would . . .

He stopped.

She gave a keening sound of protest.

He shushed her. "Lean forward now."

Her hands landed on his chest and instinctively, she groped for anything that would bring him joy. Evidently, mere contact was enough, for his heated skin chilled with goosebumps.

"You are a darling," he said, as with his hands on her bottom he raised her above him.

Dimly she realized what he was doing; he was going to enter her, take her, vanquish her innocence. If she could have spoken she would have told him to hurry.

He fitted them together without fumbling—of course—and then he said, "Pamela. Look at me."

The tone of command penetrated her wonderful daze, and she opened her eyes.

His sinful gaze watched her, fervent and so grim he clearly took this business of defloration seriously. "Listen to me. You have to do this."

What did he mean? She shook her head.

"Yes, you have to. You're on top. You're ready. Please. Take me inside you."

Enough of her reason returned for her to realize his stratagem. This wasn't fair. If they did it his way, she couldn't blame him afterward. She couldn't claim that his expertise had swept her away or that she'd been seduced.

"It's the only way," he said. "If you want me . . ."

She did. She wanted him so much, and regardless of what happened after, she had made her decision and she would always have this evening.

So, tentatively, she began to lower herself onto him. At first she slid—the oil, she realized, eased the way.

"That feels . . . so good."

Surprised by his thickened tone, she looked at him. The cords in his neck stood out, color stained his cheeks, and his eyes were half-closed. He gasped beneath her as if he were in agony . . . but he wasn't. That was passion. She recognized it, she knew not how, but she was transporting Kerrich beyond the mundane. Her body was carrying him to a magical realm, and this, *this* was what she had wanted. She had mastered the man beneath her. And how much she loved command!

As she moved down further, discomfort made her pause.

He groaned, an ardent, desperate groan. "Please."

"You're too big," she told him.

His hips jerked beneath her, sending him deeper, making her gasp on a shard of pain.

He stopped himself with obvious reluctance, and he stared at her worshipfully. "You are the most beautiful woman I've ever seen."

She lifted herself slightly, allowing the ripples of distress to fade.

He must have thought she was punishing him, because he said, "I mean, more than beautiful. You're intelligent and witty . . . please, Pamela, if you would just finish, I would do anything for you."

"Anything?" She held herself still, readying herself for the pain that must come.

"Climb mountains. Swim . . ." Gripping her hips, he stared at her pleadingly.

"Oceans?"

He nodded.

"I don't want that. I just want this." Taking his hand, she positioned it between her legs.

His smile looked more like a painful grimace, but he touched her as he had before. He touched her just as she wanted.

And she plunged down. Oh, God, he hurt her. It hurt, but he kept caressing her and the pain mixed with the passion, and she didn't know what to do but to rise and plunge down again. He was assisting her now, moving his hips, helping her catch the primal rhythm. Her fingers clutched at him, her frantic breath caught in her chest, her heart beat out of control, and she was ecstatic. The motion, the tumult, the joy felt like riding the wildest stallion toward the tempestuous night. It was hot, it was sweaty, it was crude, and she loved it.

He loved it, too, for he made breathless, inarticulate sounds of encouragement as he strained and writhed beneath her. Everything narrowed itself to one square desktop, and that square encompassed all the universe. She was here, living now, aware of everything and carried beyond. Her thighs ached from the exercise, her knees hurt from contact with the hard wood, she had a stitch in her side, but Kerrich was inside, deep in her womb, luring forth a response, and she wanted that response so badly, waited for it with such desperation, nothing else mattered.

When the spasms caught her up, she cried out her joy. She wanted to press herself down on him, to savor the climax of this fiery ride, but Kerrich couldn't pause. He urged her on, and she went willingly, his need spurring hers. They moved together, faster and faster, until beneath her he gave a shout and held her hips tightly against him, and climaxed while she . . . well, she had never stopped.

CHAPTER 20

Slowly the passion that consumed her senses retreated, and Pamela began to feel again. Once again she smelled the scent of attar of roses, and thought the flowers must be burned by the fires of wanting. Goosebumps rose on her skin as her perspiration dried. Between her legs she felt full and damp, sore and well-pleasured. Her thighs ached, her knees hurt, and when she looked around . . . dear heavens, she sat nude on a naked Lord Kerrich, on his desk, in the middle of his library, while beeswax candles blazed with their white light and the flames flickered on the hearth.

She was completely exposed. She could never pretend this hadn't happened. She had agreed to—no, insisted on—consummation with no hope of denial. A blush climbed from her chest to her forehead, and she looked everywhere but at Kerrich.

"Don't," he commanded.

She glanced down at him sprawled beneath her, then glanced away. "Don't what?"

"Don't give me your regrets. That wasn't a calling card you gave me. That was your virginity, and I will not have you say you repent it."

She looked again, and his play of features demanded as much as his body had a few moments ago. "Then I won't *tell* you."

He smiled at her, a winsome smile of great charm. "Don't repent it, either."

"No . . . no." She wouldn't. Rational or not, she had made the decision to know him carnally, she was an adult woman, and she would take any consequences that transpired. Moreover, it occurred to her that, given the chance, every sane women in the civilized world would choose to experience amorality with Kerrich; Pamela would have to keep this a secret or the man would be inundated with offers.

"I can't keep it a secret forever!"

Bewildered, he shook his head. "What?"

Remembering his reputation, she added morosely, "Everyone already knows."

"Knows . . . what?"

"That you're an expert at this. That you can bring a woman ecstasy."

Stretching his hands up, he hooked his hands under his head and looked unbearably brazen. "Did I bring you ecstasy?"

She sat up a little straighter. "You know very well what your capabilities are. You don't need me to tell you."

"But I do." He let his appreciative gaze travel up her body to her face. "It's a little-known fact, but men need to be encouraged before they can perform. You should praise me constantly, and if you do, I'll personally guarantee ecstasy every night of our married life."

In perplexity and desperation, she asked, "Why are you pursuing this? I told you I wouldn't wed you."

"I always planned to marry, although not yet, but you are . . ." He hesitated for a telling moment.

"Convenient? Without interfering relatives? Pretty enough?"

He visibly wavered. "Well . . . yes, all of those things. And I like you, I enjoy talking with you, my marriage would fulfill the queen's wish, and you wouldn't expect more from me than I was willing to give."

"Why are you spoiling a wonderful moment?" she asked in despair. "You're a rake, and rakes are safe. A rake doesn't want to marry."

"I don't *want* to, but if I must—"

"I don't know where you earned the reputation for honeyed words. You're insulting." He opened his mouth to argue, and she spoke right over him. "I can't marry anyone. Especially not you. Don't you understand? I want what my mother never had. I want a whole man. Or none."

His mouth twisted wryly. "Which parts do you find me missing?"

In a vain attempt to bring back their accord, she leaned down so her nipples brushed his chest and let her mouth hover just above his. "If you were missing any parts, I wouldn't know, would I?"

"I wouldn't tell you, either. Why won't you marry me?"

Leaning her arms on his chest, she explained, "I want a complete husband. I don't want to share him with other women. Nor even one other woman. I want to know he means his marriage vows and will love me forever and ever."

"Perhaps . . ."

"No." She put her fingers over his lips. "Don't even suggest it. You want things, unreasonable things, like a wife who loves only *you* and trusts *you* implicitly."

She was right, he realized. He didn't even understand it himself. This very morning he'd considered marriage nothing more than an undesirable future obligation. And he must have the devotion denied his father or he would have no wife at all. Grandpapa would say Pamela's and Kerrich's shared parental disappointments gave them common ground for a marriage. Yet when Kerrich looked at the idea logically, he knew their betrayed hopes divided them as surely as the greatest chasm, for it would take a miracle for either one of them to trust through the difficulty and the years of marriage.

On the other hand, he felt he could spend the rest of his life right here, inside Miss Lockhart. Inside Pamela.

So she would have to learn to trust him, become devoted to him, and then wed him, because marriage was what he wanted.

Slowly, he rose onto his elbows, then up on his hands, and looked her in the eyes. "We are not done here yet. Not until I convince you."

She opened her mouth to argue, and he smoothed his lips against hers. She resisted for one long moment, then she softened against him, female, pliant, warm, tender. She wrapped her arms around his neck and pressed herself against him, and inside her his organ stirred to life.

Damn, it wasn't possible. Not so soon.

He slid to the edge of the desk, placed his hands under her bottom, and lifted her as he stood. She made no objection; indeed, she clung as he wanted her to, her strong legs wrapped around his hips, her slender arms clasping his neck.

Where did he want her? He'd already had her on the desk, and never would he work there without remembering the rise and fall, the heat and excitement, the sweat and the moans. Tupping Pamela had been everything he had ever dreamed in his wildest adolescent fantasies, and now he would live his dream again.

Where else did he want to build a memory?

On the rug. Clasping her hips tightly to his, he tumbled to the floor before the fire. The thick Oriental carpet cushioned his fall, he cushioned Pamela's, and they were still one. For some reason, that mattered more than it should.

"Are you all right?" He laid her flat and knelt over her, holding her hips high, keeping himself inside. "Did I hurt you?" He brushed her hair out of her face, trying to see if she was in pain, if he should remember his background as a gentleman and let her go.

She returned the favor, brushing his hair off his forehead. "You didn't hurt me. Only a little, and the pleasure more than paid for the pain."

"So I can do this?" He moved his hips a little, testing her while watching her face.

Her eyelids drooped. "That's very intense."

"Intense?" He did it again. Her tissues were still swollen from excitement and tight with her virginity, and her passages clung to him, rubbing him like the tightest fist.

Her chest rose and fell as she took a deep breath. "Yes, I'm sensitive now and that—" She grabbed his shoulders when he moved again, and her nails dug into his skin.

He scarcely felt the pain as his cock finished hardening within her. She lifted her hips toward him, and he whispered, "Pamela, stop. If you don't lie very still, I won't be accountable for my actions."

She lifted her hips again, and this time she added a little swirl.

He didn't think she knew what she was doing; her eyes were closed, and she wore the expression of a woman discovering lust and reveling in it. But he had to grind his teeth to remain in control. He had to. He ought to. Ought to . . . he entered her to the hilt, then drew himself almost all the way out, and heard her moan. He ought to let her take her enjoyment of him.

He pushed his way back in again, taking his time, allowing her body to adjust.

She wrapped her arms around his buttocks, pulled him tightly against her, arched her back, and so suddenly he was caught by surprise, she came to orgasm. Holding him where she wanted him, she surged against him in shuddering waves, grinding herself against him, using him like . . . like a woman uses a man.

If he could have laughed, he would have. Instead, the fever caught him up and he lost all sense, all decency, and every bit of the discipline he had spent years developing. He thrust himself into her, once, again, taking his satisfaction on Pamela as if she were just a mistress and not the one he loved.

No. She was not the one!

But he couldn't pull back. His body held him in thrall, and he poured his seed into her, uncaring of the consequences. She was his, and he would put his stamp of possession on her.

When he finished, he collapsed on her, almost unconscious and completely empty. She had all of him there was to give. If, by some stroke of outstanding luck, she demanded he service her again tonight, he would have to resort to the French method . . . and if his lips could have smiled, they would, at the thought of the rapture that would bring her.

Slowly he became aware that his weight was pressing her into the carpet, that her hands were stroking down his back, and her small, incoherent whimpers had become words.

"That was so good." She smoothed his hair back over his ears. "You are so good. You make me happy. I'll never stop wanting you."

Bone weary and yet so contented, he lifted the worst of

his weight off of her. "Did I hurt you that time?"

"Yes." She smiled at him, a spent smile that probably matched his own. "But it didn't last very long."

His eyes narrowed on her. "It lasted long enough, didn't it?"

"Funny. I thought you would remember." Her smile slipped. "We can't ever do this again. We have a child in the house. Your grandfather is here. Your cousin—"

"Let's not forget the servants." He was sarcastic.

She was earnest. "Yes, the servants. You might not think about them, but I am one."

He rolled off to the side. "You are not!"

"I'm the governess." Cautiously she stood, moving as if every muscle ached. "I'm also a lady, and I work for a living. I am neither above stairs nor below stairs, and the servants will make me very aware of what they think."

"If they dare, you tell me and I will—"

"You can't dismiss them all." She picked up her clothing.

Observing the stretch of muscles beneath that glowing skin gave him a primitive sense of accomplishment. He'd made her his.

She continued, "Every one of them knows. They've probably got their ears pressed against the portal right now."

Savagely, he gazed at the door. If he jerked it open now, how many servants would fall in the room? How many could he terrify with one loud shout? Remembering the earlier, incoherent and extremely identifiable sounds he and Pamela had made, he said, "We could have been quieter."

Wide-eyed with instantaneous dismay, she covered her mouth.

No! He wanted to take the words back. He adored her soft moans of arousal, the louder notes of orgasm, the fading whimpers of exhaustion. Going to her, he wrapped her in his embrace. "Not you. It was me who shouted. I was the one who was too loud. You were very ladylike."

In the stinging tone he had come to relish, she replied, "I have never heard a lady make sounds such as I did."

He chuckled. "No, you wouldn't have, would you? But you were not loud." He didn't want her self-conscious and embarrassed the next time. Although, damn it, she was right about one thing. He couldn't treat her like a mistress if he wanted her to wife. His grandfather would take him to task. Hell, *Beth* would take him to task. He would have to convince Pamela another way. But he had charm in abundance, and she had proved to be susceptible. With patience and seduction, he would bring her around to his way of thinking.

Releasing her, he went behind the screen and fetched the green velvet robe. He brought it and reluctantly held it out for her to put on. The curve of hip to waist, the long legs, the glimpse of breast . . . he couldn't believe he was dressing this woman when all he wanted was to take her to his room, place her on his bed and marvel at her perfection. "I will walk you to your bedchamber, and should we meet anyone I will make it clear you and I have been having an innocent discussion in here."

"For *how* many hours?" She slipped her arms into the sleeves. "In our nightclothes? Or rather—*your* nightclothes?"

"*And* that they are to treat you with the greatest respect or they will find themselves personally thrown into the street by me." Turning her toward him, he rolled up the overlong sleeves and frowned at the hem that draped about her feet.

"You take your role in my downfall very seriously."

Outraged, he said, "That was not a downfall. How dare you call it a downfall?"

Her mouth, wide and rosy from his kisses, quirked in a smile. "That was a misnomer. Actually, it was more of a slip."

That pleased him no more. "A slip?"

"A . . . pleasurable interlude?"

"Yes." He nodded. He agreed with that. "Very pleasurable. Also, I would like to point out the obvious. Any tinge of disgrace would be readily wiped clean by a judicious application of the wedding ceremony."

Her wide, rosy mouth tightened. "No."

"Every woman has the right to refuse." He bowed. "Just as every man has the right to pursue."

"No," she repeated with a hint of desperation.

"However, for the moment I accede to your wishes and I will stay away from you in every carnal sense."

"I'm so grateful," she snapped caustically.

He donned his robe. "You should be."

Cautiously, he opened the door. He saw no one. Moulton was nowhere around. The footmen were gone from their stations. He gestured to Pamela and she joined him, then they crept up the stairs. No one walked along the corridor at the top. The silence was spooky.

"They're avoiding us," Kerrich said.

"How kind of them." Pamela sounded as if she meant it.

He supposed she was right. Regardless of how firmly he put down any pretensions, Pamela would be made uncomfortable by their mere presence. This was better, this lonely trek down the hallway to her bedchamber.

They stood before her door, two people parting company, knowing that tomorrow in front of the others they would have to pretend nothing had happened, and unsure how to say good-bye.

"Thank you." Pamela said at last. "You made that so . . ." She glanced up shyly.

He had never seen her shy before, and he was charmed. "You were wonderful, too." Then he cursed himself for his prosaic phrasing. "What I mean is, I've never had an experience like that. I just wish . . ." He leaned one hand flat against her door.

"Yes, I wish . . ." She glanced around at their solitude. "Do you think that maybe . . ."

Beneath his robe, his organ stirred, incorrigible and valiant. "You just told me *no.* We just agreed . . ."

"You're right. Of course you are, but just this once . . ."

"Yes! All right." He had the knob turned and the door opened before she could say another word. They tumbled inside, and as he shut the door, he said, "Tonight, for the whole night. *Mais oui?*"

In the meager dawn, Kerrich stood and gazed at Pamela, slumbering and exhausted after her first night of love. She was a beacon that drew him when he should be gone. So why did he linger when, if he waited longer, the servants would be stirring, his grandfather would awake, he would meet Lewis in the corridor, and Pamela's reputation would be ruined beyond repair? Just because she refused to wed him was no reason to treat her so shabbily, and forcing marriage by exposing their liaison would begin the union in acrimony.

There was no reason to resort to those measures—yet.

He laughed softly. He held all the power in this mismatched pairing, and that was the way it should be. A grateful wife, an infatuated wife, worked to please her husband. A wife like that could never become like his mother. And after all, how hard could it be to wed and live happily? His idiot friends did it all the time.

Tying his robe firmly around his waist, he opened the door and stepped out into the corridor.

"My lord."

The whispered summons startled Kerrich, and his fists clenched automatically.

Then he saw a figure in the shadows. "Moulton," he snarled. "What in the devil are you doing here?"

"I wouldn't dream of disturbing you, sir, except we have had a development." Moulton beckoned Kerrich toward the stairway.

Recalled to their shared duty, Kerrich followed him down to the library. The door was closed, but a glimmer of light showed underneath. Moulton opened it and gestured Kerrich inside.

Kerrich entered. He stopped in mid-step. The room had been ransacked. Drapes torn down, chairs overturned and cut open, locks on his desk broken, and every document he owned scattered. Furious, Kerrich turned on Moulton.

Moulton held up his hands. "I was following Mr. Athersmith tonight, my lord, on what was obviously a butterfly folly. This is the work of professionals."

"But . . . why? We've given Lewis every opportunity to search for information about the bank's finances, and left him plenty to find, too."

"It would appear the counterfeiters have discovered you are working for the government, and this is a message to you to desist."

"Desist? And let them counterfeit my banknotes? Are you mad?"

"Well." Moulton smiled that chilling smile he never showed in his persona as butler. "If you do not, they could kill you."

CHAPTER 21

Pamela stepped out of her bedchamber, vaguely sore in unmentionable places, late for the classroom, and skittish about what the day would bring. Her reputation must truly be in shambles with the housekeeping staff, and she feared their reprisals. She'd seen it happen to other girls; the servants would snigger behind their hands, smile knowingly, wink and make overloud insinuations about her and Lord Kerrich.

And she was not wearing her disguise any longer, and she missed that protection.

One of the serving maids stood in the corridor, arranging a great array of red roses in the vase on the table. Her mouth popped open as Pamela walked toward her. "Good morning, Becky," Pamela said.

"Good mornin', miss." Becky bobbed a curtsy. "Please, miss . . ."

Pamela stopped and braced herself even as the scent of roses wrapped her in memories. "Yes, Becky?"

"If ye don't mind me sayin' so, ye look beautiful this mornin'."

"Th-thank you." Pamela took another breath. Lovely scent. And the maid had been civil.

Pamela walked on.

One maid. Perhaps the tale wasn't all over the house. Or perhaps Becky liked her well enough to ignore it.

No matter. Pamela was not a helpless child like the girls whose reputations had been destroyed by one illicit night. Those girls cowered and blinked through tears, looking longingly while the man—the seducer—pretended not to see.

Pamela would never be like that. She had too much pride. She had refused Kerrich's proposal of marriage!

Of course, it was the proposal that almost had her cowering and tearful. That temporary insanity of his had frightened her half to death, and only when she argued had he withdrawn his offer. And why had she been frightened? She hated the answer even while she faced it.

She had wanted to accept. To throw caution to the wind, to take her chances on a rake . . . and spend the rest of her life weeping as he nightly walked out of the door.

No, that was not the life for her. She'd done the right thing, and this morning he would undoubtedly be grateful to her and ashamed that he'd ever even mentioned it.

She walked toward the classroom, past a maid polishing a mirror—the same mirror, over and over again, sneaking glances at Pamela. Striving for a degree of normalcy, Pamela said, "Good morning, Sheila."

Sheila jumped as if caught doing something she shouldn't, curtsied and hurried away. Then, before she turned the corner, she spoke, all in a rush. "Miss Lockhart? Ye're pretty."

"Thank you, Sheila." This wasn't as bad as she'd feared. The servants seemed unaware of the private events of the previous evening. Had Moulton somehow maintained his discretion? So were the servants truly ignorant? That seemed almost too good to be true, but—

A cheerful voice behind her said, "'Ow are ye this mornin', miss?"

Pamela glanced at Dorothy as she passed by, her arms full of linens. "Good morning."

"Ye're lookin' fair pleasin', miss."

Pamela relaxed. Maybe it was true. Perhaps they hadn't thought anything about closed doors, the robes, the long silence. Strange though it might be, perhaps her transformation did occupy all their attention. After all, none of the servants had seen her true appearance before. No powder. No rouge. And dry.

Her own reflection in one of the wall mirrors caught her attention, and she stopped to gaze on herself. Her appearance *was* pleasing this morning. She had discarded those annoying dark spectacles, her complexion glowed with its natural color, she still wore knitting needles in her coiffure, but rather more loosely, and her dress was . . . not good. She had packed only Lady Temperly's dresses when she'd come to Lord Kerrich's. She could scarcely complain that she had to wear the dowager-styled kerseymere now. At least the purple changed her eyes from plain blue to an intense violet. Very attractive, should she run into . . . well . . . anyone who was interested.

So with a poise that no longer felt feigned, she walked into the classroom—and her aplomb failed her.

Kerrich was there. Kerrich and Beth, heads together, laughing. Kerrich . . . dear heavens, with the morning light shining around his head and his coat of dark blue travel wear, the man was *audibly* handsome.

Smoothly he came to his feet, smiling at her in an intimate manner that had her blushing. How did one react to the man who had last seen her naked, panting, and desperate? How could one behave habitually when she remembered how he looked, his arms upraised, his nude figure gleaming in the firelight?

Blessing the discipline instilled by years of courtesy, she dipped into a curtsy. "My lord."

He bowed, still looking at her, still smiling. "Miss Lockhart."

He said nothing else, but hearing the deep, smooth, honey tones brought up memories of his voice calling her name, begging, demanding . . .

He watched her as if she pleasured his gaze as she had pleasured his body.

Suddenly she couldn't remember if she'd buttoned her dress, or pinned on her collar, or dressed her hair. Her hand crept up her buttons to her throat, then to the chignon . . . yes, she was buttoned and pinned. Only his gaze suggested she was unclothed, and that because he was a self-confessed rake and rogue.

Beth's awe-struck voice broke into Pamela's jumbled thoughts. "Miss Lockhart, you look so beautiful."

"So beautiful," Kerrich echoed.

Primly, Pamela said, "True beauty is on the inside."

"So the wise tell us." He stepped closer to her, crowding her with his height and breadth. "But I say a little beauty on the outside never hurts."

Just being in his vicinity, breathing his scent and gazing into his sin-colored eyes, was enough to make her lose her head. She almost agreed with his absurd statement.

Rake and rogue, she reminded herself. She knew very well what to think of both of those conditions. She had only to recall her father, gone without a word. Taking her watch out of the pocket of her skirt, she looked at the curlicues on the silver case. She had only to remember her mother, grieving and alone. But . . . Pamela had lived all her life and schooled all her responses by those memories, and right now, those moments seemed far away and irrelevant.

As if the watch burned her hands, she dropped it in her pocket.

Perhaps Kerrich was not so like her father. Witness his true affection for Beth.

Self-conscious, she glanced at the watching child. His affection *was* true, wasn't it?

Beth sat at her desk, her hands folded in her lap. "I'm ready for my lessons, Miss Lockhart."

She looked as innocent as a babe, but Pamela recalled her carefree escape the day before. "Do you have your books and your slate?"

"Yes, Miss Lockhart." Beth almost sang the answer.

"She was just saying how ready she is," Kerrich said.

They both looked far too satisfied, and Pamela answered tartly, "As long as she wasn't saying how very much she wanted to return to the racetrack."

She couldn't believe it when the two exchanged guilty glances. "Didn't you two learn your lesson yesterday?" she demanded.

"Lord Kerrich did." Beth rubbed the pocket in her pinafore. "He learned not to bet the horses against me."

"I'm not taking her to the track again," Kerrich hastily assured Pamela.

"He's kind of a crabby loser," Beth confided. "Miss Lockhart, did he ever tell you why he took me?"

"You shouldn't call Lord Kerrich a poor loser. It isn't polite," Pamela said. "And no, he never informed me why he took you to that dreadfully inappropriate place." She glared at him.

He didn't notice. He was glaring at Beth. "I came to the classroom this morning on a different errand."

"I just thought Miss Lockhart might understand why you took me if you explained—"

Kerrich interrupted without remorse. "I have both sad news and gratifying news. We won't be able to go to my estate in Norfolk, after all."

"Oh, dear." Pamela had looked forward to introducing Beth to the countryside, and to being there herself.

"The gratifying news is, we can't go because we have an invitation that can't be refused." With a flourish, he removed a folded, stiff paper from his pocket, and showed them the seal. "Because it comes from Her Majesty herself!"

The blood drained from Pamela's head, and she snatched the invitation from his hand.

He chuckled as he watched her, obviously reading her alarm as excitement, and recited the invitation as she read it. " 'Her Majesty Queen Victoria, sovereign and monarch of the British Isles, commands the presence of Devon Mathewes, the earl of Kerrich, and his ward, Miss Elizabeth Hunter, at a reception at Buckingham Palace three days hence at four o' the clock in the afternoon.' "

Pamela sighed in relief. She hadn't been invited.

"Yes, isn't this good news?" Kerrich exclaimed.

Beth didn't look as if she thought it was good news. She looked petrified—and guilt swamped Pamela. If Pamela were going, she would be there to comfort and instruct Beth.

"I knew as soon as we allowed Beth to participate in society that the queen would hear about it," he said. "One of those dear, gossipy ladies must have rushed right over and told her."

Kneeling beside Beth, Pamela tucked a few stray strands of hair into the child's short braid. She was glad to be excluded, but in penance she would ruthlessly coach Beth in the three days before the reception.

"Victoria must be in a ferment of curiosity to have put us on the guest list so quickly," Kerrich continued. "This reception has been planned for months."

"You have done everything we required of you," Pamela said softly to Beth. "You have proved your bravery beyond doubt."

Impervious, Kerrich charged on. "Before, I wasn't invited because it's one of those family events Prince Albert dotes on, and I'm not seen as respectable enough to mingle with parents and children."

Pamela told Beth, "You will dress in your prettiest gown, the one with the ruffles which you have so longed to wear."

"Of course, I wouldn't have gone anyway, but all that's changed now. All because of Beth. Look, it's written here on the side, 'Miss Elizabeth will be presented to Her Majesty Queen Victoria at six o' the clock.' " He looked down and realized something was going on right beneath his nose. "Why aren't you happy?"

Annoyed by his insensitivity, Pamela snapped, "My lord, you are like the rooster who thinks the sun rises to hear you crow."

He looked startled, but apparently not even her impudence was enough to ruin his expansive mood. "I've been blathering on. Well, I'm pleased. You have both done well." He inspected Beth's pale countenance. "What's wrong?"

"She's never met our queen before," Pamela said.

"Of course she hasn't. That would be the idea."

"She's nervous."

"I am," Beth said in a small voice.

"You? Nervous?" Clearly, Kerrich couldn't imagine such

an instance. "You're not afraid of me. Why would you be afraid of her?"

"Because she's the queen. She's important," Beth declared.

Pamela plucked her handkerchief from her sleeve and covered her mouth with it, but nothing could contain her muffled laughter.

Kerrich's lowering scowl promised retribution. Then he knelt beside Beth. "I have known Her Majesty for years, and I assure you, she is very kind, very young, and very pretty. She is easily charmed, and you are charming. You will win her heart immediately."

Beth jollied up. "Really?"

Pamela might have been offended that Kerrich so easily reassured the child when Pamela herself couldn't. Instead she saw the good use he made of his glib patter, and she was grateful.

"I have my faults, but I'm not a liar," he told Beth. "I have complete confidence in you."

A cautious smile broke over her face. "I'm not a liar, either," she told him. "I used to be afraid of you. Now . . ." She flung her arms around his neck.

He returned the hug with obvious surprise, then stood her on her feet and rose. "However, the consequence of all these good tidings is that I have to go to Norfolk to check on the bank. I had planned to do it when I was at Brookford, but that's out. The servants are even now seeking Mr. Athersmith so he may accompany me, and the carriage is waiting. So . . ." He swatted Beth on the rear. "I'm ready to go, but I forgot my fawn kid gloves. Could I send you to seek out my valet and get them from him?"

Beth beamed at him and curtsied. "Gladly, Lord Kerrich."

She ran out of the classroom while Pamela gazed after

her with proud tenderness. "That was very good of you, my lord."

"Further proof that there isn't a woman I can't charm."

Disconcerted by the cool declaration, she looked and found him stalking toward her, wearing an expression of absolute licentiousness.

"After all, I charmed *you*, Miss Pamela Lockhart, did I not?"

She backed up and tried not to be charmed all over again. "My lord, your charm is of concern to no one but yourself."

"When did you again start calling me 'my lord?' " Catching her by the shoulders, he held her in front of him.

"We agreed this"—she shrugged her shoulders—"would not be a good idea."

"We *agreed* you would call me Devon."

"We did not agree that," she answered indignantly. "I yielded to your demand under the greatest of blackmail."

"So you did." He smiled at her, that winning smile that made her remember just what form his blackmail took. "I could make you surrender again."

"Unwise, my lord, unwise!" Her heart thrummed, confirming the excitement she denied within her mind.

"I'm going to be gone for two whole days."

"Farewell." She held out her hand as if to shake his. "Have a pleasant journey."

He brushed her hand away, moved so close he crushed her petticoats, and slid his hands off her shoulders and down her spine to her bottom. "We should share one last kiss before I go."

She clutched at his arms even as she said, "Certainly not!"

"After all"—he bent his head to hers and lifted her up toward him—"with the carriage waiting outside and the child returning, we can take it no further."

Somehow her lips found their way to his. They strained together, and he feasted on her like a starving man. No matter that they'd loved too many times last night; as she tasted him, the hunger rose in her, sharp and prodigious. Breaking off the kiss, he bussed her cheeks, her forehead, her chin while she clung to him and wished they were alone, it was night . . . and all the rights and wrongs of their situation had vanished.

When his hand slipped to her breast, she thought she must burst into flames. And a flaming governess seemed a poor excuse for a teacher. "Beth will return."

He caressed one last time, then admitted, "I know." Leaning his forehead against hers, he stared into her eyes. "I know. If you married me, I would shower you with kisses like that every day."

She still gasped and trembled, but she said, "You promised!"

"What did I promise?"

"That you . . . you *agreed* not to press me for marriage."

"I didn't. Last night. But I have reconsidered. You should take me. I'm a good man. You'd never know about my mistresses."

She got her breath back in one long inhale. "You mistake goodness for discretion. Please, my lord, release me."

He did, rather abruptly, and his voice rose. "You won't accept money and you scorn discretion. What will it take to make you marry me?"

Now he was acting as she expected a thwarted man to act. Petulantly. "I don't wish to marry, and that is no surprise to you. I *told* you I would not. You *know* about my father." She touched the watch in her pocket.

"I am not your father."

"Neither are you the man I would ever choose."

Fists on hips, he gazed at her through narrowed eyes.

"*Ever* is a long time." His smile beamed forth so suddenly she blinked. "So I will ask you every day."

Had he been using his disapprobation to test her resolve? "I still don't understand why you would wed me at all."

"Because your body calls to me to fill it."

"My lord, we are in a classroom where innocent children learn!"

"Because I find myself in a violent ferment of desire which not even a night of you has fulfilled."

"Sh!" She glanced toward the open door and prayed that one of the servants hadn't heard.

"Because I can bear the thought of your company for the next fifty years with equanimity."

Prepared to shush him again, she found herself saying flatly, "A high compliment, indeed."

"I am not the kind of man to tell silly tales to the woman he plans to spend his life with, and I did not think, Pamela, that you were the type of female who wished to hear such tales."

"No." *Yes*. "No." She couldn't bear this. A male human was nothing more than a primitive creature who disregarded his heart, loved with his brain, and thought with his organ. Without a doubt the attractive ones were worse. She'd seen her mother die of grief for a man.

Now here was Kerrich, and who was he really?

And why did she care?

Anxiously, she searched for a topic of innocuous conversation and blurted out one of her worries instead. "I hope there's no trouble about the library."

He stiffened. "The library. What's wrong with the library?"

"We left a bit of a mess last night when we . . . when we left last night."

He stared at her as if he had just caught her stealing the

silver, then he released a slow sigh of what sounded like relief. "Don't worry. Moulton has closed it up today, and he's taking care of it."

"Good." *I'll only have to be embarrassed by Moulton.* But there was no use bringing that to Kerrich's attention. He didn't even know most of his servants' names. He certainly wouldn't comprehend being embarrassed by a minion's insight. Picking up her pointer, she twirled it in her hands and carefully avoided looking at him.

Part of the trouble with Kerrich was that he wasn't offended when she snapped at him, not even now, when she had discarded the façade of sour Miss Lockhart and became young Pamela. He was gorgeous, rich, titled, and so indifferent to sentiment that he planned to use a child to keep a fortune in his already wealthy bank. Yet he was spending time with Beth, apparently for the pleasure of her company. And he had succeeded in seducing Pamela, yet still he insisted he wished to wed her when he should be wiping sweaty drops of relief from his forehead that she had refused him!

Beth ran into the room. "Lord Kerrich, your valet says you have the gloves in your greatcoat."

"Ah, how foolish of me." He touched his finger to her nose. "Thank you so much for helping me."

Beth beamed beneath his praise.

When Beth had met the queen and his scheme came to fruition, he would show his true colors. He would demand Pamela show respect when she felt none. He would coldly discard Beth. He would pay Pamela off and go seeking another lover.

Then the earth would be round, the sky would be blue, the sun would rise in the east, everything Pamela believed in would be true, and her life would return to normal.

CHAPTER 22

"How was your trip, my lord?" Moulton asked late the next afternoon as he helped Kerrich off with his coat.

"As foul as foul can be." With an imperious gesture, Kerrich waved away the swarming footmen. "I discovered the whereabouts of the mysterious disappearing Mr. Athersmith."

Moulton lowered his voice. "He was at your estate in Norfolk?"

"Not at Brookford, but he had been at the bank." Kerrich stripped off his gloves and stuffed them in his hat. "On my business, he told my employees."

"And they believed him?"

"Why would they not?" As Kerrich walked past, he handed the hat to the footman. "I have confided my troubles in no one."

Moulton trailed him to the vase of roses displayed prominently on a table. "Of course, you're right, my lord. What did Mr. Athersmith do at the bank?"

Leaning down, Kerrich sniffed a particularly lovely blossom and thought of Pamela. "He stole a large quantity of the special, watermarked paper on which we print our notes. Concluding they worked on my command, my employees helped him carry it out. They were pleased with themselves."

Moulton stared in blank amazement. "The ballocks of the man!"

"I didn't know he had it in him," Kerrich said wearily. "Any developments here?"

"Mr. Athersmith has disappeared from London, although now I know why, and without him we're no closer to discovering the creator of this plot."

"You weren't doing too well *with* him."

"No need to be critical, my lord," Moulton said, and then proceeded to be exactly that. "Although the officials at the Bank of England are the least efficient I've ever worked for. They insist on using their own people where we professionals should do the job, and this is the result. We're left with nothing but a cold trail."

Pulling a rose from the bouquet, Kerrich twirled it in his fingers. "Perhaps Lewis's band will return to my estate to do their printing."

"We're watching the site—or at least the bank officials claim someone is—but the villains realize you have knowledge or they wouldn't have shredded your study. And to be frank, they can abandon that printing press because they can afford a new one now." Moulton was tight-lipped with frustration. "If we can find your cousin, my lord, we will arrest him, regardless of your wishes."

Kerrich nodded. He'd done what he could to rescue Lewis. The Mathewes family name would suffer, but Kerrich was damned tired of worrying about his cousin when he had a queen to pacify and a betrothal to enforce. "As long as I'm not going to hang with him."

"Is that what they told you?" Moulton shook his head. "Not a chance, my lord."

Kerrich had thought the bank gentlemen were bluffing; cheering news to know he was right. "Good. I'm planning on marrying, and prison would interfere."

Moulton's smirk blossomed. "If I may, I would offer my congratulations and say you have chosen a lovely young lady."

Presumptuous, of course, but for the moment Moulton was the butler, and a good butler always knew what was happening in the house. "Don't tell her that," Kerrich advised. "She'll give you a lecture on the shallowness of outer beauty."

"Quite." The two men exchanged a grin.

Kerrich gestured toward the closed door of the library. "How is the mess?"

"I told my men what happened, and we've confided in a few of the trustworthy footmen. Told them there was a robbery, but you wished that no one be alarmed. We've been quietly cleaning it up. It looks acceptable, if somewhat denuded. I've kept it locked, for I've had to keep an eye on some of the maids. They're incredibly curious."

Finally, Kerrich asked the question he'd come through the door wanting to ask. "Where is Miss Lockhart?"

Moulton proved himself not only one of the sleuthing world's most efficient operators, but also an accomplished source of information. "She is upstairs with the child," he said. "Shall I send for her?"

"Have her come to the drawing room."

When Kerrich walked in the drawing room, he wondered why he hadn't said the game room or the lounge or the ballroom. He couldn't relax in this room. He couldn't even sit down. His mother had decorated this chamber. He had deliberately left it as it was so he would always be reminded of that day after his father's death when he had found her in the embrace of a stranger. Why tonight did he choose this room in which to meet Pamela? Was his mind hinting that he should rethink his determination to wed any woman who affected the emotions he had constantly and carefully safeguarded?

He'd always thought his wife would be a woman of little mind and average beauty, one who let him do all the thinking, one who would not be a temptation to other men, or a temptation to him. Pamela was not what he'd planned, and he knew if he gave up on his scheme to wed her, she'd be relieved. So why not—

"My lord, you sent for me?"

The sound of her crisp voice halted his wayward thoughts. She was here—the no-nonsense, frank, sparkling Miss Lockhart and the handsome, passionate, determined Pamela. Two women blended into this one, this perfect woman. The woman he wanted. Every time he saw her, he grew more and more sure. He had to have her.

He would just make sure she never knew the depths of that need.

She still wore a dowager gown, bunched at the shoulders and wide at the waist. Her hair was pulled back as tightly as it had ever been, and the knitting needles were back in place as if that would halt his passion—and disguise hers. She was frowning, the ferocious frown she had used with such success when she had played the role of the sour old governess. Unfortunately for her, the gown and the coiffure poorly camouflaged her figure and her loveliness, and without her disfiguring cosmetics that frown lent a piquant air to her even features and made Kerrich want to kiss it away.

Of course, probably he would want to kiss away any expression she wore, save an expression of longing.

Extending the rose, he said, "I missed you."

She closed her eyes, obviously not in ecstasy. "My lord, we have agreed that the other night was an aberration, not to be repeated, and I must beg that you don't say such things to me."

Pamela was too intelligent, too saucy, too sure of herself, and even in that ridiculous ensemble, far, far too beautiful. Taking advantage of her closed eyes, he sprang across the room to her side. "I love to hear you beg."

Opening her eyes, she jumped back.

Ah, she wasn't nearly as impervious as she would like him to believe. Certainly the way she viewed him bespoke some emotion, even if that emotion was nothing more than alarm.

"Depth and passion hide in the rose's scent." He held the flower before his nose. "Don't you agree?"

"One would have to travel far before one finds a person who does not love the scent of roses."

He brushed the flower underneath her chin. "The scent reminds me of a transcendent evening I spent with the lady I will wed."

She tried to hold her breath. He saw her try, but she couldn't. Not and say what she was driven to say.

"I don't want to be reminded, and I'm not going to wed you." Taking a breath, she refilled her lungs with the scent of the rose, and her expression perceptibly softened. "You sent for me, my lord?"

"I want a kiss." Before she could refuse, he quickly added, "It was a ghastly trip. I've got problems at the bank, and not just the difficulty threatened by Queen Victoria. I've uncovered treachery, too"—he rubbed his aching forehead—"and that of the kind that breaks my heart. All that sustained me was knowing you were here in my house and when I got home, I would get—" He broke off. What had gotten into him that he prattled on in such a manner? Ladies should be protected from life's difficulties. With his best irresistible smile, he said, "You're being incredibly patient with my complaints."

She looked at him as if he were mad. "No. I thought you were talking to me as if I were—" Now she broke off.

"My wife?"

She was shaken; he saw it in her face. But he was no less disturbed. The casual, occasional conversations he had foreseen for his marriage did not include intimacy of thought and experience.

Stepping up to him, she wrapped her arms around his neck. "One kiss."

His wife should be a decoration on his arm, a hostess in his home, a mother to the faceless, nameless and well-behaved children they would breed.

Her fingers tangled in his hair.

He didn't want his wife thinking she had the right to know his business or share his concerns.

She pressed her lips to his.

He didn't want his wife thinking at all.

Then *he* wasn't thinking. He dropped the rose and gathered Pamela close, lifting her onto her toes. The scent of her, the feel of her, the taste of her was what he needed to clear away the hurt of a cousin's continued betrayal, his worry about the queen's threat and the rapidly approaching reception. They kissed as if they were lovers reunited after a long and painful absence. As if together they made one whole person. As if they were in love.

Her lips opened beneath his and she accepted his tongue gladly, then sucked at it with gentle pressure. The eroticism of her action brought his imagination to life, and he dreamed of lying flat on his back while she used her mouth on him.

They needed more time together. He needed more privacy to tempt her as he knew she could be tempted. He wanted to possess her, over and over, until she desired him so much she would willingly call him master.

Knowing Pamela, the loving would have to be prolonged and intense—and if he were lucky, she would hold out for a long, long time.

The scent of rose surrounded them. He looked down to see they'd crushed the blossom beneath their feet, and Pamela—Pamela was melting in his arms.

Using all his persuasive powers, he said, "We can't continue in this manner. We must be together."

He meant in marriage, but she said, "Yes. Now. Shut the door." Her willingness and her demand caught him by surprise, but he wasn't a fool. If her desire for him was inexorable, he would not object.

"Not in here," he said. Not in here, with the ghost of his mother and her lover mocking him.

Taking Pamela's arm, he hustled her out the door and toward the library. Moulton saw them and without in any way revealing his thoughts, sprang forward, key extended. But as he fit it in the lock, the door swung slightly on its hinges.

Both men stopped. The door was open. Gently, Kerrich put his finger on his lips to indicate the need for silence, then shooed Pamela back. Like a charging brigade, Moulton slammed the door back and dashed through the entrance, Kerrich on his heels.

There, sitting at the desk viewing all the account books, sat Lord Reynard, a glass of whisky at his elbow. The old man's mouth was puckered, and he stroked his chin as he viewed the aghast Moulton, then Kerrich. "Interesting stuff you have here, Devon. Complete nonsense, of course."

Kerrich exchanged a glance with Moulton. "Sir, I . . ."

Lord Reynard looked beyond them. "Ah, Miss Lockhart, are you a part of this conspiracy, too?"

Kerrich saw her peeking around the door, and said hastily, "No, sir, she's not."

"Then, much as I hate to interrupt your wooing, perhaps she should leave."

Kerrich went toward her, but she backed away as if he were the carrier of some dreaded disease.

"I left Beth with Corliss." She didn't look at him. She didn't look at anyone. Her cheeks were red, and her spine was as stiff as ever Miss Lockhart's had been. "I must go back. If you would excuse me, my lords." Curtsying, she hurried off.

"I embarrassed her." Lord Reynard made a tsking noise with his tongue. "And just when things were going so well."

"Yes," Kerrich murmured, looking after her. "I wish I hadn't . . ."

"No use wishing you hadn't, yet. There'll be plenty of time for that after you're married. You'll wish you hadn't said this, and swear you hadn't done that . . . you are going to marry Miss Lockhart, aren't you?" Lord Reynard leveled a stern gaze on him.

"I have asked her, sir."

"Beg her. Women like men who grovel."

"I am not so far gone as that, sir."

"Really?" Lord Reynard got that grandfatherly smirk on his face.

"If you would excuse me, my lords." Here Moulton tried to make his escape, with a bow and a few murmured phrases.

"Shut the door, Moulton, and stay," Lord Reynard commanded. "I told you before—I recognize a man from Bow

Street environs when I see him." He waved a hand at the chairs before the desk.

Both men seated themselves, Kerrich with resignation and Moulton with great discomfort.

Lord Reynard folded his hands before him and leaned forward. The amiable old gentleman was gone. They faced the man who had been raised in poverty, taken control of a bank and made his family's fortune through shrewd intelligence and utter ruthlessness. "Now. A few of my old friends still have connections in the Bank of England, and rumors of counterfeiting are starting to swirl. These books"—Lord Reynard pushed the dummy accounts away—"are fraudulent. So it's time to explain to your old grandfather just what's going on."

Lord Reynard's genial tone didn't fool Kerrich, and he said, "You see, sir, Lewis met this girl . . ."

When Kerrich had finished the tale, the old man pursed his lips. "I never knew Lewis had it in him."

Leaning back in his chair, Kerrich said, "Neither did I, but he's having an affair with some great lady, he's in love with Miss Fotherby, and he's involved in stealing from the Mathewes Bank and the Bank of England."

"Busy boy," Grandpapa commented. "But I don't care. I've known that lad since he was in nappies, and Lewis's mind isn't convoluted enough to think up such an intricate plot to counterfeit money."

"No, my lord," Moulton said. "We know he is working for someone, but we cannot find out who."

"I knew the boy was in trouble, but I had no idea how much." He turned to Moulton. "Is he going to hang?"

Moulton looked grim and nodded. "The best he could hope for is transport."

"Damn. I hate to see that happen. He's my sister's grandson." Lord Reynard sipped his whisky. "But you have to catch him first. Do you know how you're going to do it?"

"No, sir," Moulton said.

Lord Reynard put his glass down with a snap. "Then I'll tell you."

Pamela crumpled the note. She couldn't believe Kerrich's gall. He summoned her to him *now*, when the queen's party was not four hours hence and she was supervising the maids as they prepared Beth.

Although the maids didn't really need any supervision. Today, with no struggle, Beth had taken a bath. Her white, ruffled gown with the blue velvet sash was laid out. So many cheerful, helpful maids were crowded into the bedchamber, Pamela didn't have a place to sit, but still . . . she wanted to be there for little Beth. The sweet child needed her for reassurance.

Going to Beth, she knelt beside her. "Darling, Lord Kerrich demands to see me."

"All right," Beth said brightly as she turned her head to let Corliss take another rag curler out of her hair.

"But I won't go if you want me to stay here with you."

Beth nodded and watched her hair bounce in the mirror. "You can go."

"Your happiness is more important to me than Lord Kerrich's summons."

"I'm happy. Go ahead." Touching the newly formed

curls, Beth asked, "Corliss, I want these forever."

The maids laughed indulgently, and Corliss said, "Really, Miss Lockhart, there's no need for you to stay. When it's time to go, we'll have Beth ready to meet Her Majesty, and you know you can't refuse the master."

For one brief moment, Pamela was horrified. Did everyone know she couldn't refuse Kerrich?

Then she realized Corliss meant she couldn't refuse the master's *summons*. "No, I suppose I can't." Reluctantly, she stood up, edged toward the door and out into the corridor.

Moulton spoke quietly from the shadows. "Miss Lockhart, this way."

Startled, she caught her breath.

"Beg pardon, miss. Lord Kerrich has instructed that I bring you to him." He led her down the long corridor with its blaze of candles and on every table a vase of roses. Then they walked into the gallery, their heels clicking on the polished hardwood floor. They passed open guest bedchambers rich with color and fabric, through a game room with a billiards table, and at last they turned into the other wing. The family wing, with the family bedchambers.

Pamela's cheeks burned. Kerrich didn't mean for her to come to his bedchamber . . . did he? Just because she had given him an inappropriate invitation yesterday, and just because his grandfather had been in the library, and just because she and Kerrich had been left frustrated—that was no reason for Kerrich to think he could call for her any time he wanted a romp. Hadn't she been humiliated enough in front of Lord Reynard?

Moulton stopped before the double doors that led to the master suite and flung them open. Stepping back, he bowed.

Cheeks burning, lips pressed together, fingers knotted, Pamela looked at him.

In a rush, Moulton said, "No, miss! It's not like that.

Please, no one but me knows where you are and I wouldn't . . . I am the soul of discretion."

There could be no doubt. He *was* the soul of discretion, or word of her downfall would be all over London by now. Still she hesitated until Kerrich stepped into the doorway. He hadn't changed yet; he wore a plain white shirt with the sleeves rolled up and trousers with no boots, and he sported an impish grin.

"Come in." He gestured. "We haven't much time."

The words were ominous. His expression was not.

"Stop glaring," he said. "I have a surprise for you."

Although still disinclined and braced for a fight, she tentatively entered the chamber.

"Not the kind of surprise you're obviously imagining." Circling her, he stepped behind and placed his hands on her shoulders. "Miss Lockhart, you should do something about that salacious turn of mind."

He sounded so happy, and she wished she were anywhere but here. For she struggled with the strong suspicion Kerrich thought that she was also attending the party.

A suspicion that immediately proved correct. "I had hoped to catch you before you started to get ready."

Moulton shut the door behind her, sealing her into the richly decorated room with Kerrich. A fire burned on the hearth, candles were lit everywhere, and a vase of roses bloomed on a table placed beside a comfortable armchair. She looked longingly back at the entrance.

"I have something for you." Taking her hand, Kerrich kissed it lingeringly, then pulled her toward his bed. The massively carved and ancient monster was swathed with bed curtains of rich blue-purple and accents of scarlet and gold.

There, on the coverlet, lay a gown. A beautiful gown. A proper gown. A perfect gown of gleaming gray taffeta, with black net over rose taffeta decorating the modest neckline. The sleeves were flared, the cuffs decorated with the same net and rose taffeta, and around the hem of the full skirt wound another stripe of rose and net. If she'd been offered her choice of gowns to wear to the queen's reception, this was the one she would have picked—and her heart sank.

"This one was my favorite," he said, "but I had Madame Beauchard deliver several."

Delicate lady's unmentionables in her size were stacked beside the gown. A lacy chemise and matching pantalettes. A corset of the finest silk. Crisp petticoats. Thin stockings and, on the floor, gray slippers.

He had thought of everything.

It would have been so much better if Kerrich hadn't laid eyes on her until she kissed Beth good-bye and it was too late for a confrontation. Then she wouldn't have to try and make excuses, and she could at least put off her explanations. So she stared at the exquisite thing and said, "It's lovely, but—"

He held up his hand. "I know what you're going to say. You can't accept a gift like this from a man. Not even from me. But you can, you see. I'm taking the cost out of your wages."

She wheeled on him. "What?"

"*Now* you're looking at me." With the ball of his thumb, he brushed her lower lip. His lips quirked, and he looked unbearably pleased with himself. "Let me give you this. It would make me very happy and, if you wish, you may consider it a bonus toward the success of our project."

She hated to wipe that expression off his face. She really hated to, but when she thought of going to Buckingham Palace, her fright rose up and almost overwhelmed her. "Thank you, but"—she swallowed—"where would I wear it?"

For a long moment, he stood immobile. His gaze swept her, noting her complete lack of preparation, and she could see his mind working, calculating, and coming up with the right answer.

His eyebrows tilted devilishly. "Did I say you could wear a different gown?" he asked. "I've changed my mind. You will wear this gown, and you will wear it to Her Majesty's reception this very afternoon."

She hated this dread that stole her breath and turned her hands cold. "I can't."

She would have explained further, but he smiled and stepped closer, crowding her against the bed. "Beloved, there is nothing you can't do." He removed the knitting needles from her chignon. He touched her collar, and it fell to the ground. He had Pamela's buttons undone and her corset loosened before she thought it possible, and her petticoats fell in a froth around her feet.

Of course. He was stripping her. No doubt he planned to stuff her into the gown and drag her to the queen's reception.

"I can't go, I wasn't included on the invitation, and one doesn't drop in unannounced on the queen."

"You are not unannounced." With a yank, he peeled everything down, leaving her clad in her chemise and stockings.

The man could give lessons on how to undress a woman. Would-be rakes would line up for miles.

"When I responded to Her Majesty, I responded for Grandpapa and you. Grandpapa, because he is my houseguest and one of her favorite friends, and she is very loyal to her friends. You, because you are Beth's governess and no one, not even Victoria herself, expects me to handle a girl-child on my own." He smiled into her eyes.

She saw the steel behind that pleasantry. "It's not so

easy. I've met Her Majesty." Pamela walked a delicate line. She didn't want him to remember, yet she wanted him to understand. To let her off. "Years ago when she was a child."

"Really." He stripped the coverlet off his bed, and laid it, and the gown and its accoutrements, flat on the floor. "I wish I had known that. I would have mentioned it in my note to Queen Victoria."

"No!" In a turmoil, she watched him throw the blankets back and bare the sheets.

"But you have told me so little of your past, you are almost a stranger to me in almost every way that matters." Placing his hands on her waist, he hoisted her up onto the mattress. "Yet we communicate in one way very well. Shall I remind you?"

With a shock, she realized she had been foolish. Kerrich hadn't been stripping her to force her into that gown. He had been stripping her to . . . to . . . "You can't do this!" she protested.

"Yes." Grabbing the waist of her pantalettes, he pulled them down and sent her tumbling backward. "I can. You used me to rectify the wrongs done to you. Now I'll use you to cure my frustration, and this, at least, is fair."

Clawing at the sheets, she tried to right herself. "No, it's not!"

"You were revenging yourself on other men. On boors who treated you badly." He spread her legs. "My frustration is with *you*."

"No. We don't have time. No. Kerrich, no."

He mounted the bed and grabbed her flailing wrists, and imitated her protests. "Yes. Yes. Pamela, yes."

Her heartbeat picked up when he placed both hands over her head and held them there.

"You are the most recalcitrant woman I have ever met."

He pushed her chemise up around her neck. "I do something so thoughtful it amazes even me. Something which would send every other woman of my acquaintance into paroxysms of ecstasy." Still kneeling between her legs, he looked her over.

All over. The breasts, the waist, the patch of dark hair between her legs. With a dip of his head, he took her nipple into his mouth and suckled, then licked it repeatedly until she squirmed against the sheets. She ought to kick him. She ought to . . . She lifted her foot.

"Don't even consider it," he said. "You owe me a cure for my frustration."

"I don't owe—"

He bit her nipple. Not hard, but enough to bring her arching off the mattress.

He stripped off his pants with one hand. "I was afraid you would object to the fact I'd bought you a gown. Can you believe that? I imagined you would be so conventional as to worry about the propriety of a man buying something as personal as clothing for a woman not his wife. But no. Not you. You have to be different."

In desperation, she said, "This isn't nice."

"It certainly isn't." His long finger slid smoothly inside of her. "That's why it excites you."

"No." She writhed, extracting the sensation of his hand against her. "It shouldn't." What kind of woman was she, to be aroused by the scent of Kerrich, the warmth of him above her, his grip on her wrists and the threat of his possession? Aroused when she should be indignant at being exploited and handled and overcome.

"Try to be honest about one thing, at least." He kissed her neck. He nipped at her ear, then ran his tongue slowly around the rim. "Tell me you want this."

From somewhere, she managed to summon enough pride to say, "No."

Sitting back, he smiled at her, that wicked, luscious mouth mocking her feeble denial. "When I'm inside you, I'm going to get all the way in, right to the mouth of your womb"—his finger stroked up, not far enough, but up—"and you're going to want me so much you'll wrap your legs around my hips and lift yourself to me. I'm going to move in and out slowly"—he imitated his threat—"then faster, and all the time you're going to be just on the verge of climax. You'll beg me. Can't you imagine your own voice crying out, saying, 'Please, Devon, please,' and it'll be better than this because it'll be my cock, stretching you wider and longer, pushing you as far as you can—"

"Please, Devon."

He chuckled, damn him. He chuckled.

But hastily he shifted, positioned himself at the entrance of her body, and just as he promised, languidly entered her.

Heaven. It was heaven. It was so good. She gasped, trying to get enough air, trying to fill her lungs so she could scream with . . . with pleasure so acute it was almost pain.

"You're still new." He spoke right in her ear. "You're still so tight. I have to move slowly so it doesn't hurt. It doesn't hurt, does it?"

He knew it didn't. He challenged her with his tone. When he released her hands, she was going to show him . . . his pelvis rested right on hers, and the heat of him warmed her all the way through. Her legs moved restlessly, her feet stroking the sheet. The rocking motion pressed him against her again, and again, still at his own leisurely pace.

She whimpered and tried to make him hurry, but he wouldn't. The muscles inside her quivered with each stroke. They wanted to spasm. She wanted . . . devil take him, if he would just bestir himself instead of keeping to this deliberate rhythm, she could finish this.

Then she remembered how he'd predicted she would wrap her legs around his hips. Wanton. Opening herself to him like that. She wasn't giving herself today. He was taking her.

But he wasn't doing it right. She lifted her hips, trying to find that perfect snippet of passion that would bring her to climax.

"You're too impatient. You have to learn to prolong your anticipation."

The swine chided her! She was ready to melt, and he was lecturing. If she opened her legs all the way, if she rubbed her legs against his, perhaps he would understand . . . and he would be inside her so deeply. Right to the mouth of her womb. Just as he promised. Wrapping her legs around his hips, she deliberately tightened her inner muscles on his organ.

He stopped. He looked down at her. Not a trace of amusement remained on his face. His eyes were red-rimmed, his nostrils flared, the skin that stretched across his features was flushed with hectic color. And he asked, "Pamela, what do you want?"

She tossed her head from side to side, trying to deny him, but finally she said, "You. I want you. All the way in. Now."

He gave her himself. In an explosion of heat and motion, he thrust into her, filling her all the way, satisfying one need, creating another. The mattress rocked and creaked. She moaned and he groaned. When he released her hands, she clutched at his hair, his shoulders, his back. Anything to try and save herself from the devastating passion that swept her along. Swept them along.

Climax struck her like a bolt of lightning, starting deep

inside and radiating outward, consuming her entire body, shaking her soul. He wrapped his hand in her hair. He held her still and stared into her eyes. As she trembled with her rapture and he lunged to reach his, she heard the firm demand of his mind and his body.

Mine, he declared wordlessly. *You're mine*.

So she closed her eyes to shut him out and instead savored every last twitch and spasm, both his and hers.

They were done. The silence that fell was absolute. Her heartbeat slowed. She got her breath back under control. She got her *self* back under control.

But she didn't have the nerve to open her eyes until he said, "I'm feeling more like it. How about you?" He lifted himself away before she had time to look at him, time to respond. "I'll certainly try not to think of this when I'm speaking to Her Majesty, and I suggest you try and control your wayward thoughts, also."

He sounded for all the world like a man who regularly encountered earth-shaking experiences, and found this one rather commonplace.

The mattress creaked as he descended from the bed.

In slothful movements, she rose to lean on her elbow and watched him fasten his trousers. "I'm not going."

Picking the beautiful new gown up off the floor, he tossed it on the bed. "Cease your missishness and dress yourself at once."

He wasn't arguing. He was ordering. He placed the undergarments beside her with no sympathy for her plight at all. And she was still weak. Her legs still shook. Her thighs were damp. Her hair straggled around her shoulders. She felt . . . well, she felt as if he'd succeeded. As if he'd used her. Or as if . . . as if he'd offered her more than she, trapped in the remains of her childish fears, had dared accept.

"Get up," he said.

Pamela dragged at her snarled chemise, tucking her knees up against her body and dragging the hem down as far as it would go. "This reception is the culmination of your plans, my lord. When you take Beth up to meet the queen, you will be pronounced a respectable person and all your troubles will be over."

His eyes narrowed on her. "I don't understand your complaint. Did you think I would deny you credit for all you have done for the child?"

She lifted her chin, concealing the depths of her fright with a waspish tongue. "This world is divided into people who do things and people who get the credit. I do things. *I* don't need to go to this reception to prove myself Her Majesty's respectable, hard working subject."

"You ought to be spanked," he said in a falsely affable tone. "But I don't have time."

In the flash of his temper, she saw a glimpse of the real Kerrich, and he frightened her. "Please, I can't." She grasped the bedpost. "Those people know me."

"What people?"

"The nobles. The *ton*. The people who know about my father." If only she could conceal herself from his freezing indifference! "They'll look at me and pity me. I won't go."

"Those people don't matter."

She glared into his eyes. "To you! You're the earl of Kerrich! No one dares laugh at you or make condescending comments about how low you've fallen or offer false sympathy for your losses."

"Oh? When my father died and my mother began her rampage through the male population, I was ten years old. Do you know how many fights I fought for her good name? Which was more than she ever did!" He was livid. So livid he was shouting. "Do you know how many times I broke my nose for that woman?"

Pamela backed up against the bed post and shook her head.

"Twice." He held up two fingers. "Then she left me. Left me with Grandpapa and went off to the continent with the first of her traveling lovers. She still drops in every once in a while and doesn't understand why I'm not more fond. When she betrayed my father's memory in the basest way and abandoned me to the laughter of fools." Slowly he clenched his fist, then pointed one of his fingers at her. "You're not going to abandon us like that."

"I'm not trying to abandon you."

"Beth deserves better than that, even if you think I don't."

He made her so angry, with his callous disregard and his attitude that everything affected only him. "Don't you understand? I don't want to be humiliated."

"You're going to have to face them sooner or later," he said. "It might as well be now."

She sat there on the bed, clutching her chemise in both her fists and doing her best to convey scorn. "I would think, since you have been through this, that you would be more sympathetic."

"More sympathetic to being abandoned?" Gripping her ankle, he dragged her toward him. "Or more sympathetic to female megrims?"

She kicked at him, but he set her on her feet beside the bed and stripped her chemise out of her grip and off over her head.

Stepping back, he looked at her. And looked at her again. The frantic rush of activity stopped. He licked his lips as he stared at her body, but she now recognized the signs of his arousal, and this was not arousal. This was more like dawning horror and desperate comprehension.

She began to think, to suspect . . .

Drawing in a hard breath, he said, "No." He dove at her and she raised her hands in self-defense, but he had her out of everything, even her stockings, and he seemed not even to notice her bewildered resistance. Turning her to stand before the fire, he stepped back to view her. "Don't move," he commanded.

Self-conscious at his incredulous inspection, she covered herself with her hands.

"Damn it, woman, put your hands down."

She looked at him, defiant, acutely aware of her nakedness, and desperate to escape this scene.

"You," he said, and his voice shook. "Do you know who I am?"

Had he remembered that long-ago night? He had, she was sure of it. "You are Lord Kerrich."

"I've seen you before, haven't I? Years ago, the party with King William for little Princess Victoria. At Kensington Palace. You were the girl in the window."

She thought begging to be allowed to miss the reception was the worst humiliation she could endure, but it was nothing compared to this.

"I was angry," he said. "I took the boys out to the garden. I told them I was going to scare the girls, and when I started climbing the trellis, they ran away."

This was like the dream where she stood on the street before an oncoming carriage and was unable to move. Unable to scream.

"I saw you, alone in a bedchamber, changing your clothing." His open-handed gestured indicated her whole figure. "I saw you nude."

Any wise woman would have been pretending ignorance by now, instead of standing still, fists clenched, in a panic as he reminisced about a time she had done everything she could to forget.

"You lying little jade." His eyes sparked with fury. "You saw me. You know me! You always knew it was me who fell—" He paused.

"Into infamy?" she asked gently. If it was too late, it was too late. He knew her. "Yes, Lord Kerrich, I recognized you immediately as the notorious youth who dangled upside down and naked before the nobles of the age." Proudly, she straightened her shoulders. "Now may I put on my clothes?"

CHAPTER 24

Pamela stood before Kerrich without a stitch on, and she looked as poised as she had on that foggy night so long ago when he had first noticed her—and wanted her. Damn the woman, did nothing shake her? "No, you may not put your clothes on," he said harshly.

"You were a conceited swine even then." She passed judgement with cool disdain.

"I can't believe you lied to me for so long about something so important."

"I didn't lie."

"By omission—again." He clutched his head in disbelief. "Just as you did about your appearance."

"So you've told me all of *your* truths?"

"We're not talking about *my* sins." He took a turn about the room. He was a man. Men didn't have to be honest about certain things—like emotions. "That is beside the point. How long have you remembered?"

"Always." Pamela shrugged. "Never. What difference does it make? We only met the once. It was of no importance."

"No importance? How dare you say it was of no importance? That night haunted my dreams for years. It still haunts my dreams"—no wonder he'd dreamed of that body with the horrible Miss Lockhart's face attached!—"although now I know why."

"That evening was a long time ago," she said, "and within a fortnight my father had abandoned us. I never think of it. I scarcely remember. I want clothes."

"I've been trying to give you clothes all afternoon, and if you'd just taken the damned things I wouldn't know even now." That face. That body. He'd been a boy infatuated with a girl for the first time in his life. She hadn't cared; she had been brought there by her father to be company for the child-princess, and Kerrich had been given to understand she dared not fail in that commission. Looking back, he realized Pamela had been intent on being the perfect daughter, as if that would somehow procure her the perfect father. Kerrich and his clumsy bids for attention had been secondary, and had elicited only scorn.

"I'll take them now," she said.

"Damned right you will." Picking up the undergarments, he flung them at her.

She caught them and dropped them into the chair. Except the chemise, which she pulled over her head as quickly as possible. "I saw you, too. Well, actually, first I heard you yell. Then I saw your face for a split second before you slid off my windowsill. When I went to the window and opened it, I could see you again. Hanging by one leg of your trousers. From the trellis. With that famous full moon twirling in midair."

"Do we want to talk about what we saw that night?" The chemise reached her knees, but the firelight behind her showed right through the gossamer fabric. "I saw you. With that rich body, the high, heavy breasts, the curve of your hips and your long, long legs. And you looked at me with your sorrowful eyes and all I wanted to do was comfort you." His voice rose. "Right before I plunged into scandal!"

She sat on the chair, crushing the starched petticoats, and pulled on the filmy new stockings and garters. "I know you saw me, just as I know you fell. Must we drag our pasts out in the open when we've got a party to prepare for?"

"I slinked and worried for months. I was sure my mysterious goddess at the window would tell. Or that someone who knew me had seen. But no one ever came forth." He paced across the room. "But I knew someone had freed me from my trousers. I heard two girls' voices from the open window above me, felt that poker prodding at my leg, and when it ripped—"

"Are you complaining about the job I did freeing you?"

"I knew it." He turned on her. "I knew it was you!"

"Because I have to say, I did the best I could considering that I thought you would want the job done quickly. In addition, the princess arrived in time to see me grabbing the poker. She was only nine, but she already behaved regally, and she insisted on giving me advice the whole time." She was standing, struggling with the corset.

"Turn around," he ordered.

She glared at him for one moment of defiance. Then good sense prevailed, and she did as he commanded. After all, she couldn't dress herself, and he doubted that she wanted to call a maid to view the shambles in here.

Speaking to the wall in her brisk, no-nonsense tone, she said, "I can't believe you are still fretting about this. It was a boyish prank. It failed spectacularly and you were exposed in an embarrassing manner. But I suppose, knowing you, you're worried that I'll tattle it about. I won't. If I didn't before, I don't know why I would now. No one knows and I don't know why anyone would care."

"The queen is using it to blackmail me."

She tried to turn. "What?"

He jerked her back around by the corset strings. "Her Majesty has the trousers, she has the poker, and she's threatening to tell society the identity of the mystery man who was the full moon on the foggy night. How else do you think she got me to adopt the brat?"

"Threatened to take her money out of your bank? But no, you said you didn't need the money."

"And I don't bow to financial blackmail. Which she knew. So she had an alternate plan."

"You mean . . . all of this—me, Beth, the lessons, the party—everything was to protect you from the revelation of a twelve-year-old, silly piece of gossip?"

"People will laugh!" he roared.

"You're the earl of Kerrich. What do you care if they laugh?"

With a sense of gratification, he pulled the corset tight enough to give her a lovely line in her dress—and offer her some discomfort. "I shouldn't care if I'm laughed at, heh? But your sensibilities are too delicate to bear facing people who might remember the scandal of your father's abandonment."

"Do you dare compare the insignificance of your bare bottom with the very real tragedy of my family's disintegration and disgrace?"

"As you have so kindly pointed out to me, it was twelve years ago." Tying off the corset, he turned her to face him. "No one is going to remember."

"That might be true, but my father died less than a year ago in France in the arms of yet another of his ladies. She apparently had fallen for his charm." Pamela cleared her throat. "Her husband took a dim view."

"Good God."

"Her husband caught them *in flagrante delicto*. He barely

missed his naked wife when he shot my father." Her gaze flickered toward him, then away. "That, I believe, has revived the scandal in all its glory and added a luster which cannot be denied."

"I am so sorry." Not about the scandal, but about the death. She might sound stalwart, but he'd seen the glitter of tears. Taking her in his arms, he held her closely. "It must have been like losing him all over again."

She jabbed at his stomach, and when he didn't release her, she pinched him. "Save your condolences. I scarcely consider the loss."

He released her. Clearly she didn't want his solace, but he could see the tangled skein that held her in its coils. Or perhaps he understood because he had been a lost child, too. "He was your father. You must have mourned him."

"Mourned him?" Wondering how to explain such matters to such an obtuse man, Pamela scowled at Kerrich. She hated this, but if talking about her father and his stupid disgrace would release her from her duties at Buckingham Palace, she would talk. "I didn't mourn him. I mourned my *mother*."

"Of course you did." He spoke very slowly, as if speaking to a dim pupil. "Your mother died in a state of grace, without ever spoiling your youthful dreams of motherly perfection."

"I didn't think she was perfect." Pamela said quickly. Until her mother's death, she had scorned her mother's meek acceptance of disgraceful fate. Afterward . . . well, perhaps she had idealized her mother a little too much.

"But your father—early on, you were forced to see his faults. So when he died, did you mourn him?"

"Do you know what my father was like? All charm when he wanted his way, and all sulking when he didn't get it. Always looking out for some new woman to chase, and always bored when he got her. Always spending money we didn't have on something he didn't need because he thought that would make him happy. My mother always put her own needs aside so he could have what he wanted because she wished him to be content." She pressed her hand to her forehead; the remembering gave her a headache. Or perhaps that was the press of tears behind her eyes. "As if anything could ever have made him content. He left when I was fifteen, old enough for me to know what he was—a man running from his ailing wife and his judgmental daughter."

"But you still loved him."

"No!" She drew a fierce breath, then lost it in a quivering sigh. "Yes. I don't know."

"Of course you loved him. You fear me too much."

"What are you talking about?" Her throat almost closed up, and she massaged it with her palm. "I don't fear you!"

Almost to himself, he said, "You won't marry me." Then he looked up at her. "And you won't let yourself love me."

"Not every woman in the world is going to love you."

"But you want to."

She would never get involved with a man who understood women. She would never get involved with another man at all.

"I'm the first man you've ever let yourself get close to," he said. "Aren't I?"

What was he trying to do? Snatching up the petticoats, she pulled them on and turned her back on him. "You know you were my first."

"Your first what? Your first *lover*?" He came around to see her face. "You can't even say the word. I'm your lover. I make love to you. We wallow in touching and kissing and fornicating and loving. You admit to all of it, except for the loving. I know now what I miss when I'm with you, and that is the quiet whispers in the dark after all the passion is spent. The whispers of 'I love you.' "

"It would be a lie." Yes, it would. She tied the petticoats and reached for the dress. "You don't whisper to me, either!"

He was relentless. "You pretend to be asleep or"—he gestured toward the rumpled bed—"you pretend not to see."

She wanted to deny everything, but watching her father lie his way through a swath of maidens had hardened her resolve to be honest. "I don't want to love you."

"I know that." Taking the gown from her, he slipped it over her head and helped her with the sleeves. "From our first meeting, you tarred me with the same brush that tarred your father, and regardless of the evidence never have you let yourself change your mind. You see only the rake when you see me, never the man."

Was he right? He fastened the porcelain buttons at the back. She had supposed her heart ached because of the weak and frivolous longing for a man like her father. Did it instead ache because she wouldn't allow herself to love the heroic man of her dreams?

"You can walk away from me if you like, but still I say, whether or not your father was wholly a villain, you still loved him, and because you won't admit it you can never love a man. So will you mourn your father or will you die an old maid?"

Facing him, she was defiant to the end. "There are worse things than being an old maid."

"Lonely. Embittered. Poison to anyone who tries to get near you. Always keeping your father's watch with you as a reminder that people can hurt you, and you should push them away." A knock sounded on the door, and Kerrich walked to it and laid his hand on the knob. "Yes, there are worse things than being an old maid." He eased it open a crack.

"My lord," Moulton said, "there has been an incident at the Bank of England."

Pamela saw Kerrich's attention leave her, leave the room, leave the house.

"So my grandfather was right." Kerrich sounded amazed and gratified.

"Lord Reynard read the situation correctly, my lord."

"Get my horse. I'll be right there." Not bothering to shut the door all the way, Kerrich went to the closet and pulled out a pair of well-polished black boots, a crisp clean shirt, a blue waistcoat and a black coat.

As he stripped off his shirt, she went and stood in front of him. "What do you mean, you'll be right there? You're due at Buckingham Palace in less than two hours."

"Something important has come up." The clean shirt went on and he tucked it into his trousers.

"Something important?" She snatched up his waistcoat and held it hostage. "What would you call Beth's introduction to the queen?"

"Less important. Excuse me." He tried to take the waistcoat and when she wouldn't give it up, he went back to the closet and brought out a dark green brocade and shrugged into it.

Pamela followed him as he walked to his coat and picked it up. "You can't do this. You can't abandon Beth."

"The child will be well cared for without me." He stopped and looked her over. "Assuming you're over your histrionics and will do your duty as governess and accompany her. My grandfather will take my place, and I'll be there when I can."

"This is just the kind of behavior I should have expected from a dilettante such as yourself. You commit yourself to a scheme and then can't carry it through."

"Considering your behavior today, I would have to submit that people who live in glass houses shouldn't throw stones."

His cool mockery fired her indignation. "Quite the contrary. I'm going to the party. You are not. You are cold and uncaring."

He put his arms into his coat as if he hadn't heard her.

"You had me get a child for you when you didn't intend to keep her—"

"Him. I wanted a lad, remember?" From a drawer in his cabinet he removed a black silk scarf and collar.

"You don't intend to adopt Beth, do you?"

"You always knew that."

"Yes, and I'm damned for going along with your despicable scheme. I knew better, but I—"

"You wanted the money." He picked up his boots and showed them and the neckwear to her. "I'll go downstairs and find my valet to help me don these. I would ask you, but your resentment is too large for you to get close."

He left her standing there, swallowing hard and not crying.

He opened the door all the way. "Blast!" Stepping out, he stared down the corridor.

"What?" she asked.

"Beth," he said.

It took her a moment to realize the door had been partially open. She forgot her own troubles. She swallowed. Dear God, Beth had come seeking comfort or to show off or just to tell them it was time, and she must have asked a servant and found them—and heard them talk about her hopes and how they were never anything but foolishness.

Rushing to the door, she looked out at the empty corridor, then up at him, sick with worry and horror.

"She'll understand," Kerrich said with pigheaded nonchalance. "She'll be fine. What time will she be presented to Her Majesty?"

"Six o' the clock. You mean you aren't going after Beth? You hurt her!"

"I'd say we both hurt her." He groped for his pocket watch, then strode over and plucked it from his jewel case and looked at it. "I'll do everything in my power to make it to the palace—but I have to go."

She could scarcely breathe for disappointment. "How does a man like you look at himself in the mirror? You *are* like my father."

He stared at her as if he didn't know her, then took her by the arm and inexorably pulled her toward him. Looking down into her eyes, he said, "And you're like my mother. You don't know a diamond when you hold it in your hand."

CHAPTER 25

"We didn't believe the young man could be so violent, my lord."

Kerrich stared at Mr. Gordon, agent for the government, in absolute disbelief. "So you let Athersmith get away?"

"He had a pistol! We weren't prepared! Who would have thought that in broad daylight so bold a thievery could take place!" Given a listener, the makeshift guard would go on making excuses for hours. "He just walked right in. He loaded up paper to print banknotes. He took our ink! Then when we apprehended him, he shot at us."

"A single shot pistol?"

"Indeed!"

"If it was empty, what further harm could he do?"

"He was waving another! Besides, people were in the lobby! Customers were at the windows. The bullet knocked a chip out of the venerable statue at the end of the lobby!" That was clearly the greatest indignation.

Luckily Moulton walked into the now-deserted lobby of the Bank of England before Kerrich gave in to his urge to strangle Mr. Gordon. Kerrich left the man without apology, and speaking in an undertone to Moulton, mocked the man's feeble defense. "Yes. Who would think they would want to steal from a place where they store money?"

"I did warn you, my lord, of the government men's pathetic inefficiency," Moulton said. "If they had consented to warn the regular guards, none of this would have happened."

"They didn't give warning to the bank's guards?"

Moulton smiled in a fed-up manner. "It is the government, sir."

Kerrich strode with Moulton outside the bank building on Threadneedle Street. Leaning his hand on one of the mighty columns, he took a breath of fresh air and asked, "What information did *you* glean?"

"According to the government men—and we have established how effective they are—there was no diversion of any kind, yet somehow Mr. Athersmith walked into the storeroom in the back of the building, removed fifty reams of watermarked paper and several crates of the special, jet-black ink with which they print the banknotes. He placed them on a handcart and was on his way out the front door when he was spotted—by the bank guards."

"Hurrah for the bank guards! But if there wasn't an accomplice, how do the government men account for Lewis's near-success?" Kerrich asked in frustration.

"Unfortunately, even the bank guards are uncertain how he got so far, and my only man on the scene came back from supper into the midst of the shouting of 'Stop, thief,' the customers screaming and running, and that damned pistol." Moulton shook his head. "I'm sorry, my lord, but not even my men will argue with a lunatic holding a gun."

"So Lewis got away," Kerrich said.

"He's gone."

"There was no sign of an accomplice. No diversion."

"Not according to the government men or the bank guards."

"Are they lying or are they idiots?"

"As for the government men, I would have to choose for idiots, my lord. But the bank guards should have seen something and they claim they didn't."

"Keep questioning them. See if you can drag some version of the truth from them." Kerrich looked out the door and into the afternoon sunshine. This incident, muddled, confusing and frustrating as it was, was nothing compared to what he had fled at home. He thought of Beth and her inopportune discovery and of Pamela and that disagreeable scene they'd enacted. Now he had to go to Buckingham Palace where the queen held his trousers ransom and Beth and Pamela stalked the halls, out for his blood.

He was going to have to grovel before all three. The snarl of muddled affection and hurt feelings was just the reason that, when women were involved, he eschewed emotional relationships. Yes, he much preferred the shallow, the vapid and the silly.

Unfortunately, neither Queen Victoria, Pamela nor even Beth fulfilled his qualifications. The evening was going to be an execrable experience.

Pulling out his pocket watch, he looked at the time. "If I hurry, I can just make Beth's presentation to Her Majesty."

"You'll be at Buckingham Palace, my lord?"

Turning to Moulton, Kerrich glared as if he held Moulton responsible for the bloody mess his life had become. "Indeed. I have to go make merry."

Two hours ago, Pamela couldn't have imagined she could travel to Buckingham Palace, the new royal residence, and that she would be anything but preoccupied with her own personal torment at meeting the queen and seeing so many society people who knew her identity and background.

But as Kerrich's carriage inched forward in the line that would deposit them on the wide stone steps, she thought only of Beth. Beth, seated on the back-facing seat across from Pamela and Lord Reynard. Beth, clad in her ruffled dress, white stockings and black leather slippers. Beth, blessed with that combination of sensitivity and street wisdom that made a mockery of Pamela's attempts to explain the unexplainable.

"Lord Kerrich wanted a child to make himself look respectable," Pamela said.

"I know." Beth had her face pressed to the window, watching the milling of carriage runners and footmen outside.

"I agreed to get him one."

"You got him one," Beth said in an even tone.

Hesitantly, Pamela told the bad part. "We both always knew the child would not be adopted." In a rush, she added, "But I wanted him to adopt you. I encouraged him to spend time with you because I knew he would fall in love with you."

The afternoon sun shone through the windows, and Pamela plainly saw Beth roll her eyes.

Worse, Lord Reynard snorted.

If Pamela wasn't justifying her actions to that pleasant old man, she had no chance of convincing anyone. Especially not Beth, who was the one who really mattered. "Lord Kerrich would be here with you right now," Pamela said, "but he had something very important to do."

"Oh, indeed?" Beth pressed her face against the glass as the carriage inched forward. "I'll wager *you* don't even know what it is."

"No. No, I don't." Pamela didn't even know why she

was defending him, except that his absence hurt Beth even more than she'd already been hurt, and this child deserved better. "But I know he wouldn't have gone unless it mattered greatly."

Beth looked straight at Lord Reynard. "It's the counterfeiting, ain't it?"

"Isn't it," Pamela correct automatically. "What counterfeiting? What are you talking about?" She found herself ignored by both other occupants of the carriage.

Lord Reynard looked taken aback, and the normally genial old face became stern and still. "Young lady, what do you know about the counterfeiting?"

"I overheard Mr. Athersmith talking about it at my party."

"You were eavesdropping?" Pamela asked in censure, but for all the attention the other two paid her, she might as well have been speaking a different language.

Leaning forward, Lord Reynard put his face down to Beth's level. "Do you understand how important this is?"

"Yes." Beth shrugged. "No, not really."

"Counterfeiting is a very bad crime," Lord Reynard explained. "Like stealing without having the courage to face the victim."

"Mr. Athersmith was sure in trouble about it."

"I don't understand. Lord Kerrich and Mr. Athersmith are investigating a counterfeiting?" Pamela scrambled to catch up.

Lord Reynard said, "Beth, I need you to tell me—who was Mr. Athersmith talking to and what was he saying?"

"He was talking to a lady. Upstairs, where they weren't supposed to be."

"A lady? You mean, a female?"

"A lady," Beth insisted. "I didn't see her, because she was being so mean to him I knew they wouldn't want to know I was there." She looked delightful, feminine and childish, and she swung her foot back and forth as she bounced on the padded leather seat.

But her gaze was perceptive and Pamela could see that Lord Reynard was taking her seriously.

"She talked like a noble lady?" he asked. "Not a servant, then. Miss Fotherby?"

"No! 'Cause this lady said if Mr. Athersmith wanted Miss Fotherby, he had to be clever and rich. He had to stop galloping off at the mouth, and not drink, and she took his bottle away from him." Beth wrinkled her nose. "Besides, I heard Miss Fotherby talking. She's got a little voice and she squeaks a lot. This lady sounded deeper and annoyed like Mrs. Fallowfield when we orphans were feeding the mice."

Pamela's mind whirled. She'd never experienced such confusion. A crime had been occurring right under her own nose, and everyone knew about it except her. For precisely this reason, she always advised young governesses not to get involved with their employers. "Mr. Athersmith was trying to get some money by . . . by trapping a counterfeiter?"

"Ooh, I don't think Mr. Athersmith is a good man," Beth said.

Pamela thought of the affable young gentleman who looked so blond and upright and, when compared to his cousin, seemed the epitome of virtue. "Mr. Athersmith is involved in the counterfeiting?" Her voice rose.

Beth judged Mr. Athersmith with the astute perception of a child. "He's not important. He's poor, and he's one of those fellows that wants everything everybody else has, except he wants it the easy way." Seeing Pamela's wide-eyed horror, she added hastily, "But I could be wrong."

"Of course you're wrong. Mr. Athersmith is . . . proper

and good." Pamela glanced at Lord Reynard, expecting that he would defend his great-nephew, but he was staring out the window. Still trying to gain some comprehension, she asked, "Even if it's true about Mr. Athersmith, why would a lady be interested in counterfeiting?"

For the first time, Lord Reynard looked at her, and he acted as if she'd uttered something profound. Rubbing his chin, he asked in a thoughtful tone, "That is just what I've been asking myself."

CHAPTER 26

Kerrich straightened himself as best he could in the antechamber of Buckingham Palace, but there was little to be done about his windblown hair and wrinkled neck cloth. One didn't appear at Queen Victoria's afternoon reception in such a state, but neither did one ignore the invitation, especially when one was in deep trouble with both his orphan and his betrothed. It was bad enough that he had left them to arrive on their own with only Lord Reynard in attendence. If he missed Beth's presentation, he shuddered to think of the punishment he would suffer under the hands of all three females. Not that he hadn't had a woman angry with him before, but this time he doubted if his usual shower of atonement trinkets would heal the breach.

Lord Albon was going down as Kerrich ascended the stairs, and Kerrich's heart sank. "Tell me the reception's not over."

"No, of course not. But I made the required appearance, now I'm off to meet my ladybird."

Kerrich pressed his hand to his chest. He could breathe again.

"The queen's in the blue drawing room," Albon said.

"But you're looking a little rumpled. Been falling out of windows lately?"

With a hearty *ha ha!* and a punch on the arm he passed Kerrich, and Kerrich stumbled on a step as he turned to stare at the fellow. What had Albon meant by that? It had better have been a random comment on Kerrich's dishabille and not what Kerrich feared it was.

But when he passed a group of matrons on the landing, they grinned at him with most unladylike mirth, and one of them winked at him. As he climbed the second flight, a cold sensation crept down his neck and he glanced back to see them watching him, or, more specifically, his buttocks, in what could only be described as a lascivious manner.

This wasn't good. This wasn't good at all. Indignation began to mix with uneasiness, but still he hoped he was imagining things.

In the upper corridor, when he could hear a multitude of voices, he paused before a mirror and finger-combed his hair and straightened his coat. Then, taking a sustaining breath, he stepped into the blue drawing room.

Everything appeared to be normal. Brown marble columns rose to the gilded ceiling. Classically carved murals decorated the panels above the doors, flung wide to connect the blue and bow drawing rooms. Ladies and gentlemen stood in groups, chatting and smiling. The children were nowhere to be seen; no doubt their fete took place in another chamber.

As Kerrich strolled into the room, he scanned the throng for Pamela and Lord Reynard. At the same time, he anxiously attended any snippets of conversation he could hear. At first, the discourses sounded bland enough. He overheard a complaint about the size of the room, altogether too small. Some people had never been to Buckingham Palace, for this queen was the first to use it as a royal residence, and the gossips claimed she found that the drains were faulty, the windows stuck shut and the bells would not ring. Buckingham Palace was a disgrace and a dreadful waste of money.

But as Kerrich walked farther into the chamber, the occasional titter assaulted his ears. As he glanced around, he saw smiles slanted at him. And the ladies continued to behave oddly—every time he turned, he found at least one of them examining his backside. Damn it. Damn it, this couldn't be happening. Not today. Not when so much had already gone wrong. Not when so much was at stake.

When he ran into Tomlin, he was relieved to see his friend, but that lasted only until Tomlin grabbed him by the arm.

"You sly old dog," Tomlin roared. "A full moon on a foggy night!"

At that one phrase, all Kerrich's suspicions were confirmed. Rage hit him hard and low. Rage and the instinct to shush Tomlin, to cover up, to hope no one else had heard. But it didn't matter. His surmise were true. This was how Pamela had chosen to get her revenge. While he'd been at the Bank of England, saving the country from ruin, Pamela had been here at the queen's reception, telling his secret to everyone. Everyone knew. Everyone was laughing at him. The moment he'd been dreading for years had finally come, and he wanted to howl out his wrath.

He couldn't.

Not with Tomlin still babbling on. "You were the famed full moon on a foggy night? All these years and you never told *me*, your best friend?"

Kerrich thought of and discarded several strategies in rapid succession. All of them involved denial, and denial, he knew damned good and well, would never succeed. Not against this scandal. Not against this truth.

He retained the presence of mind to smile a crooked smile and continue walking. "I didn't want to brag. I thought you might feel somehow"—he glanced pointedly at Tomlin's crotch—"inferior."

Putting back his head, Tomlin laughed heartily. As always, Tomlin was good-natured, and as always, he shambled along beside Kerrich, clumsy and prone to trip over his own feet. "You're famous, man!"

"I would have said infamous, myself." Kerrich glanced around, carefully avoiding eye contact with anyone. "Does everyone know?"

"I heard it as soon as I walked in the door."

"I'll be constantly assaulted with it then, I suppose."

Tomlin laughed again and nodded. "I'll wager you have a scrapbook hidden somewhere with all the caricatures and lampoons from all the gazettes."

"I don't, and as much as I want to discuss this with you, I have something more pressing on my mind right now. Have you seen Miss Lockhart and my charge? We're supposed to be officially presented to Her Majesty at six, and it's nearly that now."

"Saw Miss Lockhart pacing between the blue drawing room and the bow drawing room." Tomlin cocked his head as if he didn't understand Kerrich's mood. "You're certainly taking this calmly."

Kerrich pulled out his pocket watch and checked it. "Taking what calmly?"

"This full moon on a foggy night revelation."

Looking deliberately surprised, Kerrich said, "It was no revelation to me. I've known all along. Now if you'll excuse me, it's bad form to make Her Majesty wait."

As he walked away, he congratulated himself on a good performance. His ruddy cheeks could be blamed on the heat, his slight smile was one he always wore on formal occasions and, he flattered himself, he appeared completely ordinary. No one looking at him could know the wrath that rocked him with every step. No one could guess that, in his mind, he was picturing himself with Miss Lockhart, wringing her neck. While he had his hands on her, he would roar out his displeasure until she never dared vex him again. Then he would withdraw his suit with the most withering sarcasm of which he was capable, and after that he would never see her again. Never. Not unless he had the happy occasion of tossing her a coin when she begged at his gate because she was so devastated she could never work again. Yes, that was it. He could see her now, in rags, her beautiful face smudged and her hair prematurely gray, begging him to—

Pamela caught his sleeve before he realized she was there. "My lord, I was hoping you would appear."

Torn from his walking daydream, he looked at her. This was no smudged, ragged, haggard prune. The handsome gown that he had chosen for her swirled like a silver cloud. Her blue eyes picked up the shades of gray and glittered with a combination not unlike a drift of clouds on a sunny day. Her hair, airily draped and curled, softened her countenance into a parody of sweetness. She looked like the embodiment of his sweetest dream—when she had actually executed his greatest nightmare.

Pulling him toward an unoccupied corner, she said quietly, "A terrible thing has happened."

The last of his discipline vanished. He was livid, absolutely livid, and he scarcely maintained the presence of mind to keep his voice down. "Did you think I wouldn't hear the moment I walked in the door?"

"You . . . know?" She glanced around, pale and daring to pretend innocence when she had betrayed him as soon as she set foot in Buckingham Palace. "Other people know?"

"Know? Everyone knows, and they've done nothing but tell me about it in one way or another since I came in."

Her forehead puckered and her eyes widened. "They know where Beth is?"

"With my grandfather, I would suppose."

"Lord Reynard found her? He went after her. We've both been searching, but without success, and if you're saying—"

"What are you talking about?"

"About . . . Beth." She examined him. "What are *you* talking about?"

Taking her arm, he backed her into a corner. He pulled himself up to tower over her, and he glared into her eyes. "I'm talking about you telling everyone my secret."

"Your secret?" The little harpy wasn't cringing as she was supposed to, and she blinked in obviously feigned confusion. "You have a secret? All I know about is that nonsense at Kensington Palace and you can't be worried about *that* at a time like *this*!"

"Everyone is laughing!"

She held up her hand to halt him. "I believe we are talking at cross purposes, my lord. Let us understand each other. You are unhappy because somehow the truth of your youthful indiscretion got out and people are discussing your bare posterior."

"Among other things, and don't use that patient, tutorial tone with me."

"I, on the other hand, have a *real* problem."

His command clearly had had little effect on her, and he hadn't seen that expression on her face since she'd changed from the old Miss Lockhart to the young Pamela. But he recognized it. She wanted to rap his knuckles—or worse.

In a crisp, no-nonsense tone, she told him, "Beth arrived at the palace with Lord Reynard and me, but as soon as we entered, she disappeared. She was incredibly distraught. I fear she has run away."

"This is your terrible thing that happened?" Kerrich was trying to absorb the new information and not succeeding well. "If she disappeared right away, when did you have time to betray me?"

She stared at him as if he were demented, or worse. "I didn't betray you. Why would I care to? My only concern is that child, loose in the palace, wandering the halls. Perhaps she's lost."

"Nonsense. How could she get lost in here?"

"She's from a small orphanage and before that, a small home," Pamela snapped. "You tell me."

Kerrich looked around the long room, saw the smiling, chatting guests, thought about the size of the palace, and for the first time since he'd found Pamela, comprehended the seriousness of his predicament. The mystery of the counterfeiting genius was still unsolved, his cousin was on the loose, Queen Victoria was expecting to see him, child in tow, on the hour, Beth had disappeared, and he'd just proved to the woman he wanted to wed that he was not only a selfish noddy-pate, but also that he had no faith in her and her discretion. Assuming Pamela was telling the truth and had not spread the story of his upended and naked debut—and now that it was too late he saw no reason to doubt her—he would have to wait to discover the sly busybody who had informed against him, for now he had to find Beth, and make amends, and . . . this day couldn't get any worse. "Tell me where you've looked."

"I've walked all the rooms with guests in them. I didn't see her, but she's small and she probably wants to hide from me because she . . . is disappointed in me."

"Did you ask the governesses if they'd seen her?"

"No." Pamela wrung her hands. "I've been afraid to ask

anyone for fear the news will spread that we are not responsible enough to care for a child, and that will ruin everything we've worked for. At the same time I think I'm being foolish for caring about something as trivial as the queen's good opinion when Beth is lost."

Kerrich had seen the expression on Beth's face when she'd heard them fighting. He doubted that she would do anything foolish; she'd proved herself savvy in every way. But she might very well be willing to see them embarrassed, and they had little time before their presentation to Queen Victoria.

That brat. To leave them standing before the queen and stammering out an explanation! Yet at the same time, he had to appreciate such a heady revenge, and he knew damned good and well that Beth had no incentive to cooperate. Not if she thought herself used and soon-to-be-abandoned.

"She isn't lost," he said with assurance. "She's hiding. But we need to find her." Untangling Pamela's hands, he placed one on his arm, then led her through the crowd toward the bow drawing room. He could feel her trembling, and in as soothing a tone as he could manage, he said, "Let's find the chamber where the children are playing and question them, and we can talk to the governesses, too."

Pamela's fingers flexed on his arm, and in a voice he had to lean close to hear, she said, "Devon, she was angry with me because I led her to believe you'd give her a real home. A place where she could stay forever."

He searched as they walked, and whenever he looked at someone, they smiled at him as if they were imagining him naked. He never smiled back. "She was angry with me, too."

"Yes, but I always knew that you were . . . that is, I thought of myself as better than . . . I just didn't realize how much I had betrayed my own integrity by making promises I couldn't keep."

She was insulting him. Blatantly, horribly. But she sounded wretched, and he did know what she meant. More than that, he wanted to comfort the woman who just now faced the results of her deal with the devil. "Beth is a bright girl," he murmured. "She'll come back."

"But will she come back in time to be received by the queen? I suppose being presented to Queen Victoria is trivial, and I know Beth was nervous about it, but I think it would be a moment for her to remember forever." Pamela bit her lip so hard he winced in sympathy. "That honor might make up for the great hurt I've inflicted."

"You haven't hurt her!" he muttered. Pamela was too hard on herself. She expected honor and virtue when she was only a woman, and a woman who made her living by working for men like him who . . . who for the past few years had forgotten most of what he knew about honor and virtue. "You plucked her from the orphanage, you made me accept her, you taught her lessons and deportment—she knows what she owes you."

"I promised myself I wouldn't let the child be hurt by your plan, and she was. Beth was—is—so hurt."

Her distress convinced him to take a hard look at himself, and what he saw made him faintly ill. He had been raised with his father's and grandfather's good examples before him; when had he strayed so far that he no longer expected himself to be honest and kind and responsible? When he compared himself to Pamela, he grew frightened at the man he'd become.

They had almost reached the bow drawing room when Herr Muller stepped in front of them. He had arrived in England as a servant of Albert's, and in the short time since the queen's wedding, he and Albert had done much to organize the household. Herr Muller arranged the queen's receptions and kept them on schedule, and everyone did as he told them.

Now he stood before them, hands behind his back, and in his high, sharp voice said, "Lord Kerrich, perhaps you have forgotten. Her Majesty awaits you."

"I haven't forgotten."

"Then I must request that you come with me now. Queen Victoria is most interested in meeting your ward."

"I don't have my ward with me," Kerrich said. "I haven't collected the child yet."

Herr Muller blinked as if he didn't quite comprehend. "This is an informal reception, but you are expected to show yourself on time. You will have to explain everything to Her Majesty. Follow me now, please."

"Oh, no." Pamela's voice was less than a whisper.

Kerrich hesitated, but he had no choice. He didn't know where Beth was. He could be searching for her for the next hour. His monarch called; he had to respond. Steering Pamela through the crowd behind Herr Muller, he said, "I'll explain. She'll let me go look for Beth."

"Her Majesty is a martinet for protocol," Pamela said softly. "She will not like this at all."

Pamela was right. She knew the queen, and no matter what happened, the next few minutes would be an ordeal for them both.

He saw Albert first, towering over the crowd. Then the crowd parted, and there was Victoria standing beside him, short, twenty-one years old, rather plump, and smiling with the kind of vivacious enjoyment she had experienced so seldom in her regimented life. They stood, framed by an arch, against the wall. Their afternoon garb was handsome but not excessive. They carried no scepters and wore no crowns.

Yet no one would mistake them for just another couple. No one crowded the royal couple; a wide area stood empty around them. They were clearly monarchs doing their duty, and right now that duty was to socialize with the families of the realm.

He recognized many of the people around them. They were the intimates of the court, influential people whom Victoria had known for a long time and liked. They were also the bastions of society and friends of Kerrich's, although he never made the mistake of thinking they weren't thoroughly enjoying the humiliation of his unveiling.

Lord and Lady Pitchford stood as far apart as it was possible for any couple to stand and still be together. Probably they had been fighting about Bully-Boy and his antics. Oh, horror. Kerrich glanced around. Was that little brat here?

Of course, Colbrook grinned at Kerrich and mouthed, "Full moon on a foggy night." The bastard.

Looking thin and elegant, Lady Colbrook stood close by a window where a ray of sunshine picked up the sparkle of her discreet cut diamonds and turned her graceful pale yellow silk the same color as her pale blond hair.

Kerrich was surprised to see Lord Swearn—wasn't he supposed to be with his family at his estate in Suffolk?

Lady Albon stood there alone. Of course, Lord Albon had been rushing out the door to his mistress as Kerrich walked in.

Herr Muller stepped forward and announced them. "Lord Kerrich and Miss Pamela Lockhart."

Kerrich heard a murmur, then like the dunderhead that he always was, Lord Colbrook exclaimed, loud enough to be heard, "Look at her! I told you Miss Lockhart was a beauty. Guess she was pulling the wool over Kerrich's eyes, heh?"

Beside Kerrich, Pamela flinched.

For the first time, they recognized Pamela as the same woman they had seen in his home. A murmur of astonishment rose, and he recalled his own incredulity as the guise of the unattractive female had washed away in the rain and this beauty had taken her place. Yes, his friends would enjoy that she had cozened him—he was far too rich and successful for them not to revel in that—but their amusement at his expense would lead them to gossip about her father. Pamela was right. This would be an ordeal for her. He wanted to put his arm around her and comfort her, but now was not the time, and after this day he'd be lucky if she ever allowed him to touch her again.

"My lord Kerrich," Queen Victoria called out, "how good to see you at this gathering of respectable *families*." She emphasized the word *families* as if he might never have heard it before.

With a rush of pleasure, he realized the queen no longer held the whip hand over him. The tale of his full moon was out; she couldn't blackmail him with its release any longer. A horrible irony abounded in this situation; he no longer needed the child, yet he had her and her governess, and he wasn't sure he could ever be happy without them.

Kerrich and Pamela stepped forward and bowed, then walked to the royal couple and bowed again.

"I haven't had the pleasure of your company for too many years, Miss Lockhart." Queen Victoria held out her hand to Pamela. "I have much missed my dear friend."

Now that the moment had come, Pamela's nervousness seemed to have disappeared. She was the epitome of poise as she curtsied and took the queen's hand. "As I have missed you, ma'am. But of course, I have followed your celebrated life with much excitement, and may I offer my congratulations on your coronation and marriage?"

Victoria beamed and wrapped her hand around Albert's

arm. Marriage had made her happy; Kerrich supposed he couldn't begrudge her that, although he could and did blame Albert for her sudden unyielding demand for respectability.

Respectability. He didn't have it, and there was the matter of the queen's nest egg in his bank.

Where was Beth?

"And what have you been doing?" Victoria said. Then, with a sly, sideways glance at him, "Or should I say, what are you doing with Lord Kerrich?"

Kerrich realized his mistake at once. When he had sent his reply to her invitation, he had simply listed Pamela's name. He hadn't thought to list her occupation, or that the queen would attach undue importance to the fact he was bringing a lady.

But Pamela's dignity never flagged. "I am the governess to Lord Kerrich's ward."

Victoria had been well trained. Her dismay showed for only a flash. "I'm sure you're a wonderful governess." Then she looked up at Kerrich and demanded, "Where is your famous ward?"

Devil of a good question. "Your Majesty, my ward is—"

"Right here, boy," Lord Reynard said from behind them. "I have her by the hand."

CHAPTER 27

In unison, every face turned toward her and Lord Reynard, but Beth wasn't going to let that sick rush of shyness show. She didn't look at Lord Kerrich and Miss Lockhart—whenever she thought of them being so sneaky, she still got kind of mad—but instead kept her gaze fixed on the queen, who wasn't very tall and was smiling at her as if she'd never seen a girl as adorable as Beth. Which maybe she hadn't, because Beth was well aware she had never looked as fair as she did now. She loved her lacy white gloves, and she loved her ruffly dress, and she really loved her blue velvet sash. When a girl looked this good, she *ought* to get to meet the queen.

But she couldn't seem to move, so Lord Reynard gave her a little push.

As she walked forward, Lord Kerrich met her and put his arm around her shoulders. Together, they faced Queen Victoria. "Your Majesty, this is my ward, Miss Elizabeth Hunter."

Beth curtsied just as Miss Lockhart had taught her, and she must have done it right because the crowd murmured with approval, the queen beamed, and Prince Albert—Beth knew it was Prince Albert because she'd seen his caricature in *Punch*—smiled at her like he liked her, which he should because she had such bouncy curls.

Holding out her hand, Queen Victoria said, "You are a dear girl. Come and speak to me."

Miss Lockhart said pretending to be brave was the same as being brave, and she had called Beth a lion, so Beth marched right up to the royal couple and took the queen's hand. "How are you, Your Majesty?" she asked.

That was the polite way to open a conversation, so Miss Lockhart said, but apparently not many people asked the queen that because someone in the crowd laughed really loudly, Prince Albert developed a sudden cough, and the queen tittered as if caught by surprise. Then she frowned into the crowd until the muted amusement died down, and when it had, she said, "I'm fine, thank you, Elizabeth. How are you?"

"I'm fine, thank you."

Now Beth was out of conversation, but the queen took over. "Won't you tell me how you became Lord Kerrich's ward?"

"He fetched me from an orphanage." That wasn't the story they'd agreed on. Beth could almost feel Lord Kerrich's consternation, and she hoped Miss Lockhart was squirming. It wasn't that they'd been mean or anything. They'd given her good food and nice clothes and she'd got to live in a really nice home for a little while, but it made her sore that they'd given her hope, too. So what if she was only a tyke? She'd lived in that orphanage enough to know that hope was a lot more important than that other stuff and when the hope was false and it got jerked away—well, it hurt. It hurt a lot. Beth was still feeling bruised.

But as Lord Reynard said, into every life a little rain must fall and holy stones, you've had a few deluges, but you're all right, aren't you? The old fellow was correct, so Beth said, "Yes, I was put in an orphanage. My father died while resuing Lord Kerrich from some bad guys, so Lord Kerrich hired Miss Lockhart. Together they looked and looked for me. And since they've found me"—she smiled back at Lord Kerrich and Miss Lockhart with practiced adoration—"they've been so good to me."

Lord Kerrich was staring at her rather grimly. He knew she was getting a little of her own back with her dramatics. But Miss Lockhart was pressing her lips together like she was trying not to cry, and Beth realized Miss Lockhart was really scared that Beth didn't like her anymore.

As Lord Reynard said, everybody makes mistakes and Miss Lockhart made a corker, but she's already berating herself about it and worse than you could and don't you think that's enough? So Beth sent an extra bright smile toward Miss Lockhart, and instead of making Miss Lockhart feel better it must have made her feel worse because she had to fumble for her handkerchief. So Beth tried again to make her feel better by announcing, "I want to be a teacher just like Miss Lockhart and go back to that horrible orphanage and teach those tykes—I mean, those children—so they can be good people, too."

"That's so lovely!" Queen Victoria clapped her hands. "Elizabeth, you've touched Miss Lockhart so much she's weeping."

"Yes." Now Beth was starting to feel bad. No matter what she did, Miss Lockhart just cried harder. So she did the best thing she could think of. "Your Majesty, do you think when you're done with the food here at the party, I could take it to the orphanage so they'll have something good to eat?"

The whole drawing room quieted down really quickly.

"They don't have much besides porridge"—Beth thought

she might have done something wrong, but she didn't understand what—"and just the stuff left on the plates would make them so happy they'd jump around like fleas on a dog."

Now the queen smiled.

The tension in the chamber relaxed, and Prince Albert snapped his fingers. "Herr Muller, you will take care of this."

This Herr-fellow bowed brusquely.

Queen Victoria brushed back Beth's curls. "That is very good of you to think of your less fortunate friends."

"They'll be happy," Beth said earnestly.

Directing her voice to Lord Kerrich, Victoria said, "I must say I am impressed with your reformation. Aren't you, Albert?"

In his deep, accented voice, Albert said, "Most impressed, my lord. I hope to see you and Elizabeth here again."

Lord Kerrich bowed, but he didn't say anything. Beth guessed he didn't want to promise *that*.

"So if you would like to come and visit me after the reception, I believe I have something of yours that I should return." Queen Victoria's eyes sparkled mischievously as she spoke, and Beth wondered what the queen had that made Lord Kerrich scowl.

"I would say it no longer matters whether you return my possession or not, for somehow"—he frowned at the queen like he was the devil—"the whole world knows anyway."

The queen's eyebrows shot up as if she were surprised. She glanced around at the crowd, then she looked at Lord Kerrich and shook her head decidedly. "Not me."

"Who?"

Queen Victoria looked at Miss Lockhart, who had managed to stifle her tears, but Miss Lockhart shook her head, too. It was like they all were talking and not making sense, and the only thing that Beth didn't mind was that everyone in the crowd looked as bewildered as she felt. Except for Lord Reynard, and he always looked like he knew everything. Beth guessed that was what happened when you got old.

"Come and see us anyway," Victoria commanded. "We will discuss the other matter."

They sure had a lot of matters. Then with a start, Beth realized they'd been dismissed. She'd had her audience with the queen, and it was over. But for just a few moments there, it had been grand.

Pamela watched as Kerrich put his arm around Beth's shoulders again, and guided her away, setting the stage for the next presentation. His Lordship and the child walked between her and Lord Reynard, and as the crowd shifted and another subject was given an audience, the attention left them.

What other matter would the queen want to discuss? Then she remembered—the Mathewes Bank affair still needed to be settled.

Lord Reynard offered his arm to Pamela. "I'd judge that a rousing success."

Pamela walked with him after Kerrich and Beth. "So it was, my lord." A complete success. Her Majesty not only considered Kerrich to be shepherded safely into the fold of respectability, but from Victoria's pleasant smile Pamela guessed there would be no more talk of changing banks. So the plan Kerrich had proposed that day in the study of the Distinguished Academy of Governesses had come to fruition.

Of course, the tale of the full moon on a foggy night had surfaced, but regardless of Kerrich's belief, that wasn't Pamela's fault and had not been mentioned in the original deal. Yes, she had succeeded, and would receive all the moneys owed her. The Governess School would survive and prosper. Her task was done.

She blinked away another round of tears. This wretched, inopportune weakness had to stop, or people would begin to suspect that she and Lord Kerrich . . .

"Where did you find Beth, my lord?" Pamela asked, and hoped that husky note in her voice didn't betray her.

"She found me, and rather bitterly railed against you and Kerrich, but she's a clever girl." Lord Reynard kept up with Kerrich and Beth as they stepped into the less-crowded bow drawing room. "With very little help from me, she talked herself around."

"Thank you, my lord," Pamela said from the bottom of her heart. And, as Kerrich and Beth came to a halt in a curtained alcove, she said, "Pardon me." She watched her own hand reach out for Beth's shoulder and touch it. "Beth," she said softly, and waited in one second of agonized anticipation.

Would the child spin around with a smile or a scowl?

But it didn't matter. Pamela had to hug her, to confirm she was safe by holding that slight, warm child. As Beth turned, Pamela sank to her knees and embraced her.

Beth didn't push her away. Instead she hugged Pamela back and piped, "I'm sorry, Miss Lockhart, for worrying you."

"No. No, I'm sorry." Pamela held her away, looked into her eyes, and apologized from the fullness of her heart. "I am sorry."

"I know. Lord Reynard explained it all to me. I know about . . . money and such. I would have done what you did, too." Beth grinned and waved her arm back toward the queen. "Did you see me? Wasn't I great?"

Ah, the inevitable rebound of youth. And its incredible complacency! "You were very great. Everything went well."

"Except Her Majesty acted funny when I talked about the orphans."

Lord Reynard interceded. "One does not tell the queen of England that her orphans are suffering."

Beth wrinkled her nose. "But they are."

"Especially not then," Lord Reynard said.

"But it was only one small gaffe, and because it was the result of a generous heart, Her Majesty easily forgave you," Pamela said.

All the time they were talking, Kerrich circled them like a worried dog, glaring at them and then glaring at any stray onlookers. Now he snapped, "All right, ladies. Enough mawkishness. Get up, Miss Lockhart, we have visitors bearing down on us."

"Ah, lad, you're such a sentimental fool." Lord Reynard leaned on his cane and grinned tauntingly at Kerrich.

"Claptrap," Kerrich muttered.

Pamela stood up, Beth's hand tucked in hers. She felt as if she had dived into a dark tunnel and barely made it out the other side, and she wasn't sure all of herself had come through intact. In fact, she suspected she had changed, although just how she hadn't yet discovered.

The entire group of Kerrich's intimates had followed them.

Lord Swearn walked up with Lady Albon on his arm, and greeted them.

The pairing of these two startled Pamela. At Beth's party, Lord and Lady Swearn had seemed *so* married. But these two had that sparkle in their eyes and that spring in their steps. Pamela knew without a doubt they were indulging in an affair.

Lady Colbrook appeared next, and just as the first time Pamela had met her, she appeared perfect, intelligent and perceptive.

Her husband trailed behind her, glowering. Pamela didn't know what had made him so unhappy, but she hoped Lady Colbrook told him to think before he spoke. Or if that wasn't possible, to speak more quietly. Someone needed to; the man was a social menace, and how Lady Colbrook, with her charm and natural social graces, put up with him, Pamela did not know.

"Miss Lockhart, how good to see you again." Lady Colbrook smiled without a hint of condescension.

"And you, my lady." Pamela curtsied, thinking that the ordeal of subtle and not so subtle interrogation had begun.

Lord Colbrook said heartily, "You're looking much differ—" Lady Colbrook's elbow struck him in the rib cage and his breath whooshed out. "That is," he wheezed, "you're looking well."

Pamela avoided looking straight at him. "Thank you, my lord."

"It was touching to see Her Majesty with Beth." Lady Colbrook included Kerrich and Pamela in her comment.

Pamela realized—Lady Colbrook had changed the subject! Pamela wanted to weep with gratitude. She didn't know if she could have kept her poise as she evaded questions about why she had disguised herself. And when someone dug for the details of her father's death! Ah, then Pamela would have longed to use her wit to cut them off.

But Lord Swearn easily followed Lady Colbrook's lead and spoke to Beth. "Yes, you certainly impressed our sovereign."

"Thank you, my lord." Beth squeezed Pamela's hand and beamed.

Pamela squeezed back. Their excitement was mutual;

perhaps Pamela would come through this reception without any more surprises.

"The queen is interested in children." Lady Pitchford arrived in time to hear the comments. "She's increasing."

"Increasing." With child? The queen was with child? But she'd been married for less than a year. Surely it wasn't possible that this woman, so much younger than Pamela, could be . . . in a stupor, Pamela repeated, "Increasing."

Kerrich looked startled. "Her Majesty appears plump, yes, but—"

The married women looked on him, the ignorant male, pityingly.

Of course. Pamela almost staggered beneath the impact of the report. The queen was expecting a child.

"We'll have a royal babe ere the year is out," Lady Colbrook said.

Lord Pitchford appeared and declared, "She's knocked up. Poor Albert."

Pamela lightly touched her fingers to her own midriff. A child.

Beth tugged at her hand. When Pamela leaned down to hear her, she whispered, "Is it true about the baby?"

"I don't know." Pamela didn't know whether she answered Beth or spoke to herself about her own sudden and overwhelming alarm.

"Poor Albert?" Lady Pitchford's bosom heaved with indignation. "Poor Victoria, I would say. She's the one who'll have to have a child ripped from her loins."

The Tomlins rushed up. "Did we miss it?" Mrs. Tomlin asked.

"I would say it's just getting started," Lady Colbrook drawled. "But let's halt everything right here. We'll have no more of your loin-ripping, Lady Pitchford. There are gentlemen and children present."

Certainly Beth's eyes were wide as she listened to the conversation.

"We missed Beth's presentation?" Mrs. Tomlin insisted.

At the nods all around, Tomlin grinned impishly. "But we have to make conversation about something. Let's question Kerrich about the full moon on a foggy night!"

That jerked Pamela back to the immediate issue.

"No." Kerrich glanced at her. "Let's not."

Swearn was grinning, too. "But—"

"No." Kerrich was adamant.

So it was true. Everyone *was* laughing about his youthful exploits . . . and he had immediately decided Pamela had betrayed him. Probably still thought she'd betrayed him.

She couldn't be having a baby by a man who thought her deceitful and treacherous. They had scarcely been together . . . only the few times . . . that night in the library . . . and afterward in her bedchamber . . . and earlier today.

Quite a few times, really.

Pamela hadn't thought this affair through. She hadn't thought at all.

Colbrook began to say something. Something vulgar, no doubt.

Lady Colbrook ruthlessly spoke over the top of him. "If we're going to talk scandal, let's talk about what happened at the Bank of England today."

Pamela's attention honed in on Lady Colbrook.

Everyone's attention honed in on Lady Colbrook, but Kerrich swiveled to face her and spoke so sharply, Pamela winced. "How do you know what happened at the bank today?"

"I was there," Lady Colbrook said.

"You were there," Kerrich repeated.

Beth tugged at Pamela's hand again.

"Yes, and can you believe it? There was a young man

there with a gun, and he shot at a guard." Lady Colbrook drew herself up indignantly. "I could have been killed!"

"How awful!" Mrs. Tomlin exclaimed.

Lady Colbrook spoke clearly enough that her voice reached everyone. "I was riding by on the new gelding Colbrook bought me—"

"The gray that Wilcox sold," Lord Colbrook said proudly.

"—and lost control of the creature."

"But you're the best rider I've ever seen," Lady Albon said.

"A dog spooked the horse," Lady Colbrook snapped.

"Was he robbing the place?" Lord Swearn sounded stern. "Did he get away?"

"Why were you riding by the bank?" Kerrich asked.

Lady Colbrook sighed in annoyance. "Yes, he got away. He fired a gun!"

Pamela noted she didn't answer Kerrich's question.

Beth tugged at Pamela's hand again, and loudly whispered, "Miss Lockhart!"

Lord Reynard moved closer to his grandson.

Pamela realized Kerrich hadn't heard Beth's revelation about the lady and Mr. Athersmith. She looked down at Beth and lifted her eyebrows.

Beth nodded excitedly. "That's her."

"But she's so agreeable." Still, Pamela's heart raced with excitement.

"Lady Colbrook, tell me what you were doing at the Bank of England," Kerrich said.

Lady Colbrook's wave of the arm included everyone in the group. "If you'll just be quiet, I'll tell the whole story."

A strange man's voice intruded, and for a moment Pamela couldn't place the frenzied, infuriated tones. "The whole story, my lady?" he said. "Or just the parts you made up to gild your own damnable precarious image?"

Like a stage villain, Mr. Athersmith stepped out from behind the curtains with a cocked pistol pointed at Lady Colbrook's heart.

CHAPTER 28

Lady Colbrook kept her composure admirably. She didn't scream, didn't cower. Instead she confirmed Kerrich's suspicions with a single phrase. "How did *you* get in here?"

Lady Albon ducked and shrieked. Mrs. Tomlin shoved her husband behind her out of harm's way. Pamela took Beth by the shoulders, pushed the child behind her, and backed away.

Kerrich stepped between Lady Colbrook and his cousin. "Lewis, this isn't wise."

"Wise?" Lewis's voice shook as he tried to angle around Kerrich and still keep his back to the wall. "Wise? What is wisdom to me? I'm ruined. Everyone at the Bank of England saw me."

"You were the one stealing from the Bank of England?" Lord Swearn flushed ruddy red and his lips drew back from his teeth. "You lived in my house. You taught my son. You . . . you beast."

"See?" Lewis's trousers were torn at the knee, his hair stood on end, he audibly drew breath after painful breath. "See? I can't stay in England or I'll hang, and I can't leave England because Miss Fotherby, the girl I love, is here."

"My daughter!" Swearn started toward Lewis. "How dare you even speak her name?"

The gun swung toward him. "This is your fault. You told me I was too poor to have her, so I searched until I found money!"

"You didn't find it, you stole it!" Lord Swearn shouted.

Lord Reynard stepped between the men, and held Lewis's gaze. "Lewis, you're at Buckingham Palace."

"And I'm acting improperly," Lewis mocked the old man. "What will the queen think?"

"Don't be stupid, lad," Lord Reynard said crisply. "The royal guards will kill you."

"I've nothing to lose." Lewis's voice shook.

Kerrich wanted his grandfather out of there, and at the same time knew an appeal would not sway him. After all, Lord Reynard was the man who had taught him it was better to die for your principles than to live in cowardice. The devil fly away with Grandpapa!

Someone in the crowd screamed. "A pistol. That man has a pistol!"

More screams followed, and people scattered for the exits, carrying Pamela and Beth with them. Kerrich's gaze met Pamela's as she turned in the doorway and sent him one last glance.

He wanted Pamela and Beth safe, and at the same time he hated to see them go. He wanted them to see what he'd been involved in, why he'd left them to travel to Buckingham Palace by themselves. Selfish. He was selfish to the bone, but if he had to die, he wanted to do it honorably and in the arms of the woman he loved.

Kerrich almost laughed at himself. Right here, right now, with a gun pointed at his chest and death staring him in the face, he could admit he loved Pamela. He loved her—and he had made no provision for her.

She disappeared from the doorway, and moved to sudden desperation, he murmured to Lord Reynard, "If I'm hurt, you'll take care of Pamela and Beth."

"I will," Grandpapa answered. "But I'm warning you right now, boy. Don't get hurt."

Lewis glanced around. The gun wavered. Kerrich jumped toward him. And Lewis once again leveled the pistol on Lady Colbrook.

Again Kerrich stepped between them, holding out his hand. "Lewis, I recognize that gun. It's mine, one of my matched pair of dueling pistols. So give it to me."

With a bitter snicker, Lewis said, "You don't get *everything* you want, Devon."

"Young man, this is so dramatic!" Lady Colbrook snapped. "If you don't care if you live or die, why don't you just shoot yourself?"

Lewis's eyes bulged with fury. "Because it's all your fault." He pointed his other hand at her, and the gun waved wildly. Lord and Lady Pitchford turned and ran, but Lewis didn't seem to notice. He saw only Lady Colbrook. "You're the one who thought up the counterfeiting. You're the one who told me what to do. I did what you told me."

With absolute, icy composure, Lady Colbrook asked, "Who's going to believe that?"

"I do," Kerrich said. Lewis hadn't been meeting a lady for licentious purposes as he and Moulton had thought. He'd been meeting her to get his instructions. "You were at the Bank of England to create a diversion for Lewis. You failed and left Lewis to take the consequences."

Lewis inched along the wall, trying to get into position for a clean shot at Lady Colbrook.

She ignored him to stare at Kerrich for a long, considering moment. Then she shrugged her bare, pale shoulders. "Ah, well. As long as you already *know*. The truth is, I didn't fail. I made a lovely diversion by slipping from my horse and pretending to be hurt and fainting artfully. I did so well Mr. Athersmith almost got the paper outside. Then he rammed the cart against the doorframe and, as if the noise weren't enough, knocked the paper off onto the floor and broke one of the bottles of ink."

"Not all of it, and I was hurrying!" Lewis said.

"I told you not to hurry." Contempt lashed through her tone. "I told you if you just act as if you're supposed to be there, no one would notice you."

"Cherise!" Colbrook exclaimed, obviously bewildered. "What are you saying?"

She ignored him like the insignificant trifle he was. Speaking to Kerrich, she said, "If Mr. Athersmith had been cool, he could have convinced those stupid guards to help him pick up the paper and carry it out. But no. He had to shiver with guilt. When they inquired what he was doing, he pulled out a gun and shot it off—"

"I didn't mean to!" Lewis cried.

"You never mean to. If I had the proper staff, I could organize the world." She flipped open her fan and fanned herself languidly. "But good help is hard to get these days."

Kerrich looked around. At the both entrances to the drawing room, the crowd rumbled and shifted, senseless people too fascinated by the drama to appreciate the danger. Here in their small group, they all stood with their mouths open, staring at Lady Colbrook as if they didn't know her. As they didn't. None of them knew this imperturbable organizer of high crime.

"I didn't realize it at first," Lewis said. "She can do anything, and it doesn't matter if she gets caught. No one's going to hang her. She's noble, and she's a woman. No one in the government is going to admit a woman made mock of them."

A faint smile played around her mouth. "That is so true."

Kerrich still stood between Lewis and his target. Lewis still held that pistol pointed at Kerrich. He didn't think his cousin would shoot him, but the pistol shook with Lewis's continuous tremors, and his eyes darted madly about. He was panicked. Guns were notoriously flighty. If Kerrich tried to grab the pistol, it could misfire, and Kerrich had no desire to die for someone as reckless as Lady Colbrook, or at the hand of someone as foolish as his cousin.

"This is asinine," Colbrook objected. "My wife couldn't be working for a counterfeiter and me not know it."

"Working for a counterfeiter?" Lady Colbrook was obviously stung by his lack of comprehension. "I don't work for anyone!"

"There!" Colbrook nodded, satisfied. "See?"

"Everyone worked for me. I thought up the whole plan." Lady Colbrook chuckled, her voice a pleased contralto. "I picked my men, five of them, thieves who knew how to take orders, and I thought that we should first test our capacities on Kerrich's banknotes, but I always knew the glory would be to counterfeit notes from the Bank of England. Mr. Athersmith was my only mistake."

Kerrich couldn't let this standoff continue.

"For God's sake, Cherise!" Colbrook exploded. "What the hell are you talking about? We're rich. You don't need money!"

Lady Colbrook put her fingers to her forehead in exasperation. "Colbrook, you are so pedestrian. I didn't do it for the money. I did it because I *could*."

With deliberate carelessness, Kerrich stepped aside to allow Lewis a clear shot at Lady Colbrook.

"What are you jabbering about?" Lord Swearn asked.

"Women don't commit crimes because they *can*."

Lady Colbrook viewed him with a sneer. "You mean, your dear Lilly doesn't do that, don't you? But Lilly has seven children. I have two, and I've raised them and married them off. Nerissa married a marquess and Daniel married an heiress, so you can't say I didn't do well by them. But I ask you, what am I supposed to do now? Sit and needlepoint until I wither and die? I think not, Lord Swearn." Her gaze dropped to his arm where Lady Albon's hand rested. "And Lilly knows about your affair and is pleased for the respite, although she wonders what Lord Albon will do when he finds himself raising a child who looks like you!"

Lady Albon leaped away from Swearn while Swearn sputtered, "Well . . . not really . . . didn't do it . . . damned woman . . ."

Lewis's hand tightened on the trigger. As the pistol thundered, Kerrich shoved Lady Colbrook aside. Then he flung himself at Lewis, butting him in the chest and grabbing him around the waist. Kerrich had him. He would have knocked Lewis flat if not for Tomlin. Dear, bumbling Tomlin, who always tried to help and always ruined everything. Tomlin jumped into the fray. With all his weight behind him, he rammed into Kerrich. Kerrich lost his grip on Lewis. Lewis escaped, scrambling up and sprinting the length of the drawing room toward the wide entrance.

People screamed and scattered as he came at them, still holding the smoking, single-shot pistol.

Kerrich yelled, "Grab the bounder!" but panic swept the crowd in every direction.

Lewis dashed into the corridor.

Kerrich followed, his feet pounding on the hardwood floor, his breath coming fast.

The two of them darted from side to side as people dove to avoid them.

Half-turning, Lewis flung the pistol at Kerrich.

Kerrich ducked and kept running. Running toward the stairway. As Lewis rounded the curve, Kerrich lost sight of his cousin for a few precious seconds. He skidded around the corner.

Lewis was hesitating at the top of the stairs—while the queen's guard mounted the steps.

Pamela and Beth led the uniformed men. The governess and the child. They were almost upon Lewis.

Kerrich's blood ran cold. He shouted a warning

Pamela and Beth looked up. The guards looked up. Pamela pointed.

No one could have stopped Beth. She was just so fast. The child darted up the remaining stairs and hit Lewis at the knees, knocking him forward. He fell down the stairs almost at the guards' feet.

Kerrich sped toward his cousin, trying to reach him before—

—before Lewis drew the other pistol from his pocket.

"No!" Kerrich roared.

"Brat!" Lewis aimed at Beth.

Pamela stepped in the way.

Even as the guards leaped on him, Lewis shot.

He hit her. Dear God, he had shot Pamela. She collapsed where she stood, then tumbled down the steps.

She couldn't be dead. This wasn't right! He should have taken the bullet! Kerrich beat Beth to Pamela's side, but only just. Her cries of "Miss Lockhart!" mixed with his voice repeating, "Pamela. Pamela." Gently, he turned her face up. She was alive. Good. But blood bubbled from her shoulder and spread into a rapidly growing pool that stained the shattered silk. "Get a doctor," he shouted. "A doctor!"

"Yes. I can do that. I'll get a doctor." Beth raced down the stairs.

Kerrich pointed at a hovering footman. "Escort her." He didn't think Pamela was conscious when he picked her up, but she screamed with the pain. Behind him, he could hear the struggle with Lewis, but he didn't care. He had to get help.

Someone grabbed his arm. He looked into Queen Victoria's face. "Find me a bed," he ordered. "Find me a bed now."

"Follow me," she said, and she led him to a state bedchamber.

"Herr Muller has already sent for my physician," Victoria said as she threw back the blankets. "Don't worry, Kerrich. Miss Lockhart will survive."

"Of course she will. I will accept nothing less." He laid Pamela on the sheets. Her lids opened and her eyes were glazed with pain. Her face was white, sweat beaded her upper lip. Blood bathed her torso, and Kerrich swore, using words Victoria had probably never heard. "Fetch me a towel. Quickly!"

He didn't wait for it. Grabbing a tasseled pillow, he pressed it on the wound.

The door opened and shut. People were talking in the corridor outside. Victoria disappeared.

Grandpapa sank down on a chair beside the bed, looking every day of his age. "Put a rug on her," he ordered. "Keep her warm."

Where had everyone come from? Where did they go? But it didn't really matter. Only Pamela mattered. She'd been shot with his own gun! Hand trembling, Kerrich covered Pamela with a blanket. "I need scissors."

Suddenly Albert was at his side, handing him a pair. "Will you cut the clothing away?"

Kerrich tossed the pillow aside. Together the two men sliced through the neck of the gown and peeled it back. As they pulled the cloth, the wound bled more. Pamela moaned. Albert handed Kerrich a pad made from a towel. Kerrich pressed it on the wound.

The door opened and closed again, and Beth appeared. "I've brought the best doctor in London!"

Kerrich glared at the man taking off his shabby coat and rolling up his sleeves. "Quickly, man. Save her."

"Aye, ye're fortunate, m'lord. If ye had a fancy physician, the lady'd have no luck atall." He said "at all" as if the two words were one, and Kerrich realized he was Irish. "But I'm Paddy McEachern, an' I've been diggin' bullets out of every man, woman and child in Ireland for years. Now I'm workin' the docks here in London. I know what I'm doin'." His claims were as exuberant as a blast of Irish whisky, and as he spoke he leaned over Pamela. Raising her eyelid, he observed her, and when the other eye flashed open, the doctor said, "Ah, she's awake. That's good."

"Lord Kerrich, the queen's physician is on his way," Albert said.

Lifting the pad, the doctor grimaced at the sight of the wound, then leaned his head close as if he were listening. Raising his head again, he said, "Could be worse. Could be better. I won't know until I go diggin' for the bullet."

"Why could it be better?" Lord Reynard asked.

Dr. McEachern's attention flickered toward the old man in the chair, then returned to Pamela. "The reason it could be better is because if the wound were closer to her arm, I would know the bullet hadn't nicked her lungs. Probably didn't," he added quickly. "Can't hear her wheezing at all. But I won't lie to you. If her lungs have been touched, she hasn't much of a chance."

Kerrich's own lungs froze in the clutch of agony. "Blast you, just fix her."

Dr. McEachern drew a long black cloth cylinder out of his bag, and nodded at Albert. "That gentleman's not fer believin' me credentials." He looked at Kerrich. "But this is your wife, I think. Will ye let me do the task? I promise ye'll have as fine a job as any can do in London an' beyond." Unrolling the cloth, he laid it out across the bed.

Kerrich found himself unable to stare anywhere but at the row of bright sharp instruments tucked into pockets in the black silk.

Dimly, he heard Beth say, "I won't go, Lord Reynard. I'm staying with her."

But Beth's words didn't mean anything, because Pamela could be dying.

"Will ye let me operate on her?" Dr. McEachern spoke to Kerrich as he drew forth a long, thin, shiny scalpel. "It's up to you, sir."

Kerrich didn't have a choice. The queen's physician wasn't here and Kerrich doubted he had experience with gunshot wounds, anyway. In a hoarse voice, Kerrich ordered, "Operate."

Dr. McEachern turned brisk. "She's conscious, so I'll need people to hold her. Sir, will you?"

Obviously, he didn't know Albert's identity, and Albert didn't enlighten him. He just came around to the side of the bed beside the doctor and grasped Pamela's arm. Kerrich climbed on the other side of the bed and held her.

"She's going to fight," Dr. McEachern warned as he prepared to make the first incision.

He should have said she was going to scream. Because she did, loud and long and shrill, and she didn't let up until

Dr. McEachern held the bullet in his forceps.

Then, into the blessed silence, Dr. McEachern said, "Good news, m'lord. I can safely say her lungs weren't touched."

CHAPTER 29

"Lord Kerrich wanted to take you to his house to recover, but I told him that would not be proper. When he offered Lord Reynard as a chaperone, I was forced to point out that, although Lord Reynard is elderly, he is also a male person and unsuitable as a duenna for a young, unmarried lady." Queen Victoria sat beside Pamela's wide, sumptuous bed in Buckingham Palace, stitching a needlepoint chair cover, just as she had done at noon for precisely one-half hour every day since Pamela had been shot.

That had been over a fortnight ago, but Pamela still found smiling a trial and talking an effort. Everything wearied her, perhaps because, although there had been no infection and the wound had healed in a marvelously efficient manner, her heart ached all the time.

"I must thank you again for allowing me to remain here." Pamela sat up and tried to shift the tumble of pillows into some comfortable position. "I do have a bedchamber at the Distinguished Academy of Governesses, although not nearly as grand as this one." This bedchamber had gold brocade draperies and a counterpane, rich maroon wallpaper, and cheerful paintings on every wall. "Every day when

Miss Setterington visits she asks me when I'll be well enough to return."

"There is no rush." Queen Victoria stood and plumped the pillows directly behind Pamela's head, then helped her recline again. "You're still dreadfully wan, and that bruise on your face is turning a most ghastly shade of yellow."

Pamela touched her own cheek. The stairs had left their mark on more than just her face. She resembled a calico cat with brown and yellow marks up and down her entire body. For one moment, she suffered as she wondered if that was why Kerrich so seldom visited, but she knew that wasn't true. Any man who kissed the formidable and disguised Miss Lockhart wouldn't be so shallow as to see bruises, or even a scar left by a gunshot, as barriers to desire.

And that was the problem, wasn't it? When he did take time out of his busy life to visit Pamela, the queen chaperoned them, or Hannah did, or one of Her Majesty's ladies-in-waiting, and while he stood beside her bed, he treated Pamela with the utmost respect and admiration.

Pamela hated his respect. She spat on his admiration. She could scarcely bear his polite, well-meaning conversation. If he wished to speak with her honestly, as he had done before, no one's presence could have hobbled his comments. Pamela understood what he was telling her without words.

The fire had burned out. He no longer desired her.

Queen Victoria's voice intruded on Pamela's own personal purgatory, and with a start Pamela realized Her Majesty had reseated herself and had been speaking for quite a while.

"So I told Lord Kerrich that Lady Colbrook tricked the story out of me months ago. I had no idea she was so clever, although later events certainly proved she was. I assume she spread the tale of Lord Kerrich's . . . um . . . bareness outside the window that very night to try to cause a diversion from her own activities." Queen Victoria was shaking her head in amazement. "He is still angry about that."

"Yes, but he would be, wouldn't he?" Pamela's gaze rested on the vase of roses beside her bed. Every day the old roses were replenished with fresh ones, and every day she inhaled their scent and remembered Kerrich's passion, then inhaled again and wondered if the scent of roses would ever again bring her delight. But she never asked that they be removed.

"He was willing to do anything to keep that tale quiet, even adopt that adorable girl." Victoria grinned wickedly as she stitched. "I've never forgotten that night at Kensington Palace. We were most amused. He was the funniest thing I'd ever seen, hanging there in all his glory, and I told him if you hadn't insisted that discretion was the better part of kindness, I would have tattled on him immediately."

"Was he properly appreciative?"

Queen Victoria glanced at her, her eyes full of mirth. "He didn't appear to be, although it might have gone better if I hadn't laughed."

"All men take it ill when a woman finds them an object of mirth."

"Yes, but I've made it up to him." The queen dismissed his disgruntlement with a wave of her needle. "I told Albert Kerrich was a good man. After seeing him with you and Elizabeth, Albert believes me now."

"Kerrich has been everything that is kind." And respectful and admiring. Not at all like the Kerrich she had come to love.

Love. That was the awful part. She loved him, and he didn't even desire her.

The wretch!

If only she hadn't been shot. Then she could stand up to him and tell him what she thought of a man who abandoned a child—oh, for a good cause, to be sure—but he had left Beth to go to meet the queen with only Pamela and Lord Reynard as support. She'd tell him what she thought of men who substituted respect and admiration for flaming desire. And most of all, she'd tell him . . . well, she'd tell him she was sorry she'd screeched at him. That she wished everything hadn't ended so badly. That his reputation for seduction was in no way inflated. That their affair could never have worked because . . . because she had trusted him no more than he had trusted her. They'd made so many mistakes. They'd told so many half-truths. And she just wanted to ask him if he had cared at all.

Queen Victoria stood, rubbed her back with her hands, and in an irritable tone said, "I just can't sit. It's not comfortable."

In the last weeks, the royal pregnancy had developed to the point that it could not be hidden. Pamela couldn't keep her gaze off the queen as Her Majesty wandered to the window and stared out across the London skyline. "I understand," Pamela said, but what she felt when she gazed on Queen Victoria was not understanding. It was uncertainty. Her own monthly courses hadn't arrived, but *surely* that was because of the trauma her body had suffered.

The queen turned and faced her. "I know what you're thinking."

Heaven forfend.

"You're thinking I should do more to punish Lady Colbrook."

"I wasn't thinking that at all, Your Majesty. I haven't been told what happened to Lady Colbrook."

"Oh." The queen fidgeted with the fringe of her silk

shawl. "Lady Colbrook is under house arrest, and we have advised her husband, who should be the head of their household, that a long trip abroad would be appropriate."

Aghast, Pamela stared. "After all that she did . . . devising the plan to counterfeit banknotes, organizing her crew, recruiting Mr. Athersmith . . . and that's all?"

"Yes, and do you know why?" Victoria didn't wait for an answer. "Apparently she bragged that the men in the government policing forces would never admit a woman had so tricked them, and she was right."

"You jest."

"She deliberately created a diversion in the Bank of England by losing control of her horse and requiring that she be carried into the lobby and carrying on so that people crowded around and Mr. Athersmith almost succeeding in stealing those supplies." The queen shook her head. "They didn't even realize she had done it on purpose! They still prefer to blame everything on Mr. Athersmith because he's a man, and because he's dead."

Pamela plucked at the sheet. In great indignation, Beth had told her that Mr. Athersmith had wrestled his way free from the guards and somersaulted onto the marble floor below the staircase. He hadn't survived the fall, and that disappointed Beth, for she wanted him alive and suffering as Pamela suffered. Pamela could only think of that pleasant-looking, earnest man who loved a young lady, yet whose appearance, personality and value always paled into insignificance beside the radiance that was his cousin. "A man's pride is a very odd creature," Pamela said, "and it drives him to peculiar behavior."

"I think that is good of you to be so understanding of any man after . . . after the difficulties you've had since your father . . ."

Pamela covered her eyes with one hand. The good hand.

The other arm was still in a sling, because any time she moved it, it ached and pulled so dreadfully she was in tears. This was a good gunshot wound, the best, Dr. McEachern said, and the queen's own physician gravely agreed. She had been lucky.

So what had it been like for her father, shot and left to die? What kind of agonies had he experienced as he writhed alone?

Pamela hated that Kerrich was right. She had never mourned her father, and now it was catching up with her. Now that she was weak and wretched, her father walked her dreams.

"I'm sorry," Victoria said. "I should never have mentioned that dreadful time. I just wanted to offer my condolences on the deaths of both your parents."

"Thank you, Your Majesty." Pamela picked up the silver pocket watch she kept on her pillow and looked at it.

Queen Victoria took that as a hint, and gathered up her belongings. "You're tired."

Hastily, Pamela flicked a tear away. "Perhaps. Just a little."

"My physician says you'll feel better soon. Why don't you take a nap?"

"Yes. Thank you. I will." Except that when she did, her father was there. Day and night she saw him, charming, handsome, feckless. When she was a child, she had loved him for the charm. When she was an adolescent, she hated him for the fecklessness. Almost everything he'd ever done was unforgivable, yet right now, as the pain of the bullet lingered, she remembered the early times when he had swung her on the swing, sung her to sleep, and carried her on his back. He had been her father, all she had of him was a watch, and her love for that loving, winning man had never been completely vanquished.

So as Her Majesty slipped away, Pamela covered her face again and cried for him, all the heartache he had caused and the bitterness of all those wasted years.

She cried for herself, for all the lonely years ahead. Kerrich was like her father in his charm and his comeliness. But he wasn't feckless or irresponsible. He'd been on a secret mission. He cared so much for his grandfather and his family name he had gone to great lengths to change his image from rake to upright member of the nobility. Only now that he no longer cared did she realize it.

She . . . she had been so afraid of being like her mother, dedicated to a man who disdained her love, that she'd refused to encourage the best man she'd ever met. Beneath the shield of her hand, she smiled a watery smile. Perhaps not the *best* man; he had his faults and she was well aware of them. His conceit. His hauteur. His tendency to take advantage where a gentleman should not. But he was the man she loved, faults and all.

She had alienated him, and now she had to live with the consequences.

At some point, she must have slipped into slumber, for she came awake with a start when Beth whispered in her piercing voice, "Miss Lockhart, are you asleep?"

Pamela chuckled. Beth always made her happy. "No," she whispered back without opening her eyes.

Beth tiptoed away, then at the door whispered again, "Come *on*."

Pamela's eyes popped open.

Kerrich stood framed in the entrance holding a bouquet of red, white and pink roses.

The mere presence of the man brought a tingling to her shoulder—among other places. That dark, ruffled hair, that sensuous mouth and the twice-broken nose. As if his countenance weren't enough, his shoulders filled his dark blue coat to perfection, that light blue waistcoat was brimming with his broad chest, and she didn't dare look at his trousers because she remembered . . .

And when he stared at her like this, she was no longer aware of her wan complexion or the pain from the gunshot or the aches from staying in bed too long. When he stared at her with those sin-colored eyes, she wanted to remain in bed longer—with him in it.

"Miss Lockhart, I know you are tired of being asked how you are, but tell me, then I will let the matter drop." He strolled to the side of the bed, each movement a symphony.

The voluptuous scent of the roses reminded her of just how virile he could be. "I'm fine," she said.

"No. I didn't defy the queen and sneak past the guards so you can tell me a polite lie. You must tell me the truth." He took her hand, and the warmth of their two palms together made her want to sigh worshipfully. "Just this once."

The truth is, I love you. "The pain grows less," she said. "Three times a day, Dr. McEachern makes me move my shoulder as far as I can, and I think that helps."

Beth piped up. "She cries because it hurts so much."

"Don't . . ." *Tell him about her weakness.*

His hand tightened on hers. "The doctor's hurting you?"

"The forced movement is helping. Even the queen's physician admits that."

He glared at her as if she had made him angry. And anger, she had to admit, was a passion of sorts, and better than respect and admiration. Abruptly, he said, "I must tell you the truth."

Pamela had heard a man start a speech like this before. Her father had told her the truth not long before he walked away.

Kerrich continued, "I know you don't want to hear this,

but I must express my gratitude to you for helping apprehend my cousin."

She supposed he might think she had helped kill his cousin.

"None of those other people even thought to go get the guards. Only you." He smiled down at the child at his side and stroked her hair. "And Beth."

"Lord Kerrich, aren't you going to give her the flowers?" Beth prompted.

He started as if he'd forgotten the roses he held. Then he laid them on the pillow beside Pamela. "They're beautiful," he told her, as if she needed instruction on appreciating them.

"Yes. Thank you."

Beth pulled up a chair and slouched in its depths, observing them with bright-eyed interest. "He's sent *all* the roses."

Pamela tried to look into his face, but the intensity of his gaze caught her and she had to glance away. "That is very good of you, my lord."

"I'm glad you think so. But I must finish all I wished to say."

Of course he had to finish, else she think the roses meant that he wished her to remember how the scent of roses had encircled them as they came together on his desk.

"When you brought the guards," he said, "it was further proof that you're a remarkably intelligent woman, marked for success in every battle of life. Me, I was like all the rest of the men, not even thinking a lady could be the villain."

"You figured it out pretty fast," Beth observed.

Heaven knew why, but Pamela felt moved to comfort him. "So you did, my lord, and you took effective action."

"Not effective enough, or you wouldn't have been shot."

He looked out the window as if he couldn't bear to look at her anymore. "By my own cousin, with my own pistol! I felt so guilty. I would have done anything to have taken the bullet for you, and at the same time, I was overcome with awe for your bravery. You never even thought, you just stepped in front of Beth."

Beth chimed in, "She's the bravest person I ever met."

"She is!" he said to Beth. Then with vigor and directness, he leaned over Pamela, placed his hands flat on the mattress, and said, "You listen to me talk and all I'm saying is that I'm grateful to you, that I'm full of remorse that you were hurt, and that I cherish your fearlessness. But I have one more very important thing to say."

What? That you will never forget our time together? That you hope we can remain friends? Pamela moved to save herself any more of this excruciatingly painful farewell speech. "Yes, I think I know what it is, but I would spare you because I have good news. Since Her Majesty knows me and she has met Hannah, and I have proved myself to be—"

"A loyal subject," Beth prompted.

"Yes. And so respectable." Pamela smiled with a fair amount of irony and rigorously avoided Kerrich's gaze. "As Hannah is, also." *Although Hannah truly was respectable and Pamela was just one of Kerrich's former conquests.* "Her Majesty has offered to give the Governess School her personal recommendation."

"That's very interesting," he said with patient politeness. "What does it have to do with us?"

"Simply that with the queen's recommendation, overwhelming success has blessed the Distinguished Academy of Governesses. Hannah has had three experienced and highly esteemed governesses come to us for placement, and she has found them positions and been paid for that service." Pamela was proud of her steady voice and business-like demeanor, especially considering her reclining position and informal attire. "Also, we have a full classroom of young ladies whom we are preparing to go into service, and every one of them is spoken for."

His brow puckered. "I'm sure I'm pleased for Miss Setterington."

"When you have paid the money you owe us, we'll be on solid financial ground."

Beth sat straight up in her chair and stared in consternation.

Lifting his knee onto the mattress, he loomed over Pamela. "You . . . you want me to pay you?"

"What you owe us." She had to look at him now. His face was right in hers, so close she could smell the minty scent of his breath. "I did fulfill your demands, my lord."

He just stared at her.

"I mean, your demands that you be represented as a respectable, compassionate man who is worthy to handle the queen's money. Together, Beth and I have done that."

He still stared as if he couldn't quite believe that she had the nerve to dun him. Then, as abruptly as he had risen above her, he backed away. He stood a decent distance from the bed and said, "Would you rather I paid you or Miss Setterington?"

As if trying to get her attention, her heart gave a hard thump. She took a calming breath and ignored it. "If you would just send the amount to the Distinguished Academy of Governesses, we would be most grateful."

"Of course, as I am grateful to you for the success of this mission."

Slapping her forehead, Beth groaned loudly.

They both turned and looked at her.

Pamela found herself on unsteady ground, wanting to

keep the child herself and not wanting to cut the affectionate ties that bound the orphan and the earl. "My lord, I imagine you will wish to return to your previous penchant for manly living, and such habits would not be suitable for a girl who will soon become a young lady. So I'll keep Beth."

Neither Beth nor Kerrich said anything. They just stared at each other, and Beth's lower lip wobbled.

Which had the effect of convincing Pamela that she knew best. "But please, my lord, promise you'll visit whenever you wish."

Lord Kerrich tore his gaze away from Beth and backed toward the door. "I'll have Beth's clothing sent to the academy, along with my payment for your services." With a brusque bow, he walked out.

Beth scrambled to her feet and stared after him, then stared at Pamela, then stared back at the empty door. "Miss Lockhart, you've ruined everything!"

Pamela just wanted to burrow under the covers and cry, but as always she had to keep her chin up. "No, really, darling, someday you'll understand—"

In a rush, Beth asked, "Did he ever tell you why he took me to the horse races?"

Pamela thought perhaps she didn't want to hear this, and with a faint heart, she said, "No. No, he never did."

"He took me because I was going to cry. He knew I was faking, but he didn't care. He couldn't stand it. And he said the reason he'd take me again is because it made me smile. He's a nice man, Miss Lockhart, and"—Beth's eyes filled with tears, and this time she *wasn't* faking it—"we're never going to see him again."

CHAPTER 30

"Kerrich, tell me, why did you want to come to this racetrack?" Tomlin groused as he tromped through the muddy grass on the way down the hill to the rails at the front. "You hate the Hippodrome. The horses are second-rate, the jockeys are pathetic and the people who frequent the track are unfashionable." He leaned closer to Kerrich. "And I've hidden my wallet because half of them are thieves."

"Dreadful place," Kerrich agreed. The autumn breeze ruffled the hair on his forehead, but nary a cloud marred the clear blue of the sky. No storm would rip through the throng today to reveal secrets better left unexposed. He observed no saucy, fresh-faced girls in pretty dresses to wager with, and all the women were clearly strumpets out plying their trade. But the crowd was loud, the second-rate horses were running, the pathetic jockeys were riding and his clumsy friend Tomlin was with him. Just ahead of them two footmen carried his grandfather in a sedan chair, and Lord Reynard prodded them with his cane when they jostled him too much and yelled at the people who got in the way.

Kerrich hadn't enjoyed an outing so much for well over

a month. "Don't know what anyone sees in this place."

Tomlin sighed. "You've been acting oddly since your cousin died. I know it's a disgrace to have a criminal in your family, but let's face it—most of us have a horse thief or two hidden in the ancestral closet. It's not as if the two of you were close."

Kerrich grimaced. "Sadly, no, we weren't, and it's hard to grieve for a man who would aim for a child and shoot a woman."

"Dastardly," Tomlin said. "How *is* Miss Lockhart?"

"Fine, last I heard." Kerrich pretended disinterest. "She left Buckingham Palace and returned to her Governess School."

"Oh, that's right. The Distinctive School of Instructors."

"The Distinguished Academy of Governesses," Kerrich corrected. "I'm sure her life is easier now that she's no longer living under my auspices, and my life has been richer since she and the child moved out."

"Children can limit you." Tomlin nodded. "I know. Got three of my own. And that orphan girl you had was a handful. That Beverly."

"Beth."

"Yes, that's it. Beth. Have you seen her?"

"No, I . . ." *I miss her too much to go see her. I'm afraid she'll reproach me for failing to obtain Miss Lockhart's affections. And if I see her, I'll want to keep her.*

"Better that way," Tomlin said. "Clean break. Less painful. And you know how children are. She'll forget you right away. A couple of years, and she won't even recognize you on the street."

They reached the railing at the front, with its full, unobstructed view of the mediocre races.

Kerrich stared at the oval track, imagining glimpsing Beth at some distant date. She'd be beautiful, intelligent, well-grounded with common sense and stuffed full of manners. And she wouldn't even know him.

Everything about the concept reeked.

The footmen placed Grandpapa's sedan chair on a flat piece of ground and pulled the supports from the rings. Lord Reynard thanked them and flipped each of them a coin, then planted his cane in the grass, placed his hand on the gold knob at the top and surveyed the area like a king on his throne.

Tomlin asked, "So Kerrich . . . when are you going to start living like a bachelor again?"

"What do you mean?" Kerrich snapped.

"The child isn't living with you. Neither is the formidable Miss Lockhart. Yet you haven't been to the club. You haven't been to the theater. You aren't tupping a mistress. You're so damned dull you might as well be married."

Kerrich lifted his monocle and glared at Tomlin, but he could think of no retort. He *had* been dull, but whenever he went to the theater he thought how much Beth would enjoy it, and when he rode his horse about town, the damned creature had a tendency to wander toward the location of the Governess School. Then Kerrich would imagine he saw Pamela in every lady below the age of fifty, and it got damned embarrassing trying to explain he hadn't meant anything by his breezy comments—and they were always breezy.

"Don't try and blame your monkish conduct on me, boy." Lord Reynard lounged in his chair. "*I've* been going to the club. *I've* been going to the theater."

"*You've* been spotted in the company of the dowager countess of Anson, you cradle robber, you." Tomlin hiked up his trousers and squatted beside the old man. "You should tarry with women your own age."

"There are no women my own age," Lord Reynard said tartly.

Tomlin cackled like a hen who'd just hatched a set of chicks, and the young footmen who stood guard behind their little party tried hard to hide their laughter.

Standing, Tomlin shouted, "Swearn! I see you've got your eldest with you! Require a chaperone now, do you?" And off he went to visit with an embarrassed-looking Swearn and his censorious son.

He left a rather clamorous silence behind. Never mind that the spectators were walking about, laying wagers and waiting for the next race to start. Ever since the counterfeiting affair had been settled, Lord Reynard had been watching Kerrich and waiting for . . . something. Kerrich wasn't sure what, but he hadn't delivered and Lord Reynard had made his disapproval clear.

Leaning against the railing, Kerrich clasped his hands and muttered, "I do not know why I ever liked such a tactless, nosy oaf as Tomlin."

"Because he tells you the truth."

Kerrich scowled.

Lord Reynard had risen and stood beside him, frail and hearty, old and eternally young, with his cane clasped in one hand and his hat tipped at a jaunty angle over one eye. "You know, son, in your adolescence, I tried my damnedest to be a good substitute parent, and I think I succeeded."

"Yes, sir, and I—"

"Shut up." Lord Reynard shook his finger under Kerrich's nose. "Just shut up, and put that demmed monocle away. It looks ridiculous."

Kerrich stuffed the monocle into his pocket and wished his grandfather weren't always so blunt.

Lord Reynard closed his eyes. "Where was I? Oh, yes. I listened to your youthful writhings, I was tactful when you were foolish, I allowed you to make your mistakes and kept my mouth shut. All really arduous tasks, as you will discover when you have your own children—if you're ever smart enough to get married." He paused.

Kerrich didn't know if he was supposed to talk yet, but he said, "Yes, sir."

"Your luck just ran out. I'll let you get away with ill-considered, imprudent and irrational, but you're being just plain stupid. What the hell are you doing letting Pamela Lockhart slip between your fingers?"

A race started. The crowd began their long-necked, wide-eyed concentration on the horses. Kerrich watched glumly, and when the race was finished and sounds of relief and disgust exploded around them, he turned to his grandfather. "I didn't let her slip between my fingers. She doesn't want me."

"I saw the way she looks at you. Of course she wants you. You've made a mistake." Lord Reynard pointed toward the top of the hill. "Go to her and fix it."

"I tried to . . . to fix it. When she resided at Buckingham Palace, I sneaked in to see her. I was hoping she'd tell me she would marry me."

"So you proposed to her?"

"Not exactly."

Leaning his elbow on the railing, Lord Reynard examined his grandson from hat brim to boots. "You wanted her to propose to you?"

"No! That would be expecting too much, I think."

"You wanted her to tell you she loved you?"

"Yes." Kerrich sounded defiant, even in his own ears.

"Why didn't you tell her that you loved her?"

His grandfather knew. His grandfather knew that Kerrich loved her, and he wasn't mocking Kerrich about his vow never to love, or crowing that he was right. Grandpapa was clever that way. So Kerrich answered, "If I told her I loved her, she'd win."

Lord Reynard's bafflement appeared to be real. "Win . . . what?"

"She'd hold the power in the marriage, and I'd be like my father, a beggar at my own table."

"What the hell are you talking about?" Lord Reynard tapped Kerrich's chest hard with his cane. "Your father wasn't a beggar at his own table! Don't you remember their marriage at all?"

Despite the warm sun, chills ran up and down Kerrich's spine. "I remember Mother smiling at Father and hugging him, but—"

"Your mother adored your father. Yes, she's the kind of woman who has to have a man, but she hasn't remarried. Do you know why?"

"She's been with so many gigolos no decent man will have her," Kerrich muttered.

"Damn! I hate it when you're deliberately obtuse." Another set of horses came out of the starting gate. Lord Reynard didn't stop talking, but he did lower his voice in deference to the bettors. "Your mother is a wealthy, noble widow. She's attractive and knows how to make every old man young again and every young man a virile giant. Any man in England and on the continent would be glad to wed her, but she's never loved a man since your father."

"She had a damned funny way of showing it." Kerrich's voice vibrated with old, carefully preserved fury.

"There were never any other men for her while your father was alive. He was a generous man, and he would want her to be happy now. So if she loved him and made him happy when he was alive, and he'd wish her nothing but the best now, what are *you* bellyaching about?"

From the depths of his ancient anguish, Kerrich confessed, "They laughed."

His grandfather followed his conversational wandering without trouble. "They? The other young pissant aristocrats like you?"

"Yes! And the adults, too."

"So your indignation isn't for your father's sake, or about your mother at all. It's about you and your pride."

With immense reluctance, Kerrich nodded. "It sounded so much better before."

"Before you realized you were a selfish young snot-nose?" Lord Reynard stared him in the eye. "Don't worry, I've known it for years. Listen, boy, I don't know the recipe for success, but I know the recipe for failure, and that's trying to listen to everyone. Hell, every ass has an opinion. That laughter is envy, and what they say about your mother is nonsense. I've known her since she was a child. She's a good woman—and you're a great deal like her."

Kerrich sprang back. "I am not!"

"You were always searching for the woman you loved in every face and in every body. Think, boy, how much like Miss Lockhart all your mistresses have looked."

Because I've been wanting her all my life. The thought sprang into Devon's mind, alive, rising with the beauty and peril of an asp from a basket with the aid of a charmer's flute. With a shock he realized—he would never want another woman again. Only Pamela.

Because when Pamela loved, she gave herself completely. When Beth was angry with her, Pamela didn't waste time wondering how it would be if Beth rejected her or whether she would be hurt by that rebuff. She had just reached out for Beth and embraced her. Pamela's wholehearted dive into love frightened Kerrich; how did she dare without protecting herself first? And how could he make her love him like that?

Kerrich and Lord Reynard leaned against the rail and watched the horses start around the track.

Into the silence, Kerrich burst out, "I wouldn't care what anyone thought, if I could have her on my terms. I want to know I'm going to be happy."

"So you're looking for a guarantee of happiness, are you? You think as long as you're the man in command you'll be happy? What about her? What if she's not happy?"

"I can make her happy."

"Boy, if you think you can *make* that woman do anything, you don't know her at all."

The race finished while Kerrich wretchedly pondered that insight. Lord Reynard was right. He didn't know Pamela. That was part of her appeal. The truth of her remained beneath layers upon layers of complex personality and evasive smiles. But he caught glimpses of the core of the woman, and each time he liked her more. Loved her more.

Lord Reynard groaned and clasped his arm. "I'm tired, and while I'm usually hesitant to give you the benefit of my experience, I'm ninety-two and might not live long enough for you to get smart."

"You're eighty-four, Grandpapa."

"Stop sassing me and help me sit down."

Surprisingly, Kerrich wanted someone to tell him what to do, so he gave Lord Reynard his arm and assisted him while he sat. Then he squatted beside the old man. "Tell me."

Lord Reynard tapped Kerrich on the forehead, right between the eyes. "Marriage isn't about who's in command. It's a partnership where you stand or fall together."

"But to get Pamela, I'd have to sink my pride completely. I'd have to grovel."

"If it makes you feel better, lad, I groveled for your grandmother." Lord Reynard grasped one of Kerrich's wrists. "Tell me something, boy. When you saw Lewis take aim at your woman, did you jump for joy?"

"No!" Kerrich didn't want to think about that awful moment when he dove for Lewis, knowing all the while he couldn't make it.

"When you were holding her and the doctor dug out that bullet from her shoulder, did you think, 'If her lungs are hit, I'll be rid of her'?"

"No!"

"I saw your face. All you could think while she screamed was that she could be dead soon, and you wanted everything to be different."

Kerrich clutched at his composure. "I wished I could have saved her the pain. Of course I did."

"If you were so bloody indifferent, why didn't you get a footman to hold her? You could have left the room."

"No!" Pulling a handkerchief from his pocket, Kerrich blotted the sheen of perspiration from his forehead. "That is, I felt responsible, and thus should be there."

Lord Reynard pulled out his pocket watch and looked at it worriedly, shook it, raised it to his ear.

"What's wrong?"

"I was afraid, with the load of manure around here, that the works on my watch would be ruined."

"Grandpapa, that is not funny!"

"Ah, you've lost your sense of humor." Putting the watch back in his pocket, Lord Reynard leaned forward and lowered his voice. "Have you thought she might have taken seriously what you poked at her in fun?"

With a glance at the footmen standing sentinel, Kerrich

did the same. "Do you mean, have I thought she might be increasing? Yes, I've thought of it. In fact, it's . . . likely. I deliberately didn't use the French sheath because I thought if every other method of getting her to marry me failed, she'd have to come to me and—"

"Wait." Lord Reynard put his hand on Kerrich's forearm. "You thought that woman would come to you and beg—"

"I didn't say beg!"

"—beg you to wed her because she was with child?" Lord Reynard's fingers tightened, and he burst into laughter. It was an insulting laughter, one that mocked Kerrich's intentions and his intelligence.

Unfortunately, Kerrich knew he deserved it. He waited patiently until his grandfather had finished, then handed him a handkerchief to wipe his wet eyes. "I don't want her to marry me only because she's increasing."

"You're a picky bastard, aren't you?" Lord Reynard sighed. "You're in love with a quick-witted woman who has as much pride as you do and who doesn't need you. She'll survive without you. Hell, she'll prosper without you. And why do you love her?"

"Because she's quick-witted, proud and capable." Kerrich hated this. He was handsome, he was wealthy, he was well connected and he had nothing to offer Pamela that she desperately needed. He had only love to offer, and he could take a chance and offer it, or never tell her and regret it for the rest of his life.

"This is what you do," Grandpapa instructed. "You figure out what you want. Then you tell her. Then you ask her what she wants, and you listen to what she says. Then you give it to her, and maybe she'll take it, and you in the bargain, and maybe someday, if you don't blunder too badly, she'll love you."

Kerrich stared at his grandfather and remembered the

fantasies she had shared. "I already know what she wants."

"Then what are you waiting for? Give it to her."

"Yes. Yes, I will, but first . . ." Confession was good for the soul, Kerrich told himself. "Grandpapa, I *was* the full moon on a foggy night." Then he braced himself for Lord Reynard's amazement.

Instead, Grandpapa said, "Did you think I didn't recognize the Mathewes family jockum? I've been holding one of my own for eighty-nine years."

"Eighty-four," Kerrich corrected automatically. His grandfather knew? He knew?

Kerrich smiled, then chuckled, then roared. All these years, Kerrich had been so careful to keep the truth from his grandfather, and he always knew?

The footmen stared, his friends gathered around and tried to convince him to tell them the jest, and the wagerers laughed as if Kerrich's merriment tickled them, too.

When Kerrich had recovered enough to talk, he told the onlookers, "You'll have to get the tale from Lord Reynard. I'm off to make my darling's dreams come true."

CHAPTER 31

Hannah hurried toward the study, her brow knit with puzzlement. A gentleman had arrived, Cusheon said, and had requested her presence, but the gentleman refused to give his name. By the butler's smirk, it was obvious he knew, but he shook his head and refused to answer when she questioned him. "Go on down, Miss Setterington," he said before he hurried off toward the kitchen. "You'll approve."

Pamela was occupied with teaching the class called "Maintaining the Proper Governess Decorum," so Hannah didn't bother her. Indeed, Hannah didn't bother Pamela with almost anything, since her friend had not recovered from the gunshot wound as Hannah had hoped. She had begun to suspect Pamela's problem was not so much a residual weakness as a melancholy of the spirit. Not even Hannah's vivacious projections of fame and fortune for the Distinguished Academy of Governesses could cheer her, and when Pamela was not excited about making money, Hannah diagnosed serious problems. Man problems.

She had subtly questioned Beth about Pamela's experience at the hands of that despicably handsome Lord Kerrich, and Beth had just as subtly evaded her. Unhappily, the child was disconsolate, too, and that left Hannah with no recourse but to wait until one of them opened up to her.

She had already waited over a month.

The door to the study stood open. She sailed in—and it shut behind her. Swinging around, she found herself facing Lord Kerrich, his hand flat against the door, and a giggling Beth.

He bowed. "Miss Setterington, I hope you will forgive this unorthodox intrusion, but I have a favor to ask of you."

His arrogant assurance set her teeth on edge. "What would that be, my lord?"

So he told her.

"I don't understand why you can't travel with Beth to Brookford House." Pamela sat on her bed and watched as Hannah packed a bag for her. "I'm still weak from my wound."

Hannah ignored her.

"There's so much for me to do here."

Hannah held up a plain, white pair of pantalettes and frowned at them. "A little lace trim would not go amiss, Pamela."

"For what purpose?"

"I find those little furbelows cheer me." Hannah folded the pantalettes and placed them in the bag. "You could use some cheering."

"Have I been glum?" Was that why Hannah insisted Pamela go on this dreadful trip that would end in her seeing Kerrich and hearing his voice? Because if that was it, Pamela could change. "I'm glad you told me. I'm just tired, that's all. I'll make an effort to be more blithe."

Hannah put down the petticoats she had deemed travel-worthy and took Pamela's hands. Looking right into her eyes, she said, "Dear, I'm not trying to tell you I don't need you here. It took the three of us, Charlotte, you and I, to start the Distinguished Academy of Governesses. Without the support, knowledge and combined income of all of us, we could never have succeeded so quickly. But we have reached the time of which we dreamed. The school is organized, the placement agency is popular, and the whole structure needs only the lightest of hands on the reins. A chance like this, a chance to travel to Brookford House, should be seized and enjoyed."

"But you—"

"Beth likes me very much, but you are her particular friend and dear guardian. You must take her."

The only time Hannah sounded this firm was when she was speaking to a recalcitrant student.

Pamela put her hand on her back. "I hate to mention it, but the place where the thief stabbed me is painful, too."

"He stabbed you on the other side." Hannah stuffed Pamela's boots into a second, still-empty bag. "I think to travel you should wear your new light blue dimity with the white flower pattern—"

"I should be still in half-mourning for my father," Pamela objected. Besides, she'd picked out that color because Kerrich had once suggested she would look lovely in that shade, and to wear it in front of him seemed an admission of sorts.

"You're almost out." Going to the cupboard, Hannah brought out the gown. "Besides, you never cared before."

"I do now." Pamela did, too, and was prepared to be stubborn about it.

So Hannah proposed the perfect solution. "Then you shall carry my gray cashmere shawl with the embroidered flowers along the hem. They're blue, too, and will match the dress, and the gray will make everything proper." Hannah laid the gown across the bed next to Pamela, then took her by the shoulders and looked into her eyes. "You don't have to stay at Brookford if you don't wish to, Pamela, but you are going. And Pamela?"

"Yes?"

"You might think about leaving your father's watch behind."

Shade from the magnificent oaks dappled Pamela, Beth and Lord Reynard in the luxurious open carriage as it traveled along the wooded drive toward Brookford House. The wheels crunched as they rolled over the gravel and the breeze carried a hint of autumn. The huge park boasted an extensive wilderness and a fishing pond, all of which Lord Reynard had pointed out with pride. To Beth's great excitement, she spotted a deer, and even Pamela found reluctant serenity among the green, red and gold leaves.

"Coachman," Lord Reynard said, "stop at the top of the rise."

The trees thinned. The carriage slowed. The house came into view.

Pamela's mouth dried. A green sweep of scythed grass swept from the shore of the lake to the edge of the stone piazza. The Italianate house rose three stories high and stretched twelve windows wide, an architectural marvel of rosy stone and Ionic pilasters. The peak at the top of the portico was rife with intricate floral carving. A stone railing surrounded the roof, and chimneys of various heights rose above it all. Overall, the effect was one of mellow beauty set among the sylvan hills.

Beth exclaimed, "Bless my soul. This one's bigger than the one in town!"

"Much bigger," Lord Reynard said. "Almost two hundred rooms, with forty-seven bedchambers and twenty baths—with plumbing! It's really too big for a single man and, as Devon has recently discovered, it's a dreadful place to housetrain a puppy."

Beth giggled.

The carriage lurched onward.

Lord Reynard said, "Devon bought it in Norfolk so he could be close to me. I live not far from here, Miss Lockhart, on the Mathewes family estate."

"Oh." Pamela found herself wanting to fidget as the drive wound closer and closer. "How pleasant that the two of you are close."

"Devon's a good grandson and a fine man." Lord Reynard nodded. "Don't you think so, Miss Lockhart?"

"A very fine man." If he hadn't been, Pamela wouldn't be in this state of apprehension. Brookford House loomed, inundating her with the impression of wealth and comfort. A small group of people stood lined up on the steps, craning their necks as the carriage approached.

Then she saw *him*. Kerrich, standing on the piazza waiting for them to arrive. The house became nothing but a backdrop, a place where he could be viewed, and she was lost. Drowning in desire and need and love, seeing only him and wanting to launch herself into his arms.

As the carriage came to a halt and the footman opened the door, he strode forward, as handsome and arrogant as the first time she'd seen him in the study of the Governess School. But this time, his gaze danced from one to another, and he smiled broadly. "Welcome to my home!" he called.

Beth did what Pamela longed to do. She jumped from the carriage into his embrace. Her arms wrapped around his neck, his arms clasped her close, and he spun with her in a delirious dance of joy.

"I missed you, Devon, I missed you," she said.

"I missed you, too, Beth. There's been no one to laugh at me when I lose a wager on the horses."

His back was turned to the carriage, but Pamela could have sworn she saw him kiss the top of Beth's head, and she swallowed. Beth had pined for him; apparently, he had missed her, too.

Setting Beth on her feet, he said, "Your horse has been lonesome without you, so I hope you're prepared to ride her as much as she wants."

"Yes!" Beth yelled.

Pamela began to remonstrate, but changed her mind. Conduct was less encumbered in the country, and Beth would calm down soon.

The footman extended his hand, and Pamela reached out to take it, but Lord Reynard said, "Age before beauty, young lady, age before beauty."

Startled, Pamela pulled her full skirts back as he tottered to his feet, and when he pointed at the second footman and said, "You'll have to support me, also," she thought nothing of it.

Until he had wobbled his way down and let the footmen lead him over to Beth, leaving no one to assist her except Kerrich, and he had a hot, intent expression that she recognized as . . . well, that didn't look like respect, admiration *or* gratitude. Moreover, he held his hands behind him as if he had to physically restrain himself from snatching her from the carriage.

His clothing didn't reflect country ease. He wore an almost formal dark green suit, black waistcoat and silk neck cloth. His shiny boots glittered in the sunlight, and his smooth chin must have been shaved within the last hour. The rose in his lapel drew her gaze; it was gloriously red and perfectly formed, a bud on the verge of full blossom. Gorgeous. Taken altogether, he was gorgeous.

The new gown that Pamela had resisted wearing now seemed scarcely good enough, and she was grateful for the quality of the cashmere shawl and the frame of her blue-trimmed hat, which, she knew, brought out the blue of her eyes.

Kerrich pitched his voice to reach her ears only. "Welcome, Miss Lockhart. I have imagined you here at Brookford, and the reality is a greater gratification than the dream." He took one white gloved hand from behind his back and held it out to her.

"Thank you, my lord, for inviting me." Painstakingly, she laid her palm in his.

The contact was like rain after a drought. Like spring after winter. Like the first time in a long time that the man she loved had touched her.

But he didn't love her.

His fingers closed around hers and he helped her to her feet, then steadied her as she set foot onto his property. He gazed at her with the greed of a miser catching his first glimpse of gold.

He said only, "You look well. I worried that you would take on too much after you returned to work, but you appear to be robust."

"Yes, most robust. I am very strong." Silently, she winced. She made herself sound like a prizefighter, savage and grunting.

"Your strength is one of the things I most admire about you." He stood so close he filled her gaze, and she could smell the scent of starch from his clothing and the sweetness of the rose in his lapel. "But I feared you might overestimate your stamina."

"On the contrary, Miss Setterington and Beth have quite coddled me." She found herself glancing up into his eyes, then away, as if the elegance of his brown eyes with their heavy black lashes was too much for a mere woman to contemplate.

"Good," he said.

"What?" What were they talking about?

"Good that Miss Setterington and Beth coddled you."

His lips formed the words with glorious precision, and all she could do was admonish herself not to behave like a fool. "Lord Reynard and Beth are waiting for us."

"No. They went inside."

How did he know that? He'd been looking at her every moment.

With tender hands—well, she considered them tender, probably they were only polite—he turned her toward the house. "I have people I would like you to meet."

"As you wish." She would likely have agreed to anything he said. Then she realized he meant the crowd on the stairway. The servants, she supposed, but why would he want her to meet them?

Placing her hand on his arm, he brought her to the bottom of the steps. "First, let me introduce the butler, Mr. Dawson."

The perfectly groomed, slightly rotund butler bowed.

"Mr. Dawson." Pamela nodded.

"My housekeeper, Mrs. Bell."

The thin and erect housekeeper curtsied.

Why was Kerrich introducing her? "Mrs. Bell," Pamela echoed.

"The head cook, Mrs. Smith." Kerrich gestured to a broadly smiling, apron-clad woman. He continued as they walked up the stairs, naming each servant. "The senior downstairs footman, Ralph. The senior downstairs maid, Betty. The senior upstairs footman, Roger. The senior upstairs maid, Joyce. The cook's assistant, Paul."

Why was Kerrich doing this? "Mrs. Smith." Pamela smiled politely and repeated after Kerrich. "Ralph. Betty. Roger. Joyce. Peter."

Gently, Kerrich corrected her. "Paul. The cook's assistant is named Paul."

With a shock, Pamela realized—Kerrich knew them. This careless, arrogant, domineering peer of the realm knew each one of his servants, what they did, what their names were. She looked at him, wide-eyed.

"I learned their names so I could introduce you properly," he said.

"I see." She had imagined an incredibly uncomfortable visit, with Kerrich treating her coolly if he noticed her at all. Now he was introducing her to his staff as if . . . her mind veered away. She couldn't think that. She didn't dare. Instead, she concentrated on remembering the servants' names.

At the top of the stairs, she had made it through the ordeal with no more mistakes. Glancing toward Kerrich, she discovered he wore half a smile and satisfaction like a second skin.

For some reason, his confidence snapped the steel back into her spine, and she straightened, gestured down the long line of servants, and in the crisp tones of Miss Lockhart the elderly governess, she asked, "Where is Moulton, my lord? Did he remain in town?"

"Mr. Moulton refused my excessively generous offer to remain my butler and has returned to his investigative firm."

With difficulty, Pamela absorbed that information.

"He did, however, offer me a position there should I ever desire." Kerrich smiled openly. "Which of course I shall accept if my plans do not come to fruition. What is the use of being safe if you're not happy?"

She thought it a rhetorical question, but he paused as if expecting an answer. "I'm afraid I don't know," she replied to him and herself.

What plans?

"Exactly," he agreed. "Now you must come in and tell me what you think of Brookford House."

Two footmen had left their places in line and held the polished doors wide. Kerrich guided her into a soaring foyer whose marble columns directed her vision upward to a blue-painted ceiling decorated like the sky with clouds and a stylized sun.

"The house wasn't originally in the family." Kerrich led her slowly forward, his hand over hers as she craned her neck to look above. "Brookford was built in 1790. When I was looking for a country estate I found it and fell in love. I confess I have changed very little, but perhaps you like a more modern style."

She thought she restrained her enthusiasm admirably. "This is most beautiful. Very calm and welcoming."

"Just what I thought," he said with an irksome contentment.

It was as if he saw through her propriety to the woman beneath. Dreadful man, did he dare think he understood her?

Worse—did he?

"The servants are setting up refreshments in the conservatory," he said, "but if you aren't too tired from your journey and wouldn't mind stretching your legs a little I'll give you the brief tour of the downstairs."

"I would like that." Perhaps it was vulgar curiosity, but Pamela found herself wanting to view the vastness of Brookford House.

They walked along through the door at the end of the foyer and into the picture gallery, another long, high room with huge pastoral landscapes in gilt frames and a few portraits, some darkened with age and some bright with new paint.

"As you may have guessed, we haven't a lot of family portraits." He pointed at one of his grandfather, another man obviously his father and a youthful Kerrich. "Until Grandpapa came along, the family was noble, but poor. Not that my ancestors ever starved, you understand. The old Mathewes estate provided a decent living, and I can safely tell you that the men in my family are excellent providers. We always take care of our wives and children."

Again he seemed to expect an answer, so she said, "An admirable trait." What she really noticed was that he still held her hand trapped between his arm and his palm and showed no indication of letting her go, and the warmth of the contact distracted her from studying the picture of him as she would have liked.

He led her into another room, a library much like the one where he worked in London, with comfortable chairs, bookshelves on either wall that went on forever—and a desk. A wide desk similar to the one where they . . . without warning she blushed, all over, at once. Not even Miss Lockhart's professional serenity was proof against the sight of that broad, shiny surface.

"My office here at Brookford." He walked her right through, but she thought he must have noticed her discomfort, for he strolled with ever more obnoxious confidence. "This corridor leads to the conservatory."

As he ushered her through, she thought strongly about suggesting that a meal shared between the two of them would be inappropriate and asking that she be led to her bedchamber where she could rest. He would understand then that he knew nothing about her and had no reason to feel confident about anything. He would never have to know that with his help, she had healed from the pain of her father's abandonment and had left the silver watch behind at the Distinguised Academy of Governesses. She would escape with her pride intact and her emotions in shambles.

Drawing herself up, she made ready to annihilate him with her dignity and her indifference—when abruptly, he stopped.

"Matilda!" he snapped. "What are you doing?"

CHAPTER 32

Kerrich's sharp tone startled Pamela, and the greyhound of perhaps three months yelped. In a flurry of long and scrambling legs, Matilda ran away from the stain she'd just left on the Aubusson rug and hid under a table. Landing on her belly, she peeked out, her big brown eyes worried.

Kerrich dropped Pamela's hand and strode forward. "Bad dog. Bad dog!"

Matilda started crawling toward him, tail wagging.

Pamela was irresistibly charmed. By the dog, and by the master. "She's a darling."

"I've had Jimbo and Bailey—they're my other two greyhounds—for years, but recently I decided I should get a new dog." He picked up the gangly animal and glared into her eyes. "Right now, I can't remember why." The little dog whined and her tongue licked at his face, and he spoke directly to her. "And kissing isn't going to get you out of trouble, Miss Puddles!"

Pamela couldn't control her grin, or the mawkish sensation of indulgence she experienced at the sight of the suave, wealthy, confident Lord Kerrich brought to treacherous sentimentality by a puppy.

"Hey, there!" he shouted.

A footman and two maids arrived on the run.

"Matilda needs to be taken for a walk." He handed the dog to the footman, who bowed and backed hastily away. "Julie and"—he hesitated—"Dora?"

Both maids curtsied.

"Matilda has left her calling card." He pointed. "There." The maids were smirking, too, and Kerrich scowled at the three women. "Stop that!" Striding to the far door, he stood aside and said, "If you would come this way, Miss Lockhart, I believe we have a small repast laid out for your pleasure."

Pamela walked toward him, her plan to bow out discarded, but her dignity intact. She would eat with Kerrich, carry on a conversation with him, and let him know by her demeanor that she didn't mourn their previous intimacy, scarcely remembered his unflattering marriage proposal, and was doing very well without him.

Like the rest of his house, the conservatory glittered with all that was resplendent, a glass-enclosed room where potted flowers bloomed in pots and strawberry plants set small green fruit. A linen-draped table sat in the center covered with an artfully arranged plate of cold meats, cheeses and condiments. A massive marble vase filled with roses stood off to the side. Two chairs were drawn up facing the imposing view from the windows into the garden where chrysanthemums bloomed.

Kerrich held the chair for Pamela. Still enthralled by the view, she walked over, began to sink down—and Kerrich exclaimed, "Stop!"

She half-turned to see him scooping a large, gray-striped, slumbering cat out of her seat.

"I forgot. Luke likes to sleep in here." He held the limp

cat as she sank into the chair, and asked, "Do you want to hold him?"

"Of course," she said doubtfully, "if you're sure he's alive."

"He's just old." Kerrich laid him in her lap. "And spoiled. The housekeeper spoils him."

Kerrich looked chagrined enough that Pamela eschewed challenging his blame of the housekeeper. Instead, she petted the cat, who proved himself to be among the living by draping himself upside down across her knees and purring. With the afternoon sun slanting in and the scent of flowers rich in the air, the conservatory exuded peace. She relaxed against the back of the chair.

Then Kerrich placed his hands on her shoulders, and she stiffened.

"I suppose it's pathetically obvious what I've been doing," he said.

She took a careful, controlled breath. "Showing me your majestic possessions."

"Yes, and letting you know that . . . that without you to share it with, it means nothing."

Her breath caught. She coughed abruptly and violently, and clutched at her shoulder where her almost healed wound now throbbed.

"Are you all right?" He leaped to pour her some wine.

She nodded and took a sip from the glass he thrust into her hand. "Thank you. Sorry." Her voice was choked. "Whatever I'd expected you to say, it wasn't that."

"Why else do you think I had you come to Brookford?"

"To bring Beth?"

"If I didn't have time to fetch Beth myself, I have many trustworthy servants to perform the task." Kneeling before her, he rubbed the cat's wide belly. "No, I wanted you to see that I have all you want. I have a house in the country.

It's not a cottage, but you said you like it and if you wanted, I could build you a cottage. I have cats. Barn cats and house cats. You could take a kitten as a pet. Or two kittens. As many kittens as you want. I own dogs. Greyhounds, good dogs, they have the run of the house." He gestured outside. "I have a beautiful garden. Flowers. A rose garden. Lots of books to read, and for you, all the time in the world to read them."

Confusion buffeted her. Nothing about this day, nothing at all, was as she expected. Groping for understanding, she wanted to be absolutely clear about his intentions. Cautiously, she asked, "Am I to assume you are renewing your suit for my hand?"

"I never withdrew my suit for your hand!" His haughty indignation went ill with his supplicating position on the floor. Then he caught himself. "I just never knew I would willingly beg you to marry me."

She watched him absentmindedly pet the cat as he tried to make himself appear humble. He was very appealing like this. Not particularly believable, but appealing.

When he realized she wasn't going to answer, he said, "Although I know you don't need any of my things, I will bribe you if that will convince you to marry me."

"Do you think I'm the kind of woman who would marry a man for his possessions?"

"If you were, you would have taken me the first time I proposed."

She liked that he realized the truth.

"But there are other reasons for us to marry. Not that I want this in any way to influence your choice, but . . . I think that you might be going to have my child."

"Of course," she breathed. Of course. Somehow he'd discovered she was expecting and he thought . . . he thought what? That she would *have* to marry him? If that were the case, he'd be clomping about, arrogant and proud, demanding his paternal rights.

"Of course? Does that mean *yes*?"

Her hands fluttered to her waist. "Yes."

His eyes grew large, and he asked, "Would you excuse me for a moment?"

Bewildered, she watched as he stood, went to the window, tucked his thumbs into his waistcoat—and grinned. Foolishly, broadly, as if he couldn't help himself.

After a moment he swallowed, put on a serious face, and came back to kneel before her. "Forgive me." His hands flitted over her and finally settled, one on her shoulder and one over her hands. "I know that sometimes women don't feel well when they are increasing and you might not be particularly happy knowing that if all does not work out well between us you will bear a child out of wedlock, but—I have dreamed my whole life of having a child . . . with the woman I love."

Oh. Oh. He'd said he loved her. When he looked at her like this, and she felt the slight tremble of his fingers over hers, she thought . . . she felt . . . well, euphoric.

When she didn't reply at once, he said, "I know that might be hard for you to believe. My reputation is not good and your experience with your father doesn't incline you to believe me—"

"You're nothing like my father," she said. She might have lately mourned her father, but she suffered no illusions about him. She knew very well that if her father had gotten one of his mistresses with child, he would have left nothing behind but a trail of dust.

"I'm not. I can assure you of that by telling you I have known several women in the biblical sense, but I have no children, because I always, always use a sheath. I didn't with you. Never. Not even the first time." Kerrich moved closer, crowding her knees. "Do you know why?"

"No." Her lips formed the word, but she made no sound.

"Because I knew you were going to be difficult. I knew I would need every weapon in my arsenal to keep you, and if that included getting you with child, then I was willing to use it." She tried to jerk her hand away, but he threaded their fingers together. "Despicable, I know, but you're everything I've always been afraid of."

She had no idea what he was talking about. "Afraid of?"

"You're what *every* man is afraid of. And what every man wants. You're so clever that it doesn't matter that you're beautiful. When I kissed the ill-favored Miss Lockhart that first time, I told you I was testing you, checking that you hadn't fallen in love with me and so would present yourself naked in my bedchamber."

"Thus saving yourself trouble," she said bitingly, remembering his rejection and her embarrassment.

"But in truth, I kissed you because I had forgotten what you looked like in the wit of your conversation and the pleasure of your company." He drew a small, wooden, intricately carved box from his pocket and opened it. Inside a ring of pearls and sparkling blue saphires rested on a bed of black velvet. "For the touch of your hand I would crawl through a horse stable on my stomach. If you wished, you could be the worst kind of tyrant and I would love it, and you. I had to realize that I trusted you not to do that, and submit myself to your rule. Please marry me. I'll always be faithful, and I can never be happy without you."

He had been so sure she was going to say yes. He had groveled before her! But she had taken the ring, the ring he'd spent hours designing just for her, and asked that someone take her to her bedchamber because she was more tired than she'd realized.

He hadn't seen her since. She had sent down an apology and a request for a dinner tray, and of course he'd accepted the apology and sent up the dinner tray and tried to understand where he'd gone wrong. He'd offered to fulfill her dreams. He'd assured her he wanted their child but knew that, without him, she would be able to care for it and herself. He had told her he loved her, which he had never told another woman because no other woman had captured his heart and soul.

Now, Kerrich hoisted himself out of the chair in the library where he'd been brooding, leaving Jimbo stretched out on the floor before the fire. Stopping beside the old dog, he petted him under the chin, thinking how easy life must be when one had been gelded. Unfortunately, that was not a solution Kerrich would consider for himself. Taking a candle, he mounted the stairs and strode along the corridor toward his bedchamber.

As he had tucked Beth into bed, she had told him it was his overconfidence. She said Miss Lockhart must have sensed overconfidence because no matter what he said or did, he still knew himself to be handsome, wealthy and of good character.

He had to admit Beth was right. His confidence was one of the bedrocks of his temperament, and so he would tell Pamela.

With his hand on the doorknob of his room, he stared down the corridor toward the wing where Pamela was sheltered. The temptation was almost irresistible. He wanted to go to her, to take her hand and again beg her to wed him. Then, if she didn't agree, he would strip her naked and make her see sense.

But he feared the trip to Brookford had been difficult for her. She was increasing, she had suffered a gunshot wound and she needed rest. And who knew? Perhaps tomorrow he would wake and go down to breakfast, and she would be there smiling, pouring his tea and proclaiming she wished to marry him.

If not, he would refuse to let her go home.

According to his grandfather's counsel, which Lord Reynard had given freely during dinner, kidnapping was a bad choice of methods to deal with a proud woman. But when pressed, Grandpapa had declared that if Pamela continued to prove difficult, kidnapping might be the only acceptable solution, although he did question how Kerrich would trick her into speaking wedding vows. Kerrich decided he would deal with that difficulty when he encountered it.

With a sigh, he opened the door and slammed it behind him.

A fire burned on the hearth, roses were scattered over the sheets on his downturned bed and someone—a female—rose out of the chair before the fire. He had a brief moment of thinking, *Not the senior upstairs maid again!*

Then his brain processes froze.

Miss Pamela Lockhart turned to face him, and she was totally, lushly, starkly naked. She stood with her feet slightly apart, her chin up, and her hands behind her back.

She smiled, a rather tremulously wicked smile that gave hope even as it aroused. "My lord, forgive my intrusion. I know how it irks you to have women arrive in your bedchamber without clothing, and I would not intrude on your hospitality without taking the precaution of trying to please you. So because I am like all the rest, and I'm here only because I love you without cease, I decided to wear this." She extended her hand.

He had to try several times before he could tear his gaze from the body for which he endlessly lusted to a mere limb with five fingers . . . one of which was decorated with a sapphire-encrusted, pearl-decorated, love-given ring.

"Will that amount of adornment suffice?" she asked.

Her eyes glinted so merrily it was obvious she knew the answer, but she had led him on too long. He had to clarify, "Only if you agree to wear it *every* night in my bedchamber."

"I will wear whatever you like every night in *our* bedchamber."

He allowed himself one moment of relief before snatching her into his arms. "The ring alone will do."